W9-CCC-903

RIDERS

TOR TEEN BOOKS BY
VERONICA ROSSI

Riders

RIDERS

VERONICA ROSSI

TOR®
TEEN

A TOM DOHERTY ASSOCIATES BOOK
NEW YORK

RIDERS

Copyright © 2016 by Veronica Rossi

A Tor Teen Book
Published by Tom Doherty Associates, LLC
175 Fifth Avenue
New York, NY 10010

www.tor-forge.com

Tor® is a registered trademark of Tom Doherty Associates, LLC.

The Library of Congress Cataloging-in-Publication Data
is available upon request.

ISBN 978-0-7653-8254-2 (hardcover)
ISBN 978-1-4668-8779-4 (e-book)

Our books may be purchased in bulk for promotional,
educational, or business use. Please contact your local bookseller
or the Macmillan Corporate and Premium Sales Department
at (800) 221-7945, extension 5442, or by e-mail at
MacmillanSpecialMarkets@macmillan.com.

First Edition: February 2016

Printed in the United States of America

0 9 8 7 6 5 4 3 2 1

For Andy, Wes, and all those
who have dedicated their lives
to protecting freedom

CHAPTER 1

W hen I open my eyes, all I see is darkness.
Can't move . . . can't speak . . . can't think through
this jaw-grinding headache. I hold still, waiting for some clarity on where I am or how long I've been out, but nothing
comes. What I know for sure: I'm tied to a chair, gagged, and
my head is covered with a hood that reeks of sweat and vomit.

Not what I expected from a rescue.

My neck creaks like a rusty hinge as I straighten, and the
darkness comes loose and starts to spin. It spins and spins and
my stomach throws in the towel, and it's spinning, too. Hot
spit floods into my mouth. I know what's coming next, so I
pull deep breaths, in and out, until the urge passes and I'm
okay again. Just sitting here sweating bullets in this chair and
this hood.

I can't believe this. They *drugged* me. Gave me some kind
of sedative, because I am *way* too calm right now. Probably
painkillers, too. I can't feel my shoulder and that cut was deep.
My deltoid looked like raw steak. Even I should still feel a
gash that bad.

Nice. Well done, US government. The whole world is going
to hell, pretty much. I'm one of the few people who can help—
and this is what they do?

I turn my focus to listening. Every so often I hear feet shuffling or a throat clearing. I pay attention to the sounds, trying
to figure out how many men are guarding me. Two is my guess.

A radiator clicks on behind me and keeps clicking, like
someone's tapping a wrench against metal. Heat builds on my
back like sunshine. Strange in all this darkness. After a few
minutes it shuts off and the quiet stretches out. My back is

just starting to cool when a door whines open. Footsteps come toward me and stop. Then a chair scrapes across the floor.

It's game time. Answer time.

"Take off his hood," says a female voice.

There's a tug, then a rush of cool air against my face, and my eyes slam shut against the brightness. I'm not expecting it when the gag goes next, tearing out a few layers of my tongue with it.

"Take your time," says the woman.

Like I have a choice. For a few seconds, all I can do is try to get some moisture back in my mouth. I pull against my arm restraints, riding out the urge to rub my stinging eyes. It takes forever for the figure in front of me to come into focus.

A woman—in her forties, I think—sits behind a small wooden desk. She has olive skin and dark hair, eyes as black and shiny as wine bottles. Her navy-blue suit looks expensive and she has a PhD kind of vibe, like she knows everything about something. And wrote a book about it. A civilian. I'd bet anything.

"Hello, Gideon. I'm Natalie Cordero," she says. "I'm going to be asking you some questions."

She folds her hands in front of her and pauses, letting me know she's in control, that she talks to guys like me every day, but I know for a fact that's impossible. No one else in the world is like me. No one.

A whiff of her perfume reaches me—a floral-citrus-musk combo that's strong, a scent bullhorn, but better than the stench from the hood.

Two men stand behind her. The guy wearing a Texas Rangers baseball cap is massive, the size of the door he's guarding. The other guy's more compact, has a dark complexion and wrestler ear. He rests a hand on the Beretta in his belt holster and gives me a look like, *Just give me an excuse to use this.*

Both have full beards, wind-chapped faces, and are dressed in jeans, hiking boots, and Patagonia jackets, but they're special ops. Delta or SEALs. You don't get that kind of stance, relaxed but totally alert, without earning it.

I recognize them. They were part of the unit that busted me out of Norway today. Or yesterday . . . or whenever that happened.

Natalie Cordero assesses my shirt and cargos, the dried blood, the burnt patches, the crusted mud, the top layer of fine ash. I've looked better, I'll admit. Then I follow her eyes to my shoulder. Through a tear in my shirt I see that my captors—who are supposed to be my allies—put a compression bandage on my cut. That was cool of them.

"Water?" Cordero asks.

It takes a couple of tries but I manage to scrape out some words in reply. "Yes. Yes, please."

The bigger guard in the Rangers cap brings over a plastic bottle with a flexible straw. His face is ruddy and square, brickish. Graying beard, blue eyes. He's the guy who knocked me out in Jotunheimen. But I didn't really give him an option. I lost it when Daryn stayed behind. I didn't expect her to do that. Never saw it coming and totally lost it. That can't happen again. I can't lose control of this situation, so I focus on getting my bearings as I suck down water, replenishing my dehydrated body.

I'm in a small room with pine walls and floorboards. Even the trim is pine, so. Either I was eaten by a tree or I'm in a cabin. There's a window to my left with checkered blue curtains. No light or sounds bleed through, so either it's nighttime or the window's been blacked out. I'm going to go with both. The only illumination in the room comes from an iron lamp in the corner with no shade, just a bare bulb that's either a trillion watts or my eyes are extra sensitive from the drugs.

A cool draft seeps through the two-inch gap beneath the

door. It's not easy smelling anything beyond Cordero's perfume but I catch stale carpet smell and woodsmoke. As prison cells go, it's pretty cozy.

"I should've asked before," Cordero says when my water break is over, "would you prefer that I call you Gideon or Mr. Blake?"

I was right. She's not military or she'd have called me "Private Blake."

I swallow again, my throat feeling better. "Ma'am, I'd prefer you untied me and told me where I am." I instantly want to punch myself for the *ma'am* thing. She's *detaining* me. Screw manners.

She doesn't answer, so I try another question. "Are we still in Norway?" Nothing again. I look to the guys at the door. "Are we back in the States?"

"I can't give you that information at this time, Gideon," Cordero says, deciding for herself what to call me. I'm eighteen, probably half her age, so I can see why she didn't go with "Mr. Blake."

"Why can't I know where I am? Why all this?" I nod to myself. "I'm not going to run. *I* called *you* guys, remember? For help? How about cutting me free?"

"When I'm done questioning you, you'll be released."

"Released?" It's so messed up, I have to laugh. "I haven't done anything wrong."

"No?" She leans forward, her gaze narrowing. "You inflicted millions of dollars of damage on Jotunheimen National Park. You don't think that's wrong? American taxpayers are paying for that damage. The American public paid to bail you and your friends out of that mess. You're lucky the media hasn't caught on yet. You almost caused an international incident. You do realize that? Until I know exactly what you were doing in Norway and why you chose to destroy acres of pristine parkland, you aren't leaving this room. I mean that, Gideon. You might as well get comfortable."

"You think this is about damaged land? About *money*?"

"If I thought that was all this was, you wouldn't be here."

I'm not sitting here and playing this game. "You really want to know what this is about? I'll tell you. Pure evil is out there. We're in trouble—and I don't mean American taxpayers. I mean humanity. I mean *everyone*. And you're looking at one of the only people who can do anything about it. So what do you say you untie me?"

"Not happening, Gideon," she says, disregarding everything I just said. "And before you become belligerent again, let me tell *you*. Losing your temper won't help anything."

This is a huge waste of time. I need to get out of here. Find the guys. Get the key back. "Where's Colonel Nellis?" I trust my commanding officer. I want to talk to him, not a stranger.

"This incident has gone above the jurisdiction of the US Army," she says.

"Who are you with? The Defense Department? CIA?"

"Let me spell this out for you. *I* ask questions, *you* answer them. That's how this works."

There actually wasn't any spelling in that, but whatever. I'm done with this. Time to bring the wrath.

I reach for my anger, for my sword, for Riot.

I get nothing. I'm powerless. The drugs have neutralized everything. I'm completely zeroed.

It makes no sense, none, so I start yelling. She's making a huge mistake. I'm one of the good guys. She has no idea who she's talking to. Everything I say sounds scripted and insane but it's true. It's the truth.

Cordero checks her watch. "Seems it's about that time again." She looks over her shoulder at the guy with the Beretta. "Get him under control."

Beretta slides a small black pouch from a cargo pocket. He pulls on latex gloves and takes out a hypodermic needle as I keep yelling and thrashing against the bindings, getting absolutely nowhere.

The bigger guy, Texas, comes around my chair and puts me in a rear chokehold. "Relax," he says. "Relax."

Which is the last thing I'm going to do, but then stars flicker against the pine walls and the room dims, then *I* dim. I'm not yelling anymore, I'm passing out.

Beretta sticks the needle into my forearm and depresses the plunger. A slow burn spreads through me. My face goes numb. My muscles relax. I relax.

I don't want to relax, but I relax.

Texas releases me and I suck in air. Gulp it down. Oxygen is the best damn thing ever created.

Beretta shines a penlight into my eyes.

Bright light.

Doesn't feel good.

Close eyes.

I'm vaguely aware that I reacted too slowly. Reactions shouldn't happen in steps. Unless it's only one step. A single, self-contained step.

Yeah . . . that seems right.

"The kid's cooked," Beretta says as he peels off the gloves. He and Texas step back, posting up by the door again.

Keeping my head up becomes my new goal. It's not easy. Reminds me of balancing a basketball on my finger. While trying to process information through it. Except my head isn't actually a basketball, it just feels like one.

Yep. The kid's cooked.

Cordero unfolds her hands. She drums her fingers on the table, watching me. "Ready to talk now?"

"You have no idea how big this is . . . what's happening. You have no idea who I am."

It takes me a second to realize that the words hanging in the room are mine.

Not good.

Cordero's fingers stop drumming. "Why don't you tell me?"

I come so close to blurting it out, blurting *everything* out, I almost feel like I did it. Something's not right. A prison break is happening in my mind. All my thoughts want out. My story wants out. Images of the past few weeks crash around in my head demanding freedom. Holding them back's a full-body effort. I'm tied to a chair but my heart's doing a triathlon. My face goes hot and the back of my throat starts to burn. What the hell did they just give me?

Cordero waits. "Okay, Gideon. We'll try again in half an hour." She pauses at the door. "I can do this all day. Can you?"

After she leaves, I let my head fall forward where it wants to be.

Breathe, Blake. Breathe.

I could've handled that better. But was I supposed to tell a stranger what's going on? Who I am? *What* I am?

No way. Cordero would've panicked. She'd have lost her mind. But the words are still on my tongue. They're right there.

I'm War, I want to say.

I am War.

CHAPTER 2

It takes me less than a minute to realize that I have to answer Cordero's questions. The drugs have wiped out my entire arsenal of abilities. I'm stuck in this chair until I give her what she wants. There's no other way. I have to talk.

The taller guard, Texas, leaves to get her but she waits the full half hour before coming back, like a parent making a point. *Don't test me, Gideon Blake. I mean what I say and I say what I mean.*

She brings a black file with her that makes a slap when she drops it on the desk. My military record. It's pretty thick considering I only shipped off to Basic a couple of months ago after high school, but I've already had a notable run in the Army.

Cordero tucks herself under the desk. "I'm glad you came around." She flips open the file, then waits like she wants me to say thank you.

"You should've covered the electrical outlets," I say instead.

Her dark eyebrows go up. "Excuse me?"

"If you didn't want me to know I'm back in the States. Just a tip for the next time you unlawfully detain someone."

"Noted. Any other suggestions on how I can do my job better?"

"Yes. As soon as we're done, Nat, the *second* we're done, you untie me and get Colonel Nellis."

Cordero's mouth lifts at the corners. Not a smile, exactly. More like a close cousin to a smile. "Stop calling me 'Nat' and we have a deal."

I nod, but I'm actually not sure it's going to work. Everything I said sort of just slipped out. My thoughts are still up in arms, tired of being stuck in my head. I have to keep consciously beating them back and hoping they stay there.

A muffled voice in the hallway draws my attention to the door. Sebastian, Marcus, and Jode left Norway with me. Only Daryn didn't. The guys must be here. Probably in adjacent rooms being interro-questioned by their own Corderos. I bet Marcus hasn't said a word, but I can just imagine the verbal diarrhea Bastian and Jode are slinging. Neither of those guys needs drugs to spill.

Thinking about them reminds me of Daryn again. This time I really sink into the memory and she's twisting her long hair over one shoulder and smiling at me.

What are you looking at, Gideon?

You. I'm looking at you.

How am I looking?

Perfect, I should've said. But I didn't.

"Gideon? Are you with me?"

Whoa. Not at all. How long did I just zone out? Priority one: Get these drugs out of my system. They're slowing me down too much. I won't stand a chance against the Kindred doped up like this. I need to get this debriefing done, find the guys, and get back in the fight.

"Yes," I say. "I'm with you."

"Good. Let's start with the accident at Fort Benning." Cordero reads from the folder. "The last record we have of your whereabouts is dated six weeks ago. You suffered extensive injuries during a training incident. The report states that you fractured your femur, radius, and ulna . . . cracked ribs . . . severe concussion. It says here you were unresponsive for over two minutes. You had just been declared dead when you resuscitated." She looks up from the file. "Tell me what happened during that exercise. You were parachuting?"

I nod. "But it didn't go right and . . . I bounced."

Behind her Texas and Beretta exchange a look. *Dumb boot,* I bet they're thinking. *Incompetent little turd.*

"Bounced?" Cordero asks.

"Hit the dirt at a very high velocity."

"Yes. I have that here, but I'd like to hear the full account in your own words."

Right. My own words. But now I can't seem to start. Going through this from the beginning will use up precious time. How can I sit here, talking, when the Kindred are out there hurting innocent people? On the other hand, if I tell Cordero the situation without any lead-up, she'll either panic and make hasty decisions, or think I'm crazy and refuse to believe me— neither of which I want, so. The fastest way out of this room really is to tell the whole story, and that jump was definitely square one. The beginning. Or the end, depending on your perspective. Death usually is the end.

"Walk me through it, Gideon. Moment to moment," Cordero says, like she's sensed I'm finally ready.

"Okay. The accident."

CHAPTER 3

You have my military record, Cordero, so you know the lead-up: how I'd literally boarded a plane for Fort Benning, Georgia the day after I got my diploma in May. It'd been a long senior year, not a lot of fun for me, and I couldn't wait to put high school behind me and start doing something I actually cared about.

I spent the summer going through Basic Training, then Advanced Infantry Training, then Airborne School, finally ending up where I really wanted to be—the Ranger Assessment and Selection Program. RASP is the gateway for becoming a Ranger, a soldier in the 75th Ranger Regiment. My dad had been part of this elite combat unit once and I was determined to become part of it too, even if it killed me—which is actually what happened, but I'll get to that.

RASP, in a nutshell, is eight weeks of pure punishment meant to weed out anyone who's not supposed to be there. The program puts you through constant physical and mental tests on almost no food and even less sleep. Intense. But my Ranger buddy and I were both in it for the long haul. Cory was from Houston, a couple of years older than me, and relentless. He'd face a twelve-mile run in full combat kit with a grin and his personal motto: *Nobody ever drowned in their own sweat.*

Four weeks in, our class had been reduced by around half, to fifty guys. We were pulled away from the steady stream of road marches and weapons drills for a parachute jump. Most of us had just gotten our jump wings in Airborne School, and they wanted to keep our training fresh in our minds.

We loaded into an Air Force C-130 just after 10:00 a.m. Cory and I took our seats side by side, how we'd pretty much been for the past month. As the plane's propellers fired up, the anticipation of the coming thrill erased the aches that had been piling up in my body. By the time we were in the air, I found myself grinning. Like every other five-jump chump.

My first jump a few weeks earlier had required a leap of faith just to get out the door. But then the canopy had opened four seconds later, right on time like it was supposed to, and I'd relaxed, and it had been amazing. It was real quiet and peaceful on the way down, and you couldn't beat the view.

This jump would be my sixth. Since it was only intended to refresh our training, we were jumping Hollywood-style, which meant we weren't wearing our weapons, rucks, or combat load. Without all the gear, I felt more comfortable, and I knew it would also give me more time on the descent. Jumping from a thousand feet, the whole thing never lasted much longer than a minute—combat jumpers need to get on the ground fast—but without all the battle rattle weighing me down, I might get a few more seconds in the air than normal.

I sat back. Compared to the stuff I'd been doing, this was going to be a treat.

Listening to the drone of the engines, my eyes moved over the guys sitting in jump seats against the outside skin of the aircraft and in rows down the middle. It'd been a long time since I'd felt like I was in the right place, doing the right thing.

Then Cory dug an elbow into my side. "Good, Blake?"

The question sounded casual but I knew it wasn't. The week before, we'd been pulling an all-night march on Cole Range—acres of Georgia woods reserved for our training—and we got talking about the worst things we'd ever been through. I was so sleep-deprived, hungry, and sore, I let slip that nothing had ever felt tough since my dad had died August 2nd of the previous year. Which happened to be a year ago, that very day. I was sitting on that plane on the anniversary of his death—and Cory had remembered.

But I had it under control.

"Good, Ryland," I replied. Then I flipped him off as a thank-you for asking.

In the center aisle, the jumpmaster started going through the jump sequence. *Get ready, stand up, hook up, check static line, check equipment, sound off.* I went through each check, along with the fifty guys around me. Airborne School put thousands of soldiers through this process every month and every part of it ran like a well-oiled machine.

As we approached the drop zone, the jumpmaster opened the door and cold air rushed into the plane. Sweat rolled down my back as the adrenaline buzzed through me. The feeling of toeing right up to the edge of my limits was familiar. I'd leaned pretty hard on it over the past year because it made me forget exactly what Cory had just reminded me of.

The jumpmaster gave the go command and the guys at front of the line started exiting, one after another, handing their static lines to the safety by the door and launching into the sky.

We moved quickly. In seconds it was Cory's turn. He jumped through the door and disappeared, and then I was up. I took my last steps on the plane and threw myself out. As the air current grabbed me, I locked my feet and knees together and hit a good exit position. The plane's engine noise receded rapidly behind me. As this was a static-line jump, my chute would autodeploy. My job was just to make sure that happened properly.

Setting my hands on my reserve chute, I counted off like I'd been trained to do. "One thousand, two thousand, three thousand, four thousand."

What the . . . ?

Where was the tug?

I looked up, searching for an open canopy like I'd seen in my previous jumps.

It wasn't open.

What I saw above me was a twist of pale silk. The canopy had rolled into a tight line. I instantly recognized it as a parachute malfunction—a streamer, also called a cigarette roll because of the way the parachute looked.

It offered no lift capability at all so I was still in a dead free fall. I shot past Cory, then saw him above me, suspended by his canopy and looking the way I was supposed to be looking. In the rush of the wind, I thought I heard him yell my name.

Then time went into slow motion and my training kicked in.

I ripped at the handle on the reserve chute and watched in disbelief as the reserve went straight up into the main, still streaming above me, then as the two wrapped and twisted together.

At this point, I knew I had a real mess on my hands but I stayed right with my training. It'd been drilled into me that the proper reaction to a reserve that failed to inflate was to reel it back in hand-over-hand and throw it back out, away from the main. As many times as it took. For the rest of my life. So I did that. I pulled and reeled in my reserve like I was in a tug-of-war for the ages.

I hadn't missed a beat in my reactions, everything felt like instinct, but some part of me was stunned that I was suffering a double malfunction, every jumper's worst nightmare. They were incredibly rare—but not rare enough for me right then. The drop zone was coming up fast. Really fast. I finally bunched my reserve into a ball in front of me. With a heave, I threw the reserve down and away as hard as I could and *wham*! My harness yanked against me, digging into my groin.

My reserve had finally opened. The main flapped next to it, still in a twist but no longer causing problems.

This should've been great news but as I looked down at the earth, coming at me like a planet-sized bullet, I knew it was too late. My velocity wouldn't allow for a safe landing. Or even a survivable one.

I had moment's thought about my father and the coincidence that was happening, the two of us falling to our deaths on the same day, then I reminded myself of the correct parachute landing fall position.

Feet and knees together. Tuck chin and elbows. Land on balls of feet, then roll to calf, thigh, arc body—

I hit so fast it felt like I landed everywhere at once—feet, ass, head.

The last thing I remember was hearing the crunch of bones in my arm and my legs breaking. And that was it.

I was done.

CHAPTER 4

"What happened after you fell?" Cordero asks.

There's a new intensity in her eyes. Same with the guys guarding the door. They've been indifferent so far. Almost bored. Not anymore.

"After I fell?" I say, buying myself a second to shake off that fall and get my heart to settle back down. Did I just say everything I think I said? Did I tell her about my *dad*?

Stay on topic, Blake. Answer the question. Only what she asks. But even that's not so simple. What do I say here—the truth?

I fell, then my bones snapped, and then everything went quiet and I was floating in the stars, surrounded by them, breathing them, feeling them, dead, I knew I was dead, but I still heard guys yelling, felt Cory doing chest compressions, keeping my heart going, then something cinched tight to my left wrist and the life surged back into me?

No way. I'm not telling her that. She's not ready yet. But these drugs in me are wicked.

I think it.

Words come out.

That's dangerous.

And my recollection feels too sharp. Too real. Just now it felt like I slipped into the past. As I was talking, my mind dove much deeper. I could see every detail. Feel every sensation. I literally just relived my death.

"Gideon?"

"Yes?" I was droning again. Basketball brain is bad news. The fact that the Kindred are out there and I'm stuck in this chair is even worse news. The radiator's going again. I didn't even hear it go on.

"What happened after the fall?"

"I woke up in the hospital. Walter Reed Medical Center. I'd been in ICU for a few days when I came around. My mom flew out to be with me but I only have a vague memory of that. Of anything from those days, actually, because I was either unconscious or drugged. Kinda like right now. By the way, Nat, Natalie . . . Cordero. I have a supersensitive stomach and it's not liking whatever you gave me. Puking's a personal specialty. I hope you're quick."

"Your files from Walter Reed are interesting," she says, without missing a beat. "You were released within a week of being admitted." She looks up, her eyes going a little wide. "That's awfully fast."

"Awfully so."

"Where did you go afterward?"

"I was transferred home. I'd stabilized much sooner than the doctors expected. They couldn't seem to get a good grasp on what needed to be fixed. The status of my injuries . . . they described it as 'dynamic.' The docs did what they could, set the major bones—the femur and tibia—then decided to give the swelling a chance to subside before bringing me back for further assessment."

"Your injury status was *dynamic*?"

"Constantly changing."

"Thank you, I know what it means. Where's home?"

"Half Moon Bay, California."

"And what happened there?"

"Things got weird."

Cordero sits back in her chair. She threads her fingers together. "Tell me about the weird," she says.

So I do.

CHAPTER 5

O kay. Home.
      I was only there for about a day, but a lot happened in that time. It was when I first started noticing that things with me weren't right.

From the second I woke up, I was so disoriented that I didn't recognize my own room. I remember thinking the desk and the surfboard hanging over the window looked familiar before I realized they were actually mine. And my body felt strange. Not how I expected for being so busted up. I had air casts on my left leg and arm—I'd fallen on that side—but I didn't feel any pain. My muscles only felt swollen, like they'd been stuffed with cotton balls. I chalked that up to all the pain meds I'd been taking.

Another strange thing about that morning was being alone. For days I'd been under the constant care of doctors and nurses at Walter Reed, then during my transfer home. Before that I'd been surrounded by guys all the time, in a nonstop flow of activity. You could call RASP a very *dynamic* environment. But that day in my room all I heard was the far-off hum of Highway 1. I was hyperaware of not having anywhere to be for the first time in months, so I just stayed there for a while, staring at the stripes of sunshine on my window blinds, absorbing my new situation.

Mom hadn't moved anything in my room since I'd left home. My desk was still crowded with baseball trophies. My camping gear and backpacks were still piled in the corner. My graduation cap and gown were still thrown over the back of my chair. Everything looked too flimsy and bright. Like toys compared to the gear I'd been using in the Army.

After a minute or two, I rallied the courage to take a look at myself. My injuries could have definitely been worse but they were no cakewalk, either. Beneath the air casts and my clothes, I knew I was black-and-blue. Stitched up like a quilt. A real mess. Once the swelling went down, it was possible I'd need surgeries in my arm, wrist, and leg, followed by months of rehab before I could even think about getting back to Fort Benning. I'd been told at Walter Reed that could all take up to a year, but I'd refused to consider what that really meant in front of my mom and the doctors. Now I did, and it just about killed me.

I don't expect you to understand this but enlisting in the Army, it was . . . um. It was a really good thing for me. I'd been in hell since my dad died. But RASP had turned things around for me. It was something positive when I'd needed it, and lying on my bed that morning, I couldn't accept the setback I'd just been dealt. That I was going to miss *a year* while I healed. I couldn't do that. I couldn't go back to how I'd been before.

As that sank in, anger moved through me like nothing I'd ever felt before. A feeling way bigger than frustration or disappointment. It was *rage*. Rage that felt like heat inside me, a fever to the millionth degree. So much it seemed measurable, like if you had the right lens, the right equipment, you'd see thermal waves in the air around me.

I was on strict orders not to move unless absolutely necessary. Parts of my femur had shattered and had only just been set. Right then, I couldn't have cared less. With that anger sizzling inside me, I couldn't lay there any longer.

I shifted to the edge of the bed, slid my legs off the mattress, and sat up. A head rush hit me hard, my pulse a shrill cry in my ears, and the room carouseled around me, but I knew there'd be more. I braced myself for the pain I knew was coming.

It never did. Aside from dizziness and anger that felt like

burning cordite inside me, I felt okay. My left arm and leg felt puffy and a little numb, but that was all.

My mom had left a note on my bedside table beneath a glass of water and my bottles of pain meds—a pharmacy's worth. She was on a quick run to the grocery store. I was supposed to take my next doses as soon as I woke up because I was already two hours late. She'd also left my crutches leaning against the wall. I passed on the drugs, grabbed a crutch for my healthy arm, and stood.

Still fine.

I kept going.

To walk with only one side of my body, I had to drag my crutch in a half circle ahead of me, then step, then drag, then step, sort of like a human compass. I figured that out as I left my room and made my way into our short hallway, past the pictures of me and my twin sister, Anna, playing naked on the beach as babies, then me with braces and zits in Little League uniforms, then me with braces and zits before junior prom. I attribute most of my mental toughness to growing up walking that hallway day after day.

I gave myself a goal to get to the front door because setting goals is how I do things and I needed to keep moving. I needed to feel like I could still get around on my own. If I could just get past the front door, it'd be a sign that I was back in control, and already recovering.

As I hobbled into our small living room, I noticed some moving boxes stacked under the window and stopped. Anna's painting of the ocean had been taken down from its spot above the couch and leaned against the wall. Our bookshelf was empty except for two framed photos. One of my dad kneeling by a swordfish on his best friend's fishing boat, the other of me as a scrawny-ass kid riding a two-foot wave like I was the king of everything.

The signs were all there. We were selling the house.

I hadn't expected that, though I should've. My mom managed a seafood restaurant by the harbor. She made an okay living but she was paying for Anna's college. I tried to help. I gave her as much as I could from my Army paychecks, but it wasn't much. Without my dad's income, I knew we couldn't stay in our house—the house my dad had built—and give my sister a college education. Still. I hadn't realized we were that close to selling. I hated that my mom had to handle this—the sale, a move, her *life*—alone. But I didn't know how to help. How could I take some pressure off? Especially now that I was busted up?

Hobbling past the moving boxes, I made it to the front door and stepped outside. The concrete walkway felt cool under my right foot; my left was safely encased in the air cast.

Half Moon Bay, where I grew up, is a small town southwest of San Francisco right on the Pacific Ocean. It's a fishing town and a surfing town and the smell there is a combination of lobster traps and highway exhaust and tourist restaurants. You know the smell of fish and chips? That's home for me. A hundred percent, it's home. It's the best smell in the world. I'd missed it, but now I couldn't stop thinking about the move. Soon this *wouldn't* be home. Where would my mom go? And everywhere I looked I saw memories of my dad. The street, where we used to throw the baseball. The driveway, where he used to wash his truck. His workshop, in the garage.

I'd already lost him. Was I going to lose these memories of him, too?

My next-door neighbor, Mrs. Collins, was out tending the roses along her picket fence. Mrs. C had just retired after being a nurse for forty years. Her husband had flown F-4s for the Air Force in Vietnam. Mrs. C had never had kids, so she'd sort of adopted Anna and me as unofficial grandkids. She loved to bake and had this great sense of humor. The day I enlisted, she brought over an olallieberry pie with a note that said, *Dear Gideon, The Army is a fine path too, I suppose.*

As much as I liked her, I was in no mood to talk. But I shuffled over to her anyway, because I knew my mom would never hear the end of it if I didn't say hello.

"Hey, Mrs. C," I said, trying to settle myself down. The personal anger atmosphere I'd developed was still with me, this searing heat that seeped from my skin. "How you doing today?"

"Gideon?" Her eyes met mine. They seemed foggy, like she wasn't really focusing on me. And she'd frozen in place, letting the long red rose she'd just clipped fall to the grass.

"Mrs. Collins? You all right?"

She blinked. "Of course I am. I didn't expect to see you."

"Sorry. Didn't mean to startle you."

"I didn't say you did. What is it you want?" she demanded, her cheeks jiggling.

I didn't really register her question right away. It seemed too harsh, and her gaze had gone from foggy to granite. "I was just walking to the beach."

Actually I'd been hoping she'd heard about my accident and would offer to bake me a get-well pie, but not anymore. She was starting to freak me out.

"*Liar.*" She pointed the clippers at me. "You're not going to the beach, young man. All you're doing is standing there wasting my time!"

"Uh, *what?*" I didn't understand. This was the little old lady who asked me to catch and release house spiders. Who smiled when she was sitting on her porch—alone. I mean . . . *wasting her time?* She lived for visits from me and Anna.

"Get on your way!" she yelled. She pulled off a gardening glove and tossed it at me. I dodged, but not very well with the cast and the crutches, and it smacked me on the back. "Scat!"

That sounded like a good idea to me. I dragged myself down the street, confused and shaken up. I made a mental note to talk to my mom. Mrs. C was getting up there in age. Maybe it was time someone checked her out.

I hobbled past the Marshburns' and the Harringtons' down to the end of our court. I knew better than to head into the sand with my injuries, so I stopped at the trailhead. Beyond the dunes and beneath the fog, the ocean was there, big and dependable. You could always count on the ocean to be the ocean.

As I stood there, I realized I still felt no pain in my leg or my arm. My doctors had been way off on their estimates for my recovery. A *year,* they'd told me. No way. Six months was my new target for getting back to Benning. Why not? Physically, I was feeling way better than I expected. Mentally, I had a full tank of frustration and anger to fuel me. And my pre-Army life offered nothing I wanted. My buddies and my sister were away at college. And with the house selling, I wouldn't even have that anymore. I had to get out of there.

Down the beach, I spotted the Harringtons' dog loping across the shallow waves. Jackson was more grizzly bear than Labrador. He'd been my running partner before I left home. I called him, and smiled as he came bounding over.

Ten feet shy of me, he dug his paws into the sand and stood tall, ears on high alert like he didn't recognize me.

"Easy, boy. It's me." I'd known him since he was only a couple of weeks old.

His lips curled and he bared his teeth, letting out a low, rumbling growl.

"Jackson, it's me."

He charged before I got the words out, his hackles lifting, his mouth snapping.

I swung my crutch forward. "Jackson, *back*!"

But he kept snarling and lunging at me no matter what I yelled, pushing me back toward sand where I knew I'd lose my footing. I thought ahead. If I fell, I'd use my arm with the cast to shield me from his bites.

I'd just stepped off the asphalt when Jackson stopped. His ears pricked up. Then he took off, responding to the voice I could now hear calling him up the street.

I watched him disappear around the side of the Harringtons' house, my heart banging against my chest.

What *was* that?

I'd had enough fresh air for the day. I hustled home, relieved that Mrs. C had gone inside, too. Shooting through my front door, I came face-to-face with my mom.

"Whoa! Mom! I was—"

I was what? Freaked out by a little old lady and a dog? But the sight of my mom put that all out of my mind, and it was good. Just real good to see her without being in the haze of painkillers.

I hadn't had an actual conversation with her in weeks, since before I started RASP, and there were a dozen questions I wanted to ask her. If she was doing okay with the house thing. If she was lonely without Anna and me around. If she'd considered dating again—just a yes or no answer would do on that one. I knew she'd move on eventually. She was tough, my mom. And she was young. She'd had Anna and me when she was only twenty and she took care of herself and all that. A lot of times people thought she was Anna's older sister, since they looked so much alike. Way more than Anna and me.

A second or two passed before I realized we were still standing there. Mom hadn't said a word and neither had I. For all that I'd wanted to ask her, I couldn't execute an emotional pivot. I still had this pissed-off furnace cranking inside me. When I finally spoke, what came out of my mouth was, "Were you ever planning to tell me about the house?"

She started in surprise. "We are *not* talking about the house right now, Gideon. We are talking about *you*. Were you trying to scare the life out of me? I leave for half an hour and you disappear? You're not even supposed to be out of bed!"

A grocery bag tipped over on the kitchen counter, and an apple rolled into the sink. "I'm fine, Mom. I just needed some air."

But it was like she didn't even hear me. "I called Anna," she continued. "I was about to call Cory. Don't you think I've been through enough this week? I don't think you realize what this has been like for me. Do you know how close you came to dying?"

"I'm okay, Mom. I had to get out of the house for a second. Calm down, okay?"

She didn't. She kept yelling at me, saying she couldn't believe my lack of judgment. Didn't I understand how serious my injuries were? Was I purposely trying to hurt her by hurting myself? She'd seldom laid into me that way before, with so much relish. When she finally slowed down, I told her I was going to go back to bed.

"That is a very good idea," she said, but her tone was more like *get out of my face.*

I hightailed it back to my room. Nothing felt normal and I needed to think.

I dropped onto my bed and stared at the ceiling, going through every step I'd taken from the minute I'd left the house. I'd gotten to Jackson's rabies episode when it hit me. After I saw Jackson, I'd *run* home. Awkwardly with the casts and the crutch. But not the limp of a guy with broken bones. That wasn't all. I'd stood on both feet while Mom had yelled at me. Then I'd walked right into my room and lain down. No hobbling. No drag step. No pain.

I looked down at my leg and wiggled my toes. Then I flexed my muscles inside the cast and did the math. So . . . I was two hours overdue on pain meds, I just ran up a hill with a pulverized arm and leg, and I felt *fine?*

"Gideon?" My mom knocked on the door. "I'm sorry I yelled, honey. I don't know what came over me. I guess the stress got to me. And I didn't expect to see you moving around so soon and it scared me. I don't want you to get hurt again, but it wasn't right to take it out on you."

Now, *that* sounded like my mom. Hearing the softness in her voice relaxed me a little. "It's okay."

"Can I get you anything?"

She wanted an excuse to come into my room but I had too much going on in my head for that. "No thanks. I'm going to rest now."

"All right. I'm right here if you need me."

As soon as her footsteps faded away, I sat up and stared at my leg cast, having a little argument with myself over whether I wanted to look or not.

I had an okay stomach for seeing blood. Food and drugs, not so much. But blood and injuries I could handle pretty well. Only this was *my* leg. Did I really want to see it bloated and bruised? Crisscrossed with staples?

Yes, I decided. Yes, I did. I had to figure out what was happening.

I undid the Velcro straps and pulled apart the plastic frames of the air cast.

My leg looked like my leg, with the addition of a few pale scars that were so faint I almost couldn't see them. I had no bruises. No swelling.

Right. Okay, so . . . Was I *dreaming*? Seeing things?

Panic built inside me as I unstrapped the cast on my arm next, pulling that off.

Surprise again. My arm had healed, just like my leg. Insane. Completely insane, but there was something else. Something *on* me.

A thick metal band circled my wrist. Two inches wide, and the metal itself was nothing I recognized. It looked like mercury, but it gave off a red glow. The light that bounced off it was deep red. Crimson.

My first thought was medical bracelet. It had to be one of those magnetic healing bands. But I couldn't find a clasp or a buckle. The metal ran around my wrist without a single scratch, button, or hook. And it was tight. Glued-on tight. I had no idea how it'd been put on me.

More important, I didn't see how it would ever come off.

CHAPTER 6

Y ou can stop there, Gideon."
I clear my throat, caught off guard by Cordero's inter-ruption. It takes me a couple more seconds to come back completely. Leaving the past is a slow process. Thick. Sticky. Like bellying out of a swamp.

Are these drugs even legal? Have I asked that?

"If what you're saying is true, you healed from the accident in five days?" Cordero asks.

"What I'm saying is true. So, yes. Five days."

"And no one thought this was unusual? Your mother didn't comment? The doctors?"

"I haven't been seen by a doctor since I left Walter Reed, and my mom . . ." I shrug. "She was definitely suspicious that day, but I haven't talked to her since, so I don't really know what she thought."

Cordero's eyes drop to my wrist, which is covered by my long-sleeved shirt and strapped to the chair with plastic flex ties. "Do you still have the cuff?"

I nod. "Like I said, it doesn't come off."

She lifts two fingers in the air, motioning to the guys behind her.

Texas steps forward and kneels at my side. "Don't do any-thin' stupid," he says in a thick drawl. By the door, Beretta draws the Beretta and takes aim at my forehead.

Texas tries to pull my sleeve up, but the plastic tie is cover-ing it too tightly. He looks to Cordero, who nods her permis-sion. He takes a badass bowie knife from a hip sheath, cuts the tie, and pushes my sleeve up. His blue eyes meet mine for a second—a silent repeat of the warning he just gave me—and then he takes my wrist and turns it.

"It's here. No seams." He turns his shoulders so Cordero can see.

Her chair creaks as she leans forward. She studies the cuff the same way I did that day in my bedroom, kind of in awe and confusion. That look pretty much sums up the past month of my life.

"It's clearly an alloy of some sort, but it refracts light like a gemstone. . . . Like a ruby."

I wish I'd described it that way. That sounded better than *bouncing crimson light.*

"The texture?" she asks.

Texas faces me again. He keeps his bowie knife in his right hand. With his left, he runs two fingers over the cuff. "Smooth. More like glass than metal. Body temp." Genuine curiosity flares in his gaze. "Is it heavy?"

"No. I don't feel any weight at all. Same with the sword and armor."

Bam.

It's like a silent grenade goes off. Nobody moves. Everyone looks from my eyes to the cuff on my wrist, ping-ponging back and forth a few times.

I probably let that one slip earlier than I should have. Thanks, truth serum. But I've never been the best storyteller. That's Sebastian's territory. I bet Bastian's Cordero has already sent out for popcorn and Milk Duds.

I'm the one who breaks the silence. "Should I keep going?"

Cordero leans back in her chair and absently scratches her knuckles. She looks a little less blank than she has up until now. Like maybe I'm entertaining her.

"Tie him back down," she says to Texas. "And yes, Gideon. You should."

CHAPTER 7

The next morning, I woke to the sound of my mom talking on the phone.

Actually it was more like yelling, which was what woke me.

I'd slept on my stomach without wearing my casts, and hadn't taken any painkillers since yesterday. I should've been howling in pain, but I wasn't.

I'd heard my mom raise her voice before. She was half Irish and didn't take crap from anyone. But the way she was yelling had an edge that was extra sharp. And then there was the way she'd sounded off on me the day before. What had always been pretty rare was suddenly happening a lot.

She hung up and I heard footsteps marching toward my room. The door swung open and she stood there, her mouth pressed in a grim line that reminded me of the summer I broke our front window three times in three weeks perfecting my baseball swing.

"Something came up at work," she said. "I have to go in for the next few days, but I talked to your sister. She's coming up to watch you."

This was an arrangement they'd already made. While I was recovering, my mom was going to look after me on weekdays and work Friday through Monday. Anna, who was a freshman at Cal Poly and only had classes midweek, would take weekends.

It was a Tuesday, though. Mom's call had thrown a curveball into the schedule.

"Anna has school," I said.

"Well, she's going to have to just catch up. You're more important."

"Mom, I'm—"

"Don't argue with me, Gideon. She'll be here by dinnertime. I'll have Mrs. C come over and keep an eye on you until—"

"No—that's okay. I'll be fine until Anna gets here."

Mom dropped a kiss on my forehead, reminded me to take my meds, and left.

As soon as I heard the front door shut, I threw on running shoes, shoved some clothes into my Army rucksack, and grabbed my keys. I locked up the house and jumped into my Jeep—a beat-up '85 CJ my dad and I were going to fix up but never got around to for obvious reasons.

I did all of that—dressing, packing, and locking up—with working limbs. Perfectly healthy limbs. As I took the steering wheel, the shiny piece of red metal on my left wrist caught my eye. Things were happening that made no sense, and the feeling was too close to how I'd felt after my dad died. My gut was telling me to move, because moving—running, hiking, driving, any kind of movement—always helped to chill me out. It gave me perspective, and I needed that badly. I backed out of the driveway, took the freeway south, and then just . . . drove.

When I pulled up to my sister's college apartment complex three hours later, nothing made any more sense. I didn't have a new perspective.

And I had not chilled out.

My sister's college dorm was on the second floor of a new housing unit on the edge of the Cal Poly campus, with green hills and trails all around, a heated swimming pool, and a sand volleyball court in the center quad. A luxury resort, pretty much.

No one answered when I buzzed her on the intercom system and I'd left my phone at home like an idiot so I went around back, thinking I'd climb her balcony. With any luck, the glass slider would be unlocked.

A girl with blue-streaked hair was painting her toenails on the patio of the apartment beneath my sister's. She set the red polish on a stack of textbooks by her feet and looked up at me.

This time I was ready. Mrs. C, Jackson, and my mom's reactions had one thing in common—me. I'd been riled with that burning anger around them, so maybe *I* was affecting them? It was insane, but it was also the only guess I had.

I raised my hands, showing her I meant no harm. "Hey, how's it going?" Inside, I was begging her to stay calm, grasping for inner peace with everything I had, visualizing tranquility, finding my happy place, all that, and *bingo*.

She smiled.

"Who are you?" she asked.

"I'm Anna Blake's brother. Gideon."

"Her twin, the Army guy?"

"Her twin, the Army guy."

She checked me out, which was the only genuinely good thing that had happened to me in a solid week, and introduced herself as Joy.

"You don't look very much like her."

I shrugged. "Yeah, she's prettier than I am. I try not to get jealous."

Joy's smile went wider. "You're like Luke and Leia, kind of."

"We get that sometimes. Mind if I use your railing? Anna's not there yet."

"Go ahead. Use whatever you need."

"Thanks." I tossed my ruck up to the second-floor balcony. Then I jumped, grabbing the bars above me, and swung myself up. Not bad for a guy with a broken arm and leg.

"Gideon?" Joy peered up from below. "We're having some people over later. You should come by."

I thanked her again. A party sounded like just what I needed to get my mind off things.

The sliding door to my sister's place was unlocked and slid right open, which was both good and bad. Anna really should've known better. I slipped inside and froze when I heard the snuffling sounds of someone crying.

Dropping my duffel, I rushed to Anna's room and found her rolled in a ball on her bed, her eyes pressed shut like she was trying to keep in the tears, her phone gripped in her hand.

"Anna?" Sitting on the bed, I put my hand on her shoulder. "What's going on?"

She shot away with a yelp. *"Gideon?"* Her eyes moved over me, like she couldn't believe I was real, then she threw her arms around my neck. "I've been so worried. Mom said you'd broken your arm and your leg. She said you almost *died*."

"I know," I said, hugging her back. "I'm fine, Banana. I'm all right." I was all right—everywhere except in the head.

She drew back and studied me. Like I've said, Cordero, we don't look much alike. Not just our coloring. Anna's pretty skinny. Not very athletic. She'd kill me if she heard me tell you that. And I'm . . . Well. You're looking at me. I look like my dad. Like my dad did. His height and build.

The only thing Anna and I have in common is our dad's eyes. Light blue. Same shape too, with the downward tilt at the sides. People call them soulful eyes or smiling eyes. Or Paul Newman eyes—old people always say that. But to me they're the eyes of someone who listens with everything they've got when you're talking, which is exactly my sister and it was my dad, too. So seeing Anna now, it felt good but it also made me miss my dad even more than when I'd been at home, which sucked. I'd shared a womb with my sister and almost every day of my life since. I didn't love how hard it was just to look at her.

Anna shook her head, her expression pleading for answers I didn't have. "Was the accident not as bad as they thought?"

"The initial reports might've made it sound worse. And I'm still kind of sore," I said, though I wasn't.

"Worse by *a lot*. I didn't think you'd get hurt training."

"Me, either. But you can't pick when accidents happen, right?"

That word, *accident,* felt like knocking into a bruise that wouldn't heal. It was the same for Anna, too. Grief passed over her face like a shadow. I had to look away. On her desk I saw a framed picture from Christmas a year and a half ago, all of us wearing Santa hats and grinning like loons. We were still four Blakes then. A four-pack.

"What are you doing here, Gideon? Why aren't you at home?"

What she meant was *why aren't you bedridden,* but I took the questions at face value. "I thought you could look after me here. That way you don't have to miss any classes." Then I nodded at her phone, ready to leave the subject of my non-injuries behind. "You want to tell me what's going on?"

She shrugged, smoothing her hands on her pajama pants. I'd given them to her the same Christmas from the photo. Red flannel with Eiffel Towers stamped all over them because her dream was to study in Paris. My sister was an artist. Growing up, Anna made beautiful collectible drawings and paintings and pottery. I broke shit. Bikes, bats, surfboards. Hearts. Just kidding on that last one.

"Oh. Just stuff with Wyatt," she said.

"Wyatt?" I knew the guy. He was a spoiled idiot from a private high school near our hometown. He and Anna started dating senior year when they met in a mock-Senate club. I was pissed when I found out he was coming to the same college. High school should've been the end of Wyatt Sinclair. "I thought you broke up with that loser."

"I did break up with him," Anna said. "It was mutual. I mean, we decided to end it together. He said he wanted a time-out so I gave it to him."

"Like he's a freakin' toddler? That kind of time-out?"

Anna ignored that. "He thought we were getting too serious. He said he wanted to 'experience college.'" She made air quotes. "I thought we were really done. I know he's been with other girls since. But we were technically on a break, so it shouldn't matter, right?"

What technically mattered was that Wyatt was an ass, but Anna clearly didn't see it that way. I looked around at the pile of clothes thrown over her chair and the coffee mug on her desk. I couldn't believe I was talking relationships with her when I'd fallen out of a plane a week ago. And had no injuries to show for it.

Anna lifted her phone. "He just called and said he was wrong about leaving me. He said he made a terrible error in judgment and that he wants me back."

"And you told him to screw himself, right?"

"I love him, G."

"Anna. My *ears.*"

She laughed. "Okay, maybe not. But I do like him. He's smart and he treated me well when we were together. He's coming over to talk. I feel like I should at least hear him out."

"He's really coming over? That's great! My fist is dying to talk to his face."

"*No,* Gideon." Anna's smile disappeared. "Stay out of this. It's my business."

As I stared into her eyes, I wondered if this was my fault. When our dad died I was always gone, off on my own. Camping. Driving. Just hiding out alone. I couldn't be around anyone. I didn't trust myself to be. But my sister had needed someone in those days like I'd needed no one, and Wyatt Sinclair had been there for her. He'd stepped in and been her someone, and if there was one thing I understood, it was that grief was an opponent you didn't play fair with. You did whatever it took to not let it beat you. You fought dirty against grief, period. So I understood. Anna didn't love Wyatt. She loved that he'd been there for her during the worst time in her life.

"What is that?" Anna pulled my sleeve up before I could stop her. "Is that a cuff?"

"Yeah, so?" I tugged it back down. "Can't I wear jewels?"

"It's called jewelry, for one. And you can't hate it your whole life and suddenly start liking it."

"I don't hate jewelry." I just didn't like having anything on me that didn't have a reason to be there.

"Hogwash. You don't even wear belts."

True. Belts and bracelets shared a lot of DNA, in my view. I'd avoided them up until recently. In the Army, belts were a must.

Anna suddenly looked like she'd won the state lottery. "You met someone! You did, didn't you?"

I'd never had a girlfriend, officially, and for some reason that made my mom and Anna lose their minds. In general we Blake twins were pretty screwed up when it came to relationships. Anna stayed in a bad one. I avoided them completely.

"Easy there, Banana. It's called an XT3 Band. It stands for Experimental Therapy Band, third generation. Highly classified so that's all I can tell you."

I said all this, but I still had no idea what the cuff really was. Maybe I was right?

"Seriously, what's her name?"

"You know how I feel about this. If I wanted a commitment, I'd get a dog."

"Wow." She reached for a black pillow decorated with a big sparkly skull and hugged it. "So romantic."

I made a face, because who the hell wanted to be a romantic? Then I couldn't look past the skull pillow. "Tell me something, sis. Why do we have to make skulls cute? Some things shouldn't be messed with. Guns, for example. Toilets . . . toilet paper . . . guns . . . They should just stay functional. Sparkle-free."

She rolled her eyes. "Please. If I had a bedazzled toilet, I'd love it and so would you. Don't even try to deny it. You'd love a fancy can."

I did deny it, which led to a healthy debate. Trivial discussions were the bread-and-butter of our relationship and it felt good to just be with my sister—until someone knocked on the door. Anna stopped mid-sentence and vaulted off the bed. Douche bag had just arrived.

"Hey, Pooh Bear," I heard him drawl in the living room. All pet names were inherently ridiculous but that one took first place. "How are you?"

"Honestly, I've been better," Anna replied.

"I know," Wyatt murmured. "Me too. But I'm better now that I'm with you. I've missed you, Pooh."

I grabbed the sparkly skull pillow and dug my fingers into it. *Ignore, Blake. Ignore.* "I don't know if I can do this again, Wy. How am I supposed to believe you really want to be with me? Or that you'll stay with me this time?"

You're not, Anna. Move on.

"We'll just take it one day at a time. You know I never stopped caring about you." He lowered his voice. "Anna, the others girls were nothing to me. They didn't mean anything. Not like you do."

No. . . . Did he really just say that?

I flew off the bed.

"Stop right there," Anna said, the instant I crossed the door.

I did what she said and leaned against the doorjamb. Seeing Anna upset had sidelined my own problems for a little bit, but now that sharp, tangible buzz of anger was back, seething from under my skin. I couldn't even fight it. This was about my sister. My self-control was under siege.

Wyatt gaped at me, taking a half step back. "Your *brother* is here, Anna? I thought he was hurt."

"Sorry to disappoint, jackass." Well, that came out. But I didn't care. Wyatt might have been good to Anna in the past but he was taking advantage of that.

"I told you to stay out of this, Gideon," Anna said.

"Yes! Stay out of this *please*." Wyatt pushed a hand through his preppy hair. As a general rule, I didn't like guys who styled their hair like they just woke up. Messiness should never be a goal. It should be a consequence. "God, Anna. I don't think this is going to work. How are we supposed to talk with him around?"

"I didn't know he was coming down here, Wyatt. I'm sorry."

Was she actually apologizing to *him*?

You're not sorry, Anna. You are pissed off.

Anna shook her head like she was shuffling her thoughts. "Wait a minute. You've been messing around with other girls for the past month and you're mad that *my brother* is here?"

Now, that was more like it.

Wyatt frowned, clearly surprised by the pushback. "I thought we were trying to fix things, Pooh Bear. He's going to interfere with that."

"I'm not interfering. I'm just standing here." I smiled.

"See? He's already doing it. Anna, I thought you wanted to be with me. Maybe I was wrong."

What a load of guilt-tripping crap. Don't stand for it, Anna.

"This was a mistake, Wyatt." She opened the apartment door. "I think you should go."

Wyatt stepped toward her, turning his back to me. "I came here because I want you back in my life," he said in a hushed voice. "But we're never going to figure this out if you're going to be irrational."

Irrational? That sounded good to me. *Let it rip, sis.*

Anna slapped him across the cheek. Wyatt's head whipped

to the side. For a few seconds, no one breathed. We all just stood there, hearing that fleshy echo, until Anna said, "Leave, Wyatt. Now."

He shot me an accusatory glare, like he suspected I was behind Anna's actions. I was less suspicious. In fact, I was pretty sure I'd influenced Anna's behavior. Somehow, I'd focused my anger on her and propelled her through the entire thing. But how was that even *possible*?

After Wyatt left, Anna fell back against the door. "What did I just do?"

"You took care of business. You don't need that moron in your life, sis. You did the right thing."

"I hit him." She looked at her hand like it wasn't part of her. "I *slapped* him."

"You were nicer than I would've been."

Anna shook her head, her eyes welling up. "That doesn't help, Gideon." Then she darted past me into her room and slammed the door.

I reached for the handle just as the lock clicked. "Open the door. Come on, Anna. It's his loss, sis." I could hear her crying inside—one of the worst sounds in the world for me. "Anna . . . let me in," I tried again, but it was clear that wasn't going to happen for a long while.

Excellent. I'd succeeded in making her more upset. Now what?

Behind me, I heard the quiet scuff of keys as someone entered the apartment. That had to be Anna's roommate, Taylor. The last thing I wanted was another bizarre social interaction, so.

I hustled to the balcony, climbed down, and took off.

CHAPTER 8

Like I said, moving helps to clear my head. Running's always been something I've been pretty good at. It made RASP easier for me than for a lot of other guys. By easier I mean less excruciating. Sometimes around the five-mile mark, I hit the runner's high. For me the feeling is actually mellow—real quiet and steady—but as I picked up a trail heading away from the dorms into the hills around campus, I doubted I'd find that steadiness. I had too much to figure out. The fast healing. The mystery metal on my wrist. My newfound ability to, what? Make people angry?

I already had that. I didn't need to get any better at it.

Nothing made sense and I had nothing, no theories. I didn't hit any mental dead ends because I didn't even have roads. I ended up thinking about the months just before my dad died because that was a trick my brain liked to do, pulling memories from behind my ear and presenting them to me like a bad magician.

This one was a baseball memory, right after my last game junior year. My Jeep had broken down and everyone else had already gone home, so Dad and I were stranded at the field. We called Anna, who was bringing jumper cables in my dad's work truck, then went back to the baseball diamond to wait.

We sat in the home team dugout together, watching the sun sink behind the scoreboard. The infield was freshly groomed, the chalk lines dragged clean, the bases put away. I thought about how something had clicked for me that season. I'd upped my game on every level and already been approached by a couple recruiters—small colleges that wanted me—but I knew I'd do better. I had the grades I needed and enough talent. Effort was the last piece, and that was where I really kicked ass. Come spring, I'd have a scholarship offer from a big school.

It'd been a dream for a long time. That night it felt attainable. Everything seemed possible to me in that moment. *Everything* did. And as we waited for Anna to show up, I told my dad what I wanted. What I was going to do.

When I finished, I remember he looked at me for a long moment. I felt like he was seeing a man sitting there with him, not just his son. Then he'd smiled and said, "I could go for another four years in the stands."

He believed I could do it. My fate seemed sealed. In a way, it almost felt *achieved* already. My dream was going to happen. Except he died six weeks later and I never set foot on a baseball diamond again.

Anyway.

You can probably guess that thinking about my dad didn't improve my mood. He wasn't around and never would be again, but he was one person I'd always been able to talk to about anything. I could've used that right then. Without that option, I ran until my shirt was soaked with sweat and I'd put five miles behind me.

I stopped as I reached the top of a hill. The setting sun turned the sky red, and campus spread out below me. Up until then I'd barely noticed the cuff on my wrist. Wearing it felt as comfortable as wearing nothing and it shouldn't have been that way, considering I didn't like things on me, and how hefty and snug it was. But now, as I cooled down and focused on it, I felt the slightest buzzing sensation, a beehive kind of drone humming up my arm.

That was enough for me. I had a feeling this piece of metal was responsible for everything. Time for it to go. I grabbed the first big rock I saw, braced my arm on the dirt, and slammed the rock down.

A scream detonated in my ears—high-pitched, terrible. Like someone getting murdered. At the same time, the air rushed out of my lungs and my vision went red, bright fire red, and I face-planted into the dirt. The last thing I remember was the sound of my blood pounding in my ears.

It sounded like the thunder of hoofbeats.

I think I was out for a few minutes. When I came around, the sun had just set and the sky was doing a slow bleed from red to purple. As I headed back to Anna's, I had a nice long talk with myself about staying composed.

Anna's roommate, Taylor, answered the door. In the living-room area, a few people were sprawled across the two small couches, and a pyramid of empty beer cans sat on the coffee table.

I'd already made sure my personal rage atmosphere was mild, low chance of anger. Now I followed up by sending a kind of mental message into the room before anything bad could happen.

We're cool. Everybody be cool. Just be calm.

They ignored me, which was perfect, except for Taylor, who started right in with how much she'd heard about me and how much she loved Anna and how much fun they'd been having. I countered with how much I needed a shower and took my-self to the bathroom. By the time I got out, my head felt clearer and I had a plan. I'd attack the situation like I'd been trained to do in the Army. Gather intelligence. Create a strategy. Execute on it. I'd figure out what was happening to me, then go about reversing it.

Anna was at her desk when I stepped into her room. She spun in the swivel chair, sliding her cell phone into the pocket of her jacket. "Good look, little brother," she said, tipping her chin to the pink towel around my waist. I'd been born two minutes after her and she loved to remind me that I came into this world in second place. "The girls in the apartment down-stairs are having a party. Joy said she told you about it. You're coming, right?"

"Yeah, sure. Is Wyatt going to be there?"

"I don't think so." She frowned, eyeing me more closely. "Gideon, you don't look hurt at all. You look bigger."

"Yeah?" I looked at myself. All I could really see was my stomach, so I patted it. "It's all the PT I've been doing." I'd always been athletic. Army life had just honed me up more.

"Did you do something wrong?"

It took me a second to realize what she meant. She thought the accident was a cover? "Anna, *no*. I didn't."

She didn't say anything for a couple of seconds. We could always tell when the other was holding something back, which was one of the reasons I'd been gone so much over the past year. I hadn't wanted to take any chances of dragging her down with me. Now was no different.

I rubbed a hand over my wet hair, which was already dry because it was a millimeter long. "Stop looking at me like that. It's creepy."

"You're creepy." She stood. "See you downstairs."

"Wait. I need to call Mom."

"I already told her you're here. She went atomic." She tossed me her phone and smiled. "Have fun."

When she left, I pulled on jeans and sat at the desk. My first order of business was to get information. I fished some medi-cal discharge papers out of my ruck and found the number for the Army physician overseeing my case. Because of the se-verity of my injuries, I had Dr. Katz's mobile number. He an-swered right away.

"Private Blake, how are you feeling?" he asked.

"Good, sir. I'm good . . . maybe too good."

"No such thing as 'too good' where health is concerned. Glad to hear it." I heard him tapping on a keyboard in the background. "Looks like we're seeing you in a week for some follow-up exams. What can I do for you, son?"

"Major, did you or any of the other doctors put a medical bracelet on me?"

"You have no known allergies or preexisting medical conditions. There's no need for an ID bracelet."

"Not an ID bracelet. A healing bracelet. On my left wrist?"

"I don't have a record of that, Private. I don't want to discourage you, Gideon, but a magnetic bracelet won't go far considering the severity of your injuries. Is there anything else? How's your pain tolerance?"

"Good, sir. Thank you. Nothing else."

I hung up and flipped open Anna's laptop. The apartment had fallen quiet except for a deep, pulsing bass thrumming from Joy's party.

I typed one ridiculous search parameter after another.

Unexplainable rapid healing
Manipulating rage in others
Mystery metal bracelets

Just about everything turned up the same result: superhero websites.

That was enough intelligence gathering for me.

I shut the laptop, sat back, and laughed my ass off.

CHAPTER 9

College parties were a phenomenon I had yet to experience. Unlike my high-school buddies who'd spent the past months filling up Solo cups in parties across America, I'd spent them getting my head shaved, learning to low crawl, and polishing my shoes until I could see my face in them.

Those first few months in the Army were brutal, and not only because they were physically and mentally demanding. In Basic Training, a lot of guys were slackers who didn't really want to be there and it felt like my sixth-grade sleepover all over again—a bunch of screw-offs giddy on their first night away from home. Until I got a little further along in the process and found guys more like me in RASP, I'd seriously wondered if I'd made the right choice.

I wondered that again as I leaned against the wall in Joy's living room and watched people toss back drinks and dance to pounding rap music. There were about fifteen girls packed into the small room and every last one of them was hot. I'd been almost exclusively around guys for a long time so this was a welcome change for me.

Not everyone was as happy about my attendance, though. A few of the guys at the party were throwing hostile looks at me, making it clear they didn't like me encroaching on their territory. Occasionally words like "GI Joe" and "Army grunt" filtered through the music. I even heard a couple of football players in the corner reciting choice quotes from *Full Metal Jacket*. These were probably the same guys who got choked up during the Super Bowl national anthem, moved by those three minutes of intense patriotism. And see, I had a problem with that. To me patriotism wasn't a mood or a moment. It was so much more.

I ignored them and focused on hanging out with Anna and Taylor. I was still carrying around this scalding energy, this full payload of rage that was right there, reachable inside me. Ignitable. Some part of me wondered if it hadn't been with me for a long time, only that I'd been denying it. I couldn't ignore it now. I could only try to manage it.

Taylor turned out to be pretty hilarious. She was a big Dodger fan so we almost went to blows over that, but in a good way. I was glad my sister had made a good friend at school. Just as I was starting to settle in, Wyatt showed up.

I had promised myself I wouldn't interfere again, so I hung back when Anna left to go talk to him. I couldn't help watching them though. Even that bugged me. Wyatt's facial expressions were too extreme. Like, dude. Watch the crazy eyes. Just dial it back a bit. I didn't know how Anna was doing it. She had to feel like she was talking to a pinball machine.

"You know you have nothing to worry about, right?" Taylor said, laughing at me. "She's over him. And I'm looking out for her."

She was right. And Anna was smart. My sister knew what she was doing.

When Taylor headed to the patio to talk to her girlfriend, Joy wandered over. She leaned against the wall beside me and bumped my elbow, spilling a little of her beer on my sleeve. "What's wrong, Army boy? You don't drink?"

I did on occasion but not much. I'd been cursed with a stomach that didn't tolerate a lot of things. Too much sugar, preservatives, grease. If I didn't keep a good diet, I suffered. With booze especially I paid a pretty steep price, so I had to pick my battles. This wasn't one of them. With everything going on, the last thing I needed was to lose my edge or spend the night hugging the toilet.

"Actually, Joy," I answered, "I should be physically destroyed right now, technically speaking, but it looks like I might have developed a freaky fast-healing condition with a possible side of PTSD. So I thought I'd lay off the sauce tonight. Don't want to push things over the edge, know what I mean?"

Joy cupped her ear. "What? Sorry, it's so loud in here!"

"Can't party tonight!" I pulled Anna's phone out of my pocket. "In case there's a national emergency!"

"Ohhh, got it!" Joy wrinkled her nose. "It's so, like, *noble* you do that stuff!"

So far the Army had been the opposite of noble work for me. I got a mental image right then of Cory with shoelaces of snot coming out of his nose during a swim evolution. But hey. Someday I would put my life on the line for my country, so I didn't see any harm in letting her opinion stand.

Joy and I shouted small talk at each other for a little while. She was cute and she seemed nice. She told me all about the great beaches in the Philippines, where she was from. Some place called Cebu. I wasn't sure how I was doing hitting on her.

You'll find this shocking, Cordero, but I haven't always been the specimen you see in front of you. It wasn't just the braces or the zits that slowed me down in high school. I never really *tried*. My lack of game never bothered me much, though. I'd never met anyone where it had actually mattered. Not until Daryn. But I'm getting ahead of myself.

Anna had gone back to hanging out with Taylor again. My sister looked okay. She didn't look upset. On the other side of the room, Wyatt and his preppy buddies were having a competition to see who could show the most teeth when they laughed.

My gaze went to the patio where I'd met Joy earlier. A girl stood out there with a few other people, but she clearly wasn't with them. She stood alone in front of the open sliding door. What held my attention, besides the fact that she was pretty, was her expression. She stared right at me, and she looked intense and determined. Like we were in the middle of an argument even though we hadn't said a word to each other.

She stepped into the apartment and threaded through the people dancing at the center without breaking eye contact. Her gaze felt like a challenge, so I stepped up to the plate and met it. I wasn't going to break first, but my confusion must have shown. Joy stopped talking and followed my sight line.

"Do you know that girl?" she asked.

"I think so." She sure seemed to know me. "Can you give us a minute?"

"Sure." Joy glanced at her plastic cup. "I'm empty anyway," she said, and headed off.

The girl from the patio came right up and stopped in front of me. She obviously had an agenda. It seemed like the right call to let her make the first move, so I stood there, trying to look relaxed.

She was prettier up close—streaky blond hair that fell over one shoulder and tan skin. Not a lot of makeup. Maybe none. She wore a weathered black jacket, tight jeans, and scuffed boots. A backpack was slung over her right shoulder. She wasn't a college student, though. She just didn't look it. This girl had switchblades in her eyes and *don't mess with me* in her posture. She looked like she could handle herself. Super confident.

Her gaze flicked down to my left wrist. I immediately regretted not wearing a sweatshirt to cover up the cuff. When her eyes lifted again, the look in them was such an insane mixture of curiosity, relief, and fear that for a second, I wondered if I'd met her at some point in the past, offended her, then forgotten all about her.

No way, though. This wasn't a girl you forgot. I was only five seconds into knowing her, but I already knew that much.

"I need you to come with me," she said. "Right now."

"I bet that line works on all the guys."

Like I said, no game, but she was intimidating as hell. The party swirled behind her, all grinding bodies and thudding music, but she stood there as still as a lighthouse.

"This isn't a joke." She glanced toward the front door. "We have to get out of here or you're going to get hurt."

I laughed. "Sorry . . . what?"

Her eyes narrowed. "You don't know anything, do you?"

That didn't sit great with me. It struck a nerve that was already pretty raw. "I know a few things."

"Then why haven't you found the others?"

"Oh, wait. This is about *the others*?" I straightened off the wall. "I can explain that. See, I tried to find them but the spaceship left right when I got there. Just took right off. Can you believe the others did that to me? Flaky bastards." I was being a smart-ass, but I didn't want her to leave. "Look, what do you say we try this again?" I held out my hand, because why? I guess I wanted to make this more awkward. "I'm—"

"Gideon. I know," she said. Her palm closed over mine, her fingers taking a firm grip of my hand. "I'm Daryn. Let's get out of here." She did a one-eighty, still holding on to my hand, and started towing me toward the front door.

I needed a second to process a lot of things. Her crazy behavior. The fact that she had a guy's name. The fact that she knew *my* name. The fact that she was taking me . . . where? And that it should've felt like a good thing, an awesome thing, but somehow didn't.

She stopped suddenly. I ran right into her back.

"Whoa, sorry," I said, but she wasn't paying any attention to me.

The front door of the apartment had just swung open. Three people entered, two guys and a girl. Adrenaline roared through me. I knew instantly, on a primal level, something was about to go down.

The first guy was in his mid-twenties. Short black hair, and the kind of face that had to make life easier for him. His clothes were pretty slick, modern, and he was built. He had me by thirty pounds at least, but that didn't necessarily worry me. I could handle myself in a fight. What worried me was that he looked like he could handle himself in a fight, too.

Behind him stood a shorter guy, slight build, hunkered inside a suit that was a few sizes too big. He had stringy brown hair, the cratered skin of someone who'd fought hard-core acne, and glassy black eyes that cast anxiously around the apartment. He reminded me of a possum. The girl was average height and size, around my age, with red hair in a ponytail and tons of piercings—eyebrows, nose, lip. She carried herself with the same fearlessness as Daryn—who I noticed no longer looked fearless.

"Gideon, *run*," she said, pushing me back.

The tall guy homed in on her immediately, like she was the only person in the room. He said something to the other two, and they locked in too.

Daryn kept telling me to run, but I wasn't going anywhere. Retreat wasn't my style, and she was in trouble of some kind. I didn't stop to consider that she was a total stranger, that maybe she deserved what had just shown up at the door, that maybe I shouldn't have gotten involved.

I moved right into action.

CHAPTER 10

I'm going to tell you right up front, Cordero. The tall guy's name is Samrael. I don't want to keep calling him "Tall Guy" because . . . I don't know. It's dumb. For that matter, the girl with the red hair was Ronwae, and the possumy guy with the acne and the shifty eyes, that was Malaphar.

Don't worry. You'll know them all soon enough. Plus four more because there are seven in the Kindred. Seven total. But I'm skipping ahead again.

Back to the party.

Samrael looked like he was in charge, so I went after him, ready to brawl over a girl I didn't know. The theory that popped into my head as I crossed the room was that he was Daryn's violently jealous ex. It seemed plausible considering his intense focus on her. But Ronwae and Malaphar's involvement didn't fit well with that theory.

As I pushed through the last few partyers, I saw Daryn make a break for the patio. Ronwae plunged through the crowd, following her. I made a quick decision to stay on course. The best thing I could do was prevent the two guys at the door from joining in pursuit.

Joy had reached the front door moments before me and demanded to know who they were.

"You're leaving," I said to Samrael as I came to Joy's side. "Right now."

People stopped dancing and talking as the threat of danger percolated through the apartment. They circled around, a few of them pulling out phones, ready to catch any action.

"We'll leave when we have what we came for," Samrael said.

His voice was strangely calm, almost solemn, but I heard it perfectly through the pumping rap music. There was something dangerous about the total lack of emotion in his eyes. He was looking right at me, but he could've been looking at a chair or a lamp. And his posture triggered a warning inside me. I'd spent a lot of time around guys who made their livelihood off harnessed aggression. I knew potential hostility when I saw it.

I repeated my directive using more compelling language. His attention moved more fully onto me, a palpable weight descending on my shoulders.

"Who are you?" Samrael asked quietly, giving me a detached assessment.

Pressure settled over my eyes like a headache coming on, but it quickly turned painful. A feeling like invisible fingers prying around my eye sockets and digging deeper. It shocked me. I tried to move, but I couldn't. I couldn't even speak. Black spots flickered at the edges of my vision and a hot sting spread over my scalp. Fear tightened my lungs. I knew I wasn't passing out. I could still feel the tension in my muscles, and the drumming of my heart, but I couldn't stop what was happening.

The spots melded into darkness and my field of view narrowed. Then the darkness started to swirl around me and stretch into a tunnel. My feet were planted in Joy's living room but I felt myself pulling back. Felt the party recede, everything moving further away as I sank into a whirling black funnel.

"Weak," Samrael said, "whoever you are."

The pressure in my head sharpened to spikes walking over my skull.

He smiled. "Gideon Blake . . . so much anger . . ."

I heard myself groan. I wanted to fight, but my legs and arms wouldn't answer. I had one possible move.

Pushing through the black tunnel with my entire focus, I felt myself pulling closer to the party. My gaze went to the two huge football players by the door—the same two guys who'd called me "GI Joe" an hour earlier. Their attention was already on me.

I threw open the rage throttle.

Bring it, I told them. *Fight.*

They reacted instantly, exploding forward like they'd come off the line. The larger guy bolted past me, dropped his shoulder, and buried it into Samrael's back. The other one went after Malaphar, who plunged into the crowd.

The mental hold Samrael had cast over me broke. The pain released, the lack of it so overwhelming that for a second I felt like I was floating. My eyes cleared, the distancing swirl of darkness faded back, and my limbs unlocked.

The football player and Samrael grappled nearby, trapped in a struggle. Samrael was contending with the much stronger opponent. I looked for Anna and spotted her, but no Daryn.

Samrael freed himself from the football player's grasp. With savage force, he took the guy's head with both hands and drove his knee up. There was a sickening, meaty sound as the blow connected and then gasps erupted from across the apartment. The football player's eyes rolled back and he went down, three hundred pounds dropping to the floor like a boulder.

I stepped in, already swinging as he fell. My fist met Samrael's face, square on the jaw. He felt immovable, like I'd just tried to deck the Great Wall of China. He jerked back and the inside of my hand let out an audible *snap.*

Pain speared up my arm. I grabbed my hand, my instincts firing. I needed to withdraw, assess damage. But Samrael caught me around the throat and shoved me across the living room. Pain-drunk, I could only backpedal. We knocked over a small table and sent a lamp crashing to the floor. Then my back struck the wall with so much force, I felt it crack behind me.

Samrael had me pinned. My lungs couldn't get enough air. And I must have hit my head because his face blurred in and out of focus. The room had grown dimmer with the lamp broken, but in the semidark, I saw a trail of glistening blood dribble down his mouth and over his chin.

"Fool," he whispered, but his flat eyes were alive now. "Who sent you?"

He didn't wait for me to answer. The pressure came back over my eyes and my ears. He was getting inside my head again. As the stinging spread inside my scalp, the darkness began to whirl around me. I felt myself drawing back, separating from reality.

I didn't know how to fight this way. How was I supposed to defend myself? I couldn't even *move*.

Samrael smiled. His grip was crushing my throat. I still couldn't get enough air. "You know, for a moment there I thought you weren't pitiful. I guess I was wrong, pitiful Gideon." He angled his head slowly, left and then right. "But you're not scared, are you? How about now?"

His smile went wider. No . . . it was his mouth. His mouth pushed forward, forward, forward, elongating into a muzzle or . . . a beak? What was it? A *snout*?

His skin curdled into worn leather as his skull reshaped. His eyes pulled back, sloping, the black irises stirring, lighting with something dark inside. I saw a sea of torment in his eyes. Cries of anguish, fear, and weakness writhed there. I heard howling, and begging, and—

Enough. What are you? What the hell are you? Are you an animal?

"Not animal," Samrael said. "Worse."

Monster.

"That's closer."

"Hey, asshole. You need to let go of my brother."

My consciousness lurched back into the apartment. My sister appeared in my peripheral vision. She was holding a baseball bat.

Why wasn't she reacting to Samrael's horrific appearance? Why wasn't *anyone* reacting?

Samrael looked at Anna. "Sure thing," he said mockingly. He released me. In an instant his features shifted back to normal. He was just a guy again. With a split lip leaking blood that was just a little too dark, like wine.

I took the bat from Anna. "Get out," I rasped.

I still wasn't completely myself but I had every intention of attacking if he didn't leave. Taking a life was something I'd been preparing myself for, as a soldier. But I'd never imagined it happening this way. With a bat, in front of my sister.

Samrael turned to the front door. Ronwae, the redhead, stood there breathing hard. "She's gone. I looked everywhere," she said, her voice chiseled with an accent I didn't recognize. She disappeared into the hallway.

A mild look of disappointment crossed Samrael's face, like he'd been told he'd just gotten a parking ticket. He followed her, but hesitated at the door. "Whatever you do, Gideon, whatever you *think* you can do"—he opened his hands and showed me emptiness, futility—"it won't matter," he said, and he was gone.

I looked at my sister and struggled to find words. I'd been submerged in that consuming darkness and it still hadn't fully left me. I was still kicking for the surface.

"Your *hand*," Anna said.

I looked down. The knuckles of my right hand were already swollen and red. Pretty alarmingly. I had no idea how I was gripping the bat. The pain blared like a car alarm that wouldn't stop but my injury was a second-level concern.

"You okay?" I asked.

Anna shook her head. "I guess? More than *you* are. Who was that guy?"

"Whose bat is this?"

"What? It's Taylor's."

"I need to borrow it," I said. Then I shot out of the apartment.

I shouldn't have pursued. I had a serious injury. And I'd just seen a person-monster. But the enemy was retreating and I just couldn't let that shit go. I flew out of the complex and hit the sidewalk at a sprint. Anger roared inside me, clearing my thoughts and propelling me forward, but I slowed down as I reached the street.

It was deserted. I didn't see any college kids strolling around. Both the parking lot and the housing complex were dead quiet. All I heard were my running shoes scuffing the pavement and my lungs pumping oxygen.

When I reached the edge of the parking lot, I stopped. There was something strange about how heavy the darkness seemed. How thick. The streetlamps curving down the hill were weak points of light, and I couldn't even see the main road below. No sign of Samrael.

Okay, Blake. Take a second.

I set the bat down. My quads twitched. My right hand had developed its own heartbeat. Broken bones in there, I was sure. Nice. Added some fresh fractures to the list of things I had to deal with. I heard the squeal of cats fighting somewhere close. Because of me? Definitely possible.

Now what?

Anna would be worried. I should head back. But I was tempted to walk to the nearest psych clinic and turn myself in.

What had I just *seen*?

"Gideon."

I launched two feet off the blacktop.

My Jeep. The voice had come from my Jeep, which was parked just down the street. Was that—?

Yeah. It was. Standing on the driver's seat, propped on the roll bar like she'd been there for a while, was the girl. Daryn.

"How are you in my Jeep?" I asked, walking up. That was a mix of the two questions that fired off in my head.

How do you know that's my Jeep?

What are you doing in the Jeep that's mine that you shouldn't know about?

"It's a Jeep." She shrugged. "I just climbed in." She dropped into the driver's seat. "Come on, get in."

Sure. Get in. Right. But what were my options? Go back to my sister's apartment to field questions I couldn't answer? More hospitals?

No way. It was an easy decision. Nothing made sense anyway. And I had a feeling this girl was my only shot at getting answers.

I climbed into the passenger side, sliding the bat between the seat and the center console. "Hold on, I left my keys in my sister's—"

"It's an old car, I've got it." Daryn reached beneath the steering column for a couple of wires that hadn't been there before. She twisted a piece of electrical tape over them, sealing them together, and the engine growled to life. Then she threw it into first, and we lurched into the street to the reek and shriek of burning rubber.

CHAPTER 11

She drove like she was trying to qualify for the Indy 500, pushing my Jeep past eighty—its top speed. And that was on the way to the freeway.

My throat ached from Samrael's grip. My hand hurt so much, it was making me nauseous. I couldn't stop searching the night for three . . . *monsters*? Dozens of people had witnessed the fight I'd just been in. I knew I hadn't imagined that part. But the way Samrael had transformed . . . that couldn't be real.

I looked at the cuff on my wrist. Was *it* responsible for everything? Or was I hallucinating because I'd sustained a brain injury from my fall?

Unbelievable. My best-case scenario was hallucinations.

Then there was Daryn, driving my Jeep at Mach 3 like it was nothing out of the ordinary, her hair whipping all over the place. Where did she fit into all this? The confrontation at Joy's had obviously been about her. But why had she come there looking for me? Had she known I'd get into it with Samrael?

After a couple of minutes, I couldn't take my confusion anymore. "Are you going to tell me what's going on?"

Daryn trapped her hair to the side. "Right now?"

Fair question. An open-top Jeep doing eighty wasn't the best location for a conversation. We had both shouted to be heard over the roar of the tires.

"Just tell me one thing. Did you hot-wire my car?" I felt like an idiot right when I said it. *Hot-wire* sounded like such an old-timey term, like I should've been twirling my mustache or something. *Did you circumvent my car's ignition* wouldn't have sounded any better, and too late anyway.

"Yes!" she shouted back. "That's okay, right?"

"Sure! It's great!"

She smiled at my sarcasm, which I didn't love. My *hand* was broken. Possibly my head, too. Smiling needed to be banned for at least twenty-four hours.

I pinned my gaze on the freeway and focused on relaxing. Relaxing and not fighting the pain. *Breathe, Blake.* I glanced down at the Pearl Jam cassette tape in the player. *Just breathe, like Eddie Vedder.*

Being a passenger in my car was weird.

Being a passenger in my life was weird, too.

There were hardly any cars on the freeway. The rolling hills and dark fields around us had an eerie human quality. Like the earth had knees and shoulders.

Time passed and we put some miles behind us. Ten, twenty. By around thirty my hand was still swollen but the pain had ratcheted back noticeably. Way more than it should've, but that was one mystery I wasn't going to complain about. Had this same thing happened during my first days at Walter Reed? Pain leaving first, then accelerated healing? Had I failed to notice because I'd been hopped up on drugs?

What was really getting old were all the questions piling up in my head. Would I ever get answers? *When?* Why was I making it worse by asking questions about my questions?

We exited onto Highway 1, and the hills opened to blue fields on Daryn's side, the slate-black Pacific on mine. The ocean worked its magic on me and calmed me down some, just seeing it and smelling it. All that churning life out there.

A few minutes later Daryn slowed down, which surprised me. I'd started to think we were driving through the night. She pulled into a dirt lot with warning signs about no lifeguards being on duty and proceeding at your own peril. Appropriate.

As the engine cooled down, I looked around. There were no other cars in the lot. Nothing to raise alarm that I could see. A hundred meters ahead of us, waves broke against the beach, a white line in the darkness. Fog was rolling in and the crash of the surf seemed strangely muffled. Just yesterday, before Jackson attacked me, I'd been watching the ocean at the end of my street. It felt like a week ago.

"Whenever you're ready," I said.

"Do you have any water?"

"To drink?" I was so wrong-footed, and this girl only made it worse.

"Yes, water to drink. I'm really thirsty." She reached into the backseat, unzipping my duffel, which I'd brought back to my Jeep before Joy's party.

"Hold on a second." I grabbed her arm. "You said you were going to explain."

She froze, so I froze.

"Here's a question," she said, staring me down. "Would you like to let go of me, or should I claw your eyes out?"

"*Shit*." I let go of her. "I'm not going to *hurt* you. Why did you kidnap me if you're scared of me?"

"I didn't kidnap you—you came willingly—and I'm not scared of you, either. Not the way you think." She threw the door open and jumped out.

I vaulted over my side, rounded the Jeep, and found her leaning against the door. "Daryn, I didn't mean to—" She was pressing her fingers into her temples like she'd just been hit with the world's worst migraine. She looked like she needed a second. That was about as long as I could wait. "I really need some answers."

"I know you do." Her hands came down. "I just can't believe you don't know anything."

"Believe it."

"How am I supposed to explain this to you?"

"With words. That'd work for me. Faster than drawing pictures in the sand with a stick."

She shot me a look with legitimate stopping power. Then she crossed her arms, turning to the waves, so I took the opportunity to check her out.

It was a calculated assessment for the most part. Pretty much. I was going for clues. Intel that would help me figure out how she fit into what was going on.

What I figured out was that she was on the tall side, five-nine or so, only a few inches shorter than me, and strong. I could tell she was athletic. And pretty. Which I already knew. But reconfirmed. Pretty in a messy kind of way. Sort of camouflaged by tangled-up hair and beat-up clothes. By how still she stood—the opposite of fidgety—and by the intense look on her face, like she was daring you to make eye contact with her. I got the feeling that with a good ghillie suit and the right training, she'd have made a great sniper.

A silver chain hung around her neck. The links were heavy, thick, and disappeared beneath her leather jacket. Daryn looked back at me right as I was looking at her, uh . . . her chestal region. Because of the chain, Cordero, I swear. But it must've seemed different to her. Probably it did.

I expected her to lay into me for it, but she just gave me a super-slow-motion once over, from my running shoes all the way up to my eyes, totally up front about what I'd just done on the sly. "There's no easy way to say this," she said.

"Fine. Then say it the hard way. Or the medium way. Just say it."

I was starting to break a little. My control was.

"Okay." She looked right into my eyes. "You're War, Gideon. *You* are *War*."

I did a quick rewind and playback. "Say again?"

"You're War," she repeated.

It sounded the same the second time. "Going to war? Yeah, someday. When I deploy. I'm a soldier in the US Army." I stopped there for a second because it was still new and it felt good, claiming it. "But I haven't been to war yet."

"Okay." Daryn nodded. She pushed her hair behind her ear. "That's not what I meant but that does makes sense."

"No. It doesn't. Nothing makes any sense and if this is your explanation, then it's a really shitty explanation."

"Okay. All right. Gideon . . . you're the second rider. You are War, the red horseman. From Revelation."

As she spoke, my heart squeezed like a fist inside my chest. It kept squeezing tighter and tighter. If heart cramps were possible, I had one.

"None of this rings a bell?" she said. "None of this sounds familiar? You have to have seen some signs . . . something . . . haven't you?"

Every single gear in my mind was grinding and clattering, trying to keep up with what she was saying. I turned toward the ocean. Everything I'd seen over the past week, from my fall to Samrael's monstrous face, was coming back to me. Revelation? I knew so little about it. What I knew, generally, was that it had always scared me. Wasn't it about the end times? The Rapture? Plagues and fires?

"Gideon, I know it's a lot to take in, but—"

"No," I said, something snapping shut inside my brain. This was a dream. A nightmare. I was Gideon Blake in an alternate dimension. "No, it's fine. I think I'm gettin' it. I'm War. I'm one of the four horsemen, which means I have three buddies— help me out here. I forget who they are."

"Conquest, Famine, and Death."

A chill shot straight down my spine. I shook myself like a wet dog. "Right. Those guys. And we're supposed to end the world or something?" I wanted no part of that.

"No. You're only a manifestation of War. You've been given some of the abilities of War, but for another purpose, to carry out a specific task." She sighed. "I didn't realize I was going to have to explain all of this. I would've thought it through better."

"Yeah, I'm really sorry you're having to *explain all of this* to me. If I'm War, what does that make you, Peace? Because you've got some work to do."

"I'm not Peace," she said simply, and waited for my next move.

My next move was slamming my hands against the door of my Jeep. Stupid thing to do, but the anger and confusion had boiled over inside me and I'd erupted. I'd forgotten about my busted hand, but now I remembered. Now I felt sick, I remembered so well.

Daryn jumped off the car. "Hey! Could you calm down?"

"You just told me I'm *War*. When is war ever calm? Who *are* you, anyway? You show up in my life with a trio of psychopaths chasing you and *this* is how you're explaining it? You know what? You're crazy. This entire thing is—"

She shoved me in the chest. The action surprised me. The ferocity in it.

"Don't ever call me crazy again," she said, her voice low and shaky. She stood a moment longer, like she was going to say something else. But she didn't.

She backed away and made for the beach.

It took me half an hour to move from that spot. A full thirty minutes before I went after her. When I found her, things between us didn't really get any better.

CHAPTER 12

Cordero raises a hand.

I stop and the pine room filters back to me as the beach fades away.

It's quiet in here. Cordero is legitimately gaping at me. Behind her, Texas and Beretta wear identical you-gotta-be-kidding-me expressions.

"War?" Cordero says. "War, as in the embodiment of the concept?"

"That's me." A chemical taste is seeping in my mouth from the drugs. I swallow, but it doesn't go away. "In the flesh."

Texas catches a laugh in his throat and tries to cover it with some coughing. Beretta blinks fast a few times. I get the feeling he's trying not to smack his partner.

Cordero sends them a quick, annoyed glance. She looks back at me and sighs, absently scratching her knuckles. "War," she says, more to herself than to me. Then she removes a cell phone from her blazer and checks it. "I have to step out, but I'll be back in a few minutes." Her eyes mouth curves. "Don't move."

What do you know? She's got a sense of humor.

"So you piss people off? That it?" Texas says, once she's gone. His voice is all easygoing drawl, but his posture is rigid and his blue eyes are intense.

"Something like that."

A grin appears. Half of one. "I'm thinkin' I got that superpower myself."

"Hey, kid. The necklace." It's Beretta now. Look at that. Cordero leaves and the vibe's totally different. "The one the girl was wearing. It's significant, isn't it?"

It's an observant question. Impressive, even for a guy who's probably trained to pick up stuff like that. But I'm not answering without Cordero here.

He tries again. "What's really going? 'Cause *you*? As one of the *four horsemen*?"

That's technically incorrect. I thought I was pretty clear about being an incarnation of War. But again. Not taking the bait. "You really want to be the guy that compromises this investigation?"

Beretta snorts. "You mean this fairy tale? But I'll hand it to you—you got a good imagination."

Texas tips his chin, already smiling at what he's going to say. "There's gonna be horses soon, right? I can't wait. My family trains cuttin' horses. Best in North Texas. I'm guessin' they wouldn't stack up to War's horse."

"Probably not."

"I'd be disappointed otherwise." He shifts his weight, his shoulders relaxing slightly. "Least tell us what *Death*'s like. We're dyin' to know."

"Good one." I'm actually starting to like the guy. He reminds me of Cory. "You could find out."

"Yeah, how's that?" he asks.

"You brought us in together from Norway. Marcus is right next door, isn't he?"

Texas shakes his head like *nice try*. He won't give up any intel either. But even in his silence, I get the sense he's met Marcus, and that Marcus made a lasting first impression. As he tends to.

These guys aren't supposed to be talking to me. Or maybe they were, and I failed to give them what they were after. Either way they go quiet, setting up in their positions again like drying concrete. Party's over.

I'm thirsty again. So thirsty my head's starting to pound, but as long as my stomach doesn't get involved, I'm good. My knees ache from sitting in this chair.

Behind me the radiator goes on, giving yet another encore performance. *Tink, tink, tink, tink.* The warmth slowly comes up on my back. Hard worker, that heater. The bulb, on the other hand, is doing a flickering thing, showing some signs of fatigue. *You're losing, bulb.*

Weird that I was in Norway yesterday, probably. Now I'm wherever here is. I haven't had time to think about Daryn much. Now I do.

She's gone.

Just freakin' deal, Blake. But was I really that easy to walk away from?

The door opens and Cordero enters. She sits down, smoothing her hands along her suit. I'd forgotten about her perfume, but now it's back. Like getting pelted by fashion magazines. Roses, oranges, lemons, fertilizer. I suppress a cough.

"Gideon? Ready to pick back up?" Cordero says.

I swallow. "Yes."

But she waits a moment longer, like she's making sure she believes me. Her elbows settle on the desk and she weaves her fingers together. "You'd gone to find Daryn on the beach."

"Wait. I have some demands first."

"We had a deal. I already accepted your demands. You asked for Colonel Nellis. I'll bring him to you as soon as we're done. And you'll be free to go."

"I have new demands."

Her lips go flat. "And they are?"

"I need more water. I want my legs untied. And I want to see the guys I came in with."

"Yes to your first request, no to rest." She looks at Texas, who picks up the water bottle at his feet and comes forward.

As I drink from the straw I notice him eyeing the cuff. Interesting. Maybe he is starting to believe me.

Back in our positions, Cordero's ready to go again. "You'd

been abandoned on the beach by Daryn. You said an hour passed before you went after her?"

Did I say an hour? Can't remember. "No. It was closer to half an hour."

I draw a breath, preparing to wade back into the past. I was so shaken up that night, standing by the Jeep. The muscles in my arms and shoulders had knotted with tension. I remember how the ocean smelled different than by my house. How the fog was growing thicker, like smoke rolling over the beach as I stood there, trying to make sense of what I'd just been told.

I remember Daryn, that very first day.

CHAPTER 13

"Don't say anything," I said as I approached her. She was sitting on the sand hugging her legs and watching the waves, her chin resting on a knee. "I don't want to hear another word." I didn't have room for more ridiculous explanations.

"Do I look like I want to talk to you?" she asked, without looking up.

She did not.

"I brought you water." I tossed a bottle by her feet. "And this." I dropped my San Francisco Giants sweatshirt next to her. It was cooling down and her leather jacket didn't look very warm.

She reached for the sweatshirt and pulled it over her shoulders, ignoring the water.

Confusing. She'd been so insistent about her thirst earlier. I stood there for another second, not really sure what I was waiting for. Then I said, "Okay. You're welcome," and walked away.

I wanted to head about a thousand miles in the other direction but I went maybe fifty meters. Far enough to have some space, but close enough that she was still visible in the foggy night. The confrontation at Joy's was fresh in my mind. It was fresh in my body, by way of my broken hand. But even with the fight aside, I wouldn't have left anyone out there alone. The fact that she was female made it nonnegotiable.

Two seconds after I sat down, Daryn got up and walked the other way. And, wow. That really got to me.

"Good night, angel!" I yelled. Then since I was already being so mature, I belted out a horse neigh at the top of my lungs.

Or was it a whinny? It suddenly seemed super important

to understand horse sounds. Like, just a really important thing to get a handle on, so I sat down and tried to work that out. Some part of me recognized that I was maybe in denial, but I was stuck in that gear until Anna's phone rang in my pocket.

I fished it out. My mom was calling, but the image on the small screen paralyzed me. My parents in Yosemite. Smiling, with their arms around each other. I could see Half Dome behind them. I could see part of my arm in the background, too. Flexed, because I was showing off my biceps, which were new. It was spring. Anna and I had just turned sixteen. We'd gone camping for our birthdays.

The phone kept vibrating but I couldn't make myself answer it. I didn't want to talk to my mom. I couldn't face the worry I was probably putting her through. I couldn't think of a single person I'd have answered for.

Wait, I could.

My dad.

But I knew he wasn't calling.

When the call went to voicemail, I saw a string of alerts for the dozen other voicemails and texts I'd somehow missed. There were more from Mom. From Taylor, Anna's roommate. From Griffin and Casbah. From Cory. There was even a missed call from Wyatt Crazy Eyes Sinclair.

I stuffed the phone back into my sweatshirt pocket and pressed my eyes closed, trying to unsee that photo. Trying to *think*. If Cory had called, did my commanding officer in the Army know what was going on?

Hold up. All I'd done was get into a college brawl. And that was to protect someone—it wasn't something I'd instigated. The rest was . . .

What was the rest?

I rubbed my hand over my head—my busted hand, which was feeling *a lot* better. The pain was fading away and the swelling had started to decrease, too.

But really. War?

War?

Naw. No way.

This was just a practical joke. Someone had decided I'd make a great contestant for their reality show. I shot to my feet and stared into the darkness. They were going to regret that decision.

"Where are you?" I demanded, searching for cameras. "You really want me in your dumbass show?"

The phone rang in my pocket again. I grabbed it and launched it as far as I could into the waves. It felt good. It felt great, in fact, so I kept going, hurling shells, sticks, rocks, anything I could find into the ocean. When I'd finally worn my anger down some, I dropped to the sand.

I was tired and lately being awake sucked, so.

I went to sleep.

I woke with the image of my dad's death seared into my retinas.

It was, um . . .

It was something I hadn't seen or dreamt about in a while. In months, actually. Since I'd joined the Army. But that night—it was still night, still dark when I woke up—that night everything was right there, sharp as the day it'd happened.

It was summer before senior year. My dad and I had just bought the Jeep and I was looking forward to a couple months of surfing and fishing with Griffin and Casbah. For summer jobs, Casbah was teaching little genius kids how to build rockets in science camp. Griff was helping our high school coaches with baseball clinics. I wanted to do that too, but I decided to work for my dad instead.

He had never pushed the path he'd walked on me—not going into the military or taking over his roofing business—but I got the feeling he wanted me to see the company he'd built from nothing. And I wanted to be able to look him in the eye one day and tell him it wasn't for me, if it ever came up. It felt like the right thing to do. To try out, at least. So I agreed to spend the summer learning the ins and outs of running a roofing company. Basically doing whatever he asked me to do. Sometimes that meant making pickups at lumberyards in his truck. Other times it meant lunch runs to Subway. Mostly, I was learning the labor part. The sweat-your-ass-off-in-the-sun part.

I was bored out of my skull within the first week, but I somehow survived June and July. On August 2, a Tuesday afternoon, with only a week and a half left before school started back up, Dad called me down off a house in a residential neighborhood. We'd been weatherproofing two leaky skylights. Tons more exciting than laying down roof tiles. I got into his truck and we drove a couple of blocks. One of the neighbors had seen the skylight work and wanted a bid for a new roof.

Dad hauled a ladder off the truck and climbed up to the warped wood-shingle roof of a yellow bungalow, his black notebook and yellow pencil tucked into his back pocket. I stayed in the passenger seat, the air-conditioning cranked up against the August heat, texting with my friends. Casbah had heard about a party someone in our rival high school was throwing that night and our messages were all harebrained ideas about how we'd get in. Idiot stuff like posing as pizza-delivery guys and dropping in through skylights—which I'd conveniently just learned to remove that day.

Then something stopped me. This light creeping feeling, like when you realized a spider's been crawling on you. I diverted the AC vents, but I still felt off.

I looked out my window.

My dad stood on the roof. He was looking down at me with the strangest expression on his face. I remember it perfectly.

It was a look I'd never seen before, like something terrible had happened that he couldn't fix.

The pad and pencil dropped out of his hand. One stopped, the other went rolling. I watched my dad bend down to pick them up. His knees thudded onto the roof, then his shoulder, and then it hit me that he wasn't kneeling.

He was *falling*.

The pencil dropped into the gutter, but he kept going. He kept going, all the way down to the brick walkway. As I watched from an air-conditioned truck, texting my buddies about a party.

I went around and around with those images. Seeing the ladder and that warped roof. The yellow number-two pencil. My dad's face. Basically just torturing myself for a couple hours like that until I couldn't take it anymore.

I knew I wouldn't be able to sleep again so I stood and scoped out the darkness. There was no sign of dawn on the horizon. I didn't see Daryn, or anyone else, but I waited a little longer to be sure I was alone. Then I took a closer look at the metal cuff gleaming at my wrist.

What *was* this thing? I rested my right hand over it. A hum like a mild electrical current vibrated into my arm. I waited for more but nothing else happened. "Come on, magic metal. Show me what you got." Nothing again. "*Go*, you piece of—"

A sound swelled in my ears like thunder, but deeper. A noise like an oil drum rolling. It was coming from down the beach.

I turned toward it, searching the night.

Out of the fog came the most stunning thing I'd ever seen.

A horse.

A massive horse, almost as wide across as my Jeep, coming at a full gallop.

In the darkness, and with the fog, and at a distance, I couldn't be sure, but its coat was a bizarre red color, like blood from a deep cut, but bright. A deep, bright red. Even stranger were the flashes of gold and yellow on its hooves and mane.

Flashes that looked like flames.

I knew nothing about horses but its ears were pressed back. When I added that to its speed and trajectory—fast and headed directly toward me—my situation suddenly seemed dire.

"Stop!" I raised my arms. "I said *stop*!"

The horse lowered its head and *sped up*, each massive hoof sending up explosions of sand. I only had seconds before I was steamrolled, so I did the only thing I could.

I sprinted for the water, high-stepping through the shallows until I was deep enough to dive. Then I kicked, swimming under the surface, pushing through cold black water until my lungs burned.

When I came up, I was well past the breakers. The horse had followed me a little way in. Its coat put off so much illumination, it had created a circle of aquamarine water around it, like the ocean had pool lights. Its mane had gotten soaked and hung straight against its strong neck. I didn't see fire anymore, though. I wondered if I'd only imagined that. I didn't think so.

It waded deeper into the water, toward me. A wave rushed past its thick chest and it shied back, head bobbing, but its attention never left me.

I knew this wasn't a dream. Everything felt crystal clear. The cold salt water tickling my throat. The way my sweatshirt and jeans made me clumsy as I treaded water. The ocean swells lifting me as they headed for the beach. But I also couldn't believe I was awake.

"Are you real?" I shouted over the crash of the surf.

The horse reared, making no sound as its massive hooves slashed at the night. It settled back into the water with a splash and let out a wet snort. Then it turned and trotted away, disappearing back into the fog.

CHAPTER 14

The next thing I remember was waking up to someone shoving me in the shoulder. I grabbed the first thing in sight—my attacker's ankle—and yanked the hell out of it. By the time I figured out what was actually happening, Daryn had already hit the sand.

She was only down a second before she sprang back up. "What is *wrong* with you?"

"Sorry. You grabbed my shoulder." I came to a knee and decided to stay there. I'd startled her. She'd fallen hard and looked a little shaken up.

"*Grabbed?*" She brushed off her clothes. "I was just trying to wake you up. I barely touched you."

That was possible. I'd had a terrible night of sleep. Superficial sleep. Shivering, sporadic sleep. After my swim in the ocean, I'd changed into dry clothes, but now I was damp again from the sand and the cool air. And still on edge. And still on one knee. Why again? Was I *proposing*?

I jumped up. "You just surprised me."

Daryn was giving me a steady look. She didn't appear to be thinking good things and my face was going hot, so I decided to survey the surroundings, starting with the part of the world where she wasn't.

Morning had broken. Fog was starting to burn off. No giant red horses in sight. Good. Maybe I had just hallucinated it, like Samrael's snout. Wait, that wasn't *good*.

"You went for a swim?" she asked, eyeing my wet clothes piled on the sand.

"Yep. Just felt like taking a swim." I wasn't ready to talk about the horse. Not even close.

She crossed her arms. With my Giants sweatshirt swallowing her up and her hair all sleep-tangled, she looked different than last night. Softer or something. "So . . ." She glanced behind her, toward my Jeep. "Do you have any money?"

An antsy feeling stirred inside my chest. If she needed money, she was probably heading out on her own. Not what I wanted, but I couldn't blame her. I hadn't exactly treated her great yesterday.

"Yeah," I answered. "I have money. Daryn, listen, I—"

"Great," she said. "Let's get some food. I'm starving."

She taught me how to hot-wire my Jeep, which was easier to do than it should've been, then we fell quiet as I got us on the road. After last night's fight and this morning's takedown, we were oh for two on communicating. It seemed better for now to just not try.

As I drove I became hyperconscious of the cuff on my wrist. I didn't know if I was responsible for what had happened during the night, and part of me worried a horse might suddenly appear out of nowhere, maybe galloping alongside the Jeep or sitting in the backseat or whatever. But neither happened, thankfully.

We stopped at a breakfast place called Duckies in a tiny beach town. I made sure to broadcast my make-peace-not-war message as soon as we stepped inside. With the number of truckers and bikers in there it could've turned ugly otherwise. Then I asked our server for the booth by the windows near the emergency exit, some part of me registering that I was thinking in terms of tactical advantages and escape plans. I didn't know what was happening and I wanted to be ready for anything.

Daryn and I gave the waitress our orders right away and had a bonding moment over the fact that neither of us liked coffee. It was a quick moment. Then she pulled a beat-up journal out of her backpack and started writing in it. I channeled my energy into making a multilevel structure out of sugar packets and creamer pods.

When our food came, she plowed through a stack of blueberry pancakes and I put away a plate of eggs, bacon, and hash browns, knowing it would give me heartburn, but I was hungry and needed the fuel. We still weren't talking but I had plenty of time to observe her. She ate like she was storing up for the winter. Fast. A little messy. Drowning every bit of pancake in a waterfall of maple syrup like she had reverse diabetes. Her foot wiggled under the table as she ate, which was weird because usually she seemed really calm. She'd tied her hair up in a knot on top of her head and . . .

I don't know. She looked good.

Shame she was such a head case. Probably a criminal on the run. Bummer she thought I was one of the four horsemen of the apocalypse.

When she glanced up and caught me watching her, she gave me a look, like *what?* So I shrugged, like *nothing,* and we carried on eating and not saying a word.

It was the strangest breakfast I'd ever had.

I didn't know what to make of it.

So far every second with this girl felt like coming around a blind corner.

We were waiting for the bill when she said, "Your hand looks better." She wiped her lips with a napkin. "Does it hurt?"

"Oh, this? Barely. Almost not at all. It did last night but now it's better. Weird, because it was really busted up, but now it's, like . . ."

"Better?"

"Exactly. Way better than my stomach's going to feel after this food." *Stop, Blake. Just slow down.*

"Oh, no. Do you have a stomachache?"

"No. My stomach's prime." What the hell was coming out of my mouth?

"Prime? So . . . it's okay?"

"Totally. All good."

After that I think I blacked out for a few seconds. When I came back around, Daryn had linked her hands over her head and was stretching in a way that made it an extreme test of self-control to maintain eye contact. The two guys in the booth next to ours looked over. It wasn't the first time.

"What do you think," Daryn said, tipping her head toward the window. "One-horse town?"

Okay. Here we go. "I guess you could say that."

She rested her elbows on the table and leaned in. "You've seen him, haven't you?" she asked, her voice dropping to a whisper. "Your horse?"

I nodded.

"And? Was it amazing?"

"You could say that, too."

"Will you show me?"

The bikers in the next booth looked over again. They were starting to piss me off and I already had a hot trigger from a terrible night of sleep. And from being told I was War. I could feel the anger kindling inside me and imagined it filling the space around me, a fight breaking out. I knew it was seconds away from happening.

Daryn followed my gaze. "Morning, guys," she said, all chipper. "Try the blueberry pancakes. They're prime."

Just like that, it was big grins and thanks and have-a-great-days for Daryn. With that handled, she settled back.

"Prime," I said.

Her eyes had a shine, like the sun on the sea.

She gave a little satisfied shrug. "Totally. All good." She patted the table. "Pay up. Let's get out of here."

Ten minutes later, we were driving south on Highway 1. Daryn's boots were up on the dash and she'd sunk into my Giants sweatshirt like a turtle in a shell. As eager to talk as she'd been at the diner; now she looked like she just wanted to be left alone.

"How's it going over there?" I didn't know what else to say. And I was done with silence.

She glanced at me. "Sorry. I'm just trying to figure out how to approach this. I won't be able to answer everything. Okay?"

"Okay." I couldn't understand why she seemed nervous. *Now.* Talking to *me.* How was this the same girl who winked at bikers? "How about this," I said. "I'll ask questions, you answer them. What's your last name?"

She let out a slow breath, like she was dreading this. "Martin."

"How old are you, Daryn Martin?"

"Seventeen."

"What's your favorite breakfast food? Blueberry pancakes, right? Because if they're not, I'm going to be crazy impressed by what you did back there."

She rolled her eyes, pretending to be annoyed. "The more syrup, the better."

"What's your journal about?"

I didn't expect her to answer that one but she came right out and said, "Everything I care about." She stretched my sweatshirt over her knees. "Those are easy questions. They're easy ones to answer."

"For you, they are. I didn't know any of that stuff. You're pretty much expert level on the subject of Daryn Martin."

"Maybe." She turned to her window. "But you don't want to know about me."

Actually, that wasn't true. But it was fair to say my curiosity went well beyond her, too. "Let's just keep going. We'll stop when it's not easy anymore. You came to find me last night at that party. Right?"

"Yes." She peered at me. "But I didn't expect to be sent for you first."

"Because?"

"Because Conquest is the first horseman, not War. War is the second horseman. But like I said yesterday, none of what's going on is related to Revelation. The seven seals? The events preceding Judgment Day? This isn't about that, so I guess the order shouldn't matter. You're an incarnation of War. You've been given War's abilities to carry out a mission."

"Right. Okay. Right." I couldn't drive and have that conversation. I needed to give it my total focus, so I pulled off onto the shoulder and peeled the electrical tape under the steering column apart, killing the engine. A couple of surfers were out on the water, shredding. That looked fun. I wanted to be out there, not a care in the world.

"So, this guy," I said. "Conquest. The other horseman. Wait—girl?"

"Guy." Daryn was looking through the front windshield like we were still driving. "You're all guys."

"So, no horsepersons?" It sounded ridiculous, but it was an honest question.

"No."

"What are you? Are you, like, an anj—anj—angel?" I'd been joking last night when I'd yelled that at her, but what if she really was?

Daryn shook her head. "Definitely not. I am definitely not an angel." She looked at me, really directly. The more anxious she was, the more still she seemed to become. "Seeker. That's . . . that's how I think of myself."

"Seeker."

"Yes."

"Is Seeker higher in rank than horseman? In the grand scheme, are you more senior than me?"

"Are you kidding?"

"I'm in the military. Rank matters. I just want to know where I stand. If we had uniforms with stripes on the shoulder, would you have more stripes than me?"

For just an instant, part of an instant, she looked like she wanted to laugh. "You're unbelievable. Yes. I'd probably have one more stripe than you. I'm kind of the source for . . ." She paused. "I don't know. For information. Does that bother you?"

"Why would it?"

She just looked at me.

Did she mean the girl thing? Because I had no problem taking orders from a girl. I'd been doing it my whole life, for one. My mom was the strongest person I knew. And if you were capable, I personally gave no shits what you were. For me character was character, end of story.

"Okay, this is good." I shook some sand out of my hair, scrubbed a hand over my face. "Gettin' some answers. Hangin' in my Jeep with a Seeker in the middle of nowhere."

"Cayucos."

"Say what now?"

"We're in Cayucos, California."

My gaze drifted out to the surfers on the water. Cayucos. Kye-yoo-kuss. What kind of word was that? Spanish? I was definitely focusing on the wrong things.

"How are you doing with all of this?" she asked.

"Great. Really great."

"Want me to keep going?"

"Absolutely. Keep going."

"So . . . from time to time . . . I get this sort of . . . *download* into my mind. Information, like I said before. That's how I know what I need to do, what my task is. In the last one, I saw you and the three other riders. I learned that I need to bring the four of you together so you can help protect something that's very powerful. Something that can't fall into the wrong hands."

I nodded, taking a few seconds to let that sink in. "Are you going to tell me what I'm protecting?" It took everything in me not to look right at the silver necklace I'd noticed earlier. There was something unusual about the thickness of the links. Maybe that wasn't the object, but my instincts were pinging.

"And what about this?" I lifted my wrist, showing her the cuff. "This showed up a few days ago without a manual. Any idea what it does? How it works?"

She looked from the cuff to me, shaking her head. "There are certain things I can't tell you yet. I told you that. It's safer."

"There are certain things you need to tell me, Daryn. Usually on a mission it's good to have what's called an objective."

"I agree. And right now the objective is to bring the four of you together. The Kindred are dangerous. We're already outnumbered by them. You'll be stronger as a group. *We* will be. The only way we stand a chance is together."

That actually made sense. It was the same principle I'd been learning in the Army. Ranger Battalions only worked effectively when they worked together.

"All right," I said, but I didn't feel all right. I had so many questions. A hundred. A thousand. I couldn't even focus on any one for long. But the thing I wanted to know—*needed* to know—was if I was good.

Was I an agent of darkness? Maybe the *wrong* hands Daryn was talking about were actually the *right* hands. If all of this was true, then I was *War*. I had a sketchy understanding of Revelation, but I was pretty sure the horsemen had been unleashed to cleanse the earth of evils. But I felt shaky about how things like war and famine and death could be on the good side—instruments of anything good. And from the minute

Daryn had told me I was War, that had become a huge, looming question in my head.

Am I good?

Bigger than that, possibly, was my confusion over why I had been chosen.

Why me?

I was just a dumb kid.

But I couldn't ask either question. So I skipped ahead to easier ones.

"What about the three people at the party last night? They're part of this, right? Our opposition? You called them the Kindred. They're after this secret thing I'm supposed to protect?"

"Yes. Samrael was the taller one. Ronwae was the girl, and Malaphar was the one in the suit. And there are four more who weren't there."

"How'd they know you'd be there?"

"They can sense the object when they're near it. Its power calls to them. That's why we need to—" Daryn winced, her eyebrows drawing together. "Gideon, we need to stop now. I need to figure some things out before I tell you more. I need to bring the four of you together—that's what's important."

I let out a breath, my gaze moving to the ocean beyond her. One of the surfers wiped out in style, his arms flailing, his board jamming straight into the water like a tombstone. I watched him come up and swim over to his board. He slid back on, turned toward the waves, and paddled out, ready for more.

That was how you did it.

No hesitation. No fear.

Reaching under the steering column, I pressed the tape around the wires, bringing my Jeep back to life. "Where to next, boss?"

Chapter 15

Let's stop here for a second, Gideon," Cordero says. "I have a few questions."

I nod. Breathe. Breathe and trudge out of the past.

The chemical taste of the drugs is still in my mouth, but not as strong as when I last noticed it. Cordero's perfume hasn't let up, though. It is legit breaking me down. Nose hair by nose hair.

"Okay," I say, finally feeling back here. "Shoot."

"You trusted her blindly?"

I have to think about that for a second. My dad would have said trust *is* blind. If you knew something for sure then it'd be knowing. Totally different thing.

"I'm not saying I'd bought in completely, but I was willing to go along. I knew she was my best option for figuring things out. But if you're asking me whether I trusted her from the start? I think I did. It was just a gut feeling that she wasn't going to lead me astray. But I also knew there was more to her. I could tell she was good at hiding things. At keeping things to herself. And I was right."

"About which part? That you could trust her or that she kept secrets?"

"I still trust her, even though she lied to me. I'll get to that part. And she did hide things from me, but for my own good. I'll get to that, too."

Cordero falls silent. I think I've confused her. Welcome to knowing Daryn.

I picture her the last time I saw her, in Jotunheimen. Night. The fjord burning around me. I'd been with the guys, waiting to be airlifted out. Waiting for Daryn to join us. Then I'd yelled my head off when I'd realized she'd chosen to stay behind.

Nice, Blake. Way to keep remembering this. Real helpful.

"Why did you wonder if you're good?" Cordero is asking me.

I've checked out again. I need to focus. Finish this and get back to work. The Kindred are still out there. "Because I wasn't sure."

"Why weren't you sure?" she asks.

I glance at Texas and Beretta. I know I've already said plenty that's highly personal, but this . . . it's something I've never admitted to anyone.

"Why wasn't I sure?" I hear myself say, and I know the whole story's on its way out. My mouth won't stop. I'm hemorrhaging memories and personal failures. These drugs *suck.* "You have to understand something, Cordero. Before my dad died, I had friends, decent grades, some promise in baseball. I had everything. After, I tried to keep my life the same. I tried to hang on to all that. But it was like when you're hanging on a pull-up bar. You're good for a little while. Then your muscles start to shake, but you keep telling yourself hang on. Hang on. Hang on. Hang on. But eventually it's not up to you anymore. Your muscles give out and you drop. That's what happened to me. I held on for a while. Then I dropped. I dropped, but I didn't want my mom or my sister to worry, so I tried to hide how far down I was.

"I kept going to school, but my grades slipped. I stopped playing baseball, but I'd still go to the games. For a while, I'd still go to parties with my buddies but, mentally, I just wasn't there. I didn't care. About anything. It all seemed meaningless. How was I supposed to care about calculus when my dad was gone? All I had was anger. Anger that was . . . *immense.* Immense and burning, like I was carrying the sun around inside me. I only let it go when I was alone, hiking or running. Camping. Around other people, I worked my ass off to keep it in-side. I buried it deep, except for this one time when I didn't."

"What happened the one time?"

"I screwed up." *Hold, Blake. Hold the line here.*

Cordero waits.

"It was after a baseball game senior year. I wasn't playing. I was up in the stands, watching my old team take on one of our rivals. They always played dirty and the game was tense from the beginning. In the last inning, it got a lot worse when the pitcher for the other team purposely pegged my buddy Griffin, who I mentioned earlier, while he was batting. The ball hit Griff's helmet, probably going around eighty-five miles an hour. A missile. He went down hard. His helmet was cracked. He could have died, but he didn't. He was okay, but I wasn't.

"People don't understand how easy it can happen. How fast everything can just . . . change. I watched the rest of that last inning without seeing it. I was thinking about Griff and if he'd died. Thinking about the pain his family would feel. His little brothers, Reed and Caden. His dad. His *mom*. The whole time that anger in me was stirring up. Pure fire. I waited until the game was over. Until the pitcher was heading to the parking lot to get on the bus. Then I jumped him."

"You attacked him."

"I did. I got him down on the ground and I hit him until people pulled me off. I only threw a few punches but I messed him up. The guy had to have stitches around his eye and his mouth. He needed one of his teeth replaced."

I pause and notice that my legs and my arms have tensed up and my muscles are twitching. Thinking about that night always starts an earthquake inside me. It makes me want to run until there are no thoughts left in my head.

"The only reason his parents didn't press charges was be-cause Half Moon Bay's a small town and, as it turned out, his dad had met my dad once or twice. This guy, Mr. Milligan, he was an ex-Marine and I guess some kind of loyalty among warrior brothers kicked in. No police report was filed. I wasn't eighteen yet. Nothing went on my record, so . . . I got away with it."

Cordero thinks for a moment. "You think what you did makes you bad?"

"It doesn't make me *good*."

"Would you have kept going?"

"I might have. I know I wasn't slowing down when they pulled me off him. I might've kept going. How many people have you met who have the potential to kill, Cordero? How many people have that capability?"

My eyes drift to Beretta and Texas, who've become marble lions at the door. I know they have it too, this ability to turn to darkness.

"More than you think," Cordero replies. "You'd be surprised. Sometimes the most average-seeming people are killers. You'd never know it by looking at them."

It's my turn to study her this time. Psychiatrist? Is that what she is? Something stressful. Small lines of tension crackle away from the corners of her eyes. I hadn't noticed them before.

I wonder what she's seen.

Has she met worse than me?

Cordero shifts in the chair. She rubs her knuckles, then laces her fingers together. "I probably shouldn't say this, Gideon. I *know* I shouldn't but"—she purses her lips, unhappy with herself—"I don't think that incident necessarily defines you as bad. I think it makes you human. And I believe you would have stopped yourself. I think that's what makes a person good. Not that you make mistakes, but that you recognize them. You feel remorse for them. You want to correct them and do better."

It's a surprisingly decent thing to say. And I think she's right. When I think about that day, I can't ever imagine that I'd have kept going. I do think I would've stopped myself. That day was a low point, but it woke me up. It turned me around.

Thank you doesn't seem like the right response, considering Cordero's pretty much interrogating me, so I nod.

She gives me a nod back and then draws a deep breath, putting that small moment of humanity behind us. "Where were we? I think you'd just agreed to help Daryn, and the two of you were heading to . . . ?"

"LA. To find Famine."

CHAPTER 16

Before we left Cayucos, I snapped my Jeep's soft top into place. It wouldn't eliminate all the noise on the freeway, but Daryn and I would be able to hear each other a little better. The day was sunny and clear as I drove us south, the ocean and sky to my right, blue and bluer.

I kept the conversation going. We'd finally started talking and I didn't want to stall out. I told Daryn about my parents and Anna. People get extra curious when they find out I have a twin, so that took some time. Then I told her I used to play ball before senior year.

"Catching is like quarterbacking. It's a real mix of strategy, aggressiveness, and quick reaction. You're managing the pitch count, watching the runners on base. You control the whole game behind the plate."

"Is that what you liked about it—being in control?"

"Definitely. Control's my favorite."

Daryn's smile was a quick flash. I could tell she didn't hand them out easily. "Baseball. That explains this sweatshirt. Thanks, by the way. So why did you stop playing? You said you played until senior year."

Why had I said that? "Outgrew it, I guess," I replied, avoiding the truth. I'd left out the part about my dad not being alive when I'd mentioned him. "Decided to go the Army route."

"But you didn't enlist during high school, right?"

"My contract started right after graduation, but I wanted to be ready. I spent most of this spring working out, doing stuff that would prepare me."

I was building a pretty good house of cards. The part about

me doing all that stuff was true, but I didn't want to get into the trigger that got me to enlist.

The guy I'd messed up at the baseball game? His dad, Mr. Milligan, had come to the house a few weeks after it happened. Evidently he and my mom had been talking on the phone a lot. He came by one afternoon and sat on the couch in our living room and told me I needed to get my shit together. Except he said it in a really decent paternal way that made me feel like crying my head off. I didn't, though. I'd tried a bunch of times after my dad died, but I could never manage it. I had a jam in my tear ducts or something. As he left, Mr. Milligan gave me an Army recruiter's number on a yellow Post-it, which lived on my desk for a few weeks until I finally accepted that it was exactly what I needed.

I had no idea why I was lying to Daryn about my dad. Lying sucked. I guess I didn't want her pity. Being pitiful sucked more than being a liar. At least right then that was how it seemed.

"Were you? Prepared when you got to Fort Benning?" she asked.

"As much as I could be. More than a lot of other guys. All the PT we do in RASP? The physical training? Grueling. But it could've been worse."

"You look like you're in good shape."

My brain took a quick vacation. When it came back I had to crank the wheel to keep us on the road, which was embarrassing. And confusing. Because why? I didn't like her. I mean, I didn't think so. But still.

"How about you?" I asked, trying to keep words happening. "Play any sports?"

"I might have."

"Instruments?"

"No."

"Did you grow up in a state that starts with the letter A, M, or T?"

Her lips did this twisty thing to the side.

"Isn't that how we're doing this? Process of elimination?"

Daryn brushed some sand off her jeans. "The less we do of *this,* the better it'll be for both of us."

I started laughing. I didn't know what had just hit me. Daryn laughed too, more at me than with me, but it didn't matter. I enjoyed it.

"You run a pretty good defense, Martin. You know that?"

"I've gotten better."

"Does this mean you're not going to tell me about the downloads you get? Or how often you get 'em? Or how long you've been doing this? Like, is this your first assignment, or have you been seeking—seekering?—your whole life? And, like, when you saw me—you said you saw me—was I excelling at protecting secret powerful objects? Doing epic War shit? How amazing was I, is basically what I want to know. But in specifics. Did I look really-really awesome or just kind of good? Wait, wait—I looked prime. Didn't I, Martin?"

"Are you done?"

"With my opening questions?"

She shook her head. "Wow."

"You don't have to answer."

"I know I don't." She reclined her seat and put her feet up on the dash. I thought the subject was closed because she shut her eyes, but then she said, "It's not often you meet people who are so persistent."

"How often do you meet people who are War?"

She peered at me and gave a little shrug, like *you're really not all that special.* Then she closed her eyes again. "I can't tell you what they're like. Seeing the things I do. Knowing things I can't actually explain. You'd never understand."

"Okay." I got that. It was like telling someone what jumping out of a plane felt like. I could *describe* how it felt when your feet left the deck and the air came up and hit you. How the world looked spread out below you. I could try to explain the feeling of falling. Of being so far up you felt protective of the earth, proud of it, of the entire planet. I could talk all day but it was nothing like actually experiencing it. Some things you just had to live through.

Daryn looked at me. I think my reply surprised her, the fact that I understood that I couldn't understand, and this cool sort of vibe happened, both of us connecting over things we could never really share.

I hadn't been joking when I said I'd only just scratched the surface of the things I wanted to ask her. I had questions about the Kindred. Samrael, specifically. I wanted to know if I was mortal. Could I even die? Fast healing was one thing. Being immortal was a whole different ball game.

I also wondered about the red horse and whether it had really been on fire, and if I controlled when it showed up or not, and what its purpose was in everything because I didn't need a horse. I'd never ridden one in my life. And riding something that was on fire seemed like a truly bad call. Really, no thanks. Pass.

I had an endless amount of questions. They were all I had. My world felt like it had entered a zero-gravity chamber. Things that had had weight my entire life suddenly seemed to be floating around me, moving without reason or order. There was so much to try to understand. My level of confusion was so extreme that answers didn't seem like they'd even cut it. I was on overload and Daryn was done handing out intel, so.

I reached down and pushed the Pearl Jam cassette into the player. The song that came on was "Nothingman." Hands down, my favorite. Even on cassette and through crap speakers, Eddie Vedder's voice laid down the law.

He sang to us the rest of the way to LA because it turned

out Daryn loved Pearl Jam too, which was a cool coincidence. No one our age loved Pearl Jam. I only did because of my dad, and I didn't ask why she did. I didn't want her to ask me that back. But it was okay. It didn't need qualifying. We were rock solid on it.

Pearl Jam?

Awesome.

It was something. One thing that still had gravity.

Right then, I needed it.

As we approached the LA area, Daryn sat up and twisted her blond hair into a knot on top of her head. "Don't freak out, okay?"

I wanted to tell her that was the worst possible way to keep someone from freaking out—aside from just screaming in their face—but I nodded and said, "Okay."

Her hand drifted over the silver necklace, then came to rest on the dash. She watched the freeway, studying the exits, the buildings in the distance, her stillness and concentration growing more and more intense.

"We should take the next exit," she said.

I did as she instructed.

Her directions continued. *Take a right here. Left at the next signal. Stay in this lane.*

How was she doing this?

I kept having to consciously relax my grip on the steering wheel. Awe didn't begin to cover what I felt. I'd seen a lot I couldn't explain over the past days, both with regard to me and to Samrael, but this was my first direct experience with Daryn doing something that was literally unbelievable.

We ended up at a high-rise in Studio City, where I pulled into the underground garage and parked. In a short amount of time, everything had changed. No more long sunny stretches of highway with the roar of my tires, the rattle of the soft top,

Pearl Jam playing. Now the quiet hummed in my ears and we were surrounded by concrete lit by the glare of fluorescent lighting.

On the road, the part of me that scoped out danger had been able to take a break. It'd just been me and Daryn and we'd been moving. Not much I could do but drive to keep us safe. Not anymore, though. The second we ventured into the dense population of the city, the threat factor would multiply. The Kindred could be anywhere. They could track Daryn, so we had to move quickly. The faster we located Famine and got to a safe location, the better.

"You know where he is in the building?" I asked. The things I'd been learning as a soldier came up, quick and clear. We had a lot to go over. Knowledge of terrain, routes to and from our objective, contingencies.

"Yes." Daryn yanked my sweatshirt off, tossed it in the backseat, and hopped out of the car.

"*Daryn.*" I shot after her. "You can't barrel in there without a plan."

"We don't have time to plan. We have to move fast, before Samrael finds us."

"Fast doesn't mean reckless. Fast should be slow—efficient. We need to move in a coordinated—" The garage elevator door opened. I was tempted to physically keep her from entering it, but a humming in my arm distracted me.

The cuff.

Magic metal was talking, sending energy flowing into me. I pulled my sleeve down, covering it.

Daryn pressed the button for the eleventh floor. "I know we're rushing but we have to get to him before Samrael does."

"Hold up. You said the Kindred track the object. That's what they're after. Are they after us, too?"

Before she could answer, the door slid open on the lobby level and a flood of humanity poured inside. I grabbed Daryn's arm and swam against the tide, keeping us right up front by the door as I checked every face that went past us for Samrael. Bad enough we were in a metal box. I wasn't going to get cornered in the back.

A guy in a pinstripe suit crashed into my shoulder as he rushed through the closing doors. "Dumb couriers," he muttered, shooting me a look. "Use the service elevator next time, moron."

"Gideon," Daryn said quietly. I still had her arm. I let it go. "Just ignore him."

Easier said than done. The lid on my anger had started to clatter the minute she'd jumped out of the Jeep. As the elevator went up, so did tempers. People started getting huffy, their griping filling my ears.

"—never heard of the concept of personal space—"

"—way over capacity in here and it is just *rude* to disregard the safety of others—"

"—idiot up there thinks he can use the regular elevator—"

I knew it was my effect on them. Daryn kept looking at me, but I couldn't ratchet it back. We were making a blind charge. This was a bad idea.

Finally, we reached the eleventh floor. I launched through the doors like I was back in jump school. Then I followed Daryn down a hallway, around a corner.

Moving was helping mellow me out. Not being trapped was helping too.

The cuff was buzzing. Noticeably more voltage now.

Kinda hard to ignore. Kinda wished I knew what it meant.

Daryn stopped in front of double glass doors with frosted letters. "He's in here."

"What—here?" I had to read the sign again. "Herald *Casting*?" I didn't know what I'd expected from Famine. A guy who worked in a soup kitchen maybe, or a homeless man. But this? "He's an *actor*?"

"Gideon."

"It's okay. It's fine." I wasn't going to spin on this right now. As I quickly considered what I knew about entering potentially hostile situations, Daryn pulled the door open and strolled right in.

Inside it was a waiting area like at a dentist's office only bigger and sexier, with photos of perfect people on the walls, plastic chairs around the perimeter. Lots of white and chrome.

And Samraels. Samraels sitting in every chair. My entire body went tight. Then I relaxed. The room was filled with guys who were around Samrael's age and build. They had his same dark hair and general look. But he wasn't here.

At twelve o'clock, the receptionist peered around her computer screen. "Hi there. Come on over and sign in." She dropped the smile when she saw Daryn. "Sorry, hon. This is a closed audition."

"But I'm a relative." Daryn took a step my way. Half the guys in the room had stopped reading their stapled pages in favor of looking at her. "I'm his sister."

"And?" the receptionist said. She had high penciled-in eyebrows already, but now they went even higher. "Were you planning to deliver his lines for him?"

"Well, no. It's only that"—Daryn tipped her head my way—"he can't read."

Amazingly, I was able to keep from thoroughly losing it.

Okay, Blake. Options. Any other options? Negative.

"Actually I *can* read, it's just—" What the hell was it just? I pointed at my face. "I had a minor equipment issue. Lost a contact on the way here." Then I stood there and tried to look like a guy who could only see out of one eye.

The receptionist shook her head. "Ohhh, bummer. One of those days, isn't it? I'm having one myself." She looked back to Daryn. "But it doesn't change anything. You still can't stay."

Daryn stepped closer, lowering her voice so only I could

hear. "You'll have to find him on your own. I'll meet you at the Jeep in an hour."

"No, Daryn. I can't let you leave."

"You have to. We need him. You'll be fine."

"That is not—" *Breathe. Try again.* "That's not what I'm worried about."

"I know. I'll be fine, too."

Then she was pushing through the glass doors and I was standing there. Watching her go.

Nope. This wasn't going to work for me.

I took two steps after her, and then stopped.

The cuff.

Magic metal was hitting me with a significant and striking flow of energy. Not just a buzz anymore. There was more to it. A kind of . . . knowing or presence . . . a signal that felt *here*.

I looked to my right and there he was, looking right back at me.

Famine.

CHAPTER 17

There was one empty chair in the room and it was next to him, so. I took it.

"How's it going?" I said. Having just watched Daryn leave, I wasn't exactly calm but I tried to focus on the task of getting him on the team.

"Good." He sat over his knees and rolled up the papers in his hands into a scroll.

My first impression was that he fit the bill. Even sitting I could tell he was tall. Over six feet. Lanky. He looked a touch underfed, but it gave him that model look more than anything else. Like he belonged on one of the photos on the wall. His brown hair reminded me of Wyatt's—long and shaggy— except Famine's was more natural, like it just was that way. He was my age or a little older, I guessed.

After a second of wringing the papers, he narrowed his eyes at me like he was trying to work something out. "Do I know you?"

"I don't think so," I replied. "I'm Gideon Blake."

"Sebastian. Sebastian Luna."

We didn't shake hands, which was awkward. We'd obviously avoided it. But considering all the insane stuff that'd been happening, it wouldn't have surprised me to see lightning slice down from the ceiling if we had.

I glanced at his wrist. Sebastian's cuff was different from mine. His looked like glass, smoky black, and was webbed in a way that reminded me randomly of tendons and Halloween. It was freaky looking. I liked mine better.

He lowered his head, his longish hair falling in front of his eyes. Probably secretly trying to spot my cuff. My sleeve was covering it but I realized it didn't matter. Magic metal was still sending a steady hum into me. Judging by the way Sebastian kept strangling the script in his hands, I was pretty positive his cuff was providing him with the same feedback.

I wondered what he knew. Did he know more about what was going on than I did? Wouldn't have been tough, considering. But then he hadn't met Daryn yet.

Daryn, who was Samrael's target and currently alone.

I had to keep things moving. "Did they already start?"

"A little while ago," Sebastian replied. "I heard what your sister said. I'll run lines with you, if you want."

"My sister? Oh, right. That wasn't my sister. She just said that 'cause she was hoping to provide moral support. I'm new to this. First audition."

"First one, really?" He cracked a smile. "You don't seem that nervous."

"Actually, I'm way out of my element."

"You'll do fine. First one's the hardest." He glanced at the receptionist. "I've been to a ton of these. I shouldn't be nervous, but this one's different. A big-budget cable series like this is a career maker. It can completely change your life."

"Definitely," I said. "Life. Changing."

Sebastian stretched out his legs. He seemed to be relaxing. I got the feeling he'd talked himself out of worrying about me. Either that, or he really was a good actor.

I wasn't relaxing. I needed to drop the horseman thing on him and get out of there, but I couldn't find my way in.

"Don't take this the wrong way or anything," he said, "but you're not exactly what they're looking for, you know? Young Latino cop?"

I took another look around. He had a point. "Yeah, I guess I'm not a perfect fit." I brushed a hand over my blond buzz cut like I wished it was different. "But I'm going for it anyway."

"That's the right attitude, man. Half the time, I don't think *they* even know what they want. Sometimes I don't know how anyone makes it in this business."

"Exactly. It all just seems so arbitrary and political and"— *come on, Blake, finish strong, puritanical, pathological, perforated, Panamanian*—"weird."

"You said it. This business *is* weird."

Annnd that was enough small talk for me. "Hey, so." I dropped my voice, trying to manufacture some privacy. "We should probably talk. I'm War." I couldn't think of a good follow-up comment after that—where'd you go from there?— so I pulled up my sleeve and showed him my cuff.

"You're . . ." Sebastian had stopped blinking. "You're *what?*"

"War. I know. It blew my mind too." He was starting to go a little pale so I kept talking, using my calmest voice. "Look, it'd be better if we could talk confidentially. I don't know how much you've figured out, but I think I can give you some answers. We need to bounce, though. Kinda now 'cause there's a real possibility—"

"Next group," the receptionist announced. "Head inside, please."

Sebastian shot to his feet. The guys around us were a little slower to stand, but not by much. "You should get out of here," he said, sounding almost sorry. "I don't want to talk to you."

He walked into the audition.

I got up and went right after him.

Five of us filed into a conference room, one wall of which was a floor-to-ceiling window that showed a hazy, sort of pretty view of the Hollywood Hills.

Two long tables were set up in front of it. Four women and three men sat behind an assortment of coffee cups, water bottles, and papers. They were talking and passing around head shots. Only one of them was paying attention to us— the man on the far right. He was backlit by the gloomy glow of the day, so his face was in shadow. All I could really see of him was a shiny bald head and round-framed glasses. The kind John Lennon wore.

"Form a line, please," he said, in a pissy-bored voice. "When we call you forward, deliver the first lines on page three, up to 'drowning in a sea of gray.'"

I took my place, then realized I was standing at parade rest and had to unsoldier my stance. Since I was on the end, I'd be either the first or the last guy to go.

"This is going to be interesting," I muttered.

Sebastian's head swiveled over and I saw genuine horror on his face. "*Get out of here*. I told you. I don't want to get involved."

"You're involved. All I need's five minutes."

"Man, *please*. This is really important—"

He broke off as the guy on the opposite end of the line stepped forward.

Showtime.

Compared to the rest of us, the actor was on the short side. Stocky, with a starter paunch. He had spiked black hair and ink sleeves on both arms.

"I'm Luis Alvarez." He took a huge breath, his chest expanding, expanding, expanding, then he blew it out, deflating himself.

Then detonation.

"He was like a brother to me!" He pounded his fist against his chest. "Like *my own blood*! But I'm a *cop*. I wear *a badge*. I swore an *oath*. What was I supposed to *do*? I had to shoot him!" He threw his hands out, then made a gun with his fingers and pretend-shot the casting people. *Pop, pop, pop.* Blew fake smoke off his finger. Holstered his hand. "The law is bigger than me. It's words written in black ink on white paper, but sometimes this world is gray. That's where I am. I lost my

brother and I'm *drowning*! I'm drowning in a sea of *gray*."
Blink. "Thank you."

He stepped back in line, linked his hands behind his back and dropped his head like *that, my friends, is how you crush it.*

A flutter in my gut came up, shooting into my throat. I clenched my jaw but the battle was already over. I went from zero to howling. Big, big laughing. The insanity of everything was too much. And the embarrassment. It hurt me. I was drowning in a sea of cheese.

"*Please,*" Sebastian said. "*Shut up.*"

I was trying.

"Do you have a problem with something?" Lennon Glasses asked me.

"No, sir. I apologize for that." I was still on shaky ground, but remembering my manners, my mission. "Just a bad case of nerves." This needed to end. I stepped forward. "Can I go next?"

"He can't," Sebastian said. "He'd be out of turn."

"No, I wouldn't."

"Yes, you would."

"Then we'll go in random order."

"If it's random, then I'll go next since I'm not on the end."

"Dude, do you even know what random means?"

"Yes. In this case it means I get to go first." He took two steps forward and looked at the casting table. "I'm ready."

It'd gotten pretty quiet in the room. Then suddenly it wasn't.

Lennon Glasses shuffled some papers and the other casting people huddled around him. They had a hushed but animated discussion. We'd woken them up.

Lennon Glasses cleared his throat and looked up. "We'll take Mr. Luna first since we don't seem to have your head-shot, Mr. . . . ?"

"Blake. Gideon Blake."

Total silence again. I couldn't have felt less Latino. Maybe if I'd started belting out "Danny Boy."

"Thank you, Mr. Blake. Mr. Luna, go ahead."

Sebastian shot me a little victory smile as I made myself fall back into line. Then I watched him deliver the same exact lines, except totally differently.

He took his time to start. Almost a full minute, so everyone in the room was anticipating it, focused on him, waiting for him to speak. When he did, his voice was heavy and breaking—a sound I recognized. Grief had a particular weight in a person's voice that was too heavy for words. He knew that weight. Or if he didn't, he could communicate it.

He used the silence between the lines too, which I'd never realized was part of acting until that moment. But he filled the pauses somehow. Even his breathing said something about pain. The way he bowed his head, the look on his face. The crushing, shitty, heart-killing truth of losing someone you love was in every part of him. And when he lifted his hands and stared at his open palms with the final line, the one about drowning in the sea of gray? Chills. I got actual chills from the amount of feeling the guy put into those crap lines. Sebastian made them real. He filled the room with agony and I wasn't the only one who felt it. When he was done, the entire room was in full clench.

Awesome. Awesome stuff. But it'd been at least fifteen minutes since Daryn had walked out of there, and that was way past my limit.

I dropped my hand on Sebastian's shoulder. "Well, that was amazing," I said, tugging him toward the door. "I know I don't need to audition anymore. I give my votes to him. Unfortunately we have to run. You know how it is during audition season."

Audition season? Was that even a thing?

"Let go of me," Sebastian said, trying to break free. "I don't even know you."

"Can you believe this guy? Still in character." I had him at the door by then. Almost out of there. "Thanks a lot, everybody. Break a leg."

I pushed the door open and shoved him into the hallway.

"Okay, okay! Take it easy!" He put his hands up. "Just *let go* of me, and we'll talk."

I let him go.

He lurched out of my reach, and bolted.

CHAPTER 18

I should've caught him right away. He'd only gotten a small jump on me, but as I barreled through the door into the waiting room, I ran smack into the receptionist coming the other way. I managed to catch her and keep us both on our feet; then I took a second to make sure she was okay because I'd really given her a shot. That put Sebastian a few steps ahead of me as I chased him out of the casting office into the main hallway.

"Stop!" I yelled. "Just *stop!*"

Sebastian froze at the end of the corridor and locked eyes with me, his hands planted on the door to the stairwell. Then he pushed it open and disappeared inside.

I sprinted after him and flew down the stairs, taking the steps three at a time. As I spun around the tenth-floor landing, I saw him rounding the next flight below me. We did that again on the ninth floor, eighth. By the seventh, I was gaining on him. I spun around the handrail, turning the corner, and came to a sliding stop.

Sebastian stood on the landing below. In his hand was something I had never seen before. Two black disks suspended on gleaming chains. I had no idea what it was, but I instinctively recognized it as a weapon.

"I'm sorry!" he blurted. Then he cocked his arm back and flung it.

The thing wobbled through the air, the disks rotating on the chain like orbiting planets. Not a great throw, but I was so close. It came right at me.

I lunged out of the way, executing a half somersault in midair before my ass collided with the wall. I went down, a loud *crunch* sounding just inches away from my head.

Scrambling up, I looked for Sebastian. All I heard were the receding squeaks of his soles churning on cement steps. I turned to the thing hanging from the wall and couldn't believe my eyes.

One of the disks had sunk deep into the cinder blocks. The other swung like a pendulum beneath it, making a sharp metallic hiss as it skimmed along, raising sparks, and finally stopped.

I leaned in. The disks and chain were made of . . . black glass? It looked like the same material as Sebastian's cuff. Crystal infused with darkness. And it didn't gleam so much as glow, somehow putting off a black light around it. There was a toggle at the center of the chain, a grip made of the same material.

Sebastian's footsteps echoed farther away. He was pulling ahead, but I couldn't leave. Whatever this thing was, it seemed too important to leave behind. I reached out, and hesitated. Told myself to suck it up. It just didn't look like anything I'd ever seen. Then went for it and grabbed the handgrip.

Nothing. No problem. Just smooth, cool metal.

I tugged. The disk popped out easily, like the wall was made of cork. I lifted it for a closer look. The disks tapped together on the end of the chains; then *clink,* they snapped together, one sliding over the other, locking into place.

Badass. Amazing. Incredible. I wanted to check it out further, but I had a man to catch. I secured my grip and resumed pursuit.

Sebastian had a lead of a few flights on me by then, so I didn't expect to almost plow into his back when I hit the first floor and charged into the lobby.

"Who is that?" he asked, without taking his eyes off the glass-walled entrance.

Samrael. No mistaking him this time.

He stood just inside the center doors in dark jeans and a

black coat, more casual than the businesspeople around, but he looked like he belonged, polished and sharp. A young exec.

Ronwae, the girl with the red hair, and Malaphar, the pock-faced guy in the oversized suit, were covering the two other exits to the front of the building. There was also a new addition to the posse, a young guy, maybe sixteen, seventeen, wearing a red beanie and slouched skater clothes, who strode up to Samrael's side just as Samrael spotted us.

"Sebastian, you better follow me," I said.

That time, he did.

CHAPTER 19

In the Army, you don't say you retreat. You withdraw. That was what we did. We were outnumbered, underprepared, and uninformed, so. We withdrew like the wind.

I pushed back into the stairwell with Sebastian right on my heels. Moments ago I'd seen two doors on the first-floor landing—lobby and emergency exit—and emergency was this. Now.

I exploded through it, setting off an alarm, and ran into bright, eye-spanking daylight. First and foremost I wanted to see Daryn in my Jeep, ready to burn rubber, but she wasn't anywhere.

We'd come out onto a street with no traffic. To my right were low-slung buildings with red-tile roofs, stucco walls. Sidewalks lined with huge pots of red flowers. Parked cars, all of the luxury, six-figure variety. Down the street, there was a guardhouse, but not like at Benning. This had flower boxes. Fancy trim around the windows and doors. To my left were massive gray warehouses, STUDIO 5 painted in huge red letters across the top of the nearest one.

I'd already figured where we were when Sebastian said, "It's the back lot."

The studio looked buttoned up tight, with high concrete walls bordering the perimeter. I didn't want to get stuck in there with Samrael. But the guardhouse was a hundred meters away, with nothing for cover except flowers and Porsches. We'd be seen before we could get outside. Leaving the studio would also take us further away from the parking garage, where Daryn was. I changed plans and led Sebastian deeper into the lot, hoping for better options.

The alarm from the high-rise had faded when the door closed behind us. Now it spiked, cutting through the quiet of the studio lot. Looking back, I saw Samrael and his buddies.

With no one else on the street, they spotted us right away, but Sebastian and I had reached the sound stages and if we could just get around the corner, a little farther, we'd be in . . . New York City?

We'd run into a street lined with brownstones on both sides. Steam tumbled out of the gutters. A yellow cab was parked along the curb farther down the street. The front page of the *New York Times* floated in the puddle I'd just passed.

I'd slowed down, and Sebastian came even with me. "What do we do? It's Gideon, right? Where do we go?"

I couldn't even answer him. Real fear was spreading through me as I remembered Samrael mentally beating me down. We needed cover *now*.

I turned it back up, sprinting to the nearest building—a corner market with crates full of plastic produce and silk flowers. The windows were actually paintings of scenes you'd expect to see inside, like a woman working behind a cash register. A grinning butcher holding up a ham hock. This was a façade, but I yanked the door open anyway just in case. Plywood.

Sebastian breathed hard at my side. "What do they want with *us*?"

"Daryn."

"*Who?*"

I firmed my grip on the chains. "The girl who isn't my sister. Get behind that cab and stay there." As I jogged to the middle of the street, I thought about how I'd been trained to do exactly this—fight. Partially trained. With actual firearms, not nunchuk-disk-things. But so be it. A fight was a fight.

Samrael came around the corner first. Two others jogged up next. Ronwae and the new guy, the skater with the red beanie, who went by the name Pyro, I'd learn later. They stopped on either side of Samrael. I kept expecting Malaphar, but he didn't show up.

"Did you get tired of running, Gideon?" Samrael stopped at the top of the street, but it was so quiet he spoke without raising his voice. "Or tired of being a coward?"

"Just tired of you." I brought my hand out slightly, my prethrow position. The disks unlocked, separating by some miracle, but it must've looked like I knew what I was doing.

"What do you have there?" Samrael asked.

"Nothing," said Sebastian, coming to my side. "We don't even know you, so why—"

He gasped and folded like he'd taken a gut shot, grabbing his head with both hands.

I knew what this was. Samrael had done this to me at Joy's party. Except this was over faster. Sebastian straightened again almost immediately and looked at me. "What was that? What did he just do to me?"

"Help me understand something," Samrael said. "You're both involved in this—I can sense that you know that—but you haven't been told the most salient *crucial* piece?" He laughed, and said something to Ronwae and Pyro. I didn't hear it, but it made Ronwae laugh too. Not Pyro. He stared at us with crazed eyes, shifting his weight like a hunting dog waiting to be released.

"This is stupid," Pyro said. "Let's just kill them."

"Not yet." Samrael's focus moved to me. My turn again.

The pressure started over my eyes, the sensation of thumbs digging their way into my head, probing inside. The feeling spread and turned sharper, casting a barbed net over my brain. The darkness came, wheeling around me, pulling me back as the world pushed further and further away.

I wanted him out. Out of my head.

Get out. Get out. Get. Out.

But I need something, Gideon. Where is it?

His voice was *inside* my mind.

Then I saw images. Quick flashes. Daryn at breakfast in Cayucos, writing in her notebook. Daryn sitting in the passenger seat of my Jeep, feet up on the dash. Daryn in the elevator, finger drifting over the panel to the eleventh-floor button.

This was why she'd withheld critical information about our mission. She knew what Samrael could do. He wasn't attacking. He was *searching*. Through *my head*.

Daryn is her name? Unusual. She's kind on the eyes, isn't she? And much smarter than you, it would seem. In the context of her strategy, your extreme cluelessness is almost forgivable. Where is she, Gideon? Right now, where is she?

I tried to fight back, concentrating on pulling down the net. Pushing against the pressure.

Admirable attempt, but not good enough. Let's try this again. Where—pain, pain like nails driving into my head—*is she?*

A sound ripped into the quiet of the street. It came from close, from my throat. My knees smacked the asphalt. Sebastian yelled something. Yelled for Samrael to stop.

Samrael didn't stop.

Insanity. Death. They were the only ways out of this agony. Were they close?

Yes, Gideon. Very.

No. This was just pain. I'd felt it before. Every day. Every time I thought of my dad. I could take this.

The net released suddenly, the pressure and darkness withdrawing, and then there was the lift. The huge *lift* of being free of the pain, like hot rain pouring up and down my body, running through every part of me.

I pulled myself to my feet. The disks were still in my hand, but I felt dazed and slow. Up the street at Samrael's side,

Ronwae blurred in and out, like I was seeing her through heat waves. Sebastian. Samrael and his buddies. Everyone was focused on the tricked-out ATV that had just come around the corner.

The studio cop pulled to a stop and brought a microphone up to his mouth. "This set is authorized-access only." His voice projected through speakers mounted on the roll bar. "I'm going to need to see your passes, please."

Sebastian and I were on the opposite end of the block, leaving the Kindred boxed in the middle—the weakest position to be in during a conflict—so why did I feel like they still had the advantage?

"We'll be on our way shortly," Samrael replied. "We're just finishing up a conversation."

The studio cop climbed out of the vehicle. The guy was ripped in that gym-dweller way. Loaded with muscles that had no real-world application. He pressed his shoulders back, sensing trouble. "I'm sorry, sir. Unless you show me your ID, I'm going to have to escort you off the lot."

"Gideon, we should leave," Sebastian said.

But I couldn't leave. Something was about to go down. I was sure of it.

And I was right.

Samrael made a snapping motion with his hand, a flick like he was opening a switchblade. Something appeared at his fingertips. There was nothing in his hand, and then there was something. A knife. Sebastian and I weren't that far away. I couldn't be imagining the long ivory-colored knife Samrael was suddenly holding.

The studio cop froze as Samrael turned back to him.

I broke into a sprint, straight toward him, dread shooting through me.

Samrael reached back and hurled the knife. It traveled through the air at shocking speed, but time broke down and

I saw it in pieces. Slow. The entire thing, clear and sharp. The guard's utter look of shock at seeing a weapon used against him. The knife's bizarre trail of pale light, like a comet's. And my thoughts. I had so many thoughts as that knife sailed on and on in that instant.

That man's going to die.

By a weapon that appeared from nothing.

Because I didn't anticipate again.

I should've stopped this.

The blade sank into the guard's neck. Five, six inches disappearing at the base of his throat, right beneath his Adam's apple. The force of the strike rocked him backward. He landed on the street, his keys jangling, his cell phone skidding across the pavement.

Sebastian ran up beside me.

We stood together, watching a furious moment of legs bucking and throat grasping and gurgling. Then nothing.

Just stillness.

My eyes went to the fat ring on the guard's finger. Class ring? Too far to tell. Then the piece of lettuce stuck to the bottom of his shoe. From the pretend market, or was it real?

This was real. This had seemed like a joke in so many ways, but it was *real.*

The guard was dead.

When I looked back at Samrael, he had another pale knife in his hand. It looked like bone. A knife entirely made of bone.

"Where is she, Gideon?" he asked.

"Come on!" I yelled. Inside, I'd caught fire. "You have to deal with me now!"

Samrael launched the knife. Years behind home plate kicked in. I saw its trajectory and reacted, tackling Sebastian to the ground. The disks slipped out of my hand as we hit the asphalt. The blade flew past us and went skimming along the street like a rock skipping over a lake.

"Stay down!" I yelled to Sebastian. I scrambled for the disks and came up throwing, launching the weapon well. It traveled with the same speed as Samrael's blade, the scales leaving a dark streak as they whirled through the air.

My aim was off. I'd gone for Samrael but the weapon sailed wide and low, toward Pyro. He lunged away, but not fast enough. The chain caught one of his shins and the disks twisted, lassoing his other leg. He hit the street, calf-roped.

Samrael looked at his fallen Kindred, clearly surprised. I was too, but I didn't stick around. I grabbed the back of Sebastian's shirt and hauled him up, and then behind the cab. "You okay?"

He was shaking pretty badly but he didn't look hurt.

"My life just danced before my eyes!"

I glanced over my shoulder. Samrael was still coming. Pyro had untangled himself. Ronwae was doing that shimmering thing I'd seen a few moments ago, like seeing in 3D without the glasses.

"Call your horse, Gideon!" Sebastian grabbed my arm. "That's our only chance!"

"Call my—*what did you just say?*"

"I'll do it." Sebastian's eyes closed for a beat; then right in the middle of the street, the horses appeared.

First his. Then mine.

They charged right up to the Kindred and stood there like complete badasses, providing the best equine overwatch you've ever seen in your life. That gave me and Sebastian the window we needed to get the hell out of there.

CHAPTER 20

"G ideon, slow down," Cordero says, her hand coming up.
"You're rushing."

I trudge up out of the swamp. Clear my throat. "Am I?"

The radiator's going again. *Tink tink tink.* We must be somewhere cold. Why didn't I think about that before? Wait. Did I?

"That's okay," Cordero says. Her smile is as warm as a bag of rocks. She's been intent from the beginning, but now she's intense. Getting nervous, maybe. If I'm telling the truth, what does it mean? What will it mean to her reality, her beliefs? Her understanding of the world? She's getting a taste of what I've been through.

She looks at her folder. "You said the horses 'appeared'?"

"That's right."

"What did that look like?"

"I knew that would get you."

"The horses, Gideon."

"How about this. You give me more water and I tell you about the horses."

Cordero approves the water request and Texas is on the job. Water's good. Helps my throat, my head. Drugs are starting to pull back. Chemical taste is going away. Clouds in muscles thinning. Stomach's doing okay. Brain's getting sharper. I still have a ways to go before I'm back to normal again. Maybe another hour or so. But I'll get there.

I finish the water and thank Texas, who nods and posts up again. Then I dive right in. I never liked this, but now I'm starting to hate it. This clown show of a debriefing needs to be over. "Bastian's horse was—"

"Bastian is Sebastian?"

"That's him. Sebastian. Bas. Famine. I know he's right next door."

"You were saying about his horse?" Cordero says. No pause. No reaction.

"Right. I was saying. His horse came up in the middle of the street like black smoke. First just a thread, twisting up from the ground, then a flurry of whirling, rising darkness that gradually formed into the blackest horse you can imagine. Blacker than soot. Blacker than the deepest cave. Smoke, then solid. Then *horse.* Like that.

"The mare was long and spindly in build. Leggy, like a racehorse. She moved like she was spring-loaded, totally weightless. When she did, lines of muscle caught the light. Blue, like moonbeams. Like the flash of moonbeams on that midnight coat. When she moved *fast,* she'd leave the same trails of smoky light I'd seen when I'd thrown the disks. They'd come off her legs, her mane and tail, and . . . I don't know what else to tell you. She was incredible. Fragile. Insect-thin. Haunting. But damn if she wasn't beautiful."

Cordero's dark eyes hold steady. "You're saying the horse came from nothing."

"She didn't come from nothing. I don't think anything comes from nothing. What I am saying is that I watched her materialize in front of me."

Now she does pause.

"The horse took up a defensive position for you?"

This comes from Beretta, surprisingly.

Cordero spreads her hands. "My next question as well." She sounds a little peeved.

"Yes," I answer, "but she didn't do it for me. She did it for Sebastian. My horse, in case you're wondering, came up the same way as Bastian's, except as fire. He started out as a flare, then became this small blazing inferno, then *bam.* Horse.

Huge red horse that made a ghost trail of flames when he moved."

I force myself not to add *and he was even more kickass than Bastian's*! I get competitive about my horse. We all do.

"And these horses," Cordero says, "they appeared and simply awaited your commands?"

She had to ask, didn't she? *Don't answer, Blake. Just this one question. Don't don't don't here I go.* "No. My horse, he um . . . He came up and charged me. Again. Like on the beach."

Texas grins big, his teeth surprisingly white and straight behind the shaggy beard.

"He charged you. And you stopped him?" Cordero asks.

"No. Not me. Sebastian's horse set him straight. She let out a loud neigh and my horse fell in line. Then he was two thousand pounds of lethal, fiery trouble, shooting past Sebastian's mare, taking up position less than ten meters away from Samrael."

So much for taking the humble high road.

"And Samrael's reaction?" Cordero asks.

"Well, I'm not sure because like I said, Bastian and I got out of there pretty fast. But I think he pissed his bad-boy pants."

"Really, Gideon."

"I'm serious. You have to understand, Cordero. My horse stood like a wall staring Samrael down. Red as sunset. Head high, his breath pumping in and out. He had *sparks* coming out of his nostrils. *Flames* rolled up his legs and flowed off his tail. These horses . . . they're not normal. They're predators. Warriors, a hundred percent. None more so than mine. When Bastian's horse glided up next to him like a nightmare, like a beautiful freakin' nightmare, both of them standing there, fearless . . . just *fearless* . . . I think Samrael probably soiled himself. I know I almost did."

Cordero rolls her eyes, which makes me smile.

"I do remember looking back one last time as Bastian and

I rounded the corner. Samrael was standing in that fake New York street, watching the horses with this extreme focus. With *awe*. He seemed to be discovering for the first time what we actually were. Horsemen. And to be honest, that was pretty close to how I felt right then, too."

CHAPTER 21

After we left the Kindred behind, we met up with Daryn in the garage. She was waiting right by the Jeep as planned. The relief at seeing her there, unharmed, stopped me in my tracks for a second. Samrael had shown no hesitation in killing the studio guard. I didn't want to think about what could've happened if he'd caught her.

We piled into the Jeep and I drove. Daryn and Sebastian traded quick hellos. I gave Daryn a summary of the studio lot events. Then we spent sixty miles quietly and individually processing the extreme suck of the situation.

With my pulse finally evening out, I looked up, meeting Sebastian's gaze in the rearview mirror. I was pretty positive he'd just seen his first violent death too. We were stuck in this thing, the two of us. This was happening to us both.

"I don't even know how to thank you for what you did back there," he said.

Daryn stirred, her gaze moving between us. Sebastian and I had been quiet, but she'd been more than quiet. She had a way of sinking so far into her thoughts, it felt like she went away somewhere.

"You just did," I replied. "Sorry about your flying disks, though. Those were pretty cool."

"You mean the scales," Sebastian said. "Famine has scales. In the Book of Revelation."

He paused after every comment, waiting for some sign of recognition from me. I couldn't give it to him. I'd remembered a little more about the four horsemen, but it still wasn't much. Just another reason I didn't understand why I'd been given the job. I knew they rode horses of different colors

and that they were involved in the end times. I knew generally about sacred seals being broken, setting a series of cata-
clysmic events into motion before Judgment Day. But Daryn
had said we weren't doing any of that. We were incarnations
of the horsemen, manifested for a different mission. The mission, so far defined, being the protection of an object no one
except Daryn knew anything about.

"Anyway, no worries," Sebastian said. "I have them right
here."

I glanced back and saw the weapon resting on his legs.
"Explain." I didn't like that he had a weapon. And apparent
control of his horse. I didn't have any of that. "Explain right
now."

"Wait a second. You told me you were War. I thought you'd
know. You told me you had answers."

I tipped my head to Daryn. "She does."

"Some answers. I know some things, but"—she gestured to
the scales—"the weapons, the horses. That's all you guys."

"Hey, Daryn," I said, my frustration hitting a boil. "You realize you gave me the worst mission briefing that's probably
ever been given in the history of time?"

"Hey, Gideon. This is a need-to-know situation. You know
what I need you to. I have to get you all together. You can figure out your weapons and horses then. And it's not like I
know everything myself."

That wasn't a satisfying explanation at all, but at the moment I was more interested by the scales. "How did you get
them back?" I asked Sebastian.

"Watch," he said.

I took my eyes off the road and turned. The scales disinte-
grated into a whirl of black ribbons. *Poof.* Vanished.

That made sense. He could telepathically call the super-
weapon from magic cuff land when he needed it. Should've
figured that out myself. "Our horses. Are they disappeared,

too?" We'd left our horses standing guard, and for all I knew, they were still hanging out at the studio.

"I called mine back. My guess is yours just followed."

"Perfect. Listen up, Sebastian. As soon as we get out of this Jeep, you're going to tell me how you did that. You're going to *show* me."

I sounded like the cadre in RASP, laying it down in ruthless no-BS terms, but whatever. Intel. I needed it.

"No problem," he said. "And you can call me Bastian or Bas." He shifted around in the backseat, trying to stretch out his legs. "Most people do. I only really use my full name for work. My real name's my stage name."

"That's okay. I don't mind taking all that extra time to say your full name." Not very cool of me, but I was having a hard time being so far behind the learning curve on stuff that seemed pretty damn critical.

"Gideon has OCPD tendencies," Daryn said. She pulled my Giants sweatshirt on. It felt like her sweatshirt now.

"Say again?"

She smiled. "Obsessive-compulsive personality disorder. It's an extreme preoccupation with perfectionism, orderliness, and neatness."

Was that how she saw me? Like a human graphing calculator? Great. "You missed a few, Martin. I also like specifics. Thoroughness. And winning. At everything. But I gotta say as a soldier I fully support your use of acronyms."

"Ten-four, buddy," she said.

"In the Army we say 'Roger that.'"

Her smile grew wider. "Ten-four, buddy."

For a second there, it felt like maybe she was messing with me, in a good way. Then she raised her eyebrows like, dude. Stare much? And started giving me directions that put us on Highway 15, which was toward Vegas.

"So, no Death Valley?" I asked. "For Death?"

Dumb comment, but my balance was off.

Daryn reached down and rummaged in her backpack like I hadn't said anything.

"Can't you just tell me where we're going?" I said. It came out harsher than I'd meant. Why? No idea why.

She pulled her notebook out, propped it on her knees, and started writing.

Solid brush-off. It simultaneously annoyed me and made me want to smack myself for insubordination. Did I question my commanding officers? *Hell* no.

She'd told me what we needed to do. Wrangle up some horsemen. I had to focus on that. Sebastian obviously knew more about our tools, our weapons. Maybe the other guys, Conquest and Death, would bring their own contributions. Like Daryn said, I needed to get everyone together, and fast, so we could get down to the real work of mastering our capabilities. It was our best shot at standing against the Kindred. And, no question about it anymore, it was also our best shot at staying alive.

An hour later, night was falling and Eddie Vedder was singing about still being alive as I drove past the turnoff to Barstow. I watched the sign come and go, marking a place that I didn't know, but that had pretty big personal meaning. My dad had spent six months stationed at Fort Irwin in Barstow. Anna and I were born during those months. I hadn't been back here since.

Thinking about that took me to thinking about my mom and how worried she probably was about me. Maybe I should call her. Sure. Call and say what exactly that would stop her worrying?

Sebastian leaned forward and rested his elbows on the front seats. "Is she asleep?"

I nodded. Daryn had somehow rolled into a ball in the

passenger seat, tight as a pill bug. I had no idea how she could make herself so small. My kneecaps would've exploded in that position. A lock of her hair had fallen over her face. I wanted to brush it aside.

"Gideon, I'm not even going to try to tiptoe around the bush about this—"

"Beat around the bush?"

"Yeah. I have a lot of questions, like"—he tipped his chin at Daryn—"how does she fit into this?"

"She's, um. Well, I don't know a lot." I wanted to know more about her. More and more I wanted to know more. "But she calls herself a Seeker. She's in charge."

"That's what it seems like."

I looked at him. He looked at me. It didn't seem like he'd meant it as a put-down. I rubbed my eyes and drove.

"She seems cool." He paused like he was waiting for me to weigh in on Daryn's coolness. When I didn't, he said, "You're never going to believe this."

"Try me."

"When you tackled me earlier—to save my life, so I'm not mad, I know you didn't mean to do it, I'm just saying—I scraped my elbow when I hit the asphalt. But get this. It's *healing*!" He tugged his sleeve up. "It's almost completely healed!"

I glanced at the pink stamp on his elbow. "That hasn't happened to you yet? The fast-healing thing?"

"Has it happened to *you*?"

"Uh-huh." Finally. I knew something someone didn't.

"Whoa."

"Yeah. Whoa."

Bastian lowered his arm. "Did you die, then come back with the cuff?"

"Yep. Died and came back."

"Trippy, right?"

"Total trip."

I wanted to know how he'd died, but it wasn't the kind of question you just asked.

He pushed his hair out of his eyes. "Man, it is *such a relief* not to be the only one. I thought I was losing my mind! Sorry about running back there. At Herald Casting? When you first showed up, I didn't expect it. I think I was in denial or something. So what exactly is our job?"

The guy was kind of animated and . . . I don't know. Upbeat. He reminded me of a Great Dane puppy. But I liked him. Any guy who offers to run lines with you for a bogus audition because you lost a fake contact lens is cool in my book, so I told him what I knew about us being incarnations of the horsemen. That we were supposed to protect something. That was exactly how I put it.

"So we're bodyguards?"

"Pretty much. Except minus any concrete knowledge of what we're actually guarding."

I didn't mention the chain around Daryn's neck. Containment of information was critical because of Samrael and his mind-scanning abilities. Which . . . checking, checking . . . *yes.* Confirmed. It did make me a damn hypocrite.

"We can do that, right?" Sebastian said. "We can totally protect the thing. Especially with you being in the Army. What do you think the other guys are going to be like?"

"Don't know." I wanted them to be easygoing like Sebastian. But maybe a little tougher. Or a lot.

"You think it'll be the same with the cuffs?" he asked, looking at his. "This feeling?"

"Probably." Mystery metal had calmed down. The buzzing I'd felt at the casting office wasn't as loud but it was still giving me feedback. A constant silent tone, like I'd developed a completely new sense. I was positive Sebastian's proximity did that. Then I remembered. "Hey. Sebastian. Do you have a power? Like control over people?"

I felt stupid as soon as I said it. Like I was asking if he be-lieved in unicorns. Which weren't half as weird as our horses.

Bastian nodded. For the first time since I'd known him, his expression went dark. "Yeah, I do. You don't even want to know about it, man. It's effed up." He slid back, disappearing into the backseat, our conversation at a clear end.

I spent the next thirty miles trying to figure out what it could be. Rage seemed to make sense for War, but what about Fam-ine? I was pretty hungry right then. Was he working his power on me? But I couldn't see how wielding hunger would be an asset. Then again if I got hungry enough I got angry, so . . . Did we have *the same* power? Then I remembered his audi-tion. Was *acting* his power? If so, then I was really glad I wasn't Famine.

With my Jeep running on fumes, we stopped for gas. I filled the tank, then pulled a twenty out of my wallet and handed it to Bastian.

"Get us a couple bottles of water and some food, would you? I'm famished."

Bastian cracked a grin. "That's my line."

I left him and went around back to the restrooms, where Daryn had headed. I didn't want to crowd her so I hung back a little. She didn't see me as she slipped into the women's room. About three hours later—okay, it just felt that long—she came back out.

She froze when she saw me. "What are you doing?"

I spread my hands. "I was just . . . standing here."

"Seriously?" She twisted her hair over one shoulder, then touched the necklace. I thought I saw her fingers trembling. "Were you *waiting* for me?"

"Yes. It's the middle of the night, Daryn." This was a truck stop at the edge of the desert. There was nothing around us except great places to dump bodies.

"I can take care of myself." She shook her head, scowling like I'd insulted her, and walked away.

I stood there for a second longer, trying to figure out what I'd done wrong. Oh, right. I'd tried to be helpful.

When I came around the corner Sebastian was pulling pretzels out of a brown paper bag, crunching away. I knew he'd heard my exchange with Daryn. He wasn't even trying to hide his smile.

"*Shut up*, Famine."

"I didn't say anything, War."

When we got to the Jeep, Daryn was in the driver's seat. "You should get some sleep," she said, without looking at me.

I had the feeling this was about more than just who'd drive, but whatever.

We got back on the road and shared the bag of pretzels. Then we split two Twix bars three ways—which, believe me, wasn't easy—and talked about nothing of consequence. I think we had a debate about the best pretzel shape. Daryn liked the classic twist. I liked sticks. Sebastian liked them all. Then it was full dark and there was only the sound of my Jeep eating up miles on the freeway.

I settled in and stared at the stars. Millions and millions of them. We were in true desert now. The Mojave. And I'd never seen so many stars.

After a while, I couldn't look at those stars without thinking *God*. And then thinking, *Oh my God. You're really real*. I had the answer to the greatest mystery of all time, and I hadn't even stopped to think about it.

Why? Why hadn't I lost my mind over this? I had *proof*. Why was I so . . . so *relaxed* about the biggest, most mind-blowing part of all this? But then this trickle-down effect happened, and I started thinking about every last crappy thing I've ever done in my life.

There's a lot, Cordero. I've told you a few things already, but it's a pretty healthy list. I swear a lot. More than I've been doing. I've been trying to keep it clean for you. I have anger issues. I think I've established that. I didn't go to church more than a few times a year. I hadn't prayed since my dad died. I'd literally signed up to kill people for the protection of my country if I had to, and . . . The list goes on.

Point is, I came back to that question—why me? I was nowhere close to being an ideal candidate. I mean, I believed. I think inside, in my heart, I'd always believed. But was that enough? Was it the start, or the end? Or . . . neither?

As I watched that desert sky, all that going on inside me, I felt my mind rearranging itself. It wasn't that I understood better, or that I'd made peace with anything. I still had that zero-gravity feeling, like all the anchors in my life had been pulled up. It was more that space had opened up. I realized I hadn't even had the capacity to understand before. And that night, with all those stars over that open freeway, all I felt and saw and *felt* was endless capacity.

CHAPTER 22

My eyes wouldn't stay open, so I slept. I dreamt about my family. My dad pitching to me—weird because he never used to. He couldn't because of an old shoulder injury. My sister and my mom dancing to salsa music in our living room—weird because that had never happened. And other things that made no sense. That were just a wacky stew cooked up by my subconscious. But part of what I dreamt was real. A memory that replayed perfectly for me from when I was a little kid, in kindergarten.

It was circle time and we were all sitting on this carpet map of the United States. I was sitting on New York, Anna was over by Arizona. Somewhere in the Gulf of Mexico, my teacher Mrs. Alexander was reading a book to us.

The story was about this little monster who wanted to be terrifying but was too cute to pull it off. I couldn't sit still as Mrs. A read it. It was my favorite book and I'd brought it in that day. I wanted everyone to think it was as funny as I did. Mrs. A had just given me a second warning to stop wiggling around when the classroom phone rang. She marked her spot by slipping a pencil between the pages and went to answer it.

Everyone started goofing off but I watched Mrs. A because she was acting strange. She had turned her back to us—and she never did that. Her head was bowed and I could tell she'd started crying because her back was jiggling. She hung up, wiped her eyes with a tissue, and sat back down.

She kept reading to us with the tissue in her hand. Her grip on the book was tight and her voice sounded too high.

I'd stopped wiggling.

Anna and I always downplayed our twinness at that age,

but I crawled next to her and sat close enough that our arms were touching. I didn't know what was happening but I knew I should be next to her.

Before Mrs. A finished the book, my dad marched into the classroom. He picked Anna up like she was a baby, grabbed my hand, and took us straight home.

Anna and I were sent to my room to play, but we didn't. I stared at my Star Wars Legos and listened. The television was on in the living room. My dad was on the phone. Something bad was happening in New York—New York, which I felt close to because that was where I always sat on the map.

Anna had colored half a tree then given up, pushing the paper aside. She kept telling me she was scared and I kept telling her not to be scared because Anna scared made me anxious, and sometimes it even made me mean.

The door swung open and my mom was there, checking on us.

"What's wrong, Mom?" Anna asked.

Mom looked like she'd been crying, but she said, "Nothing, sweetie."

"Who is Dad talking to?" I asked. I knew she'd protect us from whatever was happening, so I went straight for facts. If I gathered enough facts I could figure it out on my own.

"Some friends of his from work."

"Uncle Jack?" I asked. Jack wasn't an uncle but we called him that. He was my dad's foreman in the roofing business.

"No, honey. From the Army. His old work."

It was September 11, 2001, and the call he'd made was to his commanding officer in the Reserve. I'd figure that out later.

And I'd learn that he'd done ROTC through college, then served with the Fifth Special Forces Group in Desert Storm. I'd learn that his shoulder injury had come from shrapnel embedded in his rotator cuff. I'd learn, just from watching him, from listening to him talk to his buddies, about Ranger School.

Jump school. The Ranger Battalions. The Scroll. The Creed. That Rangers lead the way.

But I didn't know any of that then. I knew my dad as a roofer. A fisherman. A lover of Pearl Jam and Giants baseball. He was the guy who launched me over the waves on the beach, and who bench-pressed Anna because it made her giggle in a way that nothing else did. He was my mom's best friend, with some additional elements like kissing that seemed pretty gross because, you know, I was six. But I learned something new about him that morning.

I learned that when bad things happened, my dad stepped forward first.

I learned he was a hero. A real one.

And that I wanted to be like him.

So much. I can't even tell you how much.

Maybe I wanted baseball because of that. If I played ball then I wouldn't have to find out if I was made of the same stuff as him. Because what if I *wasn't*? What if I had nothing great or worthy inside me? Nothing to offer the world?

Forget the world. I couldn't imagine disappointing *him*.

That would have been the worst.

But then he died and that redefined what I considered The Worst.

The Worst was watching the pencil and paper fall out of his hands as he stood on a roof. The pencil roll into the gutter. My dad fall forward and roll too—and then keep going.

He fell through the air and landed on the red brick walkway a few feet from the front door.

When I reached him, he was on his side.

One cheek pressed to the bricks, like it was a pillow.

His eyes were open but there was blood pooling in his ear.

He was so strong, my dad. My height, but much bigger than me. But he looked small to me half on that walkway, half on the grass. Then again, I'd never stood over him like that. I'd never been on my feet, looking down at my dad lying on the ground.

I just had never seen that.

The stroke was what had probably killed him, the doctors told us later. But it's the fall that I remember. Every little piece of it. The pencil. The pad. The last look he gave me. The blood welling up in his ear. The fact that I stood there holding a cell phone while blood spilled down his cheek. The fact that my skin felt cool because I'd been blasting the AC in the truck on that hot, hot day. The fact that he looked small to me, and I hated that new perspective on him. The fact that I hadn't been with him on the roof, and that if I had, I could've caught him and kept him from falling.

The fact that I didn't think the doctors had told me the truth, so.

I could've saved him.

CHAPTER 23

"G ideon. Gideon, wake up."

I lurched out of a dead sleep and looked around. I couldn't understand why I wasn't in the barracks at Fort Benning. I couldn't figure out why I was in my Jeep at night with a girl. And *asleep*. Then everything came back in a flash—the cuff, Daryn. Being War. The Kindred.

Daryn was leaning over the center console, watching me. She blinked, her eyelashes a pale flutter in the dimness. "We're here."

I sat up and scrubbed a hand over my face, trying to get some brainpower going. "Where's here?" I asked.

Moonlight filtered through thick cloud cover but I could see enough. She had pulled off the freeway onto a dirt road surrounded by hard earth and scrub brush. We were in the middle of the desert. Black mountains rose in the distance, thunderheads flashing above them. Fifty meters ahead of us, another car was pulled over—just a dull shape in the darkness.

"I don't know exactly," Daryn said. "But this is where we'll find Death."

I stared at her for a second, kind of amazed that that didn't faze me as much as it should've. Then I noticed a light buzzing sensation from the cuff, similar to what I felt from Sebastian, but faint, and deeper in tone. I turned to the backseat to see if he felt it, too. He was asleep in a jackknife position, his head on my duffel.

"How do you know he's here?" I asked. "Death?"

"Because I know," Daryn said.

That wasn't enough for me and she could tell. "I saw him here. At the gas station, I had . . . visions of this." She winced. "I *hate* that word."

"Wait. *Visions?* That happened at the gas station?" I thought back. She could only mean the time she spent in the women's room. "Daryn, did you—" I was suddenly seeing these horrible images of her curled up in a metal stall with her eyes rolled to the back of her head. "Do you *pass out?*"

"If you're asking whether I can't see anything else while I have them, yes. Yes, okay? I get headaches beforehand. That's how I know they're coming. Then I fade out and I can't see anything else. Stop looking at me like that, Gideon. And take the anger down, too. I locked the bathroom door from the inside. I was fine. Can we please focus on what's important?"

She kept talking like I'd said yes. She had no idea how hard I was trying not to lose my mind. She'd been in that bathroom alone, totally defenseless. Did she think the Kindred would be stopped by a *locked door?*

"He was in that car right here," she was saying, shaking her head. "But I don't know. Sometimes what I see isn't perfect. Well, actually it is. I'm the one who has to catch up. Figure out the clues and trust that—"

"Trust that what? Trust that what, Daryn? Talk to me."

She looked out the windshield.

"Right. You want to write in your notebook for a while and pretend I'm not here?"

"No. I want to get this done."

"Weird. I want this to go on forever." I bit down, making myself shut up. This was going in a bad direction. Why was I so wound up? Was it being in the open, at night, with no concealment and a pack of murderous psychopaths coming after us? No. That wasn't it.

It was *Death.* I'd never had a good experience with death. My dad's still haunted me. And I had died and come back to life as War, so. Not a big fan, but it couldn't matter. Time to suck it up and go meet him, face-to-face.

"Was he alone in your vision-download?" I asked.

"Yes. Should I wake Bastian?"

"No. I've got it." Sebastian had negative combat instincts based on what I'd seen at the studio.

I climbed out of the Jeep. The air felt thick and hot with moisture. Charged with electricity. Thunder rumbled, close. The storm was heading our way.

"*We've* got it," Daryn said, jogging up beside me. "I'm coming with you."

The anger I'd pushed down a second ago came right back up. "Do you have any comprehension of danger?"

"Me? I wasn't the one who confronted Samrael at a party."

"But you did march into a high-rise in LA with no regard for whether he'd be there, which he was."

"I didn't know that."

"That's what I'm *saying*. We should assume the Kindred are *everywhere*." I had to readjust. Switch tactics. "I'll make you a deal. If you come with me, then I want to be there when you have the visions. You tell me as soon as you feel the headaches and I'm right there. From here on out."

In the moonlight, I saw tears pool in her eyes. Once again, I had no idea where I'd gone wrong. Not a clue.

"I've been on my own a long time, Gideon."

"Okay. I get that. But now you're not. I told you I was going to help."

She didn't say anything, and I was done. She kept too much from me. She didn't trust me. It felt like she was working against me. "Whatever, Martin."

I grabbed a tire iron from the back of my Jeep. It felt solid and heavy in my hand. Sebastian's scales would've been about a hundred percent better but he was still out and I wanted him to stay that way. I hesitated a moment, my eyes drifting to my cuff. Sebastian had said we all had weapons. What was mine?

I should've asked him earlier. How the hell had I missed that? But too late now. It wasn't like I knew how to access the weapon anyway, whatever it was.

As I came around the Jeep, Daryn planted herself right in my path. She stared up at me, her expression all determination. "I'll take the deal. I'll tell you before the next time."

I nodded. My focus had already moved onto finding Death. "Is it safe to assume you don't have any experience approaching an enemy force in the dark?"

"He's not the enemy."

"He is *Death* and the Kindred could be out there waiting for us, so we're damn well going to proceed with caution. I'll make the initial contact since—"

"I think I should."

"Negative."

"I'm less threatening."

"Exactly." I got a quick mental snapshot of her shaking fingers touching the chain after she'd stepped out of the gas station restroom. "But way to act fearless, Martin. You and Sebastian should swap tips, share some tradecraft."

Nice, Blake. Nice one. But no taking it back now, and I'd hit my argument quota for the night. My head needed to be on the mission. "Keep behind me. Stay to my right so I don't hit you on the backswing if I have to use this." I lifted the tire iron. "Got it?"

Her eyes flashed with anger. "I think I can handle that."

"Good." I stood there for a second longer, telling myself to keep a clear head. Our safety depended on it. Then I adjusted my grip on the tire iron. "All right. Let's do this."

"Ten-four," she said.

CHAPTER 24

As I approached the sedan with Daryn a few steps behind me, my pulse pounded a steady beat. I'd been taught to use all my senses to assess an environment for danger. I did that now, tuning in to the rustle of tumbleweeds, the occasional car passing on the highway, the scurrying movements of small desert life. The Kindred could be staked out in the darkness, just waiting for the right moment to strike.

My weapon was foreign, and my backup and objective, but stalking like this felt right. It was the trade I'd signed up for.

The thrumming from my cuff was still present. I tried to adjust to this new source of input. It had to be Death's energy I was sensing. If I could tune in and let it guide me, it might work as a homing beacon.

Lightning flashed, illuminating the area around me and giving me hints of what was out there. Flat land. Brush. A larger rock formation to the south. I'd have killed for some night-vision optics.

As we drew to within thirty meters I quickly reviewed my objectives. Neutralize any threat presented by Death. Get him on the team. Clear out of there. With a glance at Daryn, I closed the last stretch at a brisk pace as she followed close behind me.

The car was a silver Ford Mustang, covered in dirt. Illinois plates. Tinted windows. No sign of movement inside.

I motioned for Daryn to stay behind the car, then I tested the driver's-side door. I found it unlocked and swung it open. No one inside.

My heart rate settled back a notch. I continued to assess.

Worn black leather seats. Fast-food wrappers on the floor.

Keys still in the ignition. I turned them once. Nothing. The car had either run out of gas or broken down.

I checked the glove compartment. No registration. No papers, but I found a hand towel. A bloody one. The blood was old—the towel stank and was stiff—and there was a lot of it. It'd been soaked once.

I closed the glove compartment. Daryn was right there.

"Did—" She paused, glancing at the sky as thunder rumbled. "Did you find anything?"

I made a split-second decision to keep the towel to myself for now and shook my head. "Stay right here."

I wanted to find his tracks, so keeping hers contained was critical. I walked around the car. Sure enough there were fresh footsteps heading into the desert. I followed them a little further, confirming my guess. He had ditched the car and made for the rock outcrop I'd seen in the distance.

A normal person in distress would have walked along the freeway waiting for help. But he was Death, so. Not a normal person.

I had a hunch the car was stolen. I had a hunch he was running from something and possibly hurt. The danger factor was skyrocketing.

I looked at Daryn, reconsidering having her with me. It had seemed like the right choice so far. We were on the road. The Jeep was in sight. That had given me a certain level of confidence. But taking her into open desert at night toward a guy who drove around with bloody towels? That wasn't something I wanted to do.

"Head back and wake Sebastian up," I said, walking over to her. "Park the Jeep so the headlights face the desert. I'm going to take another quick look around here. Meet you back there in five minutes."

She nodded. "Okay. Be safe."

I watched her until she reached the Jeep, then I headed into the desert. I had no intention of checking the Mustang again, or of meeting up with her and Sebastian until I had Death. She wasn't going to like it when she realized I'd been less than honest with her, but my priority was keeping her safe. Angry, safe Daryn was better than Daryn in the hands of Samrael any day of the week.

I took my time as I waded through the darkness. As I put the road behind me, everything reduced to murky shapes, but the lightning helped my navigation, giving me X-ray shots of the terrain. Mostly a good thing, but also bad.

When the earth lit up, I couldn't process it all at once. I had to decipher the fading images in my mind. Eventually, my imagination started kicking in with its contributions.

Why did that cactus look so human?

Why had the tumbleweed looked like it had feet?

What was that dark blur across the sky?

I knew I was getting myself worked up. Not helping was the feeling in my gut that I wasn't alone. That *I* was the one being stalked.

I drew a breath, forcing some steadiness into my veins, and pressed forward.

Flash. Outcrop ahead on a downslope. Getting closer.

Flash. I was drifting left. Adjust heading.

Flash. I was looking at a creature, crouching ten feet away. Staring at me. Black as the night with white eyes and—wings? were those *wings?*—and a wrinkled face full of torment, full of pleading, and—

Darkness.

I'd frozen with the tire iron back, ready to swing. Now, surrounded by night again, I still didn't move.

I scanned the blackness around me, ready to attack. Waiting to be attacked. Every muscle in my body brimmed with violence. Overcharged. In a whiteout of mortal fear.

A breeze swept past me, hot like a breath. It carried a foul odor that made my breath catch. Then the stench was gone. Seconds had passed since I'd seen the thing, but I waited a few more before I brought my arm down.

My heart was trying to kick down my rib cage. As I searched the desert around me again, I pictured the creature's wide, pleading eyes. Blind eyes, I thought. They'd been like pearls. The way it had crouched made me wonder if it'd been scared of *me*—but that didn't mean it was harmless.

Was it one of the Kindred? I knew of four. Was it the fifth? Or was that Death? But Death had to be human—that thing definitely hadn't been—and I hadn't sensed any change in the signal from the cuff.

I made my feet start moving again. Every time the sky lit up, I tensed, expecting to see the creature again. Sweat rolled down my back and my knuckles ached from gripping the tire iron, but I made it to the outcrop without further incident.

Approaching from a slightly elevated slope, I could see the rock formation's general shape. It was configured like a horseshoe, with the open side opposite me. I had a feeling Death had put himself right at the center. It'd be an advantageous position for him. Hidden. And the opening would be the only place he'd need to watch to spot someone coming. So he thought.

I looked up, gauging the height of the near ridge. Thirty, forty feet—approximately three stories high. Steep grade, but I could handle it.

Reaching back, I shoved the tire iron through my belt and started climbing. I couldn't stop picturing the creature's emaciated body. How it'd been covered in a leathery black hide. The sharp teeth that had peeked from its withered mouth. I was pretty sure I'd seen black wings folded at its back.

Was it going to pick me right off this rock face?

Had it gone back to the Jeep?

Climb, Blake.

I channeled my concentration to the task. Rock climbing

was problem-solving. Choosing the right holds, finding the right route. I worked steadily and fell into a good flow. The wind grew stronger as I neared the crest, my shirt flapping like a flag. My lungs pumped the damp storm air, my muscles craving the oxygen. Rain was coming soon.

The climb leveled off just as my hands and forearms started to burn from exertion. Pulling myself onto the smooth shelf at the summit, I shook them out. Then the hair on the back of my neck lifted as I became aware of the energy from the cuff. It felt much stronger now. Sharper, like a radio tuned to a better frequency. I was on the right track—Death was close.

Brushing my hands off on my jeans, I moved to the edge of the shelf and checked out the view I'd come to see. On this side of the formation, the rocks stepped down more gradually, in levels that dropped to a small clearing down below. I spotted a dark shape there, but I couldn't tell if it was a person or a sleeping bag. Turning, I could see the small points of my Jeep's headlights. Farther off, the freeway.

Gravel hissed nearby. I forced myself not to react.

Okay. Not alone. The intensifying buzz of the cuff confirmed it.

Moving slowly, I set my feet and reached back, my hand closing around the tire iron.

A shoe scraped against rock a few feet to my left. Louder. Impossible to pretend I hadn't heard it this time.

"Come on over," I said. "View's nice."

The footsteps came fast—*scuff, scuff, scuff*—a flat-out sprint. I spun, caught a glimpse of a dark form blurring toward me. There was no way to dodge aside. To the side was air. I sank down, bracing, and swung the iron.

I didn't get in a full swing before he crashed into me. As I flew back, I locked my free arm into his—if I was going over so was he—and we went airborne.

It felt like we fell for a year, but it couldn't have been more than a second. We did a three-sixty in the air. I saw a flash of dark eyes. Death grabbed hold of my shirt and threw his fist at my face, but I didn't feel it. We crashed into rocks—a punch I felt everywhere. I couldn't believe he was hitting me *as we were falling*. But that could've been because I was hitting him, too.

We went airborne for another second, then struck rock again. My shoulder took the brunt of our combined weight, pain exploding in my socket, rattling all the way down into my hand. My grip gave and the tire iron clanged away.

Our fall descended a few more levels before the slope decreased, putting us into a tumble. I took a hit to the temple that blacked out my vision for an instant. My hands found his neck and I pulled him into a chokehold. But then his fist smashed into my ear and stunned me, and I let him go. When we finally reached flat terrain we flew apart and came up lunging. I remembered a takedown I'd learned in combatives training and tackled him. I thought I had him down, but he buried his knee into my stomach and flipped me onto my back.

We went on like this for a while. Beating the hell out of each other. Part of me was surprised as it was happening. I didn't lose fights. In RASP, we'd do this thing called the beef circle, where the cadre would get the class circled up and we'd battle it out, man-to-man, clearing the air of any animosities building up between us with some grappling. I almost never lost in those, even against the bigger, older guys. I'd get worked over pretty good. But I never tapped out. I've just always had another gear in a fight.

But, Death. He was strong and fast and *relentless*. Even when I'd manage to pin him, I couldn't keep him there. He was ferocious and I was taking a beating, but it only spurred me on. Because seriously? I was *War*. My pride was on the line.

"*Stop!*" Daryn's voice broke into the night. "Gideon! Marcus!"

We flung ourselves away from each other, a human supernova. Panting for breath, standing at a safe distance, we eyed each other. He stood awkwardly, favoring his left leg. I was favoring the entire right side of my body. My ears rang. My knuckles throbbed. Blood gushed from my nose and ran into my mouth.

Sebastian stood next to Daryn, looking concerned.

I leaned over and spat onto the dirt. "You *knew* his *name?*" I asked her.

At the same time Death, Marcus, said, "How do you know my name?"

CHAPTER 25

I took him in at a glance—black, my height, ripped. Hair as short as mine, shaved almost to the scalp. Worn-out clothes. Cuff on his wrist. A pale cuff—that was all I could tell. Right guy, unfortunately.

"I'm sorry about him," Daryn said.

I looked at her. *Him* was *me*? She was apologizing to Death about *me*?

"We just came here to talk," she continued. "We didn't mean to scare you or to *get*. Into. A *fight*."

She said the last part like, Gideon is *ruler*. Of. The *idiots*.

"Who are you?" Death asked her.

"I'm . . . I'm Daryn. Marcus, I think you're . . ." She glanced at me, then at Sebastian, clearly struggling to explain. How often did she have to do this? Fit the incredible into words? "You're involved in something that we know about."

"Nuh-uh." Marcus shook his head. "You don't know *nothin'* about me."

"Just shut up and listen to her," I said.

"Man, who're you telling to shut up?"

His tone. The hatred in his eyes as he looked back at me. I couldn't accept them.

I charged him. He backed away, dodging aside. *Why?* Why dodge now?

Then I realized I'd made a huge mistake.

A cold burn seeped into my fingers and my feet. It spread through my hands like ice water moving into my arms and legs. I locked up. The ground beneath me began to pull away, and a crack split across the desert soil. It went wider and wider, showing a gap in the earth that was endless. My shoes perched on the edge. Any breath I took, even the slightest twitch, would send me over and I'd fall. I'd never stop falling.

I started shaking, quaking down to my bones. I'd never shaken out of fear before but my body rang like a bell, totally beyond my control.

"Gideon?" Daryn's voice was far away. "Marcus, stop!"

This was it. Death's ability.

Fear.

I considered opening up the rage floodgates on him, but what good would it do to make him more aggressive?

Daryn was yelling for him to stop. She took a few steps toward Marcus, then staggered and came to her knees. She clutched her stomach, hugging herself, and started to rock. "No," she said. "No, no, no. Please, no."

Anger consumed me like nothing I'd ever felt before. Burning rage that shot through my cold, shaking muscles. The ice that had trapped me splintered, no room for it anymore. Not with the rage roaring through me. The crevasse disappeared in front of me, sealing closed, and I felt power—true power stirring inside me. A singular purpose. Determination to do what was right, what was necessary—and what was necessary right then was to help Daryn.

And I felt something else, too. Something in my hand that hadn't been there a second ago.

A sword.

CHAPTER 26

In my training in the Army, I'd been exposed to a variety of weapons. Rifles. Handguns of all makes and models. RPG launchers. I'd shot a fifty-cal a few times—now, that's a weapon. The fifty's *legit*. So I think you can understand, Cordero, when I say that a sword was a little disappointing.

Sword fighting was fine in the movies, for gladiators or fighting trolls or whatever. But actually using a sword in combat? Nope. It felt tardy by a couple of centuries. Of course I'd just been in an epic fistfight, but everyone knows fisticuffs is a timeless art. Point is I wasn't thrilled about the sword, but it was better than no sword, so I rolled with it.

In about a millisecond, I assessed the weapon in my hand. It was made of the same metal as my cuff—smooth, putting off the red halo of light—and the style was a mix of modern and old, a sort of a sleek claymore. Kind of cool-looking.

The fear-hold Marcus had over me had fallen away completely by then. Same for Daryn, who had stopped rocking. Bastian helped her to her feet. Seeing that she was okay, I turned my focus to making Marcus pay.

I stepped toward him, doing a badass figure eight in front of me, which I'd perfected with a lightsaber when I was seven and thankfully could still do. Part of me wanted to psych him out a little. The other part of me wanted to get a feel for the weapon. The sword wasn't weightless, exactly. It was just weight that felt known, like lifting my arm or my leg. Even stranger was that it didn't feel like I was gripping the sword, but more like the sword was gripping *me*.

"You want to mess with me, Death?" I said. "Let's go!"

Daryn looked at me like I'd lost my mind. "Gideon, what are you *doing*?"

I didn't have a chance to answer. Marcus had just produced a scythe. It materialized in a dusty swirl, extending from his hand to the desert earth.

A freakin' *scythe*.

I shouldn't have been surprised. Wasn't Death—the Grim Reaper—always shown with a scythe? Still, this was the first one I'd ever seen in person and let me tell you—a staff with a massive curved blade at the end? Terrifying. This was no ordinary scythe, either. The thing glowed in the night, soft like the moon, but it put off enough light to illuminate Marcus's face. His eyes were steady and cold. Pure glacial fury. All for me.

He extended his arm to the side like *Looky here, asshole. I'll see your sword and raise you a scythe.*

A cautious man would've backed off. Not me. Yielding would basically have told him he'd won. I was tougher and I'd prove it. If it cost me a limb, screw it.

"You really want to take on War?" I shrugged. "All right."

"What did you say? You're *War*?"

"Yes, he did." Daryn said. "Now put your weapons *down*. Both of you."

With no warning, Marcus swung the scythe in a low, sweeping arc. The thing had range, clearing eight, nine feet around him. The blade came to within about a foot of Daryn. She stood without even flinching as the sickle sliced past her, but I practically threw up my heart. I was moving before I knew it.

I shot at him while he was still on the backswing, avoiding the business end of the weapon. The scythe wouldn't be a close-range weapon. If I could get inside, I'd be safe from the blade.

Marcus had anticipated my move, and brought the back

end of the staff at me. I saw it coming and blocked with my sword. The sound as the two weapons met was deep. Thundering. A roar I felt in my chest. The collision point sent off sparks, a burst of brightness in the dark. We kept going, dealing and receiving blows. Neither of us was very good then, at that point, but what we lacked in technique we made up for in passion.

I was in the middle of a follow-through when the strength left my legs suddenly. *Wham.* Fast. One second I was getting ready to tee off on Marcus's face, the next I was on my back staring at the thunderheads above. My sword thudded out of my grip. I hadn't even known I *could* let it go.

I turned my head to look for it. That small action took all the energy I had. The sword rested on the desert soil only a few inches from my fingers. I wanted it back, but I was never going to be able to reach it. I had nothing left. Lifting a car over my head would've been easier. Straining to look to my right, I got a glimpse of Marcus's shoes. He was sprawled on the dirt next to me.

Daryn walked up with Sebastian. She crossed her arms, looking down at me, her blond hair blowing in the storm winds. Her expression was disappointed and more than a little pissed off. "How long will they be this way?"

"I don't know," Sebastian said. "Maybe a few hours? It could be longer. It's the first time I've wiped anyone out this strongly. This is awful. I can't believe I did this."

"They weren't going to be any help to us dead. Anyway, I asked you to."

They kept talking, but their voices sounded farther away. Sleep was calling to me. No. Not sleep. Exhaustion. Fatigue. A huge *lack* was yawning open inside of me. Lack of strength. Lack of hope. Lack of joy. My body felt brittle, a million years old. And fragile. Like my limbs were made of glass threads.

A fat drop of rain landed on my forehead. Another on my forearm. Painful drops. Sharp as rocks.

"It's starting to rain," Sebastian said. "Should I pull the Jeep up? I can probably get them both inside."

"Sure, let's," Daryn said. "But no need to hurry. A little rain won't kill them."

They left us there.

Above, the clouds pulsed with light, electricity splashing across the night. It was just me and Death now, getting pummeled by raindrop meteors.

And the creature, beating its wings as it flew across the stormy sky.

CHAPTER 27

The sun was rising in a clear blue sky when I awoke in my Jeep once again—this time with a pounding headache, my stomach in cramps, and my Giants sweatshirt thrown over me. My body felt like it had been tenderized.

Through the grimy windshield I saw Daryn, sitting on the hood. Her hair was up in a knot and she was talking to Sebastian and Marcus, who stood in front her. I saw no trace of the storm, or of the winged creature.

"I know you guys want answers," she said, "and I wish I could give them to you. I *really* do. But right now, all I can tell you is that bringing the four of you together quickly is the only way we'll succeed. As soon as I can, I'll tell you more. I promise."

"All right," Sebastian said, nodding. "We're almost there. We'll find Conquest, then play the rest by feel."

By ear, I wanted to say. *Play the rest by* ear.

"Man, forget that," said Marcus. "It's not all right with me."

He had the hood of his sweatshirt pulled over his head and his hands buried deep in the pockets of his jeans. His face was in shadow but I saw a cut on his cheek. I hoped his clothes hid a lot more damage, because I could barely draw a breath without talking myself into it first.

Hunkered into his shoulders and with his head slightly bowed, Marcus struck me as guarded and dangerous. And I couldn't help feeling like by adding him, our team had taken a big step backward. I hoped I was wrong. But I felt like I was right.

"So what then, Marcus?" Daryn said. "Are you going to

leave? Ignore your ability, and the fact that you can call a horse from thin air and just go about your life?"

"There's *horses*?"

"Well, yeah." Bastian shrugged. "I mean, we're horsemen."

"Tell me something," Marcus said. "Do I look like a cowboy to you?"

"We have to do whatever's needed," Daryn said. "If the Kindred—"

"I don't have to do *nothin'*," he said.

"Yes, you do," she pressed. "You do, because right now there are demons out there who are organizing, and if we don't—" She stopped suddenly, realizing what she'd just said. Then she sighed. "I didn't want to drop that on you yet. But I guess I just did."

Sebastian and Marcus weren't moving. That word— demons—had shocked them both into silence, but I'd been expecting it. I think I'd known from the first time I saw Samrael at Joy's party, but then there were the bone blades magically summoned at the studio, and the unnatural speed with which they moved. And last night, my little blind buddy. But hearing it from Daryn was still crazy. Having the confirmation. It still hit me hard.

Marcus spoke first. "*Demons* have come after you?" He didn't wait for an answer. Just did an about-face and walked away.

"I'll talk to him," Bastian said. "I'll make him hear reason."

"Thanks, Bas," Daryn said.

He went after Marcus.

My gaze went to Daryn. I'd only known her a few days. Not long. But I'd been kind of avoiding some obvious things about the way I felt around her. "Martin."

She turned and saw me, then hopped off the hood and came over, pulling the door open. "How long have you been awake?" she asked.

"Long enough."

Bastian and Marcus had stopped at the Mustang. The freeway was getting busier, cars and semis speeding past.

Daryn propped her foot on the skid bar. "He might actually be more work than you are," she said, following my gaze.

"He's the troublemaker. You'll get used to me. But about last night . . ." The situation with Marcus had gotten way out of control. I was partially responsible for that. Time to own up. "I didn't know he was going to be such an asshole, and—"

"My thoughts exactly."

"I probably deserve that."

"You definitely do. Let's just forget about it." She glanced through the windshield again. "We'll get him on board. He doesn't have anywhere else to go."

"He said that?"

She paused, then shook her head. "No."

"You know things, don't you? About us? How much do you *know*?"

She watched me for a few moments like she was thinking about how to answer. "More than I want to sometimes," she said. Then her foot came off the skid bar.

"Wait." I didn't want her to leave. I scrambled to say something. "How's my face looking? Black and blue?"

She leaned back into the Jeep and squinted a little. Her hair slipped out of its knot and spilled over her shoulder. "You have a few bruises but they're already getting better."

"Bet you wish they weren't."

"I'm glad you're healing. But I'll admit . . . I didn't mind seeing you get put in your place."

She meant Marcus, but she put me in my place all the time. "Daryn . . ." I felt like I was staring at her, but I couldn't make myself stop. She was just so steady. And pretty. "I know I wasn't very cool to you last night. I just didn't want you in harm's way."

"Thanks for saying sorry. I'm pretty sure that's what that was."

"You're correct. Thanks for interpreting my apology."

She smiled. With the desert glowing gold and amber all around, so much like her, it was a perfect smile. No secrets. No hesitation. Like she'd laid the full measure of herself on me.

It leveled me.

I reached for her hand, which was surprising to both of us. But I was already committed so I wove my fingers through hers, keeping it smooth. Under control. Maybe I even came across a little jaded, going into instant damage control.

Daryn went really still. She stared at her hand in my hand. Hers, perfect and smooth. Mine, bruised and crusted with dried mud. I could've probably thought through this a little better. "What are you doing?" she asked.

At least we were on the same page there.

"I just wanted to hold your hand for a second. It's nothing. I hold hands with people all the time."

Her smile made a small comeback, but she didn't look up. "Are you going to hold Sebastian's hand?"

"Uh, no. The thought hasn't crossed my mind."

"Marcus?"

"No." He was no joking matter. The guy was a problem waiting to happen.

"Gideon, I don't think this is a good idea."

That didn't seem like a very clear directive. "If you want me to stop holding your hand, I will. Do you?"

She met my eyes. Everything stopped. The clouds. The planets. Time. Everything. "There's something I have to tell you," she said.

Explosions of possibility went off in my head. "I'm listening." I ran my thumb over her knuckles. Her skin was so soft. We were connecting. Taking a first step.

Together. Now. Yes.

"I'm starting to get a headache."

For a second there I thought that I, Gideon Blake, had grossly misjudged the entire situation and annoyed her to the point that I'd given her a migraine.

Then I remembered and shot out of the Jeep, almost knocking her over. "You mean a vision-download headache?" I did a move with my hands like I was shampooing my head. Like that was going to clear things up. "The kind you get beforehand?"

"Yes," she said, calmly. "That kind."

"Okay. Okay. Sit down. Sit right there." I tried herding her into my Jeep but she sidestepped.

"I'm fine, Gideon. Relax."

"I'm relaxed." That wasn't totally true, but I was also completely ready to do anything she needed me to do. I was buzzing with the need to help. "I'm actually trained to handle this kind of thing."

"You're *trained* for this?"

"Definitely. There's a whole section in the Ranger Handbook. Seeker Assistance Procedures Checklist. SAPC for short. Section One-A of SAPC says, 'Secure a safe location for the Seeker'—which is you. So, sit. Please, Daryn. I know what I'm doing."

"Soon," she said. "I will soon." She was still smiling, but starting to blink slowly, the way a person does right before they're going to fall asleep. "Is this scaring you?"

"Does it hurt you?"

"The headaches a little, but not for long."

"Then I'm not scared."

"You look worried."

"Just alert. This is my vigilant face."

"I actually believe you. Gideon, can you," another slow blink, "can you keep Marcus and Sebastian away while it's happening?" She got hung up on the S's in Sebastian, slurring a little. "It's not that I'm embarrassed, it's just . . ."

"No one's getting close to you."

That should've sounded overprotective and crazy, but as I stood there, the heat of the desert sun on my back, it just didn't. I felt like I was exactly where I needed to be. Standing guard. Looking out for her.

"They're over pretty fast," she said. "Five minutes, usually."

"Okay."

"It probably says that in the Ranger Handbook. Or maybe it says three hundred seconds. You military types are so strange about time."

I mustered a smile. She was slurring more and starting to slouch. I had to fight the urge to forcibly wedge her into the passenger seat.

Daryn twisted her hair to one side, and her fingers drifted over the chain. "You know what's really beautiful? Feeling what another person feels. Feeling all their love and their fears . . . It's all just so beautiful, you know? Life?"

I didn't even know what to make of that, so I nodded.

She stared at me for a few seconds. "It's possible that I could topple over."

"Then get in the freaking car, Daryn."

"Would you catch me?"

"Of course I would."

"What about right now? Will you catch me before I fall?"

That knocked the air out of my lungs. Literally. A first for me. Lots of firsts all of a sudden.

I stepped toward her, half expecting her to ask me what I was doing, but the second I put my arms around her, she burrowed against my chest like I was her favorite pillow. Then I had one of those moments where time compresses, like your thoughts are having a car wreck, everything fast but slow. And I saw these images—fast-roping, blueberry pancakes, fire horse charging, bone knives flying, gorgeous girl making a nest out of my shirt with her face. Which was now. Happening *right now*.

She smelled amazing, like spring smells, cool, rain, flowers. And it felt incredible having her so close. I just really liked her *close*.

I cleared my throat. "How you doing there, boss?"

"I'm so good. Guys give the best hugs."

"Um . . . guys do?"

She laughed.

"You're really messing with me right now?"

"Guilty."

Yep. Liked her.

She gave me more of her weight. I was almost holding her upright now. It felt like she was drifting away somewhere, on a tide I couldn't see.

"You feel good, Gideon," she said. "I knew you would. That's why I didn't want thisss—" She went limp.

I pulled her against me and went through a hundred different scenarios in my mind in a second before I forced myself to chill out, take a breath. She'd told me not to worry, that she'd be fine, and as much as she kept secrets, I didn't think she'd lie about that.

I turned my back to Marcus and Sebastian. They weren't close but if I could've become a tank around her, I'd have done it. Shifting around a little, I tried to get it so she'd be more on my shoulder, which seemed better. More comfortable for her.

Then there was nothing left to do but count down.

Three hundred, two ninety-nine, two-ninety eight, two—

Chapter 28

"Y ou don't have to count all the way down for us, Gideon," Cordero says.

"I wasn't going to." I swallow, clearing my throat. Letting that morning fade back and this pine room fade in. "I was just trying to give you an idea. Five minutes feels like a long time when you're counting every second."

Cordero laces her fingers together. "I can imagine. I didn't mean to interrupt. Please continue. The creature you mentioned—the one with the wings. Was it one of the Kindred?"

I nod. "He's called Alevar. Creepy little dude. But I'm going to need a health break before I go any further."

I do need to use the facilities, but I also need a moment. The memory of being with Daryn is so real, it's like I can still feel her head on my chest. I have to shake it off. I just need a second to lock it back down.

Cordero frowns. "Health break?"

I was trying to be tactful but I guess she wants details, which I can respect. "I gotta hit the head. And trust me. You don't want to keep War away from a toilet when he needs one."

Texas and Beretta laugh right away. They know I'm messing around, but I've really scared the civvie. The look on Cordero's face is priceless.

"I'm just playing with you, Cordero. I drank all that water. It's just biology. You know. Natural."

"Five-minute break." Cordero pushes up from her desk. "You know your orders," she says to Texas. "Make sure everyone is on alert."

"I don't have to go that bad."

She stops at the door, her dark eyes shining as she glances back. "You don't want to push me too far, Gideon."

"Warning stands," Texas says as he unfastens my bindings. "Don't try anythin' stupid." But he sounds more casual than before. He's getting a sense for who I am. I have no intention of trying anything, and I think he knows that.

He drops the hood over my head and I muffle a groan. There's really nothing that compares to the sweat and vomit scent combo. Not even Cordero's perfume.

"What is it, kid?" he says.

"Hood stinks."

"Least it's your stink," Beretta says, and they both laugh.

Texas helps me to my feet. My legs feel spongy from the drugs and because it's been a while since I've moved. My first few steps weave. Texas grabs my elbow in a vise grip. He doesn't let go as he walks beside me, issuing commands.

Forward three paces.

Down two steps.

Ten more paces.

As I follow them, I notice the hallway sags at the center and the floorboards shake. Not just because me, Texas, and Beretta weigh over six hundred pounds combined. They feel springy and thin. Drafts sweep past from all directions. They're cool and smell alpine-clean compared to the musty warmth of the room. And this place has, like, the opposite of soundproofing. I hear everything. Passing a door, I catch voices arguing. Marcus's room, no question. Then I hear laughter—that's Bastian. Finally, I hear the steady meter of polished conversation—Jode.

It's good to hear them. I can barely sense them through the cuff. Too much crap in my blood. But I knew they'd be here. We left Jotunheimen together, the four of us. Only one of us stayed behind.

Good job, Blake. You went three whole minutes without thinking about her.

We reach the bathroom and the hood comes off. Beretta posts up at the bathroom door. Texas makes sure I don't rip the sink off the wall and . . . what? Throw it through the tiny blacked-out window? It'd be cool if I had superstrength. I check in with what I do have, searching for the sword, for Riot, and nope. Still nothing.

Texas waits behind me with the hood as I wash my hands. After being in that empty room for so long, everything is interesting and my senses feel heightened, acutely tuned to all of it. Freezing-cold tap water. Rust stains seeping into the drain. The antiseptic smell of the soap. That's all I get before the hood's back on and the world goes back to black. My hands are refastened with the disposable plastic ties. Texas and Beretta flank me again. Time to make the trip back to the room.

I picture it as we go. Turning from the bathroom into a narrow hallway with carpets worn bare at the center. Passing a small living room with cheap furniture, pizza boxes, maybe some spooky-looking government people sitting there, watching the kid in the hood walk by. I *feel* like I'm being watched. Which makes sense. There's only one reason for all this security, and for this completely unethical debriefing. This was never about money, or international diplomacy, or the press. Cordero must've gotten wind of something unusual happening in Norway, maybe from satellite photos or drone images. How much about this did she already know before I started talking?

Texas's grip clamps down on my elbow, jarring me to a halt. "Hold here. Do *not* open your mouth."

I think I hear an argument. I strain to listen. Not Marcus this time. Who? Samrael? The Kindred? "What's going on?"

Somewhere a few paces ahead of me, Beretta swears. "*Move,*" he says. "Get him back in there."

I'm yanked backward, toward the bathroom, when I hear her.

"You don't need to push me! I'm going!"

It's her.

Daryn.

I slam my weight into Texas. We crash against the wall, the whole place shuddering. He tries to wrap me up, but I throw an elbow, catch him in the nose, I think, and that gives me a second. One second to reach up and yank the hood off, and she's there. Standing inside the front door, between two men in black tactical gear, framed by the rectangle of sunlight behind her.

She looks right at me, her eyes flaring with relief.

She's here.

CHAPTER 29

Texas recovers and lunges at me. There's nowhere for me to go. My hands are tied, this hallway is tight, and he weighs almost a hundred pounds more than I do.

My forehead crashes into the pine paneling. My vision cuts out. Everything is a blur as I'm shoved back, back, back. Then I'm in the bathroom again, where Texas jams his forearm under my jaw and pins me to the wall.

"Stupid little shit," Beretta growls behind him as he yanks the door shut.

"Okay," Texas says, taking a second to catch his breath. A line of blood trickles from one of his nostrils. "Okay, listen up." He leans in, inches from my face. "You listening, Blake? 'Cause you're gonna need to hear this."

Daryn is outside. She's here.

I nod.

"Me and my buddies," Texas continues, "we've got this informal code going between us. Whenever we see or hear somethin' we shouldn't have, which happens a lot, Blake, happens a whole lot, you know what we call it?"

He's leading me somewhere. Normally I'd try to figure out where but there's no chance of me thinking clearly. She's right outside.

"Look at me, Blake." Texas digs his forearm into my throat. "Do you know what we call it? We say it's a gold-medal moment. Not sure how it started, but that's what it is. Whenever anybody says those two words, *gold medal*, we know we're in the presence of information that we should *never* talk about. Gold-medal moments go to the grave." He narrows his eyes. "You hear what I'm sayin'?"

"I hear you." I just had a gold-medal moment. Daryn is here but I'm not supposed to know. I'm not supposed let Cordero know that I know.

Texas eases back, releasing me. "I'd have done the same thing in your shoes." He drops the hood back over my head. " 'Cept I'd have gotten to her."

"I didn't want to get your ass court-martialed," I manage, finally getting my bearings.

He snorts. "Might still happen." He flex-ties my hands behind my back this time. I've been downgraded. "Keep your trap shut and remember what I said."

The walk back to the room passes in a second. I'm there before I know it, Texas slipping new ties around my wrists and ankles, tethering me back to the chair. He leaves my right hand free. Beretta hands me an unwrapped granola bar. Food is the last thing on my mind, but the fuel is important. It'll help me shake off the drugs faster. I eat it in two bites and get a stomachache. Behind me, my old friend the radiator clicks on. But the bulb is going to go. It's going to burn out and this room will go dark. Just a matter of time.

Why is she here? She's the one who left me in Jotunheimen. Is she okay? Was she captured or did she come here on her own power? I don't know what to think. I just need to see her.

Cordero comes back. She scoots under the desk and opens the file. Business as usual. "We were out in the Mojave Desert when we left off. I believe you were waiting three hundred seconds." She gives me a small, humorless smile. "What happened when Daryn came back around?"

Does she know? Does she know that *I* know?

"Gideon?"

CHAPTER 30

"D aryn, um . . ."

She came back slowly. When she lifted her head, her eyes were unfocused. Distant. And with the heat of the desert, and my body heat, she'd gone a little sweaty around the forehead. She looked like she'd woken up from a long sleep.

"You okay?" I asked.

"Yes," she said, but she looked around, clearly disoriented.

A dozen questions were on the tip of my tongue, but Marcus and Sebastian were walking back to the Jeep. I'd save my questions until the time was right. Bastian's expression didn't change when he saw us standing close, but Marcus's glass-colored eyes moved from me to Daryn like he was making some calculations.

Daryn pulled away from me when she saw them coming, sort of suddenly, putting a few steps between us. She looked at them, and at the Jeep, and not at me.

Okay, right. Message received.

"We have to go," she said. "We need to go back to Los Angeles."

We all stared at her for a few seconds; then we piled into my Jeep. No questions asked. I didn't know what had convinced Marcus to come. Believe me, if I did, I'd have done the opposite. Within five minutes of being back on the road, it was obvious that he spoiled the easy vibe between me, Sebastian, and Daryn. As a trio we'd been stable, but Death added a new element that didn't fit. He didn't say anything rude or confrontational. The guy barely talked. He sat in the back with Sebastian, totally quiet, but quiet like a fog machine. He altered the landscape of my Jeep without making a sound.

I thought of the bloody towel I'd found. The fact that he'd left the Mustang behind without a word. Obviously, he'd stolen it. He was dangerous. I didn't trust him. But I couldn't deny that the cuff on my wrist liked having him around. I felt both his and Bastian's presence through it now. Two distinct tones. But they weren't a distraction. I could choose to focus on them or not, just like with my other senses.

By around eleven, the desert heat was beating us down. We pulled over at a gas station to put the top down since my Jeep's air-conditioning was fresh air. Marcus took off his ripped-up sweatshirt. He had a detailed tattoo on his left forearm, some kind of script, the ink only a few shades darker than his skin, but what I really wanted to get a better look at was his cuff. The thing looked like it was made of alabaster—but molten, like someone had dripped wax around his wrist.

"What are you looking at?" he asked me.

I felt the cold creep of fear along my neck, that falling sensation nudging toward me.

"You want to go again?" I said, but Sebastian shot over and pulled me away,

"Chill out, Gideon," he said, and dragged me to a bank of vending machines outside the convenience store. I could still see the Jeep. Daryn was talking to Marcus. Whatever she said made him run a hand over his scalp and loosened the tension in his shoulders.

"How do you call the scales?" I asked Bastian as I watched them. "The weapons? You said you'd tell me." I needed to know how to get the sword. Marcus had command of the scythe. I couldn't be at such a disadvantage.

He nodded. "Yeah. I'll tell you."

"Do it. Now."

"Okay. Well, you have to find it *inside* yourself. Really search, and when you're on to it, you lock in." He snapped his hand shut in front of him like he was catching a bug. "It takes practice, but you'll get it."

"Tell me you're kidding."

He grinned. "I'm not. It's the truth."

"Shit."

"Hey, you got any money?"

I shook my head. How did the guy on a soldier's paycheck become the one with the money? I dug around in my pocket, finding three dollars for him, then watched him fight with the vending machine over how flat the bills needed to be.

Two girls in a white BMW on the third pump apparently thought this was adorable. They giggled, acting like he was a rock star or something.

"Hey, Bastian. Are you famous?"

He'd finally managed to get a Coke and some Skittles. "No. Not even close."

Whatever he was, girls liked it. They snapped photos of him with their cell phones as they pulled away from the pump. Bastian was oblivious.

"You eat a lot," I said.

He tore into the bag of Skittles. "Man, I love food." He shoved a handful in his mouth and offered me some.

I shook my head. "No, thanks." I liked Skittles but they turned into mini grenades in my stomach. They were harder on me than most food. "You know it's eleven a.m., right?"

Bastian's eyebrows went up. "Wow. Early." He swallowed. "Gideon, I don't mean to overstep, but we can't mess this up because of our differences." He glanced toward the Jeep. Toward Marcus. "We'll never get out of this situation if we're fighting amongst ourselves. Maybe you can just try to keep your eye on the bat."

I was with him up until end. I'd heard him screw up phrases like that before and let it go, but this time I couldn't. "Dude, it's *ball*. It's keep your eye on the *ball*. Keeping your eye on the bat would be . . . not good, man. What's up with the cliché mutilation?"

"Oh, that. I think it's because English was my second language. Shoot, no. I don't think that's it." He lifted his shoulders. "I just get 'em wrong. But at least I get my lines right. Man, can you imagine if I couldn't remember my *lines*?" He said this with devastation, like if he couldn't remember his own mother.

I stared at him for a few seconds, not sure if he was messing with me or not. Then he grinned like *gotcha*, tossed a handful of Skittles into his mouth, and chomped away.

I held my hand out. "Give me some of those."

When we got back to the Jeep, Daryn was sitting in the back talking to Marcus. She trailed off when I climbed into the driver's seat. Either she'd been talking about me or she didn't want to keep talking around me.

Whatever. I didn't care either way.

I had a horseman to find, so. Eye on the bat.

Since it was my car, and since I felt confident it would make Marcus miserable, I pushed the Pearl Jam cassette into the tape deck as I got back on the freeway and turned it up. After a couple of tracks, Bas got hung up on trying to figure out the lyrics to "Yellow Ledbetter"—an unattainable goal since they were basically undecipherable sounds with a few words sprinkled in. The song was all feeling, but he was determined. We listened to it over and over, and caught a little more each time. Metaphorically, the song felt perfect for the mission we were on.

About eighty miles outside of Los Angeles, Daryn suggested we stop for food. I pulled into a roadside diner—a place that would've looked super stylish if the year was still 1972—and scoped it out. Not a lot of cars in the parking lot. Only a few truckers and older folks inside. I asked for a table by the exit, view of the entrance, view of the parking lot, view of the entire dining area.

The Kindred had killed someone in the middle of a studio. And Alevar—the creepy bat guy—had found me in the middle of the desert. No place was safe.

Everybody ordered, and then commented on my "just bread, no butter" selection. I was forced to explain about the Skittles and my dumb stomach.

"So War has a sensitive tummy?" Sebastian said, grinning at me from across the booth.

"War has nothing sensitive, okay jackass? Eat your French toast. Who has breakfast at two in the afternoon, anyway?"

Beside me, Daryn glanced up from her blueberry pancakes.

"Dude, it's so. Good," Bastian said. "Ahhh, look at that. Delicious!"

He was having a great time at my expense. It did look damn good. Meanwhile Marcus wolfed down his burger like we weren't even there.

"There's something I need to tell you guys." Daryn pushed her plate away. She hadn't finished her pancakes and I wondered if they hadn't been as good as in Cayucos. "Are you ready?"

No one said anything. I think we all thought it was a rhetorical question. And we weren't ready for information, we were starved for it.

"LA isn't our actual destination," she continued. "We need to get to Italy."

"Then we've been driving in the wrong direction," I said. Ha ha. Then I saw the serious look in her eyes and dread started snaking through me. She was serious? "Negative, Martin. No on Italy."

"That's where Conquest is. It's where we need to go."

"I'm not going to Italy. I'm not taking this wild-goose chase international."

"Then I'll go alone."

"No, Daryn. And the problem isn't Italy. I don't know what I'm protecting. I don't know who I'm up against. I'm not hauling my ass all over the world. There are too many unknown variables. Just . . . *no*."

Marcus sank down and rubbed the back of his neck. "I'm with him," he said.

I hated that he said that. I was right, but when he agreed with me, I felt less right.

"Okay," Daryn said. "Then let's eliminate one thing."

"I vote for Marcus," I said. That got me a nice, long stare-down across the table.

"I meant one *unknown variable,*" Daryn said. I'd known exactly what she meant.

She bit her bottom lip, thinking for a few seconds. "I can't tell you what you're protecting yet. For now, it's better that only I know because . . ."

"Because why?" I already knew why, but I wanted to make sure Marcus and Sebastian did, too. "Keep it coming, Martin."

"Because it's an object. A powerful heavenly object that needs to stay hidden. Samrael, one of the Kindred, can get into your minds. He can see what you've seen. He can flip through your memories like photographs, so the less you know about what and where it is, the safer it is for all of us. What I *can* tell you is more about him. About *them*. The Kindred."

Our server came by to clear our plates, which gave everyone a moment to absorb the fact that we were walking slide shows for Samrael.

"You might have heard about the War in Heaven," she continued. "The fall of Satan, who was cast down to earth for being prideful. It's what most people think of when you imagine good versus evil. Satan defied God and for that, he was cast out along with his angels. The Kindred were subjects of Satan's. They were his servants, except the same thing happened. They were prideful and rebellious as well. They decided they didn't want to be followers of Satan, so they left." Daryn looked at me. "They went AWOL."

"Which is what again?" Sebastian asked, after a moment. He wasn't alone in needing a second to catch up to things.

"Absent without leave," I said. "They cut and ran."

"That's right," Daryn said. "They turned their backs on Satan."

"Which seems like a good thing?" Bastian said.

"But it's not," Daryn said. "They didn't reject evil outright. Only the power structure they'd been under. These are still evil beings and they've become a problem. They've banded together and gained strength. They've mutated into these, I don't know . . . these abominations. They hide behind human form, but they aren't human. And they have plans now. They want power. Independence. They've done a lot of harm, and they'll do a lot more if we don't succeed. That's what we're trying to prevent."

"Will," I said. "Will prevent."

"Yes," Daryn said. "Will prevent."

Sebastian grimaced. He looked like he was regretting the French toast.

I thought about my confrontations with Samrael at Anna's college and the studio. In retrospect, they'd seemed rushed. Samrael and his team had been quick to strike and quick to leave. They definitely hadn't wanted to linger. "They're being run down, aren't they?"

"It's possible, yes. Satan doesn't want them to rise to power any more than we do."

"So they have the devil on their tail. And they're chasing us down. Everybody's chasing everybody. What's at the end of this race? What does the object do for them?"

I needed to know what we were protecting more than ever.

Daryn's hand made the smallest movement toward the chain at her neck before she caught herself. She tucked a few strands of hair behind her ear. "It would enable them to establish their own realm of power."

"A realm?" Marcus said. "A kingdom or something? That's what they want to create?"

"They can't actually create anything. They're trying to access what's not theirs by unlocking a realm, a dimension, and they almost succeeded once already. They almost stole the object, but we have it now. We need to keep it safe until I can get it back to its rightful place." She looked at each of us. "I need your help to do that, and Conquest's when we find him."

"Okay," I said. "So we're running defense against a splinter faction of demons who are trying to build a second hell?"

"That's it. And build is a good word for it. They want power. If they can open this realm, it's possible they'll enslave people."

"*Enslave* people?" Bastian said. His face had gone ashy.

Marcus leaned over his elbows, lacing his fingers behind his head. I knew exactly how they felt, but the information was finally coming. I had to get as much as possible out of her now because I knew it wouldn't last.

"You said they're tracking the object," I said. "How, exactly?"

"I've told you that. They pick up on its energy. And they have other ways, I'm sure, but I don't know what they all are."

"You really don't know or you're filtering information as a defense measure?"

Bas frowned at me.

"What? That's not a fair question? Then what about their abilities?" I knew Samrael had the mind powers and the bone blades. Alevar had wings. It wasn't much. We had a lot to learn about our opposition. "Can we know about those? Or are we back to playing twenty questions again?"

Daryn glared at me. "I told you up front. I can't tell you everything."

"Yeah, but you're giving me just a little more than nothing." And there it was again. *Hello, temper. Welcome back.*

It was quiet for a second. Then Daryn said, "Gideon, can I talk to you alone?"

Sebastian and Marcus evacuated the booth before I could answer.

Daryn and I turned toward each other. Too close, nowhere to look but right at her, so I got up and slid across to where Bas had just been.

"Is this about earlier?" she asked.

"Earlier?"

"You and me."

It might have played some part in how frustrated I felt. But I just shrugged and said, "Give me some credit."

Her gaze fell to the table.

Wait. Was she *disappointed*?

Strike three. Strike twenty. I just couldn't get it right.

My attention pulled to the entrance, where a group of bikers covered in leather and ink filed in and began unsnapping their jackets and helmets. Not the Kindred, but we'd been there too long. My Jeep was starting to feel like shelter, even though it wasn't. But at least it kept us moving.

"I told you I'd give you one unknown. I've given you much more than that," Daryn said.

She had. It still didn't feel like enough.

As I looked back at her, I noticed that the chain around her neck fell over the outside of her jacket. On the end was a key. Heavy. Old-fashioned. Nothing spectacular, but not ordinary, either.

That was it.

It had to be the object the Kindred were after. A key that could unlock realms.

I looked into her eyes. They were steady, as always.

She was trusting me.

"We need to go to Italy," she said, quietly.

"Okay." I couldn't believe what I was agreeing to. "Okay. How are we getting there?"

"You."

I rubbed my head as I thought it over. I had a couple thousand stashed away. It might be enough for four plane tickets. If it wasn't, I could suck it up and use my credit card. I'd need to figure out flight schedules, whether we needed visas, but that was doable. We just needed time. "How soon do we need to be there?"

"Tomorrow."

I laughed. It was already past three in the afternoon. "Daryn, I don't see how this is happening."

"But you will," she said, watching me with the same expression she'd worn the first time I'd seen her at Joy's party. Like she was asking me to step up to a challenge. "We're going to catch a flight tonight. I saw us on a cargo plane."

"You *saw* us?"

She nodded. "You got us there, Gideon. Now, you just need to figure out how."

CHAPTER 31

Our first stop back in Los Angeles was my bank, where I emptied my account of the nearly two thousand dollars I'd saved from jobs, birthdays, graduation, and the Army pay I'd earned so far. It was money I'd wanted to give to Anna someday to help her study in Paris. Now I'd be using it to go to Italy. My life was taking some solid turns.

Sebastian came with me and the clerk turned out to be a guy he'd done some auditions with, so the transaction took about fifteen years to complete. I left the bank with a slim envelope of cash. Bastian walked out with a tote bag full of key chains, coffee mugs, and Post-it pads, everything stamped with the bank logo.

We headed to a sporting-goods store and went on a little shopping spree courtesy of yours truly, stocking up on warm clothes in dark colors, binos, a set of two-way radios with GPS, rope, a first-aid kit, and a bowie knife, which felt unnecessary because, you know, magic sword, but also necessary since at that point, I had a better chance of making it rain than calling my weapon. We piled into my Jeep with our brand-new backpacks stuffed with supplies, granola bars, and water bottles. Geared to the gills, but it was going to take a lot more than gear to get the job done.

Next I stopped at a shipping store to drop off one of the radios, spending a small fortune to overnight it to the Ritz Carlton in Rome, then I drove us to LAX. I said good-bye to my Jeep in the airport parking lot, which hit me harder than I expected. It felt like leaving a piece of my dad out there, but I snagged the Pearl Jam cassette and stuffed it into my pack, which made me feel a little better.

Around six, I left everyone in the domestic terminal and did some recon of the area of LAX where the shipping companies operated. A couple hours later, with the mission prep done, I met up with them and went over the plan I'd drawn up. Then it was time to execute.

We hopped on the airport shuttle. At that hour in the evening it wasn't very full, but Daryn came to my side, placing her hand next to mine on the steel grab bar along the ceiling. I noticed the chain around her neck. The key was tucked away. Hidden again.

"Almost there," she said. "One more horseman to go."

"After three comes four," I said, reading the airline signs that zipped past outside. I'd made a mistake in starting to like her. I had to figure out how to correct it. This wasn't the time to add complications.

"Gideon . . ."

"We should stay focused on the mission."

"That's what I was going to say, but you won't look at me."

I swung around so I was staring right into her blue eyes. "You have my full attention. Anything else?"

She didn't say anything, but color came up on her cheeks and her hand flexed next to mine on the bar. I knew she felt it, too. This friction between us. Like we were magnets that couldn't line up right.

Marcus and Sebastian were watching us. Not even trying to hide it.

"This is us," I said.

"It's not that I don't want that, it's just that—"

"This is our stop, Daryn." I shifted my backpack on my shoulder and hopped out. "Ready?" I asked Sebastian.

He made a sound that was either a yes or some mild regurgitation.

To reach the cargo terminal we'd need to get through two

layers of security. First, past a gatehouse that was the entry point for a large parking lot full of semis. This was where shipping companies trucked in their cargo before it was moved through another security point into the actual terminal where the planes were—which was the second breach we'd need to make, the airport itself.

The first lot was surrounded by twelve-foot concrete walls topped with concertina wire, so. Best way inside was through the gatehouse.

I checked my watch, and then Sebastian and I hustled up to it as Marcus and Daryn stayed behind. We had two minutes before the security cameras panned back.

The older man inside looked up from a crossword puzzle. "Can I help you?" he asked, with surprise. This part of the airport wasn't for pedestrian traffic.

According to the plan, Sebastian was supposed to make his move now. He looked like he might pass out, which was not the right move.

"Whenever you're ready, dude," I said.

"I can't," he said. Then he gave the man an apologetic grin.

The guard returned Bastian's smile, even though he was starting to look anxious. "You two lost?" he asked.

"No. I mean, *yes,*" Bas said. He shot me a pleading look. "We'll be leaving now."

No way. He wasn't going to flake out on me. I reached for the anger inside me, the burning potential that was always there, and let the charge ignite. I looked Bastian right in the eye and sent him a small shot of it.

"Shit!" he said, his eyes flying wide. "Gideon, what did you do to me?"

It was the first time I'd ever heard him swear. "Provided some motivation. You're on, man. We need you. Channel it, and get it done."

He looked at the guard. A second later the man's body

relaxed. I jumped through the window in time to catch him before he hit the floor.

"He looks okay, right?" Sebastian asked. "He didn't get hurt, did he?"

"He's fine. He'll just have a headache and some mild confusion when he wakes up." I set him down behind the chair and locked the door to the gatehouse from the inside so he'd be safe in there until he came back around.

I stared into the darkness. Daryn was supposed to be there any minute.

"Wow, I feel weird," Bastian said, rolling his shoulders. "Jumpy. Is this how you always feel? What's next again?"

He looked a little strung-out, his weight shifting restlessly, his jaw flexing like he was grinding his teeth. I remembered Anna crying after she'd slapped Wyatt. Sometimes using my ability had consequences that weren't great.

Daryn and Marcus walked up moments later, both looking much calmer than Bas.

"Okay, let's go. Nice and easy. We're just going to take a walk, everybody," I said, as we moved inside. To one end, busy warehouses crawled with pallets and forklifts. I took us the other way, deeper into darkness. With so many trucks in there, the lot's lights made a checkerboard of light and shadow. Killer for getting psyched out. Every truck was a place the Kindred could be hiding behind. Even with some training under my belt on staying cool under this kind of stress, I was juiced on adrenaline.

I glanced at Marcus. He was belligerent and cagey. I thought he'd be the one to worry about, but thanks to my shot of rage, Sebastian was the one who looked fired up and primed to punch something.

We arrived at a cyclone fence that bordered the airport. I could see the tarmac from where we were, lines of cargo planes, with fuel trucks and forklifts servicing everything. Reaching into my backpack, I fished out the radio/GPS and tracked the position of the companion unit I'd shipped earlier.

"Is that it?" Daryn asked. She leaned close to me and looked at the dot on the small screen in my hands. It indicated a position 146 meters dead ahead.

"That's it." I looked at the row of planes in front of us, eyeballing distances. "Third one's ours," I guessed, but the GPS would guide me right in. I slid the radio into my pocket and pulled wire cutters out of my pack, using them to create a small opening in the fence for us to climb through. Sebastian got tangled and ripped his sleeve, but we survived and made it inside. We were physically in the airport. Second breach down.

Now came the riskiest part: moving to the plane. I knew there'd be cameras everywhere, and there was plenty of activity around, so we'd have to stick close to the shadows—without looking suspicious.

We moved in bursts, with me on point and Marcus at the rear, everyone moving quietly except Sebastian, who was about as stealthy as a giraffe.

"Get *quiet* and *low*," I whispered to him.

He ducked his head, taking him to an almost invisible six-foot-two.

We'd closed to within thirty meters of the plane when I saw two men in blue mechanic's coveralls approaching. Quickly, I got everyone down behind a fuel truck.

The men came closer, strolling like they were on a break. They came to a stop around the front of the truck, close enough that I could hear one of them scratch his stubble. They were heckling each other over some bet on a football game.

This wasn't good. Our plane had to be taking off soon. I could see its loading ramp from where I crouched. We were *so* close. Sweat rolled down my chest and my back. We'd be arrested if we got caught. I'd have a record. That would make getting my old life back virtually impossible. I couldn't screw this up.

The fuel-truck guys wouldn't leave. They couldn't decide what the wager had been, twenty bucks or a case of beer. Bastian kept shifting around, his shoes scraping the asphalt. I knew he was still jacked up on the rage shot I'd given him.

Turning, I sent him a *shut up* glare.

He tapped his cuff like it was a watch. "Let me take them!" he whispered.

But I couldn't let him do that. One passed-out security person at LAX wouldn't raise suspicion. But three? I didn't want to bring that kind of heat on us. There was already too much outside of my control.

"*Gideon,*" Bas started in again.

Daryn moved to his side and mouthed, *Bas, quiet.*

The men went silent. I locked eyes with Marcus, who I knew could fight. A fight would be better than an arrest, but neither were good. I shook my head, telling him no. I imagined for an instant telling Cory this story, what was happening right now, and how he'd howl. I hoped I'd get the chance to do that someday.

The men picked up their conversation and walked away.

I rechecked the GPS. Last burst. We hustled to the 757 I'd spotted earlier. As we closed, I heard the engines running. That meant the plane was leaving soon—a good thing. I took everyone right up the ramp, then scanned the hold—pallets, boxes, no people—clear.

Or maybe not.

I heard whimpering, coming from deeper inside the plane.

"Get behind this and wait here," I said, indicating one of the containers. Then I took out my knife and moved toward the sound. The cargo was stashed in steel pallets to either side of a central corridor. It grew darker as I went, and the whimpering became louder. I followed the sound to a metal cage and knelt.

Silence.

Gold eyes stared from the darkness. I pulled my penlight from my pocket and clicked it on. A shepherd. I recognized the breed—Belgian Malinois. They were used a lot as combat dogs. "Hey, buddy. Just hang tight, I'll be back."

I checked a few labels on the boxes around me and confirmed we were on the right plane. FIUMICINO, ROMA IT. Marcus, Bastian, and Daryn hustled up.

"People were coming," Daryn said.

I heard them. The ground crew at the rear of the plane, going through the preflight checklist.

I motioned them to stay put and continued down the length of the cargo hold, moving toward the cockpit. I had three main objectives now. First, make sure the dog was the only other living cargo aboard—confirmed. Second, I didn't think the pilots would come back into the cargo hold but I had to secure the door from our side—I did that with some nylon rope from my pack. Third, find a place we could hide during the flight—located.

The floor had electric tracks—a kind of pulley system for loading the pallets—but about halfway into the hold, the tracks stopped. There, the plane had steel girders as big as railroad ties across the floor, a reinforcing belt right down the center that created a clear corridor about three feet wide. In front of this space were more pallets, which must have been loaded through the nose of the plane. I noticed a candy-bar wrapper and a cigarette butt on the floor. It looked like we weren't the only ones to have traveled this way.

I found the others and brought them over. "It's tight, but it should work."

The whine of the rear doors closing made Bastian jump. The bright overhead lights shut off, leaving only the weaker emergency lights on, plunging us into near darkness. We scattered around the narrow space and hunkered down. In ten minutes, we were in the air, the engines roaring loud and steady.

Sebastian shoved me in the shoulder. "That was *sick*! I didn't realize that was going to be so *fun*!"

"Maybe try not to yell? There are pilots flying this thing," I said.

"Stop trying to act like that wasn't awesome because it was!" He pushed me again. "You're such a badass, Gideon!"

I had to smile. "You did the hard part."

"Yeah, but you were like, 'Hold here everyone, just be cool,'" he said, adopting this super intense look that I really hoped wasn't me. "It was *sick*!"

Down the aisle, Daryn leaned forward and smiled. She didn't chime in with any praise, though, and it seemed like the moment she would've if she were going to. But that was okay. A smile was good.

Great, actually.

We'd done it. We were on a plane heading for Italy.

Reaching into my backpack for my wire cutters, I hopped to my feet.

"Where you going?" Bas asked.

"Canine rescue mission," I said, and went for the dog.

CHAPTER 32

Y ou went for the dog and . . . ?" Cordero says, when I stop.

"I got her out. It was a female."

"Nice of you, Gideon. What I'd like to know more about is the key you mentioned."

"I'll get back to it in a second. I was just wondering something." *Why is Daryn here?* But I can't ask Cordero that. I look at Texas, then at Beretta. I took the gold-medal oath. "I just told you seven demons are roaming the earth. Don't you have any questions about that?"

Cordero smirks. She opens her mouth to speak, and then closes it. "I'm waiting," she says finally. "I'm waiting until you're finished."

"Are you interested in knowing the Kindred got the key? That at the end of this, they took it in Norway? That they have it right now?"

"Of course it interests me. That's why I'm still listening."

She's listening all right, but that's kind of not even the point. Is she *believing* me, is the point. If she believes me, why isn't she freaking the hell out? Taking drastic measures? But if she *doesn't* believe me, why sit here?

Cordero rises from her chair. "Let's take another short break. I'm sure you're getting hungry. That granola bar can't have gone far. Let me see what I can do."

She leaves and takes Beretta with her.

I count to sixty before I address Texas. "Just tell me one thing. Did Daryn come here on her own?"

He ignores me. The radiator goes on and clicks for a full

minute before Texas gives me a nod that could be measured in nanometers.

Now I'm wondering *why*. Why did she come back? The Kindred got what they wanted. We lost. They won. So why is she back? Are we going after them?

Beretta returns with a cold slice of cheese pizza. I'm just finishing it when Cordero comes back, like a category 5 perfume hurricane. I'm breathing flower shops and fruit stands and turned earth smells and I can't help myself. I wince and then unwince, but it's too late. Cordero's seen.

She sits down and adjusts her chair, and sets a number two pencil on top of my file. When she opens my file the pencil rolls off the edge of the table and clatters to the floor.

I see red bricks. My dad falling through the air. And instantly, violently, the pizza tries to kick its way up my esophagus.

Somehow, I manage to keep it down.

Texas steps forward and picks up the pencil. His eyes pause on me before he gives it to Cordero. Beretta is watching me, too.

Cordero picks up on the tension. She looks at each of us, then it dawns on her.

"Oh, Gideon!" she says. "I'm sorry." She slips the pencil into the pocket of her jacket and takes out the pen she's been using. "I'm sorry. I didn't think."

I shake my head because I can't talk. It doesn't seem like her not to think. Did she do that *on purpose*? But why would she have?

There's a sense of urgency inside me, an inner burn. I was thinking of something important. Now all I can think of is my dad falling from the roof of a yellow bungalow.

"Ready?" Cordero says.

CHAPTER 33

The cargo plane was cold, uncomfortable, and loud. A lot like a military plane, in other words. The engines roared like a dozen jackhammers going off at the same time, exhausting even with the earplugs we'd bought. Marcus popped his in and zoned out ten minutes after wheels-up.

I gave Sebastian dog duties. The shepherd, Lia, had been so scared of flying she could barely walk when I got her out of her cage. I'd had to carry her over to our area. I put Bas in charge of petting her and making sure she was okay. It was what I wanted to do but he was still amped from the rage shot I'd given him. I thought maybe soothing Lia would soothe him, and I was right. They were curled up together in no time, completely sacked out.

I spent a little while locating the other radio because it still might come in handy. I found it in one of the shipping containers as we flew over Scottsdale, Arizona. It was starting to get late by then, but I couldn't sleep. I noticed that Daryn, who was on the other side of the center aisle past Marcus, couldn't either. She had her penlight out and she was writing in her notebook. I slid the radio across for her to keep. She looked over at me, dropped the radio into her backpack, and went back to her journal.

I sat back and thought about what she'd told us that afternoon at the diner. We were fighting *demons*. I'd been so focused on keeping us safe and on getting us on this plane, I hadn't had a chance to think about it yet. Now all I had was time.

As a soldier in the US Army, I was prepared to do whatever was asked of me because I believed, down to my soul, that the uniform I'd wear as a Ranger represented the defense of liberty and freedom, and the country I love. I'd chosen to serve because I could fight and because until wars stopped happening, people like me were needed. I had zero problem doing whatever it took to keep harm from coming to innocent people. Zero problem. Period, exclamation point, and freakin' *hooah*.

I hadn't had that kind of clarity since I'd become War, though. I hadn't known what I was fighting for—or really, against. But sitting in that dark cargo plane, it started coming together for me. My enemies were demons, but it was still my duty to protect the innocent. Realizing that was a huge relief.

After chewing on that for a while, I still wasn't tired. I thought about how Bastian could call up his scales and his horse so easily. I needed that kind of proficiency with my tools. For a while I tried to summon my sword by focusing on the cuff and thinking, *Here. Appear. Now.* Then I tried praying, which I hadn't done in a really long time. That didn't work but I felt better afterward, like I'd been missing out. Then I tried meditating, which I'd never done and ended up sucking at. Nothing worked. The sword eluded me, so.

I moved on.

At the airport, I'd asked Daryn to buy me a travel guide of Italy. I pulled that and my penlight from my pack and spent a couple hours reading it, paying extra attention to the maps of Rome and to the major transportation outlets—train stations, bus stations, waterways, et cetera. I'd always done okay in school, but my mind worked much better for missions. When details mattered, I was capable of storing away a ton of material. I sucked that guide down. By the time we were over Arkansas, I had a solid map of Rome in my head and some ideas for how to handle getting us safely off the cargo plane onto Italian ground.

With my eyes burning from the lateness and the reading, I

put the book away. Aiming the penlight at my companions, I ascertained that Marcus and Sebastian were still asleep. Marcus was twitching like mad, having the nightmare of his life, which pleased me greatly. A few feet past him, Daryn was only pretending to sleep. This I deduced because when I put the light on her face, she flipped me off.

I sat back, smiling at the darkness for a minute. Then I grabbed my radio, and brought it close to my lips before I could talk myself out of it.

"Special Agent Daryn Martin. Come in please, Ms. Martin. This is War. Over."

Over the drone of the engines, I couldn't hear my message register on her radio, but she did. I saw her digging around in her bag. A few seconds later, her voice came through my radio.

"Yes, Gideon?"

I pressed the talk button. "You will?"

"I will what?"

"I just asked you to come over here and you said yes."

"You didn't ask that."

"But you answered anyway. Come here."

"No."

"You're messing up the balance of the plane. We're going to fly in circles unless you come here."

"Your ego's weighing that side down just fine."

I laughed. "Is that another no?"

"Affirmative."

"What did you write about me in your notebook?"

Now she laughed but not into the radio. I heard it far away, under the sound of the engines.

"Actually, I was writing about you. You were really great tonight. Thanks for getting us here. I knew you would, but . . . thanks."

I stared at my radio. Had she written about what I'd *done*

or about *me*? There was a pretty big difference. But it was still awesome. It'd been a long time since praise had hit me that hard. Weird, because she was basically still a stranger. I'd been with her for days and I still knew almost nothing about her. That gave me an idea.

I pressed the talk button. "Daryn. Tell me three things about yourself. Think of it as my reward for a job well done. Just three. They can be anything."

There was a long stretch of nothing but engine drone. I kept waiting for her to tell me no. Bastian and Marcus were still sound asleep.

"Okay," she said, finally. "Three things. First one . . . I have a sister. Her name is Josie. Josephine. She's four years older than me and she's a science nerd. Ask her anything about the planets, or about the weather, or the periodic table or *any* random sciency thing, and she knows the answer. She's *so* smart. She knew from the time she was little that she wanted to be a doctor. I bet she'll be starting medical school soon. She wanted to go to Purdue. I bet that's where she's going. Josie—she does the things she says she's going to do. She's amazing like that and . . . and I miss her."

"When was the last time you saw her?" I asked.

"Two hundred and eighty-one days ago. And that should count as the second thing since I just answered another quest—"

I hit the talk button. "That was a subset of the first thing and don't joke around about this. I busted my ass for these so no cutting corners."

"You get mad so easily," she said, laughing.

"You drive me to it. That's why."

"So, it's not because you have a temper?"

"Don't change the subject. Thing number two, go."

"Okay. Thing number two. Well, let's see . . . I spent three months in a mental institution last year—how's that? It was right when I first started blacking out and waking up knowing things. Before I really understood. I thought I was going crazy. Literally, I thought so because my mom suffers from depression and anxiety, and it's bad sometimes. Really hard on her. On all of us. My whole family. So when I started passing out, the doctors thought it was mental illness again, only manifesting in a different way. And I guess I did too at first. My psychiatric team—I had a team—strongly suggested committing me. My parents agreed and I didn't disagree, so I ended up at this private hospital in Maine.

"I actually had to break out of there or I'd probably still be there. You'd have been proud of me. It was totally *Escape from Alcatraz*. I had to dig a hole and crawl under a fence. I gouged my back doing that. It hurt so much. It gave me a big scar that I can only see when I look in a mirror—three lines running down my back like a tiger almost caught me. It was pretty gross when it was new. But I did it. I got out and I haven't been anywhere near there or my home since."

My pulse had picked up, hearing all that. I wanted to shoot into the past and help her bust out of that place in Maine. And I wanted to know more about her. A lot more. "Why haven't you gone home?"

"Because nothing is different. This is my life. This never ends for me. I always have to leave. I always have to go where I'm needed. And it would just be too hard to see my family, then have to say good-bye. It'd be too hard for *them*. I do what I can to make it easier. A few months ago I sent them a postcard from Croatia, telling them I was traveling around the world finding myself and not to worry. I hope it helped. It's better than if they knew the truth."

I could relate to that. I'd left Anna and my mom without an explanation or good-bye.

"Are you turned off yet?" Daryn asked. "Are you picturing me in a straitjacket?"

"Was that your plan? Nice try, Martin. But it backfired. I like you even more now."

That last part wasn't supposed to come out but there it was. And there it stayed, second after second. I had no idea what she thought of it. None. My confidence was dying a thousand deaths.

Then she said, "Don't you want to hear thing number three?"

I pressed the talk button. "Sure do. Lay it on me." I was ready for things three through a hundred.

"This one's a little different. It's something I'm just realizing, kind of a revelation, and it's that . . . it's that your eyes are my favorite." Her voice had gone all gentle and soft, so I wasn't sure I'd heard her right until she kept going. "They're amazing. So blue and direct sometimes. Other times, when you're not being sarcastic or contrary, when you're listening or when you're just driving, there's such humor in them. Such humor and kindness. Then there are the times I catch you watching me, and what I see in them makes me forget everything. What I am, and what I do, and . . . I'm just a girl again. A girl who gets a million butterflies in her stomach over a boy with the prettiest blue eyes. It feels so normal. So normal and so good."

I didn't know what to say. I didn't even know how to speak anymore. My heart was going ballistic in my chest. Finally I got it together enough to respond. "So what you're telling me is that I make you feel average?"

She laughed. "Yes. You make me feel perfectly ordinary. It's the best."

"Daryn . . . Dare. Just come over here." I didn't say "please," but it was all over my voice. I wanted her with me. I was losing my mind, I wanted that so badly.

But I knew it wasn't going to happen. Every second that passed felt like she was putting mile after mile between us again. If this was her life—postcards from Croatia?—then I was beginning to understand the distance she needed. Not easy to get attached to people when you were always leaving. Coming from a military family, I knew about that.

"We should get some rest," she said. "Special Agent Daryn Martin, signing off. Good night, Gideon."

"Night, boss."

I shut off my radio. But I didn't fall sleep for a long while after.

CHAPTER 34

I woke up hungry, tired, and partially deaf, but ready to co-ordinate our ingress into Italy. Four stowaways climbing out of a cargo plane on the Fiumicino Airport tarmac were bound to attract some attention, so. Time to plan.

I stood, stretched, and put Lia back in her cage, giving her one of my granola bars. Sebastian and Marcus were both awake, but Daryn was still out cold, using my Giants sweat-shirt as her pillow.

I thought about our conversation over the radios. I wanted to get smart about depression so I could talk with her about it without sounding like an idiot. The scar on her back? Definitely wanted to see that. She'd acted like it was ugly, but no way. It just couldn't be. And the last thing she'd said? Mind-blowing.

I checked my watch and decided to let her sleep a little longer. We still had some time before we landed. We'd left Los Angeles at 11:55 p.m. Direct flights from LA to Rome took around twelve hours, and we'd gained nine hours in time-zone difference. That added up to it being night again in Rome when we'd land, somewhere around the 9:30 p.m. range, local time. Night was good. Darkness gave us more options. I set my watch. If I'd estimated everything correctly we had about thirty minutes until we touched down.

Moving to the rear of the plane, where there was more room, I presented the objective of deplaning without getting arrested to Marcus and Bastian.

"I'll handle it," Marcus said, before I'd finished. "I got an idea."

I aimed my penlight on him. "No. Not unless you run your idea by me and I approve it."

He scowled, squinting at the light. "I don't answer to you. You think 'cause you were in the Army for a month, you know everything? You don't know *nothin'* about the real world."

I didn't know who'd told him I was in the Army—Bastian or Daryn. Either way I didn't appreciate it.

"We find Contempt and I'm gone," Marcus said.

"You mean Conquest," Bas offered.

"You already found contempt, bro."

"Who you calling *bro*?" He shoved me in the chest.

I escalated immediately by throwing a punch, but Sebastian shot between us and I couldn't avoid him. I tagged the back of his head, sending him sprawling. Marcus came in and swung at me. I took a grazing hit to the forehead, but it still rocked me. My head went flying and I had to follow it. I collided with a steel pallet.

Lia was barking now. I knew Marcus was coming for more—but the sound of the landing gear whining stopped me.

Two things hit me then. Actually three. The first was Marcus, who took advantage of my momentary lapse of focus to punch me across the temple. The second was the fact that Bastian and Daryn stood nearby in a panicked discussion about how to handle us. Third was that my timeline calculations had been way off. We were beginning our descent *now*.

At Marcus's punch, I saw brightness, the painful kind, mirrors under the sun, then red like bursting capillaries. When my vision came back, Daryn and Bastian had positioned themselves between me and Marcus. They were talking, but I couldn't hear much. Just something-something-something *shadow*.

"Whose shadow?" Marcus asked Bas.

"My horse," Bastian explained. "I named her that. It seemed like she should have a name." He glanced at me, all worried looking. "Lia has a name, so why shouldn't my horse?"

"I think he should summon her when we land," Daryn said.

I stood there for a second, trying to catch up. Then I said, "*What the—?*"

The floor shook as the wheels touched down.

We all staggered, then froze. Even Lia stopped barking. We were in Rome.

Italy.

And we still didn't have a plan.

"Call her, Bastian," Daryn said. "Summon her now."

"No! Do *not* call her, Sebastian."

"I don't know what to do, Gideon! You said Daryn was in charge!" Sebastian cried. Then he closed his eyes for a second and that was it.

Shadow came up the same way she had at the studio lot—black smoke twisting and filling in the shape of a horse until she solidified and stood right there, between the pallets and the rear door. Her beauty struck me again, all hollowed-out darkness. In the murky light of the cargo hold, you could've missed her completely if she'd been standing still, but she wasn't. As soon as she took form, she started dancing nervously, the dim light catching on the shift of muscle and mane, her hooves clanging on the steel floor.

I looked at Marcus. His eyes were locked on Shadow and he looked legitimately shaken. I wondered if this was his first time seeing one of the horses.

"Go to her, Bastian," Daryn said. "You need to settle her down."

He moved right away, approaching the mare slowly. "Hey. It's okay. It's me." He put his hands out and moved closer. Gradually Shadow's movements became less jerky. Her eyes grew softer, settling for longer stretches on Bastian, and her ears came forward as she listened to him. Finally she let out a long snuffling breath and relaxed.

"That's it." Bastian reached up and ran his fingers down her jaw. "Good girl, Shadow." He turned to us, emotions flashing across his face—surprise, happiness, pride—and then he broke into a big grin. "She's awesome, right? Okay, what do we do next?"

They looked great together—both kind of spindly and *right*. A matching pair. And I thought of my horse—a creature that was aggression horseonified and appeared to be made of fire—and for a second there, I almost felt sorry for myself, except I had more urgent issues to handle. The plane was taxiing but it wouldn't be for much longer.

"Good question, Bas." My plan had involved getting into the shipping containers. We didn't have time for that anymore. I looked at Daryn. She'd set this thing in motion already. Time to make the most of it. "What's next, Martin? What are we doing here?"

"I was thinking Bastian and I will take Shadow out first? We could use her as a diversion so you and Marcus can get off the plane."

"Then what?"

She lifted a shoulder. "Bastian and I will bluff. We'll act like we don't understand the problem. If we act like we're the ones who are confused, maybe they'll think they messed up on their end. Maybe didn't get the right paperwork or whatever. We'll talk our way out of it."

"Got it. So we're going with the old *we FedExed a horse* plan. Classic. That one always works."

"Did you think of any better ideas while you and Marcus were beating each other up? Besides, there's a *dog* on board. And what other option do we have? We can't just walk off this plane."

"Daryn, twenty people parading off this plane would be better than that horse!" How was this the plan she wanted to go with? "Get rid of the horse, Sebastian. Right now." He was our best asset—not his horse.

He pushed his hands into his shaggy hair. "I can't, Gideon.

She just calmed down. She's starting to trust me and if I send her—"

We stumbled a few steps as the plane stopped taxiing.

I grabbed Bastian's shoulder. "Be ready to do the pass-out thing, you got me? Everyone get your stuff packed up, then don't do anything else unless I say so." I pulled the rope from my backpack and tied a quick slipknot at the end.

"What's that for?" Daryn asked.

"You know what's more noticeable than unloading a horse off a cargo plane? Doing it without a lead." I shoved the rope at Sebastian. "Put it over her neck."

As soon as he moved toward Shadow, the horse let out a low grunt and shied back.

"Tie her up, Sebastian."

"Are you sure?" he asked.

I wasn't. Each step he took toward Shadow only made the black mare more agitated—and then it was too late.

A gust of night air blew past me as the rear door yawned open. The ramp began to lower. Bright artificial light sliced into the plane. Sounds came next—the rhythmic beeping of a truck backing up. Voices. They were speaking Italian but the tone was universal—the sound of people shooting the breeze as they worked.

The ramp was halfway down when I heard a furious metallic clatter and saw a sleek black blur. Shadow launched herself out of the plane with the same flair for drama as her horseman, her long legs pushing her into the air, her tail lashing like a black whip.

Then there was just . . . shouting.

CHAPTER 35

I took in the scene as I ran down the ramp.

About twenty meters away, Shadow ran in tight circles, trying to find a way past the people, trucks, and other obstacles that framed her in. Every single person in the vicinity had stopped what they were doing to watch her. Two cargo handlers stared in shock, ignoring the shipping boxes that tumbled from a conveyor belt to the asphalt. A woman jumped out of a van and fumbled for the radio at her belt. Closer, a bald man dropped to his knees and made the sign of the cross.

Daryn grabbed my arm. "Gideon, look!"

About fifty meters away, two Italian customs officers burst out of a car, both carrying rifles. Sebastian saw them too, and made a break for Shadow.

"Hold on!" I caught a handful of his shirt. "She's your horse, Sebastian. You panic, *everyone* panics." I pressed the rope into his hand. "Get out there and get her under control."

Sebastian gaped at me. "I can't use this on her!"

"*Do it*, Sebastian."

"Gideon, this won't work!"

Marcus looked from me to Sebastian, swore, and then tore away at a sprint.

It was the worst possible thing he could've done. Until then, Shadow had done what Daryn had hoped—created a diversion. The second Marcus ran, we were on everyone's radar, too.

"*Stai fermo!*" yelled the two officers. They unshouldered their rifles and split targets—one on Shadow, one on Marcus.

"Go!" Daryn said. "You get Marcus. I'll help Bas."

It was the right call. I'd already made a snap decision to

follow Marcus, sensing the greater potential for problems there. I ran after him, holding up my hands so the officers could see them. "It's okay! It's okay!" I yelled. "He just got scared!"

"*Fermati!*" they shouted. "*Stop!*"

But Marcus kept running toward the terminal, so I did too. The rifle squeezed off three quick rounds—*pop, pop, pop*— and Marcus tumbled to the ground. All I could do was turn it up another notch.

Shots fired again just as I reached him. He was already getting up, but I slammed into him, putting him in an instant sprint. We made for the nearest cover, a van, throwing ourselves behind it. I pulled him against the vehicle.

"I hate you," I said, panting for breath. Blood rolled off my fingers. Mine or his? Marcus clutched his shoulder. His shoulder was bleeding. His blood.

He grimaced, in obvious pain. "Man, *shut up*."

The van was unlocked and the keys were in the ignition— first good break yet. I slid the rear door open and pushed him inside. "Put some pressure on it. Maybe you won't die."

When I rounded the van again, Sebastian and Shadow were nowhere to be seen. They'd disappeared. Daryn hunkered beneath the cargo plane's ramp, but everyone else had disappeared, too. Gunfire did that. But then I looked again, and saw two dark shapes on the tarmac. The customs officers. Facedown on the ground, with bone-colored blades sticking out of their backs.

No.

Daryn saw me, popped from behind the ramp, and came tearing over the same stretch Marcus and I had just crossed.

"No! Daryn, *no!*" I yelled.

The Kindred were here.

Samrael walked up to the officer's prone bodies casually. Four other Kindred flanked him. Pyro, the younger one, with skittish energy. Ronwae, with the red hair. Malaphar, the weasel-looking one in his oversized suit. And a demon I hadn't seen yet. A female in her thirties. Tall, with dreadlocks and a muscular build.

Samrael reached down and pulled one of the blades free. Then he straightened, looking from me to Daryn.

Daryn was halfway. Hauling. But it felt like she'd never reach me. Instinct took over and I shot toward her. I had no weapon, no way to give her cover. I did the only thing I could, putting myself between her and the Kindred.

Somehow we reached the van alive. We rounded it and I swung the passenger door open.

She jumped inside. "Let's go, let's go!" she yelled.

In the back of the van, Marcus sagged against a stack of boxes, holding his shoulder.

I shook my head. *"Bas."*

"Gideon! We have to go!"

But I was already moving, dropping low and peering around the front of the van.

The Kindred hadn't moved. They stood in a loose group around Samrael, whose eyes were fixed on me, his lips pulled into a smile.

I scanned the tarmac, the giant cargo planes and service trucks. Where the hell had Bas gone?

An invisible blow hit me over the eyes. The pain came, violent and sudden, like a door slamming over me. I crumbled against the van.

Samrael was ruthless this time. It wasn't the dull probe of fingers now. It was a screwdriver, prying into my skull. My mind gave with a *snap*. I was sucked back into the tunnel of darkness. Then an image appeared before me. I was looking at Daryn in the elevator on the way to Herald Casting. My focus moved from her blue eyes to the thick silver chain she wore around her neck.

Is this it?

I didn't want him to know.

Ahhh. So it is. Is that what you're trying to not tell me? Let's look a little more.

I saw flashes. A lightning-quick scan through my memories.

Daryn in my Jeep, curled up asleep—

Sebastian auditioning, staring at his hands—

The creepy winged guy in the desert—

So you've met Alevar, have you? Did you feel sorry for him, Gideon? He does raise sympathy, doesn't he? With those blind eyes and that 'help me' face of his. He is our weakest, but don't get your hopes up. He's still quite horrible. And you haven't met Ra'om yet. Ra'om makes up for little Alevar by quite a wide margin.

The blurring started again.

Daryn in the airport shuttle, when we'd been locked in a stare-down—

The bloody towel in Marcus's car—

Daryn at the diner outside of Los Angeles, when it'd just been us—

Well. Would you look at that? That's it, isn't it? Did she tell you this is the key?

Why was he even asking? The key was right there. Visible. The first and only time I'd seen it.

"Gideon, *please*! Listen to me! Listen to me. *Listen.*"

At the sound of Daryn's voice, the real world came closer. I was on my ass, my back against the front bumper. Daryn was kneeling in front of me, her hands framing my face, staring right into my eyes. "Come back, Gideon. Come back, come back, come back. I'll tell you three more things about me if you come back."

I couldn't respond. The connection between my brain and my mouth was down.

Daryn peered past the van, her eyes widening with fear. I imagined what she saw, Samrael closing in.

"Gideon," she said, desperately, "it's a good deal. I don't ever talk about myself, so I'd take it if I were you. Three more. Ten more. Please come back."

I tried but Samrael hooked in, dragging me back.

You think you can run, but you can't. We are always behind you. Above you. Among you. You can save us all some time by bringing me the key. It's that easy, Gideon.

Vaguely, I became aware that Daryn had gotten me on my feet and over to the passenger door. Strong girl. So strong.

More than you know.

"Get in!" she yelled, trying to push me into the passenger seat. "Marcus, help me!"

My body was coming back to me. My mind, too. I found my feet and lifted myself into the van. Then I remembered Sebastian and stumbled back out.

Daryn and Marcus swore as I lumbered around the van again—this time stepping out into the open. I couldn't leave Bas behind. I didn't do that. I didn't *do* that.

It's the soldier's training.

It's a soldier's heart, *you demon piece of shit.*

I was looking right at Samrael now. He stood thirty meters away, holding one of his pale blades at his side. Sirens wailed and flashed across the airport tarmac, speeding toward us through the darkness.

"What's the matter?" I said. "Can't take a little insult?"

He let go of me then, fully releasing my mind with a sharp recoil, like I'd struck a nerve. Then he turned to Pyro and said, "Here is your chance at last, my kin. Burn him."

Immediately, Pyro flung his arms wide. White-hot fire flared in his palms. Brilliant, condensed points. I saw them for an instant before he hurled them at me.

I dove away, tumbling onto the asphalt. An explosion cracked into the night, pushing a wave of heat past me. Hot air seared into my nostrils and deep in my throat as I drew a breath. Scrambling to my feet, I looked at the van, squinting at the brightness and heat of the flames.

Terror shot through me. It was covered almost entirely by fire.

Daryn and Marcus were in there.

I ran, the need to reach them overshadowing every other thought in my mind.

The rear door of the van slid open as I reached it, Marcus pulling it from inside. "Come on!" he yelled.

I launched myself and crashed into a stack of boxes. Daryn hit the gas, and Marcus and I went toppling to the back as we peeled out of there.

Burning, but alive.

CHAPTER 36

As we sped away from that cargo plane, I wanted to find a hangar where we could hide out and wait until Sebastian and Shadow turned up. There was no way that was going to happen, though.

The side of the van was still on fire. It was night. We were impossible to miss.

We had no choice but to keep going.

I didn't see Samrael or any of the other Kindred chasing us, but we'd picked up human law enforcement. Two Italian cop cars. Daryn lost one with her insane driving skills. We lost the other pulling onto the autostrada when it made a sudden turn that took it squirreling off the road.

Marcus was in the back, watching the car through the rear windows. He sat down, slumping against the door. When I saw his stunned face, I knew he'd used his ability. He'd hit whoever had been behind the wheel with a massive dose of fear, causing the driver to panic and jerk the wheel.

"Where was that three minutes ago?" I yelled.

"I tried!"

"You used it on the Kindred?"

"That's what I said, man. I tried, but it didn't work."

"*Shit.*" I fell back against my seat.

"You think they got Sebastian?" Marcus asked after a moment. "I didn't see what happened to him."

I said nothing. I was too pissed to respond. Bas was gone. And our abilities didn't even work on the enemy. What *use* were they? The only good news at the moment was that the fire on the van had almost burned out.

"Gideon," Daryn said. "Bas got away. It was chaos back

there, but I'm almost sure he did. We'll get Conquest, and then we'll come back and find him."

I pulled my radio out of my backpack, my fingers fumbling on the device. I couldn't believe we'd just left him. The blood roared in my ears and my face felt like it'd been torched. "Where are we going, Daryn? Where's Conquest?"

"Vatican City."

No surprise there. "It's ten p.m. local time. Are we supposed to go there now?"

She looked at me.

"Daryn. Are we supposed to go now?"

"Yes. As soon as possible."

"Because our buddy, Samrael, is probably headed there too, right? Why is it they're always two steps ahead of us? What is it you aren't saying? It's like you're *trying* to make this more difficult than it needs to be."

"What's wrong with you?" Marcus said.

I should have controlled the situation. That's what was wrong with me. We'd lost Sebastian, Marcus had been shot, and I'd taken a mental beating again because I hadn't organized and controlled the situation. I had the most training. I should've marshaled them into order. I should've established a rally point in case we got separated. But I hadn't done any of that and now we were down a horseman.

I'd grown used to getting signals from the cuff, telling me whenever Sebastian or Marcus were in the same vicinity. Now with Sebastian missing, I actually *felt* him missing. All I sensed was Marcus. Not good.

I pulled up the directions to Vatican City on my radio's GPS, handed it to Daryn, and climbed into the back. "Let me see your wound."

Marcus looked at me like he was doing me a favor, then pulled his sweatshirt off and yanked up his shirt.

Death had won the lottery in terms of gunshot wounds. The

round had gone through his deltoid, cutting clean through muscle tissue. I saw an entry and exit point, and it wasn't bleeding too much anymore. I pulled the first-aid kit out of my backpack and sprayed the wound with antiseptic, then taped it up. "Keep pressure on it."

Marcus pulled his shirt down and settled against the back of the van again. I stared into his ungrateful eyes, debating opening the back doors and tossing him out. He was disrespectful, negative, contrary, selfish. Everything I hated.

I moved back to the passenger seat and tried to figure out where Sebastian would have gone. The Pantheon? The Spanish Steps? Would he be at the Vatican? Or would the Kindred get to him first?

"Gideon, you need to calm down," Daryn said.

I was trying. I wanted to hit something and I hadn't yet. I felt good about that.

Using the GPS, I guided her through the streets to a church— a huge Gothic structure decorated with spires and angelic statues—and it hit me, finally, where I was. I'd always expected that my first time off US soil would come during my first deployment, but here I was. Italy.

"This isn't the Vatican," Daryn said.

"We're ditching the van."

We grabbed our packs and swapped the van for a dumpy-looking Fiat. I broke a window, pried up the plastic under the steering wheel with my bowie knife, and twisted some wires together. Off we went. If our mission depended on lifting cars, we'd have had it made.

Thirty minutes later, I parked on Via della Conciliazione directly across the street from Saint Peter's Square. I knew from the travel guide that the Vatican enclave was enclosed by a stone wall, and this would be our best entry point. Just ahead of us I saw the famous obelisk at the center of the expansive paved piazza. At the far end, I could see the Basilica of Saint

Peter, the row of marble sculpted saints illuminated across the top. It was an impressive place, steeped in history and art, with an air of sacredness you could feel on your skin. I focused on the security.

A pair of Swiss Guards stood about a hundred meters away, inside the columned arcade. I'd read about their arms and combat training in the travel guide. They were extremely competent warriors who probably would never have left a man behind.

I had to get this done so I could turn to tracking Sebastian down. My cuff was like its own horseman GPS. If I could get close enough to Bas, I could pick up his signal and find him that way. Rome was a big city. It might take me days, or even weeks. It didn't matter. I was going to find him.

When I felt ready, I firmed my grip on my backpack and looked at Daryn. "Anything you want to tell me that could be useful before I go? His name? Where he's supposed to be? Or do we want to keep making this as challenging as possible?"

"Jode. His name is Jode and we're supposed to find him here tonight. Somewhere here. And you're not exactly making this easy, in case you haven't noticed."

"What about Sebastian? Where are we supposed to find him?"

"I don't know."

"Then we shouldn't have left him."

"We left because we had to! Please stop acting like you're the only one who's having a hard time with this."

I shook my head. She didn't understand. Leaving someone behind went against everything I believed.

Daryn let out a long sigh. "Samrael was too close to us," she said, more calmly. "If we'd stayed there, we could've lost everything."

Could have? I thought of how Samrael had found my recollection of Daryn at the diner. She'd been wearing the chain she was wearing right now. A sacred key hung on the end, and Samrael had seen it. What if I'd already compromised us?

The urge to tell Daryn was strong. She deserved to know— she was the one wearing the thing—but I couldn't force the words out. Not with Marcus in the backseat. Not with how much I'd already screwed up. I was dropping the ball but that was going to change.

"Let's just take this one step at a time," I said. "Marcus has to stay." We couldn't walk around with a guy bleeding from a gunshot wound. We were going to have to split up. "What about you?"

"I'll stay, too," Daryn said.

Right. Saw that coming. "Okay. Keep your radio on. I'll send you a rally point location in case we need it. Otherwise just stay put. I'll be back in two hours, no matter what." I turned to the backseat. "Be ready to bring out the scythe, Death. And stay with her or I will personally end you. You feel me?"

Marcus just stared me down in response.

I got out of the Fiat but something kept me from leaving. I leaned back into the car. Daryn kept staring through the windshield. I wanted to say something to her. What? What did I want to say? Too much, and there wasn't enough time. She didn't seem to want to hear anything from me anyway, so.

I shut the car door and walked away.

CHAPTER 37

S top here for a moment, Gideon."
   "Okay."
   As the room comes back to me, I notice the lightbulb is flickering even more now and making a soft pinging sound. Standing on its last filament, that bulb. We're minutes away from a total blackout.
   I look from Texas to Beretta. Cordero.
   No one seems to even notice it.
   "You left Sebastian at the airport?" Cordero asks.
   My gaze falls to the flex ties keeping me in this chair. My hands are pulled into fists. I open them. Force them to relax.
   "I didn't mean to sound judgmental. I'm sure you had no other choice."
   "It's okay." I'm the one who did it. I'll suffer the consequences.
   "So you left him," she says, "and went to the Vatican. And then?"
   I look up. Seriously? Did she have to say it *again*?
   Cordero's eyebrows climb like she doesn't understand, but Texas and Beretta exchange a look.
   "Are you with NSA?" I ask. "CIA? I can't figure it out."
   She smiles. "Then maybe you should stop trying. I know you're tired of this but we're just about done, aren't we?"
   I nod. After Italy we went to Norway. Where we stayed until we lost the key. Where I thought Daryn had stayed. I picture her face just now, out in the hallway.
   Why is she *here*?
   "Let's move on," Cordero says. "You'd left Sebastian behind and arrived at the Vatican. What happened next?"

CHAPTER 38

It was almost eleven when I started walking the arcade. My plan was simple. One, stay alive. Two, walk the premises until the cuff alerted me to Conquest's presence. Three, get out of there. With Conquest, still alive.

Part of me actually hoped the Kindred would show up. I was routinely getting my butt kicked by them and that had to stop. I wanted a chance to give a little payback—or a lot—but I had a sword and a fire horse, sometimes, and the ability to ramp up rage in people. My tools didn't exactly make me feel outfitted for combat success.

Even at such a late hour, tourists were strolling around and snapping pictures. I tried to blend in as I noted the position of the guards and familiarized myself with the basic layout of the Vatican. As always, my focus improved with fresh air and movement. A charred smell still clung to me and my eyes stung, but I'd put the incident at the airport behind me.

I did a full lap around the piazza, orienting myself. On my second turn I spent a few minutes staring at the wing that housed the Vatican museums. Somewhere in there was the Sistine Chapel, which contained Michelangelo's famous frescoes. I thought of my sister, who should've been the one standing there, appreciating all the culture and history. Then I thought of my mom, and glanced at a pay phone nearby, picturing myself making *that* call.

Hey, Mom. Sorry I've been out of touch. Been busy protecting a sacred key from some demons. No, that's right. Demons. There's this girl who's running things. Daryn. I know, weird name but I like her. That's right. Like her, like her. Is it mutual? No. Actually I think she hates me right now. Sorry to get your hopes up. Okay. Okay, Mom. I just said I would. Mom, could you stop? I've agreed like ten times already. I promise I'll be nicer to her. Can we please talk about something else now?

Probably not exactly how it would've gone but it made me smile to imagine it. I just hoped she was doing okay.

After two hours of wandering, I still hadn't sensed Conquest and I was starting to get antsy. It was close to one in the morning and the place had cleared out. The guards were starting to get suspicious of me. Something didn't feel right. Daryn and I had found both Bastian and Marcus right away. This was taking much longer.

I radioed Daryn and Marcus, checking in and telling them I'd head back to the Fiat in fifteen minutes. Then I took a dim path that led to a wrought-iron gate manned by a pair of guards. The Vatican Gardens.

"Closed, huh?" I said, though I knew they wouldn't answer me. On the other side of the gate I saw an expanse of unbroken darkness. I'd read about this place in the guide—ordered gardens in geometric patterns, every shrub trimmed down to a perfect sphere, no leaf out of place. My kind of gardens, in other words.

As my eyes adjusted I could make out the rough shape of shrubs. A topiary hedge, then a path. My eyes drifted left, searching for symmetry, and I saw a blur of movement.

I tensed and the shorter guard caught my eye.

"Have a good night," I said, and started walking.

Casually, I reached back and made sure my knife was in the outer pocket of my pack. The path curved and grew darker as the wrought-iron gate became a high cement wall. I was alone now—not even any security guards in sight. My heart thudded in my chest. A light mist began to fall as I worked my way back to Via della Conciliazione. I needed to get back to Daryn and Marcus. I had a strong feeling the Kindred had tracked us again. We needed to leave. I couldn't lose anyone else.

The Fiat wasn't where I'd left it. As soon as I saw that it was gone I changed courses, heading away from the Vatican.

Turning into a narrow residential street, I pulled my radio out of my pocket, the soles of my shoes sliding on the slick cobblestones. "Daryn, where are you?"

I noticed that my cuff was buzzing, but it wasn't Bas or Marcus. The tone humming into my arm was new. Conquest. He was around here somewhere. My break was over; things were happening fast now.

"What's going on, Daryn? Talk to me," I tried again.

I didn't see anyone else along the street but it was dim, illuminated by a few feeble streetlamps. To either side of me apartments rose six to eight stories high, their windows in darkness at this late hour. I saw several underground garages, shadowed entryways and small alleys. All offered great places for the Kindred to lie in wait. Thinking *ambush*, I stepped off the curb and walked down the middle of the street.

The radio crackled to life. "Gideon—had to leave—we tried to—"

I only heard snatches but there was no mistaking the fear in her voice. Adrenaline shot through me. I hit the talk button. "I didn't get that, Daryn. Slow down. Tell me where you are."

"I'm sorry. I had to—"

I stopped. Stared at the radio.

Come on. Not again. Not her.

Still no answer. I moved quickly through the radio's screens to track her location using the GPS.

The hair on my arms lifted as a shadow streaked over the wet cobblestones. I felt a rush of the night air sweep past me and looked up. I saw black wings beating above me for an instant. Then Alevar landed a few feet away, touching down on the street without making a sound.

Fear shot through me. I grabbed for my knife—then froze when the radio crackled in my hand.

Static. It was just static.

Alevar crouched on all fours and folded his wings. He tilted his head to the sound, listening as he stared at me with his huge pleading eyes.

My knife was still strapped to my pack. I needed it. But his body was bent like a frog's, compact and ready to spring. He could be on me in one leap, I was positive. He could rip my throat open with his teeth before I ever reached my knife.

"What do you want?"

My voice was hoarse, my breathing too shallow.

He crept toward me, still angling his head. Intricate markings went up along his forehead and scalp, glowing faintly like his eyes. Sound, I realized, looking at his large tipped ears. He was locating me by sound, responding to the radio's soft static.

He kept coming. Was almost on me.

"*Stop.*"

He flattened his ears and went low, hugging the street. Then he extended his bony arm and pointed at the radio.

I lifted it. "This is what you want? No way."

He gestured again with more urgency. His curved talons were the color of raw steel.

"Is it Daryn? What the hell are you trying to tell me? Whose side are you—"

Daryn's voice broke into the night, a strangled cry of pure pain. Not from the radio—from somewhere down the street.

I took off running.

Alevar sprang into the sky.

Daryn had sounded close. I searched for her in the shadows

along the street, my legs churning, my backpack drumming against my lower back. Where was she?

I'd almost reached the corner when Samrael stepped from the darkness of a hidden alley, putting himself in my path.

I didn't slow down. I slammed into him, the collision like a shock wave through my body. We careened together, fighting to stay on our feet as we grappled. He was strong—I couldn't get him locked up. He broke loose and pushed me away.

"Where's Daryn?" I yelled.

As I looked into his eyes I remembered what I'd seen in them at Joy's party. The torment and pain. The fear and anguish. It was all there behind that flat gaze. Dark potential living inside him.

"Somewhere, Gideon." He smiled, enjoying my panic. "She's surely somewhere."

An invisible fist struck my forehead. I staggered back. It was him, but I couldn't go there again. The rage inside me focused to a point, to a clear and singular intention—*stop him.*

I knew I'd summoned my sword before I felt the grip in my hand.

I threw the quickest blow I could, swinging upward. Samrael lurched back, but the tip of the blade slashed his jaw. A gash opened. Dark blood streamed out, running down his neck.

"Where is she?" I demanded again.

"You're getting stronger, Gideon," he said, his eyes flicking to the weapon in my hand. He touched his neck and looked at the blood on his fingers, anger flashing across his face. "Where is she, Alevar?" he said, looking past me. "You know, don't you?"

Alevar crouched a few feet behind me. He crawled over to Samrael and bowed his head in submission, his folded wings shining with mist.

"He likes you, Gideon," Samrael said. "I sent him for the key and you've distracted him." Samrael laid his hand on Alevar, stroking the demon's smooth head. Alevar shuddered and bent lower. "Perhaps I expect too much from him. Such a crude little beast. No real thoughts inside his mind. Like. Dislike. Hate. Kill. It's about all he's capable of."

Alevar peered at me with his blind eyes. I didn't feel evil from him. Not like Samrael.

"Go on now," Samrael said, coaxing him. "I can hardly deny you the opportunity to show off for your new friend. Show Gideon your gift." Alevar didn't move. Samrael removed his hand from the winged demon's head. "I don't know why you bother to refuse me."

Alevar let out a sharp squeal, reacting to pain I knew well. He scurried back, putting himself a few feet from Samrael, then came upright and extended his wings.

They were fantastic. Enormous. Then I saw darkness leaking from the feathers. Darkness like an inky liquid that pooled at his feet. He fanned his wings, and the darkness spread, tumbling across the street in waves.

I'd seen this kind of darkness before. Outside my sister's apartment, the night I'd chased Samrael down. In the desert, when Alevar had appeared right in front of me. This had to be how he'd been able to sneak up on me.

I couldn't see across the street anymore. The light from the lamps had gone dull and cold. Shadows merged together and deepened to black. Alevar was flooding the block with darkness.

"That's enough, Alevar." Samrael smiled at me. "Not a horse made of fire but impressive nonetheless, don't you think?"

My attention pulled past him, down the street. Other Kindred were coming now, emerging from the darkness. Pyro and Malaphar walked together. Pyro's stride was tight, skittish, and he had a crazed look in his eyes. By contrast, Malaphar lumbered awkwardly, shuffling up the street. They came toward us but two other demons—the females, Ronwae and the one with the muscular build and dreadlocks—took positions on either end of the street, standing guard.

I remembered the Kindred were on the run, too. They were rebels.

Six were here. Only one was missing.

I saw no escape. They had me surrounded.

Samrael wiped at the blood under his chin again. "You know she's using you? Daryn? You're a means to an end for her. I've seen into her mind."

"No. You can't see into her mind or you wouldn't be bothering with me. And you don't have her, either. You wouldn't be here if you did."

This was a trap—for me.

Samrael stared at me. "Well reasoned," he conceded. "I am envious of her skill. I can only see into minds, but her knowledge has no limitation. She can see backward and forward. It makes her very hard to catch." He turned his palm up as he spoke. A shard of bone broke through his skin. It slid out, blade-shaped and the length of his arm. My stomach tightened up at the sight. "What must that be like for her? Has she seen your death, for example? Can you imagine that, rider? Your *death*? Pyro. Malaphar. Help him imagine it."

They came forward together, the skater and the homeless man. Harmless-looking, but not. Their stench hit me as they drew closer, the smell of rancid earth and death.

Pyro held out his hand, creating a white flame in his palm. He brought it toward Malaphar's face, illuminating the older man's pocked skin and black eyes.

Malaphar's human face flickered out, then I saw a monstrous creature like Samrael, but deformed in different ways. He had melted features. Sagging skin. He was hideous. A wax figure left out in the hot sun. Then he blurred again and I was looking at Daryn.

She smiled, but it wasn't her smile. It was nothing like her smile.

I was drawn to Daryn like I was drawn to the sea. But this girl only repulsed me.

"You will die, Gideon. Very soon," she said.

Daryn's voice. Her voice *exactly*, but the intonations were off.

"I'll be twisting the knife in your back when you least expect it."

I knew it wasn't her but my body didn't care. A sharp ache flared in the back of my throat.

Malaphar was laughing as he shifted back to his human form. Back to the weasel with the stringy hair and cratered skin. He laughed in big, hacking cackles that made Alevar duck inside his wings.

"That wasn't what I was expecting, Malaphar," Samrael said, his voice light, amused. "But perhaps it was better. Your face is a masterpiece, Gideon. I wish you could see it. I do enjoy my time with you." He cast a glance toward the female demons, who'd started to prowl restlessly. "But we can't delay any longer. Ra'om wishes to speak to you. It seems he's lost his patience for your stubborn—"

I went after him with everything I had, but Samrael was ready. He sidestepped, and swung at me with the long knife in his hand. Our blades clashed, then I dodged and swung again. I met him evenly for a few more strikes, but he was faster. Fluid. Versed in this form of warfare. I couldn't match him. He backed me against the wall of an apartment with a lightning-fast move and pinned my sword arm.

"Don't fight it, Gideon." He slipped the blade against my neck. Then that invisible pressure began over my eyes as he worked his way into my brain. "Stop struggling. Yes, good. I know it's hard for you but the sooner this is over, the sooner we can find the key . . . and kill you."

The world narrowed and pulled away from me. The whirling tunnel of darkness had become a familiar torture. I sank into it.

"You'll see him soon," Samrael said, as I sank deeper. Much deeper than I'd ever gone before. The darkness closed around me, swallowing light. Erasing everything until I couldn't see the street or Samrael anymore.

Until there was only all-encompassing darkness and I was lost in it.

Adrift.

Then I heard a low, reptilian growl and deep red eyes emerged from the dark.

Ra'om.

Demon number seven.

Seven had to be bad.

The red eyes floated nearer. I saw black pupils, sickle-shaped. Then the curve of a heavy brow covered in gray scales the color of wet stone. Each one was inches thick. The size of my hand.

Hello, Gideon.

His voice was a nightmare. Dark. Resonant. The sound of evil.

Fear flowed through me like a current.

Ra'om came closer and a huge snout appeared with long teeth, sharp as swords. His black tongue flicked against them, sizzling with saliva. He shifted, revealing more of himself. Giving me glimpses of his enormous body. Of his wings. Of the spiked ridge of his back.

He didn't deserve to be called a dragon. I had never seen a dragon as terrifying as this. The dark power I felt from him was hypnotic and hard to even comprehend.

That is the idea, Gideon. And I'm happy to know you feel so. Samrael has told me you're a tough one. Uncooperative and resistant. But I believe I can persuade you to bring us the key yet.

Ra'om pulled back suddenly, withdrawing into the dark.
Panic crashed through me. This was different than Samrael.
I didn't know what to expect. What was this?

An image took shape before me, rising out of the darkness.
My mother stood on a green hillside, her black dress flapping in a breeze. Tears ran down her face. I knew this image.
This place. It was the cemetery in the Santa Cruz Mountains
where we'd buried my dad.

Mom looked down at his headstone, and the engraved inscription came into focus.

Gideon Christopher Blake

Except that was wrong. My dad was Christopher Gideon
Blake. My parents had given me his name, only reversed.

I was seeing *my* funeral. I was seeing my mother mourn *me*.

Would that be enough to persuade you? Ra'om asked. *Or
would this?*

The image faded out, then another faded in.

Anna. My sister was on the floor of an empty room, rocking in a ball on the grimy concrete. She cried and ripped out
chunks of her dark hair. She tore at her own face with her
nails and made herself bleed as she begged me to make it stop.

Me. Like *I* was doing that to her.

Yes. I'm getting to you, aren't I? What about this, Gideon?

The image changed again, and I was seeing a party, everything dark and blurred except the golden shine of Daryn's hair.
I moved toward her, fighting through the crowd. As I finally
reached her, I saw that she wasn't alone. She stood tucked beneath a guy's arm, smiling up at him like they were together.
Then he looked right at me, and I saw that it was Samrael. And,
somehow, I knew that she was with him because I'd failed.
Because I'd let her down.

It was destroying me to see them together, but I couldn't leave. I couldn't even speak.

All I could do was watch.

Then it was me. I saw myself standing on the warped shingle roof of a yellow bungalow in Half Moon Bay. At my feet, my dad clung to the gutter, about to fall. He looked at me and asked for help. If I didn't help, he was going to die.

I reached down. I picked up the yellow pencil from inside the gutter. Then I stood and watched the strength leave his fingers. Watched as he fell and hit the red bricks of the walkway below. I just stood there.

More, Gideon? Or will you bring me the key?

CHAPTER 39

After that, I lost some time. I wasn't conscious but I wasn't unconscious, either. I was trapped in the middle somewhere.

I only remember pieces of what happened next. The dreadlocked woman lifting her head and letting out a long, baying sound. Samrael releasing me and leaving with the other Kindred. Responding to a threat that was beyond me. No more Ra'om—that was all I cared about—but I wasn't free yet.

Nausea hit me. Stomach-clenching nausea, like a concussion and motion sickness, plus the sensation that my brain had been thoroughly ransacked.

I bent over my legs and heaved, riding out the shaking in my muscles, the coughing, and the bitter taste on my tongue. It took me long minutes to regain some control. As I straightened and looked around me, I still felt weak and disoriented.

The darkness Alevar had released from his wings was lifting. Under the glow of the streetlights, the wet cobblestones looked like gold, the apartment windows like crystal. Night had never seemed so bright to me before.

I realized I didn't have the sword any longer. I had a vague recollection of calling it back just before Samrael had introduced me to Ra'om. I'd tapped into the same feeling as when I'd summoned it. A singular purpose. A clear intention. I was almost sure I could achieve that again.

So at least one good thing had come out of this.

As I found my composure, I became aware of someone watching me from the end of the street. A guy in a dark coat sat on one of the apartment stoops. Blond hair. About my age, from what I could tell. I had a feeling he'd been there for the past few minutes while I'd hacked up my intestines. I also had a pretty good idea of who he was thanks to the cuff, but I didn't go after him yet. I didn't trust myself to.

"Gideon!"

Daryn and Marcus came running from the other end of the street. Daryn flew into my arms. I yanked her close and hugged her hard, needing to feel her realness. Ra'om had knocked down some part of me that still couldn't seem to get back up.

"What happened?" Daryn said, drawing back. "Gideon, your nose."

"Don't know." I felt it now, the swelling and the pain. And I tasted blood on my tongue. "Busted it. Daryn, where were you?"

My voice sounded like it had gone through a shredder, and I was having trouble concentrating. Daryn was right in front of me, but I had to keep telling myself that she was okay. That my mom and Anna were, too.

Marcus looked away, noticing the guy on the stoop.

"We had to leave," Daryn said. "I tried to get you on the radio. I know you wanted us to stay, but Alevar saw us, then left. We thought he was going to get the rest of the Kindred."

She looked at Marcus, waiting for him to jump in and help explain.

"Has he been there a while?" Marcus asked, his eyes still locked on Conquest.

"Ten minutes."

We didn't say another word, but we both knew what needed to happen. We took off like heat-seeking missiles.

Conquest jumped up when he saw us coming. He ran down the steps and tore down the street, but Marcus turned it up, cutting off his escape route. I came up behind him. We had him boxed in.

Conquest looked from Marcus to me, like he couldn't decide who posed the lesser threat. He faced me. Wrong choice.

"Hey, man," I said. "Are you Jode?"

"Who are you?" he said, scowling at me with bloodshot eyes.

No mistaking his accent. He was English. And rich, judging by his threads. Double-breasted coat. Fisherman-style, but the kind you saw on runways, not gangways. He was weaving in place and reeked of alcohol.

That sealed it for me. I hauled off and punched him.

He fell gracefully. Knee, hip, shoulder. Like some part of him had decided, *What the heck. I'm passing out tonight anyway. Might as well get started now.*

"Gideon!" Daryn gaped at me. "What did you *do*?" She rushed over, kneeling beside him.

There was no way to explain it all. I couldn't shake the fears Ra'om and Samrael had planted in my mind. Something felt different inside me. Darker. And we didn't have time to stand around and try to convince Conquest to join up. I wasn't going to say all that, so I shrugged and said, "I came. I saw. I conquered."

Daryn sprang up. "That's not funny!"

I hadn't intended it to be funny. But I didn't clarify that either. My logical, rational mind was slowly coming back online. I had to get us off the street. Daryn and Marcus had been spotted in the Fiat, so we had no wheels anymore. We also had no Sebastian, but my first priority was getting present company to a safe location.

I crouched by Conquest and rolled him onto his back. A bruise was spreading over his cheek where I'd hit him. He let out a big snore, which got a laugh out of Marcus that honestly surprised me. I hadn't known he *could* laugh. I pulled Conquest's sleeve up. His cuff was bright white and had clean lines, more like mine than Sebastian's and Marcus's. Right guy.

Then I checked the pockets of his fancy not-fishing coat and found a wallet made of butter-soft leather. Moving through the contents quickly, I came up with a small stack of euros in crisp new bills, credit cards, and a student ID for Oxford University issued to James Oliver Drummond Ellis. No wonder he went by Jode.

Between the wallet, his clothes, the gleaming watch at his wrist, and the pretty boy face, I was starting to worry I had a Wyatt Sinclair on my hands.

Checking his other pocket, I finally found what I wanted. I held up the hotel security card. "The Great Gatsby's staying in town." I pulled the radio from my pocket and checked the address on the GPS. "His hotel's less than three miles away."

"Really?" Daryn said. "That would be so *doable* if we could all *walk*."

Three minutes ago she'd been hugging me, all worried. Now she looked like she wanted to finish the job Samrael had started.

"No problem," I said. I grabbed Jode's arm and pulled him over my shoulder. Thankfully, he had a light build. A buck fifty and five-nine or so. Also thankfully, I'd done a lot of this in RASP. Carrying Cory on my back on forced road marches had prepared me. Cory was my size. One eighty and six-one. I knew I could handle Prince Conquest.

"Race you guys," I said, settling him over my shoulders.

Marcus and Daryn looked at me like I was a nut, which felt normal and gave me a needed morale boost. Then we were off, trudging along the dark city streets of Rome.

By the time we came to the Ponte Sant'Angelo, I was sweating bullets but the adrenaline was finally leaving my body. Some of the fear, too. But I still felt like if I closed my eyes for too long, the images Ra'om had shown me would come right back.

I tried to focus on my surroundings. According to my guidebook, the bridge had stood for almost two millennia. As I passed one angel statue after another, I felt the centuries the bridge had seen. All the days and nights it had spanned the waters of the Tiber below. Looking at it, I felt insignificant. Linked to every human on the planet. Everything seemed awesome now that I wasn't in the mental clutches of a demon.

"What are you thinking about?" Daryn asked. "At this very second?"

"I was thinking that this is great," I said.

"No, you weren't."

"Was so. I'm in the moment, Martin." This moment was a lot better than the ones I'd just been in.

We walked for a little more. Marcus was ahead of us, out of earshot. He wasn't clutching his shoulder anymore. Maybe it was already healing. "Is this really what you do all the time?" I asked. "Run all over the world like this?"

Daryn shook her head. "Not like this. This is by far the most challenging thing I've ever done." She glanced at me, her eyes sparkling. "In large part because of you."

I grinned. "But who doesn't love a good challenge, right?"

"Oh, I don't know. Sometimes a challenge is just a challenge," she said, but she was smiling.

Jode was feeling heavier by the minute, but I had to deal. I'd knocked him out. He was my responsibility. "So what's your typical kind of work?"

She shrugged. "There really is no typical. It's all kinds of stuff. Always different." She pulled her hair from beneath the strap of my backpack and twisted it into a knot. She was carrying both my pack and hers. "But for example, I've found lost hikers and helped them back to trails. I've kept a couple of kids from running into the streets. I've made *dozens* of emergency calls. I kept a scared woman company when her car was stranded on the side of the road in the Oregon wilderness. I've stopped four suicides. All amazing experiences. I've been to a lot of parties—high school and college—where I've prevented rape. Those make me sick. Physically, I feel ill after those. So . . . it's things like that. Smaller, you could say, compared to what we're doing. But still really important." She frowned. "Why do I tell you so much?"

"I don't know. Do you resent it?"

"Telling you stuff?" She smiled. "Yes. Every word."

"That hurts, Martin," I said, but I knew she liked talking to me. Probably not as much as I liked it. Everything she said only made her more incredible. And she was helping me forget Ra'om. "I meant being a Seeker."

"No, I don't resent it. It's not always easy but it's a privilege. It was harder in the beginning, before I got used to it. There was one point when I felt so lonely, I wasn't sure I could take it anymore. I ended up working with another Seeker, this really great woman named Isabel. She helped so much. She's the one who told me to start keeping a journal, which helps a lot, too. I see her once in a while, whenever I need her. She's become like an aunt to me. And there are people all over the world who open their homes to me. Good people who will feed me and give me a room to sleep for as long as I need it without asking any questions. I get to see so much kindness because of this. And I'm helping people. I can't think of anything I'd want to do more than that. What about you? Do you resent it?"

"Being a horseman?" I shifted Jode onto my left shoulder. "Undecided."

My gut was telling me that no, I didn't. I'd met her because of it. I'd seen some incredible things. I knew the answer to humankind's most fundamental question. I couldn't look at the stars without feeling like God was right there watching over me. Over *everything*. A lot of hugely positive aspects. The parts I didn't love were the Kindred. And Marcus. My horse. Maybe the rage powers. Dropping out of RASP had sucked. Making my mom worry did, too. And leaving the Jeep at LAX. But other than that, being a horseman was cool.

"I bet you've been wondering why this happened to you," Daryn said.

"You bet right."

"I wondered that a lot too in the beginning." She glanced at me. "But what if it's happening *for* you? I'm not saying it is. I'm just putting it forward as a possibility. But what would you think then?"

"That's deep, Martin. I need a second to think about that." I actually needed a rest. I set Jode down beneath one of the angel statues lining the bridge. A cold whip of air rushed across my sweaty back as I straightened.

"Blake," Marcus said, turning to me. "You feel that?"

"What is it?" Daryn asked.

"Not sure," I said. I scanned the streets in the distance. They were still. It was the quietest part of night, on the verge of morning. Then I saw a shadow slipping along the far banks of the river. It could have been Alevar but the cuff was sending me—and Marcus, apparently—undeniable Sebastian signals. As the shadow drew closer, zipping up the same bridge where we stood, I could see it more clearly. It looked like long smoky threads, dark and fluttering.

I thought I knew what this was, but I had to play it safe. I focused on the feeling I'd tapped into just an hour ago—a combination of *protect, defend, serve*—and connected with a thread of power inside me. A jolt ran through my hand and I saw a flash of fire, then the sword was mine.

Yes, yes, *yes*.

Marcus came over to us. He looked at me like, *oh, so we're doing that?* A moment later, a scythe-sized tornado of pale dust flowed from his hand down to the street, forming into his weapon.

The flurry of black smoke drew nearer and slowed a few feet away. From that moving darkness, a black hoof appeared, then another, then legs, shoulders, haunches, and on up. I'd seen Shadow materialize twice now, and I was no less amazed.

This time was different, though. Sebastian formed up right along with her. One moment I was looking at ribbons of smoke. The next, there he was. Mounted on Shadow. Sitting in a black saddle I'd never seen before. Wearing black clothes and light armor I had also never seen before.

He looked nothing like himself.

He looked impressive. And terrifying.

The only recognizable part of him was his gigantic grin, which disappeared when he saw Jode slumped under the statue.

"Whoa," Bas said. "What happened to *him*?"

Chapter 40

Five minutes later, we had secured Jode onto Shadow with some rope I had in my backpack. As I tethered Jode down, I took a look at Bas's armor and Shadow's saddle. They were made of material that felt like leather in places, and of the same substance as Bas's cuff in others. Like his cuff, his armor and saddle had intricate, webbed styling. I'd never seen anything like it.

I also got closer to Shadow than I'd ever been. She was incredible. All raw power beneath a coat as cool and soft as night. I tried not to think of my burning, mean-ass horse as we set off again.

We came across a few people on the streets, but no one paid us much attention. Horses had been clopping through Rome for a long time, and with the darkness, no one seemed to notice that Shadow was a little unusual.

Our luck changed when we reached Jode's hotel. The entrance was promenade-style, so the four valets manning the front doors got a good long eyeful of the five-plus-horse of us as we walked up. When we finally reached them, they looked completely at a loss for words.

"*Ciao, signores,*" I said, in a fine Italian-Californian accent. "We're bringing our buddy James Oliver Drummond Ellis back after a big night out for his birthday. Jode here went a little crazy with the celebrating, as you can see. Too much vino. But he gave me his key card before he passed out." I pulled it out of my pocket and held it up. "And what kinds of friends would we be if we didn't make sure he was tucked in safely?"

They looked at each other. Then the oldest one said, "*Perché hai un cavallo?* Why horse?"

"She's a birthday gift from his father," Daryn said. "Polo pony."

"Champion lines," I added, patting Shadow. "We're expecting a lot out of this girl."

Daryn smiled at me. "She'll deliver. She is a beauty, isn't she?"

Definitely. She definitely was.

"*Che meraviglia! Un regalo per el compleanno,*" the valet rushed to explain to the others. He looked back at me, pointing at his face. "Signore, your nose?"

"Oh, I did that," Daryn said. "He was hitting on me."

"Yep. So she hit back. Wicked right hook. Does that . . . does that translate?"

Sebastian muffled a laugh. He stood behind us with Shadow and passed-out Jode. Marcus was there, too, watching everything in silence. He looked like he was ready to spring into action at the first sign of any problem.

"We're fine now, though," I said to Daryn. "Aren't we fine?"

She shrugged. "I'm fine. I think your nose is broken."

These ludicrous fabrications seemed acceptable to the doormen because they were suddenly all goofy about Daryn and the pretty black horse and how funny my nose looked ha ha ha. From there, it was nothing to get their help tracking down Jode's room number. They wanted to help carry him up, but Daryn and I said we'd manage. We lifted him by the arms and carried him through the swankiest lobby I'd ever seen in my life.

Once we got to the room, I set Jode on the bed. "Don't get too comfortable," I told Daryn. Then I got on the hotel phone and requested a bigger room. I expected some kickback, since it was two a.m. by then, but my request was accepted right away. Apparently if money talked, nothing was chattier than Jode's bank account.

Fifteen minutes later, Marcus and Bastian were with us as we walked into the penthouse suite. They'd taken Shadow out to the hotel's garden, where Bas had discreetly unsummoned her.

In the suite, I dumped Jode in the first bedroom I saw, then took a look around. The suite's first floor had two bedrooms and a huge living room with a bar. Upstairs, there was a rooftop patio with a hot tub and a small garden. I had a pretty good eye for spotting quality in art, from listening to Anna my whole life. Everything in the suite was top-notch.

"This place has to be worth a fortune," Bastian said.

I looked at him and found myself smiling. He was my favorite fellow horseman, and I was glad to have him back. "We need the space and we couldn't stay in the other room. Find somewhere to crash."

He and Marcus collapsed on the couches before I'd finished speaking. After the cross-country flight, the fight at the airport, and then the fight at the Vatican, we were all smoked.

I looked at Daryn. "Hey, Martin." I tipped my head to the stairs. "You and me. Hot-tub time."

She rolled her eyes. "Keep dreaming." She set her backpack down on a chair. "Will you let me take a look at your nose?"

"Sure," I said. The way she was looking at me, I'd have said yes to anything.

We went to the bathroom that adjoined one of the bedrooms. I sat on the edge of the ornate marble tub as Daryn ran a towel under some water. She came over and knelt on the rug in front of me. Suddenly I wasn't tired anymore.

She scooted closer and pressed the towel to my nose. I had a cut the bridge. With the swelling, it'd been in my peripheral vision for a while but the pain felt distant. I knew I'd already begun to heal. And I was focused on one thing only, and it wasn't my nose.

"He did this?" she said. "Samrael?"

"No. Technically, I think I did it." I was pretty sure it'd happened when I slammed into him on the street.

I felt her eyes move to mine, but I kept my gaze on the pulse beating at her throat. The necklace was right there. I didn't want to think about it right now.

She dabbed at the cut and around my mouth and chin. I felt weird having her clean up after me. Mopping up my dried blood and snot. There were a lot of things I wouldn't have minded happening between us. This wasn't on the list.

"We have to start acting together," she said.

"We will," I said. We were up against forces that were far more powerful than any one of us. Our only shot was by working together. But my team—an actor, a drunk, and a sociopath—didn't exactly inspire confidence. Still. I had to find a way to work with them. "I met Ra'om tonight."

I wasn't sure why I'd added that. I just couldn't stop thinking about him. I couldn't stop seeing his red eyes in the darkness. I couldn't think of Anna without picturing her ripping at her face. All the images were right there. Lurking. It felt like Ra'om had planted land mines in my brain.

Daryn drew the towel away. "I thought you might have." She sank onto her ankles and looked at me. "You're . . . okay?"

"Yeah." I made myself hold in place.

She stayed watching me for a long moment. Then she stood and rinsed out the towel. "Tomorrow," she said. Then she came back for another pass on my nose. "We're all together now. Tomorrow I'll tell you more."

I nodded and we went quiet for a little while. I knew we were almost done. She'd leave soon, and I didn't want that. "You told me your sister wanted to be a doctor. You, too? You seem pretty good at this."

"No. Not me."

"What did little Daryn want to be when she grew up? You owe me three more answers. You promised at the airport. I think you promised me ten, but I'll settle for three. Time to pay up."

She smiled. "Okay. Three more. Little Daryn hadn't thought

past college when her life was turned upside down. But the one thing she knew was that she wanted to keep running. She'd run track in high school."

That made a lot of sense. "What event?"

"Hurdles."

"Hot, Martin. And cool. Really cool."

"Thanks. I loved it. I was good at it, too. You're fast. Both you and Marcus."

"I'm faster. I could beat him."

Daryn laughed but I wasn't sure why that was funny.

She swept her hair behind her ear. "Okay. Second thing?"

"Fifth. Let's just keep numbering up instead of doing two rounds of three."

"We could recategorize this set as A, B, C?"

"If we were trying to make me unhappy, we could."

She shook her head. "You're so odd. Okay, fifth." She stared at the fancy wallpaper, narrowing her eyes in thought. Her mouth was curved into a smile, and she looked incredible.

I wanted to kiss her neck. Kind of badly. I also kind of wanted to bite her, too. Not to hurt her, of course. She just looked so good. All that smooth skin. She made me feel a little vampirish and crazy. I wanted to be all over her. Always. But especially when she was this close.

"I'm obsessed with Amelia Earhart," she said. "I dressed up as her for Halloween, like, ten years in a row. Every picture of me as a girl, I'm wearing aviator goggles. Not up on my head, either. I actually wore them."

"Over your eyes?"

She laughed. "Yes. I wanted to see the world the way she saw it. I had her short hair and everything. And I made everyone call me Amelia in second grade and through half of third. I still wish that was my name. Amelia Martin."

"Not as good as what you got. Daryn's perfect. Your name is. For you."

"Ew, but thanks. It's a family name." She paused, smiling at some memory. "I think running hurdles . . . I think it came out of wanting to fly."

She'd stopped fixing up my nose a little while ago. I took the towel from her and tossed it in the sink. I'd been hanging on her every word, but it didn't feel like I was getting enough. Like *we* were close enough.

"Come here," I said, pulling her up beside me.

I could tell she didn't expect that because she went quiet. For a little while, everything was quiet and we just looked at our legs. I liked her legs even better now that I knew she was a hurdler. They were strong legs that could move fast *and* jump. Badass. Didn't get any cooler than that. I liked her name better too. I felt defensive about it for her.

"Number six is kind of a confession." She peered at me sideways, letting out a slow breath. "I don't like Pearl Jam. I mean, I didn't until I met you. In your Jeep that day on the way to Los Angeles, I wanted you to like me so I might have played it up. The funny thing is, I think I'm actually starting to love Pearl Jam now, for real. One of those self-fulfilling prophecies."

"You know I like you."

I took her hands, and ran my thumbs over her knuckles. They were strong and soft, like she was. I couldn't believe the things we were saying. "I wish I didn't like you . . . but I do."

"Daryn, I want to kiss you, but I don't want to scare you away."

"Are you that bad at it?"

"Ouch. That's cold, Martin. And for the record, I excel at anything I apply myself—"

She darted in and her mouth was against mine. Making quick, gentle brushes, then it was over.

"I was worried I'd hurt your nose," she said. "That's why I . . ."

Her cheeks had gone pink.

"You didn't. My turn now?"

"Yes," she said right away.

I turned so I had one leg in the tub, then I shifted her hips my way and brought her a little closer.

"Gideon, what are you doing?"

"Just trust," I said. Then I took her face in my hands and went for it. As soon as we touched, she looped her arms around my neck, I pulled her against me, and then we were both gone. Our *I like yous* were in our mouths, our tongues, our hands. We were wrong-footed around each other so often, but not now. We were finally being honest. Completely real with each other. I'd never felt that way before. So much. So intensely. I never wanted to stop feeling that way. Then she drew away. Too soon again. But I was starting to see that I'd never feel like I got enough of her.

Her arms came down, wrapping around my waist, and she rested her head on my shoulder.

I needed a second to touch back down to earth. Get back in my right mind. Daryn's closeness wasn't helping that process along. Neither was her warm breath on my neck.

I wove my fingers into her hair. It was soft and wavy, and the color was gold in some places and went all the way to dark brown in others. No one had better hair. "I can't believe I kissed you for the first time in a bathroom."

She was holding on to me pretty tight. "What bathroom?"

I smiled. That was a good sign. "I want a shot at re-creating this in a better location. At least we weren't sitting on the toilet together, but a bathtub isn't—"

She let go of me and straightened. She wasn't smiling. The look on her face put a fist to my stomach.

She looked *sorry*.

"Okay." I nodded. "Okay. I understand. I guess we're not doing this again."

"*Do* you understand? When this is over, I don't want you to be another thing I miss."

The steadiness was gone from her eyes. There was a storm in them now.

"I don't want to be another thing either," I said.

"I didn't mean it that way, Gideon. I didn't mean for this to happen. It's just . . . you make me forget. I forget about everything when I'm with you."

"Daryn, I said I understand." I couldn't look her in the eye any longer. My gaze dropped to the silver chain.

"We can be friends, though. We can find a way . . . right?"

I wanted to say yes, but I couldn't lie to her. I didn't know if I could be her friend. I didn't have the clarity to make that call right then. I felt numb.

I felt nothing, so I didn't say anything.

Which was probably answer enough.

CHAPTER 41

The lightbulb finally quits and the room goes dark. Instant curtain drop. Darkness, like Alevar is behind it. Black so deep I can almost feel it. Cordero. Texas and Beretta. The pine walls. Everything's wiped out.

My breathing is the only sound, and it's fast. This is too much like when I saw Ra'om. But I know I'm fine. Still here in this chair, talking my head off, thanks to these drugs. Then I remember the things I just said and wince.

What the hell, Blake? Talk about the Kindred, fine. Talk about Marcus, Bas, and Jode. Talk about anything but her.

I want the gag back. Someone needs to unshackle me so I can punch myself.

Cordero lets out a long sigh. "Budget cuts," she says. "Can one of you run down a replacement, please?"

The door opens, and light and sound pour in. There's a discussion going on out in the hallway. Not a friendly one. I only hear a piece of it before Beretta steps out, shutting the door behind him.

"We can still continue this way. Can't we?" Cordero asks.

"You mean I can."

The radiator starts going again. Why are sounds so much clearer and louder in the darkness?

"Yes, of course. I meant you," she says. "Is it getting harder for you to talk about this?"

Is this getting harder for me? Yes. My thoughts are clearing. I almost feel normal again. Which is feeling like I don't want to cooperate.

"Gideon?"

"Sorry. I was just thinking for a second."

"Then this is getting harder for you. If it's helpful, we can give you another dose."

"Of the drugs?" Is she kidding? Yeah, right. Like I'm taking *that* offer. "No, I'm good. Why'd you bother with them in the first place?"

"I thought I explained that when we started. You were belligerent when I tried talking to you, and when you were first picked up in Jotunheimen. I understand your anger better now, of course."

"Because I'm War."

"Yes. And it couldn't have been easy when Daryn stayed in Norway instead of evacuating with you."

Wait.

Wait.

Did I tell her that?

I know I've *thought* it a lot. But have I actually *said* it?

Why would I have said it? I haven't gotten to that part of things yet. I'm almost sure I haven't.

Did she hear it from Daryn?

From the other guys?

I stare into the darkness, wishing I could see her face.

The radiator shuts off. My entire focus goes to the smells washing into my nose. Her perfume. Citrus and roses. And that musty smell. I *know* that stench.

"Everything okay, Gideon?"

"Yes," I say. But I don't think it is.

I need a chance to *think*.

"Then let's start again. Why don't we pretend this is a campfire story? Without the campfire, of course."

Keep it steady, Blake. Everything stays the same.

"Sure. We can pretend."

CHAPTER 42

It was Jode's fancy British voice I heard as I shuffled into the suite's living room the following morning, rubbing sleep out of my eyes.

He was pacing in front of the sofa, his blond hair sticking up like a troll figurine's. In the daylight, I was able to get a better look at him. He had a keen look in his eyes and ruddy cheeks, like he'd been out in cool weather. In his rumpled designer clothes, he looked less like he was hungover; more like he'd just stepped off a yacht. Daryn, Bas, and Marcus were spread out around the area, giving him a rundown of our situation.

I noticed that the key was resting on the chain around Daryn's neck—in plain sight. Morning sunlight poured in through the balcony, making it gleam. Apparently that piece was common knowledge now. I needed a second to get a handle on how that made me feel, which was not very special, even though I accepted that it might be the best thing for the group.

"I understand what you think is happening," Jode said. "But I can't get involved in this." He stopped pacing when he saw me. "Oh, good." He flipped a hand my way. "Here he is now. Welcome to the gathering, War. You got us this suite, didn't you? Which I'm paying for? Thank you for that."

"You're welcome," I said. I dropped on the couch and rubbed my eyes again, then my head, trying to get my brain going. I'd slept like crap. Most of the night, I'd dreamt of the images Ra'om had shown me. Even now, they seemed close. I felt like I had an evil residue inside my head.

"I know this is a lot to take in," Daryn said to Jode, "but

you have to try to accept it. We're still in danger, and that includes you, whether you like it or not. The Kindred won't be far. With all of you together, they'll be able to track us faster."

"You told me they're attracted to the key," I said.

Daryn looked at me. Straight on. Her bronzed skin seemed pale this morning, and there were faint circles under her eyes, like she hadn't slept great, either.

I'd decided to put what happened between us behind me. I needed to stay focused. I had to finish this horseman stuff so I could get back my life.

"They are," she said. "But they have other ways of tracking us, too."

They did, and I was starting to figure those out. I sat over my knees and cleared my throat. Then I told them what had happened to me on the street the night before. Finishing with that, I moved right on and described the Kindred's capabilities as I saw them.

Alevar had the night wings and could fly. We had to assume he was soaring around, looking for us. Samrael could see into our minds. Any plans we made were subject to being brain-hacked if he got close enough. He could also pull knifelike bone shards from his arm. I didn't know what Ronwae could do, but the way she shimmered worried me, like maybe she was having a hard time holding on to her human form. The female with the dreadlocks was another question mark, but there'd been something werewolfish about the way she'd prowled— and howled. Malaphar had the ability to shift form and mimic others. Pyro was the insane, fire-throwing skater dude. And Ra'om. He was in a category of his own. I'd only seen him in my mind, but I had no doubt he was real.

As I spoke, Jode stopped pacing and sat down to listen. It hit me that we were finally together, the five of us. With Bas, Jode, and Marcus there, I felt like I was getting a full chord now from the cuff—a complete signal—but it was more than

that. It was a feeling of accomplishment for having success-
fully mustered up.

When I was done, Jode pressed the heels of his hands into
his eyes. "So we're not the only ones who have these abilities,
then?"

Bastian broke into a grin. "Tell Gideon what yours is."

Jode's gaze landed on him. "I don't think it's relevant to the
discussion."

"What is it?" I looked at Marcus, but that wasn't going to
get me anywhere. He was slumped in a wingback chair, hiding under the hood of his sweatshirt like we weren't worth his
time. "What's his power, Bas?"

"He makes people want stuff."

"It's not *stuff*," Jode said. "As far as I can tell, I enhance *will*.
Determination. Whatever a person's foremost desire is."

"Wait. Your power is enhancing *desire*?"

Why-oh-why wasn't that *my* power?

"Yeah, and get this," Bas said. "For me and Marcus it was
the desire to eat. We emptied the minibar half an hour ago.
Marcus almost tore the door off trying to get it open."

"Wait. You used your power on them?" I asked.

The red in Jode's cheeks went deeper. "It was unintentional."

"He's still figuring out how to control it," Daryn said.

"The only thing that's helped is getting plastered."

"That's why he'd been drinking last night," Daryn explained. "I had Sebastian give him a bump of fatigue, which
seems to be a good substitute."

"It was a good idea," Jode said.

I looked from him to her and back again. Why did I suddenly feel like I wanted to hit something?

"What's our next move, Martin?" I asked. "Do we know
where we need to go? Because that would really help. Instead
of running around with the key, it'd be great if we could just
put it somewhere safe. Can we do that? Or is that another

thing we don't know? Probably, right? Otherwise this would be too easy. You know, sometimes it actually feels like you're working for the Kindred? I'm almost tempted to ask you to prove you're not Malaphar."

Whoa, whoa, whoa, Blake. What the hell was that?

I broke it down. Tired. No sleep. Rejected. Yes to all, but this was something else. It was that residue of darkness from Ra'om. I couldn't shake it off. It was beating me down. Now I'd crossed a line and everyone else thought so, too.

Tension filled the room. More than tension. The room filled with the anger that poured off me.

Marcus sat up and stared at me. Intense. Ready to pounce.

I had to make a smart next move, or I knew we'd end up brawling again.

Balcony. Balcony for some air.

"Actually," Daryn said. "I'm glad you said something."

"You're . . . *glad*?" I settled back onto the cushions.

"Yes," she said. "Malaphar is how this got started. Like you said, he can cloak himself in a person's voice and image. That was how the Kindred almost took the key the first time."

She paused, looking at each of us. Traffic from the city streets roared softly in the distance, filtering in from the balcony. I could feel her calm settling over us. Telling us to listen up. Big stuff was coming.

"The key has always been in the protection of one of the archangels. It was in Michael's possession until recently, when he alighted on a cliff in a place called Lagos in Portugal. A very old Seeker who lived there was close to dying, and being welcomed to the afterlife by an archangel is a privilege we're given for our service. The Kindred saw an opportunity.

"I know that Samrael couldn't have looked into the Seeker's mind and foreseen this meeting taking place. It's a way that we're stronger than them. But he must have had one of his Kindred follow the Seeker, waiting for the right moment. When

Michael appeared on the cliffs, several of the Kindred were hidden close by—and one in particular was *very* close. I'm sure you've already figured out that the old man who met Michael wasn't actually the Seeker. It was Malaphar, in the Seeker's form.

"The archangel recognized the deception, but it was too late. A struggle resulted between them. In the struggle, Malaphar pried the key from Michael's hands. It fell and struck the rocks of the cliff, tumbling away. Then it disappeared. Michael freed himself from Malaphar's grip, but the rest of the Kindred were coming. The key was safe for the moment. Well hidden. The Kindred wouldn't find it in the rocks below, so Michael fled. When the time was right, he would send someone to collect the key. And that someone . . ." Daryn's smile was somehow modest and proud at the same time. "That someone is me."

She smoothed her hands on her jeans. Calm. Taking her time.

I couldn't believe I was looking at a girl who knew angels.

"I've known about Malaphar for a while, but I didn't want to say anything before now. You had so much else to adjust to." She looked from me to Marcus. "And some of you didn't trust each other from the start. I worried it would've made things worse. What if you started to suspect each other? Or me? Or *everyone*? Can you imagine if I'd added that doubt?"

I could easily imagine it.

Malaphar. As anyone.

"It seemed better to hold on to it," Daryn continued. "I guess I think you should trust people before you doubt them. But now I see that it was naive. I think I'm the one who got us in trouble at the airport yesterday. I've been trying to figure out how they knew we'd be there. How they were waiting for us. In LA, did any of you tell someone where we were going?"

"Gideon, the bank," Sebastian said. "Remember the teller who gave me all the key chains?"

Marcus leaned over his legs, his hood shifting over his eyes. "The store where we got the radios. The guy working there kept asking about our trip and what we needed for it. Being friendly like that. I thought he was doing his job."

Daryn let out a long sigh. "Malaphar could've been either one of them. I should've warned you guys. I'm sorry, I've just . . ." Her eyes darted to me. "I've just been on my own for a long time."

"It's all right, Daryn," I said. "It's done." I didn't want her stewing over past mistakes. I'd made plenty of them myself. And we needed to get moving. The Kindred had backed off last night, but who knew how long we had? Once we were in a safe place, we could evaluate and plan. But this hotel room wasn't that safe place.

We established a few safety measures. We wouldn't talk to anyone outside our group. And we'd keep close tabs on Daryn from now on. Not only because of Malaphar. She had the key.

"What does the key do again?" Jode asked. "I don't think I got that part."

"If the Kindred gain control of it, they'll open a realm where they'll rule," Daryn said.

"Rule who?" Jode asked, rubbing his forehead. He looked almost catatonic. He was hearing all of this for the first time.

"As many innocent people as they can claim," she said. "Kingdoms need subjects."

"So they're going to kidnap innocent people and take them there?" Bastian asked. "But *why?*"

"To grow stronger. They're fed by destroying the good in human souls."

No.

No, no, no.

That was what I was feeling?

I'd given Ra'om a *meal*?

Okay, Blake. Easy. The missing piece of your goodness will grow back.

"We need to roll," I said, coming to my feet. I couldn't sit anymore. "Let's focus on getting to a safe location. Then we'll get down to work."

While everyone packed up, Jode and I left the suite and went back to the room he'd been checked into originally. It was still registered under his name, and he had left some money in the safe. I'd told him to leave it—we'd enjoyed almost seven Kindred-free hours and I wanted to keep it going—but when Jode had told me how much it was, I'd agreed. We had to go back for it.

We took the stairs as a precaution. I summoned my sword, which made Jode swear in ways that would've impressed even my Army buddies.

"Is this cloak-and-dagger business really necessary?" he asked as we went down two flights.

"Yes. Now, shut it. Please." I opened the door into the hallway.

The door was heavy but it hung on smooth, well-oiled hinges. It didn't make a sound—not to my ears—but Alevar heard it.

Out in the hallway, his head whipped to me and Jode. His black wings were curved close to his body, and for a moment he looked like a giant beetle staring at us. In the confines of the hallway, with its lush carpet and gilded wallpaper, he looked more terrifying than ever.

Jode cursed behind me. "What in the bloody hell is that?"

At the sound of his voice, Alevar scurried over.

I jumped back into the stairwell, pulling the door closed, but Alevar's hand shot through and grabbed my wrist. A hot jolt washed over me—and I locked up.

Stalemate.

Alevar crouched in the hallway; I stood in the stairwell. The door was halfway open between us. I had brought my sword arm up in our scuffle. The tip was pressed into Alevar's wrinkled neck.

I had also called up my armor.

I felt it, covering me from neck to feet, a sturdy weightless suit that fit like I'd been born to it.

"Let me go," I said.

He smelled foul, and had a steel grip on my forearm. As he stared at me with his milky eyes, eyes full of pleading, I wondered—had *he* been bled of goodness? Had there ever been any good in him?

"What's he *doing*?" Jode said behind me.

With shocking suddenness, Alevar released me and spun, unfurling his wings. They snapped open like sails catching the wind, slapping against the walls of the hallway.

From beyond him I heard footsteps, then a woman's voice. "This one, Bay. This is the one here."

Ronwae. I'd only heard her speak once, at Joy's party, but I recognized her strange gargled accent.

Jode tugged me back by the arm, but I shook my head. We couldn't move. I couldn't let go of the door. Alevar's wings were keeping us concealed but if we made any noise, we were done for.

The floor beneath me shuddered like someone had dropped a car. Then I heard a low growl and a sound like a viper's rattle.

Alevar shifted slightly. Through his long black feathers, I saw pieces of the hallway. Two creatures were there. One was a kind of scorpion mutation with a thick reddish shell, massive front claws, and a stinger rising from its back. It rattled softly, and shimmered the way I'd seen Ronwae shimmer—movement so fast it was a blur. Smaller creatures scurried all over the scorpion-thing, minute versions of it. This was Ronwae, I knew instantly. The other creature was a furry, stoop-backed beast. A hybrid between a boar and a bear, but deformed. With large humps on its back and limbs. Fangs and claws made to shred. It was the dreadlocked female demon—Bay.

As I watched, she lifted onto her thick hind legs and turned her shoulder, pressing it against the door of the room where Jode and I had been heading. The jamb groaned, then gave with a splintering *crunch,* and they disappeared inside.

In moments, shattering sounds filled the hallway.

Serious demolition.

Alevar's wings folded closed. He turned, looking at me with his apologetic face. Then he crawled after the two female Kindred, leaving us there.

CHAPTER 43

A ny particular reason why you've paused here, Gideon?"
Because I feel sick.
Because I can't keep talking anymore.
Because I know who you are.
"No. I'm fine."
"You're sure? Do you need more water?"
"I'm fine."
"The dark isn't scaring you? I have to admit it's scaring me a little bit. These demons you're describing sound dreadful. I'd hate to see one up close."

My muscles have turned to stone.

All I smell is Malaphar's stench.

It's been him this entire time.

Keep going, Blake. No change.

But everything just changed.

CHAPTER 44

Jode and I went back for the others, then we tore out of the hotel, charging into broad daylight.

Rome was alive and kicking. We pushed through streets bustling with swarms of tourists and locals on their morning commute. A few people snapped photos of me with their phones. I hadn't ditched my armor yet because I *couldn't* ditch my armor. I tried to tap into that focus—the inner switch I was beginning to find with the sword—but it didn't work. I couldn't un-armor, so I had to stay fluid and go with it. It wasn't the first time Rome had seen War.

As I led us to the nearest train station, I kept checking behind us for the Kindred. Then again, Malaphar could've been anyone on the street. We had to press forward and hope for the best. When we reached the station, Jode took over and handled the purchase of our tickets.

"Milan," he said, as he led us to the platform. The train was already there, passengers stepping aboard. "But we can transfer there and keep going. Switzerland, Germany, Denmark, Sweden. As far as we want, as long as we stay within the Eurail system."

"We don't have passports," I said, following him through the train.

"It's taken care of."

"You'd better not have used your name."

"I'm not an idiot, Gideon," he said. "I worked out a financial arrangement with the clerk. It's taken care of."

He took us to a premium car, which was only half full. We moved to the last two empty rows. Sebastian tossed his backpack down.

"It's taken care of," he said, in a spot-on imitation of Jode's voice. Then he sprawled out across the two seats on that side of the aisle. Marcus claimed the other side for himself. At the last row, Jode went left. Daryn went right. I froze.

Daryn scooted over, making room for me. In ten minutes, the train had accelerated to more than a hundred miles an hour. I let my head fall back against my seat. I was finally breathing evenly. It looked like we'd make a clean getaway.

As the adrenaline faded away, I started to regret sitting next to Daryn. The silence between us felt tense. I stared laser beams at the seat back in front of me, trying not to think about how I'd treated her earlier. Or how it'd felt when I'd kissed her. Or when she'd shut me down.

I flinched when her hand came to my shoulder, not expecting it.

"This is amazing," she said quietly. Her fingers drifted over the material of my suit, exploring. "Can we talk, Gideon?" she asked.

I didn't deserve the concern I saw in her eyes, but I wanted it. The problem was that I wanted a lot more than her concern. "Sure," I said. "What's up?"

I had to find a way to deal. We had to be able to work together.

Bastian popped over the seat in front of us. "I'm going to the food cart, does anyone—whoops, sorry. I didn't know you were . . ." He sank back out of sight.

Daryn turned toward the window, resting her head against it. A few minutes later, she was asleep.

That was pretty much the rest of Italy. Daryn, sleeping against the window beside me.

I slept too, until Venice, where I woke up in my regular clothes, no more armor. I was glad, but a little disappointed too. My armor had instantly become my favorite piece of horseman gear. After wearing it, my shirt and cargos felt too flimsy and loose. Nowhere near as comfortable.

In Venice, we transferred immediately to another train. We went on, taking whichever northbound trains left the soonest, went the fastest, and made the fewest stops. In Switzerland, we got a sleeper car with four beds and a small sitting area. Since there were five of us, the couch became my bed. In the privacy of our own car, we were able to talk about the Kindred. Somewhere around Frankfurt, I started making a list of their strengths and weaknesses. I worried about the tiny Ronwaes I'd seen crawling all over her body. Jode did, too.

"Like hordes," he'd said. And pointed out something I hadn't considered. Bay had had lumps under her thick grizzled pelt. I'd thought they were just part of her build. She'd been stacked with muscles. But Jode thought there was something more to them and came up with the theory that Bay also had tiny she-wolves, only they were hanging out *inside* of her. As I thought back, I agreed it was definitely possible. The female demons might actually be multitudes. From this we concluded that we were in even bigger trouble than we'd previously thought.

With Jode on the team, we would add a bow to our arsenal—Conquest's weapon. Not that he'd seen it yet. But even with that addition, I wasn't sure how we'd do against hordes. It just didn't feel like we had enough.

We learned a few things about each other during those couple of days on the trains, too. Made a little small talk. We were still basically strangers, but we all tried. Except Marcus, who didn't try at all.

Jode was nineteen, like Sebastian. He'd grown up in London and was in his first year at Oxford. The Ellises had owned land for generations but had recently—as in this century—

expanded into banking. From what I gathered, his family was in the business of making truckloads of money.

Jode knew about everything. We learned that we could throw out any random name or place, and he could Jodepedia it for us. The flip side was he came off a little superior sometimes. A lot of the time. Until his power came up. The ability to raise *will* leaned a lot toward raising *emotion,* and that just did not fly with the ole' British stiff upper lip. On the upside, he was able to figure out how to control it without Bas's help.

Jode told us that when his life had been turned upside down after an accident, he'd gone to the Vatican, hoping to find answers in the Vatican Library. He and I didn't talk about how he'd stood by while I'd coughed up a lung, or how I'd punched him for it. We were able to put our past behind us. Unlike Marcus and me.

Bastian was the fifth of seven kids. He was born in Nicaragua but his family had moved to Miami when he was little. He'd mostly grown up around there, then relocated to Los Angeles a year ago to pursue acting. He didn't say so but I could tell he came from pretty humble roots—the opposite of Jode—and I had a pretty strong feeling Marcus was in the same camp.

Bas was the entertainer of the group. He had stories about everything, all extremely random and great. He'd say these things like, "Hey, G. Did I ever tell you my truffle story?" And you'd wonder how a truffle story could possibly be any good. Next thing you knew you were howling. You were picturing Bas coughing up truffles like owl pellets into a prop sink in front of fifty people. We got along pretty good, Bas and me.

Bas also mentioned that his life went sideways after an accident and, just by coincidence, we figured out that we'd all had those cuff-delivering "accidents" on the same exact day. August second. We knew we'd actually died on that day, or should've died, but we didn't talk about the details. Too personal. On a couple of levels, for me. My dad had died on that same day, only a year earlier.

Marcus slept through most of Central Europe. On purpose, I thought. But Daryn and I came to a sort of unspoken truce. We started treating each other like business associates or something, which was weird. It was weird for all of us. Everyone knew it was weird. But it was the best I could do, and same for her, probably.

She didn't share much about herself, unsurprisingly. Mostly, she wrote in her journal and listened to us, or talked about mission-relevant topics, except for once when she told us she'd grown up in Connecticut. A swanky sounding place called Darien.

"Daryn from Darien," she'd said. "Go ahead and laugh."

Coincidentally, Jode knew Darien, Connecticut. He'd yachted there or something, so they talked for a little while about that, which was adorable. Rich people comparing notes on their country clubs and summer homes always warmed my heart. Bastian and I sort of just listened like paupers.

I did some sharing of my own. A little about Anna. A little less about the Army. Not much, though. I felt claustrophobic and edgy. Not like myself. I knew it was still the aftereffect of Ra'om and Samrael in my head. We'd left them behind, I was pretty sure, but the nightmares stayed with me. My only defense was staying awake, which I did until I couldn't. When I did sleep my mind ran a loop of my dad falling off that roof. Samrael's arm around Daryn. My mom grieving. Anna losing her mind.

Brutal. A brutal, brutal loop that never lost its power. It gutted me every time.

If this was a taste of what the Kindred wanted to do to people, a whole *realm* built for this kind of abuse and torture . . .

I had to stop them.

We needed to get that key back where it belonged.

CHAPTER 45

The door opens and Beretta appears, flooded by the light from the hallway, a new bulb in his hand.

Cordero stares at me in the semidarkness as he steps inside and removes the old bulb, replacing it with the new one. The lamp goes on and she's still staring at me.

He is still staring.

It.

Malaphar.

Now that I know, I can't see how I missed it before. The concentration in those black eyes isn't human. The way Malaphar has scratched and rubbed at his hands and knuckles. I had thought it was a habit but it's not. It's the tick of a demon, taking on the shape of a body that's just a little too small. And his death reek. He made a good attempt at masking it with perfume. Now it's so strong. It's blatant.

I don't know how to think of him. It's Malaphar, but I still see a woman in front of me. It's him, but it's her.

Cordero. I need to think of him as Cordero.

No change, Blake. Or he'll know.

"You were giving me such an immersive first-person perspective," Cordero says once Beretta's back in his post by the door. "Now you're summarizing. Getting antsy to finish this up?"

Behind me the radiator's clanging away. It needs to stop. My face is burning. This entire room feels too warm.

"I didn't realize I was doing that," I say.

"No. I guess you didn't. Which reminds me." Cordero checks her watch. "It's time for another dose."

"I told you I don't need it." I can't go back into the fog. Not now. "I'm cooperating, aren't I?"

Cordero's smile is thin, no teeth. "Yes, but things are going so well as they are. No need to change our modus operandi, is there?"

There is every reason to change our modus operandi, but none that I can verbalize. I still can't summon my sword or armor but I'm close.

I need an hour. Maybe less.

I need time.

I need to figure out why he's here.

Why is Malaphar back?

Same reason Daryn's here. It has to be.

They missed something.

What did they miss?

I need time to think.

And I need to recruit help.

"Don't you trust me, Cordero? I've been nothing but honest with you. I've been sitting here, tied up, telling you everything for the past few hours. Don't I deserve a little credit?" I look right at Texas. "Am I off base here? Because I feel like I deserve a gold medal for being such a good detainee."

His reaction to the code word is no reaction. Same with Beretta.

Nothing.

Not a blink, twitch, or hitch in their breath.

Are they that good? That cool under pressure? Or did they miss it? Or are they confused because it's not a perfect message? I'm not trying to tell them to keep quiet. I'm trying to tell them that a demon's sitting right in front of them.

"You are being very cooperative, Gideon, but you still need the dose. Don't take it personally. It's simply a safety measure."

Cordero looks to Beretta but Texas is the one to step forward. "We each had one dose," he says. He kneels in front of me, snapping on the latex gloves. Behind him, Beretta points the pistol at me.

Texas looks up. On his face is an expression I can't figure out, but that maybe is apology for what he's about to do. So much for gold freakin' medals. *Shit.*

He takes the hypodermic needle from a small black pouch, along with a square of cotton, then he pulls up my sleeve and presses the needle to my skin. I feel cool moisture as he depresses the plunger. The dose meant to go in my veins is absorbed into the cotton square.

Not into me.

Texas turns casually as he stands, making sure Cordero sees the spent syringe.

I have to drop my head because I know the relief's showing on my face. *Yes.* I have a man on my side. He knows something's wrong and Beretta must, too.

It's a start.

Now I just need time. A chance to think. To let the last of the drugs burn off.

Cordero asks me to pick up where I left off. "You were on your way to Norway," she says. "To Jotunheimen, I'm guessing. I think that's where all those trains eventually brought you. Am I right?"

I take a second to tap into the feeling I had last time when I actually got the dose. Like I had clouds inside my head. I think of Sebastian and how he can make even breathing mean something. Convey something.

I need to sell this for it to work. I need to come across as the same old gut-spilling Gideon. Bad way to put it. The same *uncensored* Gideon.

Act blunt on the outside. Get sharper on the inside.

I can do this.

CHAPTER 46

Norway was Jode's idea. We needed a safe, remote place where the four of us could work on mastering our weapons while Daryn waited for her next directive. Jode assured us Norway fit the bill.

After almost three days on trains, we arrived at the Oslo station around midday. Jode left with Daryn to go work some Ellis money magic at various travel agencies inside the station. An hour later, they came back with keys to a Mercedes van and a hold on a cabin in Jotunheimen National Park.

The former was purchased outright, in euros. The latter was free—part of a system of huts the Norwegian government provided for the pure enjoyment of the great outdoors.

This seemed a little too easy to me. It felt like were winging some pretty important stuff, but Jode knew more about Norway than I did, meaning he knew *something* about it. I had no choice but to roll with it.

Before we headed into the mountains, we stopped at a market and loaded up on food and supplies to last us a few weeks. Essentials like rice and beans. Canned soup. Crackers and chocolate bars. Then we left Oslo and drove past some of the most stunning vistas I'd ever seen in my life. Smooth winding rivers that cut through soaring mountains. Bright blue glaciers nestled in ridges. Waterfalls that dropped hundreds of feet into vivid green forests. After the past days crammed in train cars, not sleeping, on edge from Ra'om's effect on me, the views and the fresh air restored me some.

Finally, with nothing around us but raw, unspoiled nature, we reached a tiny tourist stop where a woman gave us a map and instructions for reaching our hut. There were no more roads now. We had to go the rest of the way on foot.

By then, it was getting late in the afternoon and an approaching storm was bringing in strong winds and cooler temperatures. I was tempted to spend the night in the van, considering the group's safety, but everyone else was determined to sleep in a place that was completely stationary.

We pulled on our packs and set off on a trail that climbed through dense alpine forest. Over an hour later, the trees thinned, the wind picked up, and the trail turned into pure ankle-twisting, rocky misery. Below us, a network of fjords spread out, their waters so calm they mirrored the dark clouds above perfectly.

"Where the hell are we going, Jode?" I'd already asked for the location and marked it on my GPS. But I was feeling the seventy pounds of food and supplies on my back. The cadre in RASP would've given this hike their stamp of approval.

"You told me remote," Jode replied. "Remote requires a good bit of trekking."

"You mean hiking."

"No, Gideon. I mean *trekking*."

We'd been doing that a lot, Jode and I. I'd become a human autocorrect for all his weird British phrases. He used *fancy* as a verb. *Nosh* meant food. *Bum* was ass. *Loo* was bathroom. And everything was either *bloody, brilliant,* or both, *bloody brilliant,* which to me only described one thing. Actually three: the color of my cuff, my sword, and my armor. They really were *bloody brilliant.*

"We should almost be there," Daryn said. She was carrying a pack as heavy as mine, and didn't looked winded at all. Tough girl. Tough, pretty girl.

Eyes down, Blake. Focus on the trail.

"We were told this hut is so far off the main trails, it never gets used," she added.

"And it's free, right?" Bas said, huffing at my side. He grinned at me, his teeth a white flash in the stormy light. "So it's afjordable."

That made me laugh, which I needed. A free cottage hours away from the nearest sign of civilization sounded like the opening to a horror movie to me—and I'd actually seen creatures that belonged in horror movies. I knew they were real so I wasn't exactly feeling calm.

We arrived at the location as the last bit of daylight faded out of the sky. I studied it as we approached. The location was incredible—a bluff that jutted right over a fjord, providing panoramic views of mountain ranges as far as the eye could see. But our shelter itself wasn't as impressive.

There were actually two small huts on the bluff. As we drew closer, I noticed the nearest one had a partially collapsed roof and a missing door. The other was built right into the hillside and was only slightly larger than the outhouse farther up on the hill. The hut appeared to be uninhabited, but I went ahead and checked things out first. Approaching with my sword—wishing it was my M4—I cleared the tiny cabin, finally relaxed, and took a moment to study our new digs.

Roughly ten by ten feet, the place looked more like an animal burrow than anything else. The wall abutting the mountain was made of huge stones the size of tires. The other three walls were a combination of irregular wood beams, more stones, and, plugging a few cracks, rolled-up towels and magazines. There were three wooden platforms for laying out sleeping bags, the highest one barely eighteen inches below the ceiling timbers.

A fireplace was built into one wall. Above it, rusted pots, spoons, and knives hung on a wire. They clanged together with the wind that swept through the open door like something out of a nightmare. I was starting to understand why this place was free. On the plus side, I didn't see any sign of rats or mice, and the two small windows seemed to be in working order.

"I like it," Daryn said.

No one chimed in. The place itself was fine with me. I wasn't going to miss towel service or a mint on my pillow. But I didn't like the idea of us being on top of each other again. We were all definitely in need of some personal space.

"It'll work," I said. "First choice of bedroom's yours, Daryn."

She pushed her backpack onto the top bunk. Marcus and Jode quickly claimed the other two. Selfish assholes. But I let it slide because we were all smoked and it was starting to get cold.

"We need firewood," I said. "And some kindling, before it gets too dark."

"I'll do the kindling," Daryn said, stepping outside first. I couldn't blame her. She'd just spent a few days with four bitter guys who hadn't showered in . . . well, in a few days. Frankly, I was grossed out for her.

When she left, we all stood there for a few seconds absorbing her absence. Absorbing how she changed us. Her composure was contagious. She brought something to our group that was palpable. Without her around, a tide of tension came rushing in.

After a moment, Jode sat on his bed platform. "I'm knackered. I'll just stay here."

"You don't get to pass because you're *tired*," I said. "Get up."

"I'll cut firewood tomorrow," he said, yawning. "I'm more in need of sleep than I am of a fire."

Marcus didn't even bother responding. He just crashed on the other platform.

Anger revved inside me. Did they think this was *a vacation*? Didn't they understand what was at stake?

That was the problem. They *didn't* understand. Neither of them had experienced what I had. Neither of them knew how it felt to have a demon crawling through your mind, to feel its evil linger, to be polluted by it.

"Listen up," I said, drawing on the last of my self-control. Bastian was leaning against the wall, the only one listening. He watched me closely, like he was worried about my next move. "This is how things are going to work. Daryn's in charge. She gives us orders, we follow them. When she's not around, I'm the guy you listen to. If you don't like it, speak up now."

Total silence. Marcus rolled over, turning his back to me.

Sebastian pushed off the wall and got in front of me, probably saving their lives. He herded me outside, over to the edge of the bluff. We came to an outdoor gathering area that resembled a mini-Stonehenge in the dim light—a half dozen flat stones arranged around a fire pit. Moonlight fell through the clouds in long beams and the air felt so thin and pure, it was almost painful to breathe. I sucked it down in deep drags.

"Gideon . . ." Bas said. "Bro, you gotta calm down."

I peered over the edge of the bluff. It was too dark to see anything but I *felt* the drop of hundreds of feet. I took a step back.

"I'm calm," I said.

"No, you're not. You've been amped for days. What the Kindred did was messed up. It sucks. But you have to try and take it easy on us, you know?"

I looked at him. I had only vaguely described Ra'om's

mental torture to the group—they needed to know what the Kindred could do—and now I regretted even that.

Bas sighed. "I'm just going to say this one thing, okay? I know you're not sleeping great. If you want, I can help."

"You'll . . . *what*? You're offering to put me out? You want to be my *sleeping pill*? That's *so nice* of you, Bas."

He waved a hand at me. "This is what I'm talking about, Gideon. This right here."

I checked myself—and yeah. I was being an ass. I knew I'd been this way for days. Tougher to be around. No one was ever going to call me the nicest guy in the world but this was too much. It wasn't me. I had a wound and it wasn't fast-healing. It wasn't healing at all.

"Don't take this the wrong way, okay?" Bas said. "But you gotta nip this in the bum."

I laughed. Jode was rubbing off on us. "There's really no bloody right way to take that," I said. I sat down on one of the stones and rubbed my head. My hair was getting too long. It bugged me. "Thanks for the offer, but I'll manage."

"Okay." He sat on one of the rocks and stretched out his legs. Smoke was just beginning to rise from the hut's stone chimney and the windows flickered with the glow of firelight. Daryn. She'd gotten it handled.

"That's kind of a relief, actually," Bas said. "It doesn't feel right using my ability on you guys."

"Yeah, they're pretty worthless." Our abilities didn't work on the Kindred. I didn't understand it. "Why have a weapon that doesn't work on the enemy?"

Bas smiled. "Figures you'd see it that way. But what if they're not weapons? What if we have them to learn?"

"To learn? I already knew how to be angry."

"That's not what I mean."

"Then explain."

"I feel like there's a nicer way for you to ask, but okay.

I'll give you my take on it. The things we can do, like your anger thing, Marcus with fear, me with weakness, and Jode with will . . . I think they're for us to master. Like, the weakness thing isn't something I have to *wield* so much as *work out*."

"You think your ability is weakness to help you face your own weakness?" This was starting to sound familiar. It reminded me of the conversation I'd had with Daryn in Rome.

He lifted his shoulders. "Maybe. What do you think your anger's for?"

"Pissing Daryn off?"

He grinned. "You are pretty good at that. But let me ask you this. What makes you angrier than anything? Angry at yourself—not at other people."

"Easy. Failure."

"Me, too. But failure how? Failure in what way specifically? That's what I've been thinking about. I already had this . . . this kind of hollow spot inside me. Being from such a big family, I always got lost. We didn't have enough money, you know, and I got passed between relatives. Live here for a while, live there. I went wherever anyone could feed me. I wasn't treated badly or anything like that. But I never felt like I was anything *special*. Have I told you what my parents call me? My actual parents? Cinco, because I'm the fifth kid. It means five in Spanish. It started as a joke, I think. But I guess part of me believes it. That I'm just a number. A mouth to feed. Kind of just . . . invisible."

He paused and the wind came up, rustling around us and filling the silence. "How'd I end up talking about me?"

"It's okay. You were explaining your lifelong quest for attention, so it makes sense. All is forgiven."

Bas laughed. "*Exactly,* dude," he said. Then he slapped his hands on his legs and stood. "I need some chocolate."

He headed back to the hut but I stayed out there for a while longer, filling my lungs with cool Norwegian air. Thinking about what he'd said.

I knew what my biggest failure was.

CHAPTER 47

The next morning I woke before the sun and did some recon around our hut. Our position was good, near fresh water, with great visibility, but I had to get lower in elevation to find a decent place where we could train. It took over half an hour of solid hiking to get down to the water, but I liked the grassy meadow that sloped gradually to the riverbank.

I took everyone there once they were awake, planning my approach as I wolfed down a granola bar on the trail. I was determined to start taking positive steps. It felt like the only way I could fight back against the images and the anger. Time to get stuff handled.

Reaching our new practice ground, I stepped out to the middle of the field as the others formed a circle around me. Steep granite slopes rose thousands of feet on either side of the river, framing us in and providing good concealment. High above, on a rocky projection that looked like an anvil, I could see part of the hut with the collapsed roof. Ours was behind it, just out of sight. Even if the Kindred had somehow tracked us to Norway, which I didn't think they had, Alevar would have to do a direct flyover to see us in that fjord. I hoped we'd bought ourselves a little time.

"So, here's how things stand," I said. "Daryn's waiting for drop-off instructions for the key, but we need to be ready if the Kindred track us down. That means we need to master our capabilities and our tools." I went on, explaining how that would require that we each give our maximum effort. We had to make the most of what we had and work hard. The philosophy I'd learned in RASP was not to practice until you got things *right*. It was to practice until you couldn't get them *wrong*.

As I spoke, my breath fogged in the cool morning. Bas nodded like, *yes, yes, totally with you*. Jode appeared to be filing everything I said away for future reference. Marcus crossed his arms and stared at the grass at his feet. Daryn listened, watching me with her steady eyes. Everyone was still here, still engaged-ish, and I wasn't yelling or being overly sarcastic. Good start so far.

"Okay, let's get this going," I said. "First, we'll get Jode outfitted with the bow, then go over some safety measures and work our way to doing drills."

"Can't we work with the horses first?" Jode asked. "I know how to ride."

My immediate inner answer was, *well, I don't*. With regard to that particular topic, I had decided I'd be a horseless horseman. I'd loved my armor during the few hours I'd worn it. I hadn't battle-tested it yet, but my instincts told me Kevlar had nothing on it. And the sword was starting to grow on me, too. But I wasn't excited about working with a creature that was essentially aggression in the form of fire.

"We'll get to the horses," I said. "Weapons first."

"If you insist."

"I do."

Jode frowned. I could tell my answer had disappointed Bastian too—understandable, since Shadow was awesome—but I kept us moving along, turning to helping Jode call up his weapon. Marcus walked away almost immediately and sat against a tree along the trailhead. Daryn joined him a few minutes later, creating a nice, condensed visual focal point of distraction.

So, I was going to bust my ass while he sat around and talked to her?

Unbelievable.

An hour later, with both Bas and I taking turns providing instruction, Jode still couldn't call up the bow. Daryn and Marcus chatted away over by the tree. Marcus was actually *smiling*.

"Again, Jode," I said, rubbing my tired eyes. Last night had been another struggle. I'd tossed and turned on the hard floor in front of the fireplace. I just needed *one night* without seeing my mom standing over my grave. "Keep trying. You only fail if you quit."

"That's right," Bas said. "When you fall off the horse, you need to just saddle it back up."

I looked at him. "What if the saddle didn't fall off? What if only you fell?"

"Speaking of horses," Jode said.

"No horses. Go again."

Another hour went by. Bas and I started to get punchy.

"Go to the light, Jode," Bas said. "Your most precious inside light."

"Just feeeeeeel it. Feel it like you mean it."

Jode smirked. "I'm English. I don't do anything by *feeeel*."

We kept at it, but both Bas and I had exhausted our vocabulary for explaining how we reached our powers. We did it by tapping into a certain purity of intention. A will to do what was best, what was needed, what felt right. Part of it was control, and part of it was surrender. I'd been joking, but in a lot of ways it was like finding a particular thread of feeling. I couldn't reach in and find it for him. He kind of had to work it out on his own. Finally, though, he did.

The instant the bow came up, his left arm shot straight out. "Now what?" he asked, his eyes flicking to me.

"Breathe, Ellis. Relax," I said. I took his wrist, keeping it steady, and took a close look at the weapon.

The bow was radiant white, on the verge of being hard to look at directly. In construction it was long and tapered, and looked balanced and light. The bowstring was so thin at points that it disappeared the way spiderwebs did in sunlight. It was the prettiest weapon out of all of them, no question. I thought of my sister, who had a real eye for seeing beauty. Anna would have liked that bow.

I didn't see any arrows but I had a gut feeling.

"Point it ten feet away," I said, "right at the ground and draw back on the string—*slowly.*"

"Ground," Jode repeated as he turned the weapon down. "Draw." The bowstring brightened as soon as his fingers touched it. He glanced at me, like *if this goes wrong it's on you*; then he pushed out a breath and pulled the string back.

At roughly half draw, there was a flash of brightness and the arrow appeared. Slender. Luminous. No fletching. Just a streamlined bolt of lightning.

Sebastian started hooting and slapping Jode on the back. I couldn't keep a grin off my face, either. A complete set now, the bow and arrow were even more impressive. And here was a weapon that actually made sense. That resembled a little bit, sorta-kinda, the weapons I knew.

"About time," Marcus said as he and Daryn walked up.

"What now?" Jode asked.

"What do you think?" I yelled. I couldn't contain my excitement. "Let's shoot something!"

We hiked downriver. I wanted to find a closed environment, minimizing the margin for causing damage. A shooting range, essentially. What I found was a saddle between two hills that would do the trick.

I made everyone stay put on the eastern slope while I jogged down and then back up the scree slope on the other hill. Along the way, I picked up a branch about as thick around as a baseball bat, but twice as long. I wedged it into the loose rocks, piling more at the base to keep it upright. Then I took a step back and congratulated myself. Good target. We were almost set.

Turning, I looked at everyone on the other slope, trying to eyeball the distance. Tomorrow I'd bring the radios and use the GPS to get exact distances, but it looked to be about 120 meters or so.

"Now?" Jode yelled. A flash of white appeared in his hands.

"*No!*" I scrambled up the hill like a mountain goat on fire.

Then I heard them laughing.

"*Assholes,*" I muttered. But something inside me loosened up a little. If they were messing with me, it meant they were doing something together. It was a good sign.

When I got back over to them, I found them deep in discussion about the proper archer's stance.

"I think I'm ready," Jode said.

He looked overextended and stiff, like he should be planted in a fountain, spurting water from his mouth, but I let it go. He'd gotten mentally prepared and he didn't look like he was going to injure himself. I'd get my shot at coaching him later.

"Okay, Robin Hood." I stepped back with Bas, Marcus, and Daryn. "Let it rip."

No time passed between the moment he released the arrow, and the eruption on the other hill. It happened in an instant.

An explosion cracked into the air, like an entire forest of trees splitting in half. My chest bucked at the pressure. Rocks flew apart.

Then, the aftermath—a dusty cloud lifting up, to the sound of a small avalanche rumbling down the hillside.

We practically killed ourselves rushing over there. The branch I'd set up was nonexistent. Pulverized. In its place we found a small crater about three feet wide and two deep, blackened at the center, surrounded by fine gray ash around the edges.

Serious explosive power.

"Incredible," Sebastian said.

I had to agree. It sure as hell beat a sword.

With everyone armed up, we moved into actual training. I went over basic safe-handling guidelines. Don't draw a weapon unless you plan to use it. Be aware of your surroundings at all times. Never fire without a target in mind. Then I broke us into two groups based on our weapons—aerial and hand-to-hand. It was the right thing to do from a tactical standpoint, but that left me with Marcus as my training partner, so. The potential for problems was high.

Jode and Bastian stayed behind to practice at our new firing range, Daryn staying with them, while Marcus and I headed back to the grass clearing. He brought up the scythe, I called up the sword, and we got started—using the flat of the blade and the base of the staff because we didn't want to kill each other. Actually, that's inaccurate. We did want to kill each other, but we avoided the business end of our weapons and proceeded to safely beat each other down. What we did in no way resembled sparring. The level of intensity went way beyond that. We took turns having the last say—him winning, then me—but it was pretty much always a dead heat.

Late that afternoon, with both of us covered in sweat and fresh bruises, he backed me up to the river. I stepped into water that was pure glacier melt. Water so cold it burned. I made a move to get around him and my foot landed right into a depression. Next thing I knew I was ass-planted, water up to my chest, an eighteen-inch blade a few centimeters away from my nose.

"Who're you fighting?" Marcus yelled.

"What are you talking about?" I yelled back. The cold pierced deep into my muscles. I'd only been in a few seconds, but I was already shivering badly.

"I know it ain't me," he said. Then his attention moved to Daryn, who was coming along the riverbank from our firing range.

Marcus flipped the scythe around, offering me the end of the staff to help me up. Did he care what Daryn thought of him? Or did he want to highlight who was on the winning end of our sparring exercise? Like me sitting in a river didn't make that clear enough.

I pushed the scythe away, got up, and broke into a jog. The sun had already dipped behind the mountains and my teeth were rattling. I had to get up to the hut and in front of a fire.

Daryn jogged over and met me, blocking my path to the trail. She looked at my sopping clothes. At how I was shivering. She couldn't seem to decide what to say and I couldn't look at her without picturing Samrael's arm wrapped around her, the two of them smiling.

"Gideon . . ."

Don't ask.

Don't ask if I'm okay.

"I think we should train with the horses. I think it would help."

Right. *That* was what I needed.

I couldn't even respond. I went right around her, back to the hut.

We ended the day around the stone circle. All of us together, but not together.

Jode and Bas hadn't done well in their training either. Daryn had grown quieter than normal. Marcus and I had gone backwards. We sat around the fire pit and ate rice and beans out of a pan. Passed around a couple of cans of peaches and some chocolate bars. Then I got the fireplace going in the hut and we crashed.

The next few days weren't any better. In fact, they got worse. I couldn't sleep more than a few hours a night. Ra'om's images started haunting me during the days, too. I'd find myself staring off, divided between what I was doing and seeing the worst things I could possibly imagine. I imagined them over and over.

I kept us all on a strict training routine, though. Sunup to sundown we worked with the weapons and even drilled with armor, but we made meager progress. Bastian and Jode's marksmanship with the scales and the bow held at a constant level—the suck level of marksmanship. Every day, I ran them through the basic principles of good shooting. I set up new targets and had them try different firing positions, but nothing helped.

Jode overthought everything. He was too much in his head. I'd tell him to shoot and he'd go into the history of longbowmen. He'd detail the Battle of Agincourt and how his weapon would fit in with our overall strategy. I knew the rambling was his way of stalling. When he did shoot, he was okay. Really, not bad. But he'd take a shot that was off by a few feet and that was unacceptable to him. He'd want to quit. He expected perfection, which I appreciated. But he had no patience for the failures that needed to happen along the way.

Jode kept pressing me to start our training with the horses. Bastian, too. But I kept shutting them down.

I knew we should be training with the horses. We were *horsemen*. But our weapons were higher priority—so I thought— and my horse? Didn't want to go there.

Bastian didn't give up like Jode, but his confidence with the scales was shaky, and the guy didn't have an aggressive bone in his body.

"I'm just not like you, G," he told me on the fourth day of missing targets by a mile. "I think you're barking up the wrong wall."

"You'll get it, Bas," I said. "You only almost decapitated me twice today."

"Man, I'm so sorry about that."

"Don't worry about it. Let's go again." I gave him the scales and stepped back, feeling hopeful. Ready to duck.

He got them spinning in the air above his head. He looked

pretty solid with that part. The problem was the release, which was a lot like hitting a baseball. A series of precise movements that had to flow in just the right order, culminating in a single, perfectly timed instant.

Bas let them fly. They sailed behind us, tearing the hell out of a patch of wildflowers. I wanted to laugh, but I was worried it would break him down.

"I suck at this, Gideon. Besides, I don't even think this is the right thing. How's this the right way to do good?"

"What do you mean?"

"I mean fighting."

"You're asking a soldier this?" I had to believe it played some part in doing good. Otherwise, what was my life? Or my dad's life? Or Cory's life? Or anyone who fought for good's life? "Dude, are you drowning in a sea of gray?"

Bas laughed. He shook his head and looked out over the water. "You said it yourself. You're a soldier. I'm not. I don't even know how to fight people. What do I know about fighting demons?"

That question legitimately worried me, too. How long did we have before the Kindred found us? How much more time did we have to prepare? Right then, a year wouldn't have seemed like enough.

Our best-case scenario relied on Daryn. Our Seeker needed to bring us information, a mission plan, a drop-off point. I'd have killed for a goal. For actual actionable plans, instead of the hide-and-train holding pattern we were in.

The only clear benefit from working with Jode and Bastian during that first week was that *I* started getting pretty good with the bow and the scales. The bow was my favorite—the arrows appeared to have limitless range and their accuracy was off the charts—but the more I used the scales, the more I took to them. The chains could be used to lasso, the disks were sharper than knives, and, thrown the right way, they came back like a boomerang. The weapon had *serious* versatility.

My own training with the sword didn't progress much, though. Marcus and I continued to give each other the good news—beatdowns, in other words. I hated the guy and he hated me. The only upside was that our fast healing was like a reset button. We ended the days with welts, swollen eyes, and split lips, but by morning we were usually fine and ready to wail on each other again.

All told, we spent a week training in which nothing positive was accomplished. I mean that.

Nothing.

I didn't know how to bring us together as a team. It was a failure on me as a leader. I hated the situation with Daryn. How awkward and forced things had become between us since Italy. And I was out-of-my-head tired from losing sleep and mentally fried, thanks to the Kindred. With all of that piling up, I'd become a walking bomb by the end of that week, so it wasn't surprising when things with Marcus came to a head the next day.

CHAPTER 48

M a'am?"
　　It's Beretta.

Beretta is cutting in on me.

A vicious expression passes over Cordero's face at the interruption. Slowly, she turns to face him. "Yes?"

Ye*sss*. Little demon hiss in there.

"I need to rotate out," Beretta says.

"Is there a situation I'm not aware of?"

"No, ma'am. I need to report in to my CO."

Texas doesn't say a word, but everything about him is backing up his partner. The way he's watching Cordero. The way he's standing. These guys are risking everything for me. What Beretta wants to report is the fact that something's wrong.

Has he figured out *what*?

Does he know who Cordero is?

Cordero finally nods. "Fine. But hurry back."

Beretta steps out. Now I wonder who's on the other side of that door. Are they really Army? Are they *people*? Or is Samrael out there with Ra'om? With Bay and Ronwae? They could all be here.

Cordero and I are looking at each other like nothing unusual is going on. I picture who I'm really looking at. Stringy hair the color of earthworms. Pocked. That dark, dirty suit that's oversized, bagging around the hands and feet. Spilling over his shoulders. But that was just a front too. The real Malaphar is the melted wax monster, with drooping skin and boneless limbs.

The radiator kicks on. *Tink, tink, tink.*

Perfect soundtrack for the nightmares I'll be having the rest of my life.

If I live.

"I changed my mind," I say. "Can I get some water?" Maybe Texas can cut my bindings when he brings me water. Or loosen them. Or slip me his bowie knife. *Anything.*

"But you're almost finished, aren't you?" Cordero says. "I think you'll survive."

Everything has a double meaning now.

Focus, Blake. Assess, plan, execute.

I search for my sword again, and find the thread, the focus, the feeling. The relief stops my heart for a moment. *Yes.* It's with me. I can summon it now. And I can feel Jode, Bas and Marcus through the cuff, too. They're close, like I thought. My armor's still out of my reach. And Riot is too, but I'm coming back.

I need to know why Malaphar is here. He wants something— something from *me.* Knowledge. I've been sitting here, telling him my story. He's been listening for clues.

Clues about what? The Kindred got the key.

Didn't they?

I think of Daryn at the diner outside of Los Angeles the first time I saw the key on the chain around her neck. Did she ever tell me, *actually* tell me, that I was looking at the key?

"You were saying that you and Marcus finally had it out?" Cordero says.

I'm a sitting duck, tied to this chair.

Time. Time is the only thing I can control.

Daryn is here. So are the guys. Texas and Beretta. One of them will come through. Someone will get me out of this chair before Malaphar is done with me.

I need to keep bluffing.

I need to stall.

CHAPTER 49

Jealousy was what started it.

I was coming back to the hut after a patrol hike around our area. I'd been making them every day to search for signs of the Kindred. Alone for the past couple of hours, I was completely zoned in to the quiet of the fjord, my senses tuned to all the smells and sounds of Jotunheimen.

I stopped dead in my tracks when I saw Daryn and Marcus by the stone circle. They were huddled on the same stone, their heads were bent close, and their backs were to me.

For a second I thought they were kissing.

Or about to. Or just had.

Something.

I heard Daryn laugh, and then Marcus said, "Dare, this isn't gonna work if you keep moving."

I went over to them, a volcanic pressure building inside me. "Afternoon," I said.

Daryn whirled to me. "Hey." The smile disappeared from her face. "Splinters," she said, raising her hand. "From cutting firewood."

Irrational rage spread through me as I looked at Marcus.

"I'll be at the clearing, Reaper," I said, and put myself in a forced march down the mountain.

Marcus came down five minutes behind me. I'd somehow managed not to detonate in that stretch of time. "No weapons," I said, as he joined me at the center of our practice field.

He nodded, and we went at it, fist-to-fist.

Fifteen minutes later, I'd split the skin over the first two knuckles on my right hand and picked up a collection of new bruises. Marcus had punched me above the temple. I was pretty positive I had a concussion. I'd already dry-heaved a few times, but it was Marcus's turn now. He was bent over his knees, coughing from the gut shot I'd given him.

"So we're clear," I said. "If you hurt her, I'll end you."

He peered up at me, drawing his sleeve over his mouth. "Man, you are *stupid*." He straightened. "You got the wrong idea."

"I saw you—"

"You saw *nothing*." He shook his head. "You're wrong in the head, War."

He had that right. My ears rang and I couldn't stay balanced. Saliva poured into my mouth. Puke was in my immediate future. And those were only the physical symptoms.

I was losing some piece of me to Ra'om and Samrael. I was starting to self-destruct. I remembered Marcus's question our first day there. *Who're you fighting?* I was starting to figure out the answer.

Marcus watched me with his cool gray eyes. "She was talking to me about you."

Wait. She was? "No splinters?"

"There were splinters. But there was a lot more of you." He tipped his head toward the trail. "Move, Blake. Somebody has to make sure you don't walk off a cliff."

I got moving.

We didn't say anything else on the hike back to hutquarters, but Marcus stood by and waited when I stopped to heave on the side of the trail. All three times. It was a huge step for me and Death.

Huge.

I still felt shaky when we got up there. Jode, Bastian, and Daryn were gathered at the stone circle around a fire, which had become our usual spot at the end of the day. It was only five or so, but it felt much later. The shadow of the mountain had already fallen over the clearing.

"Gideon, look at this!" Sebastian lifted a guitar in the air. "Dare got it for us!"

A *guitar*?

And *Dare*?

What?

I told him I'd be right back, then I jogged to the hut and changed into a fresh shirt, wrinkled but mostly clean, and did a quick washup before heading back outside. There were two unclaimed stones around the fire on either side of Daryn, which was perfect. Exactly where I wanted to be.

I didn't know what my plan was. All I knew was that something had to change. And I was pretty sure that I was the something.

"You're going to like this, Gideon," Jode said, flashing me a wry grin. "Sebastian here would like us to form a boy band."

Bas was bent over the guitar, tuning it. For over a week, all I'd heard was wind, fire, our weapons colliding, or our voices. By comparison the guitar sounded clear and rich, like my hearing had just gone high-def.

He looked up, grinning at me. "Think about it, G! We can be the Fjord Horsemen!"

I laughed, and then listened as the guitar story came out. While I'd gone on my recon hike, Jode and Daryn had walked down to the tourist station. Daryn had struck up a friendship with the attendant there, a woman named Isabel. As they'd left, Daryn had convinced Isabel to give us the guitar, which some tourists had left behind.

"Isabel?" I asked, glancing at Daryn. That name sounded familiar.

She nodded, and then I knew. The Seeker she'd told me about, her friend, was close by.

"The guitar's missing a string," Daryn said. "That's the only downfall."

"Doesn't matter," Bas said. "It's awesome."

"I'm glad you like it." Daryn tugged her sleeves over her hands. "I wasn't sure if any of you played, but I figured it didn't matter. If you practiced a little bit every day, you could learn. Or if one of you had some experience with musical instruments from their career, or as a hobby or whatever, maybe that person could teach the others, assuming his methods of instruction weren't totalitarian and inflexible. Or just flat-out rude. And that the *other* people, who might also benefit from learning to play, didn't interfere and create additional problems by being obstinate, negative, or easily discouraged. Anyway, I thought you'd all enjoy it."

The four of us looked at each other. We'd just been gently but thoroughly dressed down.

Bastian started plucking a tune, stumbling as he adjusted to the missing string. The thinnest string was gone, I noticed. The one that should've been at the bottom. But he adapted quickly and his fingers moved faster, playing a song that was like a chase, the notes running up and down and back up. We listened in silence as he made five strings work together. Work together *really well* to create something complete.

We got it. We heard her message loud and clear.

Bas started up on another song. I wanted to keep listening, but I had something I needed to do first. "Daryn."

She turned sharply to me, surprise in her eyes.

"Walk with me?" I asked.

She didn't say a word, just stood.

We took a trail that went up the mountain, instead of the more familiar one to the practice area. My heart thudded as we walked. It'd been over a week since we'd been alone and I had a ton of things I wanted to say. I tried to get it into some kind of order.

We stopped when we'd reached a smooth ledge. The sound of the guitar was quieter in the distance, but still clear.

"Isabel's here," I said. "Something going on? Do we know anything new?"

"No." Daryn crossed her arms. "She's just reinforcement. She'll be there to help, if we need it." She paused, toeing at the grass. "I didn't know she'd be there until I saw her. It was good to see her."

I could relate to that. I'd wanted to look at Daryn for days without checking myself, or overthinking it. Now she was right here, and I went right into binge mode on it. I couldn't look away from her. I'd missed talking to her. I just wanted to be around her again.

"You have such a knot on the side of your head," she said. "When are you and Marcus going to . . . What are you looking at, Gideon?"

"You. I'm looking at you."

Her eyes started to shine with some emotion that made my throat go raw.

"How am I looking?" she asked.

"Daryn, I—"

"Can we just hug first?"

"Yes."

I pulled her in and held her. We stayed there, hanging on to each other until we're both breathing steadier. I ran my hands up her back, into her soft hair. "How you doing, boss?"

"A lot better." Daryn turned her head and burrowed against my chest. It sent a wave of sheer kinetic *yes* through me. "You?"

"Real good."

In the distance, Bas started playing another song.

"Gideon, I'm sorry things got weird after Rome," she said, looking up at me.

"No, I am. My head hasn't been right."

"I know what you've been dealing with. I know what they can do."

"But it was still shitty of me—"

"But it's my fault too. I shouldn't have let anything happen between us."

"You don't think something's happening between us?" I didn't understand. Why were we standing there, with our arms wrapped around each other? "I mean, what's this?"

"I don't know." She stepped back. "I think it's us trying to find a way to be that's less painful."

This definitely wasn't going where I'd thought it was going. I didn't know what to do with my arms anymore now that she wasn't in them. I stuffed my hands into my pockets. Reminded myself to make smart choices that I wouldn't regret. "Tell me what you want," I said. "Let's start there."

"I want to fall into you like I just did," she said. "That's what I *always* want. I want to fall into you and hold on, but I can't do that. I'd just have to let go. I could leave tomorrow, Gideon. We'd never see each other again. I don't want you to break my heart, and I really think there's a potential you could. So let's not make this harder than it already is. Let's not create more history for me to miss when I'm alone again."

I tried to figure out how I felt, hearing all that. Terrible. Crazy. Amazing.

"Okay," I said. "I think I understand what you're saying. You want us to suffer now so we'll be less miserable later. I don't think it's going to work, but okay."

She frowned. "Okay?"

I shrugged. "I'm not going to talk you into being with me, Daryn. And I'm not going to pretend I like your decision, either. But if you want to not create history together, then let's do it. Let's stand here, in the most stunning place I've ever been in my life, and share some completely forgettable experiences. I'm in, Martin. Totally in."

"Are you being serious?"

"Yes."

"So you're okay with us just being friends?"

"Whoa, hold up. No."

"*No?* I don't understand!"

"I don't want to just be friends. If this is the plan we're going with, then I want to be *best* friends. Super tight, Martin. With handshakes, inside jokes, finishing each other's sentences. The whole deal. And I'm not budging on that, so. Take it or leave it."

I'd already passed on the *friends* option once. Not a mistake I was going to make again. I'd be whatever she let me be. Even if it was going to gut me.

She shoved me on the shoulder for messing with her, but her smile was huge. It killed me dead. Let the gutting begin.

"You suck," she said.

"I don't do anything by half measures. You know that, buddy."

She shook her head, then launched herself into my arms and we hugged it out. It felt like no hug I'd ever had with a friend ever. Nothing about it did. This new status between us was already mighty interesting.

We hiked back down to the huts, talking the whole way but I had no clue what I was saying. Inside I was replaying everything she'd said. I was looking at her and thinking, *This amazing girl just told me she always wants to fall into me.* Why wasn't it happening? I was trying to figure out how I could feel so damn good, but also feel like I'd had my ass kicked.

We got a lot of long stares from the guys as we walked up, but Bas was tactful enough to keep playing. I joined them around the fire, but Daryn went to the hut and came back with a blanket. She sat down on the same stone, right next to me, pulling the blanket over both of us like a really great, great friend. I was instantly sweating under it. Noticing her leg against my leg. The clean shampoo smell of her hair. Just noticing everything and frustrated beyond belief. But it was worth it because she kept smiling at me.

Sebastian finished a song, pushed his hair out of his eyes, and started up a new one.

"You're pretty good on that thing," I said.

"Thanks, G. I had to learn for acting." I didn't know how he was able to talk and play at the same time. It didn't look easy. "You get an advantage when you're up for a part if you have skills on your bio, so people take up all kinds of things, like tightrope walking and foreign languages and horseback riding." He smiled. "I wish I'd done that last one."

"What's on your bio?" Daryn asked.

"Mine?" Bas squinted up, like the answer was written in the sky. "Well, a bunch of stuff. I took ballroom dance lessons for a year. I wasn't very good at the tango or the foxtrot but I can kill it in the waltz. I speak Spanish, obviously. But I'm good at accents in general. I have a good ear, I guess. And I can play the piano. Better than the guitar. I have freaky long fingers. I also took a course in stunt fighting, and—"

"Stop," I said. "Did you just say *stunt fighting?*"

He grinned. "Yeah. I'm certified in Dramatic Combat. It's a twelve-week class where you learn how to make things like sword fighting and punches look real. I didn't tell you this?"

I stared at him, trying to digest this new information.

"I don't think he believes you, Bas," Daryn said.

He laughed. "It's true. I have a diploma and everything." He stopped playing the guitar. "Stop looking at me like that, Gideon. It's for the *movies.* So if I ever got a part that needed me to look like I could fight, I could pull it off. This is why I didn't tell you."

"I'm just trying to under*stand.* Like . . . you learned to play guitar for the movies, but you can actually *play* it. And you learned to freaking waltz, which I'm guessing you can also actually do. So what the hell happened? Why is combat the only thing you didn't actually learn?"

"War appears to be taking this personally," Jode said.

"Can you bloody hell blame me?"

Jode laughed. "No, *dude*. I can't."

"Maybe we could get some cameras up around here, see if it helps," Marcus said, like a real contributing member of the conversation.

Bas grinned. "It would totally help. I crush when the cameras are rollin'."

I nodded. "Now, that actually is true. Sebastian is to acting as the lions are to the Sahara. Top predator. Extremely capable."

Jode and Marcus hadn't heard about how I'd met Bas in the audition, so we told that story. Then we just kept going. We talked and listened to Sebastian play, as night fell around us. We stayed out there for hours, messing around. Finally *talking*. But I never lost sight of our situation.

The fire made me think of Pyro. The embers reminded me of Ra'om's eyes. When I looked into the darkness, I imagined Alevar crouched there, huddled inside his wings. How much longer did we have?

It was past midnight when Sebastian put the guitar down. My eyes stung from the smoke and from being overtired, but the last thing I wanted to do was sleep. I kept waiting for someone to head into the hut, start the trend, but no one moved.

Our lighthearted fun was over. With the fire burning down and the shadows rising, this was the time for ghost stories or confessions.

Jode scratched his head. "Well, I'll start," he said. "Car wreck, for me."

I instantly knew what this was. We all did.

"I was racing with friends," he continued. "The sons of my father's business associates, to be precise. Two of them whom

I knew quite well. We hated one another. The road was wet, and . . . I lost control and struck a tree. I lost the race." He was speaking in chopped bursts, like he wanted to get it over with. "When I woke in the hospital, I discovered this little bangle." He lifted his left arm, his cuff shining in the dim light. "That was how it began."

I felt like I was seeing him in a whole different light. Over the past week I'd ruled him out as a competitor, but his hesitation and fear of failing made sense now. Jode had wanted to win so badly he'd paid the ultimate price.

No one made any consoling comments. What was there to say? *Sorry you died, man.* Besides. We all had.

We sat and listened to the wind. We understood.

Then Daryn dug an elbow into my side.

"Ow—kay," I said. "I guess I'll go next." Then I told them about RASP and my parachuting accident. As I spoke, I became conscious of Marcus. Usually he acted like he couldn't care less what I was saying. Now he wasn't just listening to me, he was focused.

"Was the parachute the problem?" he asked, when I'd finished.

"No. It was . . . just something that happened. Just a really rare set of circumstances. What's even stranger is that it happened the exact same day my—" I caught myself, and looked at the firelit faces around me. It felt like a barrier moment. Was I going to trust these guys and tell them the truth, or not? Truth, I decided, and took a leap. "Because it happened the same day my dad died a year earlier."

I wasn't sure about the look Marcus gave me. Like he was seeing weakness in me. I didn't need that. Suddenly I was worried I'd just made a bad move. Then Bas spoke, pulling my attention away.

"I drowned," he said. "Strange, right? That it had nothing to do with food? Not what you'd expect from Famine."

"But it's still like you starved," Daryn said. "It was for air instead of food. But it was still a lack."

"Yeah. I guess you're right." Gratitude flashed across his features. He showed everything he felt on his face. "I was dead for almost five minutes. That's what I was told. Everybody was pretty surprised that I came back. It was so weird to see everyone crying. It scared me so bad it made me cry, too. I bawled. It was a super-soaked experience all around."

"Ocean or a pool?" I said, like it was an okay question to ask. But nothing felt off-limits anymore. If you could tell someone you'd screwed up badly enough to get yourself killed, you could pretty much say anything to them.

"Lake," Bastian said. "Lake Michigan. I was visiting a friend, and we were out there with a bunch of people on a breakwall near a lighthouse. The water was pretty rough. We were all saying how you could never survive swimming in there. That's when I got this wild urge to show-off and I jumped in. Stupid. Really bad idea. I got caught in a rip current. It caught me like a hook and pulled me away. I couldn't fight my way back. I just kept seeing the lighthouse move farther and farther away from me.

"By the time I saw the rescue boat coming my way, I knew it was too late. The water was *so* cold and my muscles felt like stone. I couldn't swim anymore. I went under, and then there wasn't anything. It's a total void until I came back around on the beach. Behind the emergency crew, I saw my buddy and the people I'd been with. Everyone was bawling. All this crying was going on around me. That's what I remember most. How scared and sad they were. How bad I felt that I was the cause of it. And then the relief of . . . *living*." He lifted his shoulders. "So that's me. That's how it happened."

Jode shivered like he was feeling the cold water himself. "And you, Dare?"

Derrr. He made it sound even more formal than her proper name.

Daryn shifted beside me. Her eyelashes were starting to look heavy. "I haven't died yet." She smiled. "I'm hoping to keep it that way for as long as possible."

"That's kind of not funny, Martin," I said.

"Agreed," Jode said.

"Right?" Bas said. "Don't even say that. What would we do without you?"

She laughed. "Oh, stop. You guys would be *fiiine.*"

I nudged her arm. "Hey, seriously. We're not letting anything happen to you."

She leaned her head against my shoulder. "And I won't let anything happen to any of you guys, either. I promise. Marcus's turn."

Marcus immediately bent over his knees and rubbed a hand over the back of his neck.

"You don't have to go," Bastian said. "No pressure."

"*What?*" I said. "How is that fair? *Yes,* pressure. Start talking, Reaper."

Marcus peered at me, and I saw something in his eyes. A rise to friendly competition, like we were playing horse. I'd made my shot. Now it was his turn.

He sat up, straightening his wide shoulders. "Beaten," he said. "Fists, then feet. Then a brick. Then I don't know."

Shit.

He'd been *beaten* to death?

Bas had come halfway to his feet. "Marcus, you got *jumped?*"

"No. I went after them. But it was going on for a while."

"Them?" Jode asked.

"Yeah, there was . . . ." Marcus flexed his fingers a few times. Unlike Bas, he rarely showed emotion on his face, but now I saw him struggle to keep it locked down. "There was five."

"You went after five people?" Jode said. "Were you alone?"

Marcus nodded.

I shook my head. I had to give it to him. That took a serious pair.

"*Why?*" Bas asked.

No answer. We'd found the limit to what Death would share.

"Did you lay down some hurt, at least?" I asked.

A slow smile spread over Marcus's mouth. "I did all right for a while."

Of course he did. Guy was tougher than anything.

Daryn shifted beside me. Beneath the blankets, a soft hand slid into mine and squeezed. I wove my fingers through hers and squeezed back.

We were coming together, the five of us.

We were finally getting it right.

CHAPTER 50

A lot changed after that day. We started training better, working harder. Pulling together on all fronts. Jode had some ideas that we incorporated into our arms training. He'd read a ton of military theory and wanted us to practice in the same location, instead of splitting up, for better team morale. He also wanted us to incorporate strategy into our sessions, and to drill at night so we'd be prepared to fight in darkness.

They were great ideas. Ones I'd been thinking about, too. We used them all. But the main change to our routine after that night was the horses. I couldn't avoid it any longer; the time had come for us to horse up.

We started first thing the following morning. As we reached our practice area on the riverbank, the sun was just coming over the mountains. Fog lifted off the water in big curls. It had rained early in the morning, and the grass felt spongy under my feet. We assembled in a circle, and it reminded me of our first day, though we weren't the same at all. We were united now. A team.

"I think we should go one at a time," Daryn said. "That's probably safest."

We'd agreed on the hike down that she and Jode should lead the horse training. Daryn had some riding experience from a few summers at camp. Jode had ridden, too. And Bas already had a good rapport with Shadow.

I looked at Marcus, and we silently bonded over the soup-sandwich that was about to happen. Neither one of us was looking forward to this.

"Okay, Bastian. Let's start with you."

His smile was immediate. Sebastian backed up a few steps.

A second later, Shadow came out of the darkness, swirling at his side.

Watching her materialize never got old. Neither did watching *her*. She was beautiful. All leggy and springy. So deep black, a fog of darkness that lifted from her hooves and mane. She was completely unreal. But Bas stood there, scratching her wide forehead like she was just a regular horse.

Shadow's attention moved around the group, taking us in, but she stayed with Bas. Really calm. Right beside him, though she wasn't even bridled. She had no tack on her at all. She was just a sleek, stunning horse. I wanted Jode's bow, but I'd have killed for that mare if she hadn't belonged to Bas.

"Gideon, your turn," Daryn said.

"I'll go last."

"Okay. Jode?"

"All right," he said. "I have to warn you, though. My horse is spirited. I've only seen him once, but it was memorable. Best you all be on the alert."

Awesome. My stomach already felt shaky. Jode had experience with horses, and if *he* was nervous about handling his mount . . . my situation was not looking great.

Jode stepped away from our circle and his eyes fluttered closed for a beat. A whirl of light sprang up from the earth beside him, brilliant slashes that wove together to form a pure white stallion—the light-positive version of Shadow, except much thicker and broader.

Jode's horse had barely formed when he spotted Shadow, laid back his ears, and charged.

Shadow lowered her head and let out a sound unlike any I'd ever heard a horse make before. Part shriek. Part roar. All terrifying.

Jode's horse stopped, his thick muscles bunching, his legs locking, but he slid a few feet, gouging long treads in the damp grass before he finally came to a halt. He tossed his head and snorted, steam rising from his nostrils like a cloud into the chilly morning air.

Shadow wasn't having any of it. She stood really still, like *Bring it. I am so ready.*

Jode's horse swished his tail a few times, then made a lazy turn and trotted over to Jode's side. Suddenly he seemed hugely bored, looking around him at the steep walls of the fjord. At us. Just super unimpressed with everything. Even Jode.

"Did Shadow just lay down the law?" I asked, trying to interpret horse behavior.

Sebastian grinned. "Yeah, dude. Without even *moving.*"

"Mares," Jode said dryly.

"Females are stronger than men in all species," Daryn said as she slowly approached Jode's horse with her hands out. "I'm surprised you guys haven't figured that out yet."

I pretty much had.

Jode's horse watched Daryn with intelligent eyes, his neck bent in a high arch. The stallion's coat was the kind of blinding white that seemed to glow from the inside, putting off a halo of light, like the moon.

Daryn extended her hand as she reached him. The stallion sniffed, moving up her arm. Then he got a whiff of her hair, which made her laugh.

"Hey, big guy," she said. She scratched behind his ears, looking totally at ease.

I wasn't totally at ease. You could've bounced a quarter off my stomach. This whole nature special that was happening was going to go south in a hurry once my horse showed up.

"Does he have a name, Jode?" Daryn asked.

"I haven't given it much thought," he replied.

"He's so pretty. Almost like a lantern. What about calling him Lucent?"

Jode grinned. "Brilliant."

"Good boy, Lucent." Daryn patted the stallion's broad neck, and then turned to Marcus. "Ready?"

His eyes slid over to me. It was early stages in the two of us getting along, but I was already pretty good at reading his mind. Since he barely talked, that was how you understood him, by his eyes or his posture. We all became good at it, but I'm completely fluent in Marcus.

At that particular moment, what he was thinking was, *I'm only doing this because I want to see* you *do this.*

He stepped back from the circle, rolled his shoulders, and then bowed his head.

Seconds passed. I was beginning to think he couldn't reach his horse when a pale flicker of movement stirred on the grass in front of him. Movement like gray leaves, spinning in an eddy of wind. As it grew into a small tornado, I realized I was looking at ashes. They solidified into longer threads that formed a hoof, an ankle, legs. On up until the horse was fully formed, as real and solid as me.

Like Shadow, Marcus's horse was a mare. Smaller than Shadow, though. Much smaller than Lucent. She was compact and lithe. Perfectly proportioned. Just by looking at her, I had a feeling she'd be fast. Her coat was a color I'd never seen before in a horse. Pale, pale gold.

She stood, looking from me to Sebastian to Daryn. Then Shadow and Lucent. Making the rounds. Sizing everybody up. Then she saw Marcus, and that was the end of the rest of us. She was all eyes for him.

Marcus hadn't moved. He looked more anxious than I'd ever seen him, up on the balls of his feet like he was about to take off sprinting. He looked like he had no idea what to do.

"Daryn?" he said, shooting her an uncertain glance.

"Go ahead," Daryn said. "Go to her."

Marcus took a few steps toward the mare and stopped. Then the mare took a few steps of her own, closing the last of the space between them. She lowered her head. She was so close her ears brushed his chest. Marcus reached up, running his palm along her smooth forehead. The mare closed her eyes and leaned into him.

And that was it. Marcus's shoulders loosened. His entire *body* loosened. He kept his hand on the mare as he moved next to her, and it was a done deal. They were good.

I shook my head. Seriously? *That* easy?

Marcus grinned at me, really loving how this was shaping up. "Ruin," he said. "That's what I'm calling her."

It was a good name for her. She looked ancient. Like she'd been dug up after a couple of thousand years in some crypt and dusted off.

"All you, War."

"Thank you, Death. I've been following along." I let out a breath as my gaze moved around the circle. Bastian and Shadow. Jode and Lucent. Marcus and Ruin. Daryn, steady as ever. Such a peaceful formation. I'd never been faced with a challenge that actually made me want to run the other way before. This came close, but there was no way I'd be the only guy who didn't deliver. No possible way.

"Okay," I said. "You'll all want to back up. My horse is extra spirited. He's kind of intense, actually. Maniacal."

"Shocking turn of events," Jode said.

"You've got this, Gideon," Bas said.

Daryn smiled. "It'll be fine."

"Totally." I was starting to sweat and my heart was racing. I had to get this over with.

Summoning the sword and my armor had become instinct, but I felt clumsy searching for Fire Horse. I was stumbling in the dark again as I searched for the zone where I felt focused, in line with my intentions to serve, to defend, to yield even as I found strength. Finally, I felt the thread that was *him*. I locked in and thought, *Come on out, you hellion.*

Everything happened pretty fast then. My horse came up like a blowtorch at the center of our circle. Rearing up, big burning hooves scraping at the sky. Pure blazing fury. Bad attitude in horse form.

All the humans in the circle scrambled back—myself included—but not the other horses. They went full-throttle— right in for a fight. Instantly, it was manes and tails whipping all over, teeth flashing, dirt flinging, an all-out horse battle.

The five of us stood at a safe distance and watched. What else could we do?

These horses were wicked and fast. Their power was incredible. And their fighting was vicious. My horse and Lucent had the advantage on size and strength, but Ruin and Shadow had the edge on speed and agility. Every movement created blurs of shadow and light, ash and fire in their wake, and the sounds they made cracked through the silence of the fjord.

"Are they ever going to stop?" Bastian asked.

"Yes," Daryn said, but she didn't sound sure.

"They'll sort it out," Jode agreed. But he looked worried, too. Even Marcus looked like he wanted to get in there and break things up.

Not me. I had no attachment to my horse. I didn't even know if I could touch him since he was, you know, burning.

As I watched, he took a wicked bite to the neck and scrambled to the side, his dinner-plate-sized hooves flinging mud and rocks everywhere. He crashed into Shadow. She slammed into a piece of driftwood and stumbled. She was going down, and my horse was, too. Big Red was going to land on her and crush her.

Shadow disappeared before he could. She unraveled into a twisting black cloud that shot away, flying off along the riverbank. Ruin broke into a gallop after her, hooves pounding along the gravel. She took a few strides, and then she transformed too, shifting to ashes. Now dark and pale blurs soared along the riverside.

Lucent and my horse, the giant slowpokes, were last to follow. Lucent became light, like sun rippling on water. Then Big Red turned into a flurry of flames, and he was gone, too. There were no horses anymore. Just slashes, shooting across the water.

It all happened in seconds.

We ran to the edge of the bank to watch them. Streaks of light and dark, fire and ash, twisting and threading through trees. Climbing suddenly into the air, and then plunging to fly over the glassy water again. My heart didn't beat for a solid minute as I stood there. Of the four horses, mine drew my attention most. I'd never seen anything so incredible. Never.

Sebastian was hooting and yelling his head off. Daryn and Marcus were laughing and jogging along the river, following the horse race. Only Jode and I stood there, incapable of even moving.

Jode shook his head. "Caused a bloody riot, your horse."

That was him, I thought.

Riot.

Later that afternoon, with the rest of the guys up at hut-quarters working on a fire and a delicious dinner of rice, beans, and canned peas, I recruited my favorite horse trainer and great buddy to give me a private lesson.

Daryn gave me instructions as we hiked down to the water: Keep talking while I worked with Riot. Be firm, but also understand that horses had different personalities, like people.

"Some are confident," she explained as we reached the training field, "but others are timid and—"

"Timid isn't his problem."

"But what if it was?"

"It's not."

She gave me a smile with a little eyebrow waggle. "I think *you're* timid."

"You do?"

"Mm-hm."

"Really?" I took a step toward her.

She saw what I was up to and took off running. She was fast—I had to step on the gas—but I chased her down. Then I lifted her onto my shoulders and windmilled her until I had to bring us in for a soft crash landing.

"You're pretty easy to do unremarkable things with," I said as I waited for the sky to stop rotating.

"I was thinking the same thing. It's going to be so easy to forget all about you."

Painful. Every moment with her was awesome and painful.

The clouds were gray and thick above us, an unbroken expanse of steel wool, stretching from mountain to mountain. We'd been there just over a week. How much longer until I saw Alevar's black wings soaring across that sky?

Daryn rolled onto her elbow. Her hair spilled over her shoulder, covering the key. "You're thinking about the Kindred, aren't you?"

She already knew I was, so I just looked at her.

Daryn sighed, her eyebrows drawing together. "I know it's not in my hands, but I feel responsible. Why can't I just know what to do next?"

"You will."

"But *when*?"

"When you're supposed to." I couldn't stay there any longer with her lying right next to me. I hopped to my feet and reached down, pulling her up. "Let's get to work."

I summoned Riot for the second time that day. He appeared in licks of flame, fire one second, horseflesh the next—*charging* horseflesh.

I lunged in front of Daryn, calling up my sword and armor in an instant, knowing that even with those I stood almost no chance against the two thousand pounds of fiery animal bearing down on us.

"Gideon, it's okay," Daryn said. "Just stand firm."

It didn't feel okay. I waved the sword in front of me. "Riot, back!"

His front hooves dug into the dirt when he was almost on us. His eyes bulged; then he jumped to the side like a cricket. Then he was off, galloping away before he doubled back and charged me again. On Daryn's instruction, I stood my ground.

Riot freaked out again, sped off, circled back, and that was how it went for about thirty solid minutes, time after time, until foam sizzled and dripped from his mouth and he finally settled to a quivering, steaming, burning stop a dozen paces away.

I glanced at Daryn. "Well, this feels like a good place to wrap for—"

"We're just getting started."

I shook my head, eyeing my horse. Riot looked spent, but still scary as hell.

Daryn had prepped me on how to approach him slowly. Talking. I had to do that now, before I lost my nerve. I got rid of my sword and armor, and then took a step forward.

"How's it going today, Riot?" I said. "I'm Gideon."

Nice. Two sentences and I'd already managed to embarrass myself. In front of Daryn *and* a horse. I hadn't even realized the last part was possible. I continued speaking as I stepped closer. "I'm sure we have a lot in common. You're clearly a stallion in top physical condition. Extremely dangerous. Badass. Impressive looking."

"Wow," Daryn said behind me.

That made me smile, which I needed. I was nervous as all get-out. The muscles in Riot's legs were twitching. His breath lifted in puffs of steam. He had gold eyes—and they hadn't unlocked from mine. He looked like he wanted to eat my head.

"Keep going," Daryn said. "And maybe try to be positive and nice? I think he can sense what you're saying."

Positive, check. Nice, check. Wait—*nice*?

Shit. Okay.

"You seem like you'll make a pretty good warhorse," I said as I continued approaching him carefully. "Once you stop trying to kill me, I think we'll do a lot better. Not that I don't appreciate your level of aggression. If we can just refocus it, I think we should be good. There's the other issue, too. Of you being on fire. But I see lots of potential once we figure that stuff out." I had almost reached him. Three more steps and I'd be able to touch him.

Riot's lips pulled back, and I was suddenly looking at *a lot* of big teeth.

"It's okay," Daryn said next to me. "That's how horses smell. He's just checking out your scent. Hold out your hand and let him smell you."

"You're sure he won't bite me?"

"No," she said, with a chuckle. "I'm not."

She was going to pay for that one.

I could feel Riot's warmth radiating around him. And I could smell him—a smell somewhere between hot pavement, hot metal, and horse sweat. I extended my hand slowly, saying good-bye to my fingers.

Riot stretched his neck, reaching forward, his mouth hovering over my palm. His breath drifted over my skin in hot puffs. I'd thought his eyes were gold, but the color was deeper. More like amber.

I noticed he had pulled back on the flames over his body. At the moment, they curled only along his tail. His jaw was solid and huge, and the strands of his mane were copper and gold and red, every thread a different shade.

"You're one of a kind, aren't you?" I said.

He was looked at me so directly. I felt like he wasn't just *listening* to me; he was *understanding*. That gave me a boost of confidence.

"Okay, Big Red. I'm going to touch you now. If you're going to burn me I'd appreciate it if . . . you didn't burn me."

I reached out and rested my hand on his neck. I felt solid muscle covered by fine soft hair that radiated heat. Warm. But I'd expected much more. He just felt like he'd been sitting in the sun.

What got to me though, after a couple of seconds, was feeling him breathe. Feeling his pulse. Feeling all the power in him. All his fire, inside and out.

If I could find a way to connect with him, it'd be mine.

He would be mine.

Maybe this was going to work out.

After that, I was on a mission to bond with him. I spent the next few days calling him up and letting him run himself out, then approaching him and resting my hand on his neck. We gradually worked up to the point where he'd let me drag my hand over his body as I walked around him. He liked this, I could tell, because he'd dial back the fire, keeping it away from me. I had yet to actually make contact with any flames on him. His red coat just felt warm, and with the weather in Jotunheimen continuing to cool, the warmth felt good.

I kept talking as I worked with him because Daryn had said I should. I told him about my mom and Anna. I told him about the San Francisco Giants and the game of baseball in general, which took forever. Riot got an education on the national pastime. I told him about RASP, which he liked the best. I'd been skipping stones into the water, in perpetual motion as usual, and he'd come right up next to me, his big hooves clopping into the shallows like he wanted to hear me better.

Even when his eyes were staring off across the fjord, I felt his attention. He listened to me even when I wasn't speaking.

After a few days, I started pacing along the banks as I talked and he plodded along beside me, his hooves like small meteors crashing by my feet, his tail blowing along, various parts of him on fire. Riot had a lot going for him, but subtlety wasn't his gift.

I quickly became addicted to the feeling of being with him. I grew impatient at the end of my training sessions with Marcus, eager to get back to Riot. I was first to rise and last to sleep, as always, but now it was because I wanted to spend as much time as I could with my horse.

Little things got me. How Riot would look over if I stopped talking like, *Why'd you stop, Gideon?* How he'd nudge my arm to let me know he wanted my hand on his shoulder. How, when we'd see the other guys with their horses, he'd become a little crazy and overprotective. And my favorite—how whenever I mentioned Daryn he'd strike a pose and torch up. Major show-off.

He was funny. Just really great company.

A couple of days into working with him, I laced up my cross-trainers and took off. He stayed right with me again, so we added running to our time together. Occasionally, we'd pass the other guys and there'd be comments. I had horseback riding all wrong, they'd say. Or they'd place bets as to when I'd jog by with a saddle on my back, Riot sitting in it. I didn't care. I loved running on my own, but with a horse keeping pace for you?

Not many things were better than that.

But there *was* something better. The more time I spent with Riot, the calmer I felt and the less I saw of Ra'om's images. I started sleeping better. My nightmares came less frequently. I could go long stretches without thinking about Samrael hitting Daryn, or seeing my father falling from a roof. At night when I looked into the darkness, I didn't see Ra'om's red eyes anymore—I saw Riot's. Every day, my horse put my head just a little more to the right. He managed the impossible: He mellowed me out.

The one thing that wasn't happening, though, was *riding*.

About a week in, as we approached the two-week mark in Jotunheimen, I knew the time had come to give it a try. I woke up and left for the river before anyone else had stirred. I wanted to be alone for my first attempt.

We'd had two solid days of freezing rain in a row, and our practice field was mostly mud now. Any day, I expected to see snow. Any day, I expected to see the Kindred.

I summoned Riot and he came right over to me, bobbing his head. He was excited to see me, too.

"What's up, Big Red?" I said, smoothing my hand over his coat. He nudged me with his head, telling me to get moving. He thought we were going for a run. "We're going to do something a little different today. Something new."

His amber eyes held steady on me. He was ready, too.

"We're gearing up now, Riot," I said. I knew from the other guys that our horses' tack came up when we mounted. I wanted to make sure Riot knew that, too. "Your saddle and bridle are coming up. Then I'm going to get on your back. I'm going to sit on you, so prepare for that, okay? Here we go."

I reached for his withers with my right hand, and grabbed a thick bunch of red mane with my left, holding tight. I saw the flash of a stirrup, jammed my foot into it, and swung up.

Everything clicked into place—both my feet were in the stirrups, I was sitting in the saddle, the reins were even in my hands—but my first thought wasn't about the gear. I'd underestimated Riot's size. I was *way* the heck up there.

The second thing I noticed was that not only had Riot's tack come up, but so had my armor—and—that I was on fire.

Flames rolled along my arms. They curled up from my ankles, drifting over my legs. I reached down and smoothed my hand on Riot's neck, and the flames there flowed around me. I needed a second to wrap my head around that little development, but Riot tensed beneath me and surged forward with so much force that I almost pitched off the saddle.

Gripping with my legs, I drove my heels down like Daryn had told me to do, and held on for my life. I hadn't expected him to be fast—he was built for power, not speed—but he was *fast*. The gravel riverbank became a gray blur beneath me, and the wind pressed against my face.

Since I had no riding technique to speak of, the saddle came up under me like a jackhammer. Cherished parts of my anatomy would never be the same, I was sure. Thankfully, I quickly realized that by shifting my weight onto my legs and slightly forward, it put me in synch with his gait. I took up the reins, tucked in like a jockey, and experienced true and profound exhilaration as we tore across the clearing.

Why had I waited so long to do this? I never wanted to stop. I wanted to ride a circle around the world.

Then I spotted Daryn and the guys coming down the trail, and the moment was over. I scrambled to recall the riding instruction I'd been given—be gentle with Riot's mouth, use my legs to control him—and made a total mess of things, giving him mixed-up cues and cranking the reins like a brute. I got it all wrong, but somehow Riot understood what I wanted. He slowed down, trotted right over to everybody, and came to a full stop.

Sitting up in the saddle, with Daryn and the guys watching me, I was feeling pretty big-time, but my first instinct was to play everything down. Just a regular morning, tearing around a fjord on my gigantic fiery steed.

It didn't work. I felt a grin coming on and I couldn't hold it back for anything. I knew I looked amazing up there, with my armor and horse. All burning. I mean, how often did you see *that*?

"What's up, guys?" I said, and reached down to pat Riot's neck.

I heard someone snicker, and I peered at them. "What?"

Marcus scratched his jaw. I could tell he was trying not to smile. "Your horse, man. It's the way he moves."

"It's called knee action," Daryn said.

"Riot's is quite high," Jode added. He frowned and pressed his lips together, but I could hear him sputtering.

"It's cool, G," Bas said. "He sort of . . . prances. Reminds me of those Irish river dancers. You know, the ones that—"

He couldn't even finish. He started howling. Suddenly they were falling all over themselves.

"It's 'cause he's so big, you idiots," I said. "He's like a tank. And look at all this mud. He has to have permanent four-wheel drive."

I shut myself up, because I was only making it worse. Riot and I had to just wait it out. But I didn't really care. I knew we were the best.

When everyone settled down, the rest of the guys mounted up, too. Shadow materialized at Bastian's feet, and came up with him. *Through* him. I watched as whirling darkness spun around his legs, then moved higher, covering his body. Bas disappeared for a second, consumed by those black ribbons, then there he was, mounted on Shadow, also in armor. Horse and rider, black from hoof to hood.

I'd seen Bas fold into Shadow a few times by then. The other guys, too. They'd also been working with their mounts every day. While Riot and I were jogging, I'd seen them riding along the banks, or in elemental form. Slashes of darkness and light, zipping through the fjords. Or in Marcus's case, a streak of pale dust. I knew Riot and I would be able to do that as well. That at some point, I'd fold into fire with him. I couldn't wait for that. We were a little behind, but we'd get it.

Jode's transition was faster, happening almost instantly—a flash of brightness, then he was mounted on Lucent. Much more than Sebastian, Jode had the Hollywood look, with the white horse and the lighter-colored armor. He was the only one of us who actually resembled a good guy.

Marcus summoned Ruin last. I watched swirls of ash overtake him, watched him disappear in a pale flurry, and then reform on Ruin's back. He had his suit's dark hood pulled up as he settled back into shape, casting part of his face in shadow, but it didn't hide his smile.

Daryn stepped back, getting a little distance. "You guys look *scary*," she said.

But we all knew she meant *scary good*.

I looked around me. It was our first time that way, the four of us mounted up.

Red, white, black, and pale.

A bona fide posse.

CHAPTER 51

Sounds impressive," Cordero says, dryly. "I wish I could've seen you that way."

You have, I think. *You have.*

"And your relationship with Riot sounds really touching."

As I watch her, I can't help but wonder. Does she have any idea how much I *didn't* say just now? Can she tell?

My relationship with Riot isn't *touching.*

Riot *changed* me.

I told him things I've never said to anyone.

I told him about my dad.

I remember it—walking along the river's edge one afternoon, his reflection flickering in the water. Me, talking. Putting everything I'd been carrying around for a year into words. All the anger I felt for sitting in a truck doing nothing, when I could've been saving my dad's life.

I'd lost it. I'd sat down on the gravel and cried like a baby. Everything became clear to me in that moment. How my anger had actually been guilt. How my guilt had actually been a crutch. How that crutch was what I'd been using to avoid the pain. I felt the pain that afternoon. My heart broke on that riverbank. It felt so broken, I thought it was going to kill me. But then I'd felt hot horse breath on my forehead, and when I'd looked up, there he was. Riot. Looking at me like, *I'm still right here. Get up. Let's keep going.*

And we did keep going. I did. I *have.*

Because of him.

My horse.

I never expected it.

That Riot would give me what I needed to let go. To move on.

But he did.

"I'm curious." Cordero sits back in her chair and studies me. "How does it feel to become fire?"

"Indescribable."

Cordero rubs her knuckles, and then taps her fingers on the desk. "Some people might call that a cop-out, Gideon."

"You're asking me what it's like to transform into something else?"

Black eyes hold on mine.

I instantly regret opening my mouth. I'm strapped down. Defenseless.

I glance at the door.

Where the hell is *Beretta*? It's been at least half an hour since he left.

Cordero notices. "He has been gone a while, hasn't he? Maybe he got tied up."

Cordero stands and rounds the desk, coming toward me.

"Ma'am," Texas says, "I don't think—"

"It's fine," she says, cutting him off. "I want to take a look at something."

Cordero's smart, approaching from my right. Steering clear of any chance I have with my sword.

Texas's hand drifts toward his sidearm.

"I wanted to see this up close." Cordero kneels beside me—but it's Malaphar's stench that invades my nose. She places her hand on my arm, and my muscles jump. A sick feeling climbs my throat. "Are your abilities linked to this?"

I can't even answer.

"Let's try another question," Cordero says. "You've said you can sense the other riders through this, like you're pieces of a whole. Can you sense them now?"

All I hear is Daryn's voice.

With the four of you together, they'll be able to track us faster.

The Kindred are attracted to its power.

I see Alevar on the streets outside the Vatican, pointing at the radio in my hand.

Not at the radio.

At my wrist.

At the cuff.

"You're not answering. Am I invading your personal space?" Cordero says, except it's not her voice anymore. There's gravel in it, and it's getting slightly deeper.

"Sorry, Gideon. It seems like I've made you uncomfortable." She rises and sits on the edge of the desk, right in front of me. "You've been extremely helpful so far, so I'm going to bend the rules a little and tell you something I probably shouldn't. You've been worried about Daryn, I'm sure. *Dare.* I do like it when you call her that. But you don't need to be worried anymore." Her smile is mocking. "She's here. Daryn is right outside with some of my colleagues. Isn't that great news?"

Breathe, Blake. Breathe.

Cordero smirks. "You've gone so quiet on me, Gideon, just as we're reaching the final showdown. Well, I'm assuming it's the final showdown. Maybe it isn't. I haven't heard the full story yet, have I? Let's finish up. I'm sure you're eager to see Daryn. Keep cooperating, and you'll see that she's doing fine." Cordero pauses, giving me a hellish smile. "And still in one piece."

CHAPTER 52

In a lot of ways, the night the Kindred showed up was like any other.

The five of us were inside the hut, crammed around the tiny fireplace as we tried to stay warm. Our new hobby was betting on horse races and, not surprisingly, Jode was becoming a rich man. Our betting currency—Norwegian chocolate bars—sat in front of him like a miniature stack of gold bullion.

"Never bet against me," he said, his mouth lifting in a cocky smile. "You'll only regret it."

"Can't we have other kinds of competitions?" I asked. In elemental form, no one was faster than Lucent. In horse form, Shadow and Ruin ran pretty even. Riot and I were the only ones who never won and it was starting to get old. "Tests of strength, for example."

Bas smiled. "How about which horse can plow the fastest? That'd be fun. Riot would definitely win that."

"Or which horse has the finest high-step," Jode offered.

"Or is the most conspicuous," Daryn said.

"Weighs the most," Marcus said.

They were having fun messing with me, but I could feel the tension beneath the surface.

Earlier that day, Daryn had told us she felt one of her headaches coming on. We were all wondering if this was going to be it. If we'd finally learn where we needed to take the key.

As the night wore on, despite our efforts to keep things light, it started to feel like we were on Daryn watch. Then as it grew even later, like we'd gotten our hopes up for nothing.

Jode was telling us about the whales he'd seen that morning when Daryn shifted closer to me and rested her head on my shoulder. Jode stumbled over his words, but he recovered quickly and kept going.

After a few seconds, Daryn closed her eyes.

Jode trailed off, abandoning the whales. "Gideon, do you think . . . ?"

Marcus and Bas both looked like they'd stopped breathing.

"I don't know." I wanted to take her out of there. Or make the guys leave. Not because I didn't trust them—I did. But Daryn had asked me the last time not to let them see.

Why hadn't I thought about this sooner?

I put my arm around her. It wasn't a solution. But it felt better.

Then we sat and listened to the snap of the fire and the whistle of the wind as it blew through all the cracks in the hut.

Daryn's eyes fluttered open in just seconds.

"Where'd you see the whales, Jode?" she asked. "I missed it."

No comment about delivering the key.

She'd only nodded off.

We all looked at each other like, *Shit. We need to chill out.*

Bas let out a long, stressed-out sigh. "I'm getting some more firewood." He hopped up and headed outside.

"The whales," Jode said. He narrowed his eyes. "Ah, yes. I saw the whales—three of them, there were three—near an inlet west of Gjende."

We talked about that for a while. The whales. Then Gjende, which was beyond my reach with Riot. Travel over land was slow and laborious in these mountains. But folded in with Lucent, in elemental form, Jode was almost invisible by day, like Shadow and Bas were at night. They could travel far. It gave them a lot more range than Marcus and me. Flying mini-clouds of ash were pretty noticeable, and fire? Riot and I didn't leave the immediate area very often.

After the false alarm, I was starting to settle down when Daryn's hand slipped into mine and squeezed. I looked at her, but she was staring at our linked hands.

She'd gone white. Then her eyes lifted to mine.

"I'm so sorry," she whispered.

Dread shot through me and I looked to the door. Sebastian wasn't back yet.

"What is it?" Jode said. Marcus had frozen.

I shot to my feet and barreled through the door, out into the night.

Several fires burned across the clearing, lighting the area.

The Kindred were everywhere. Not just the seven.

Dozens.

Jode and I had guessed right. Ronwae and Bay commanded hordes.

Ronwae was the one I noticed first. In her scorpion shape, she had Riot's heft, but she sat low to the ground on six segmented legs. Her thick shell looked redder than when I'd seen it before. Her claws were as long as my arm, and they opened and closed slowly, in anticipation. But they were nothing compared to the stinger that rose from her back, swaying back and forth.

She looked like more than enough to contend with on her own, but in the darkness behind her, around her, there were dozens of Ronwae replicas. Not exactly the same. Slightly smaller. Their armored shells not as deep red as Ronwae's. But still incredibly real threats.

Further away, Bay stood on top of the stone where I'd huddled under a blanket with Daryn only a few nights earlier. Even from a distance, I could see the power in her shoulders and legs, her mangy pelt and sharp claws. She lifted her head to the night—her canines were so long they resembled tusks—and scented the air, small clouds issuing from her nostrils.

Like Ronwae's scorpions, Bay's multitudes stacked the

darkness behind her, each more misshapen and gruesome than the next—a funhouse-worth of beasts.

A burst of fire erupted by the trailhead, drawing my attention. Pyro stood there, proudly showing off his fangs and the fire in his hands. Like that would intimidate me. If it weren't for Daryn and the guys, he'd mean nothing.

I didn't see Malaphar but Sebastian stood in the middle of the clearing, at the center of everything. He was standing at attention, eyes straight ahead. He wasn't focusing on me.

It *looked* like Sebastian, but . . .

I didn't think it was him.

I didn't see Ra'om, but Samrael stepped forward from the darkness in his human form, wearing a reflective jacket and pants, like an ad for outdoor gear. He smiled, totally at home with the horror show around him.

"Gideon, it's good to see you again." His gaze moved past me.

Marcus and Jode had followed me out of the hut. They had drawn their weapons, scythe and bow. Daryn stood between them.

When Samrael saw her, his smile vanished and his eyes filled with hunger. Instantly, I remembered Ra'om's image—Samrael attacking her—and rage ignited inside me. Rage that burned from my core.

"At last," he said. "I knew I'd find you."

Daryn came to my side. The key hung around her neck, gleaming against her dark jacket. She stood with her usual confidence, but I saw that her fingers were shaking.

"I wouldn't be gloating if I were you," she said. "We've been here for weeks."

Samrael's smile came back. "Yes. You were well hidden. But what's a few weeks of delay when you're building a kingdom?"

"You won't get the key, Samrael. You'll never get it."

He tipped his head. "I don't know about *never*. Why don't

we do this simply, for your sake, Daryn. For the sake of Gideon here, who's so very fond of you." He held out his hand. "Bring it to me."

"You heard me," she said.

"Another refusal?" Samrael said. "I thought that might be the case."

Time slowed as he looked up, lifting his eyes to the darkness.

Alevar.

The night demon was almost invisible in the sky, his black wings tucked like a diving falcon's. I saw him, high above. Then he was right over us, his wings whipping out, suspended in midair for an instant.

Daryn and I lunged toward the hut.

She surged ahead of me. I saw her reach Marcus—reach the shelter of the hut—then I flew back. I slammed into the ground, the wind rushing out of my lungs.

Alevar was on me. His feathers covered me, putting me in total darkness. I called my armor as his sharp claws raked over my face and my arms. I found his shoulder and summoned my sword. It pierced his wing as it came up.

He shrieked, the sound deafening. Then he lifted off me, flapping furiously as he retreated in a wounded, awkward flight.

I came to my feet in time to see Pyro launching fire in my direction. I threw myself back onto the ground, the air shaking with the explosion behind me. Heat washed over me, engulfing me.

I looked up, blinking through the searing heat. The hut was burning. Consumed with fire, like the sun was in front of me.

Where were the others?

They'd been right in front of it.

I heard my name yelled, and spun.

One of Bay's boars galloped toward me, snout wrinkled, canines bared.

Riot. I needed him.

He came up in a wash of flames around me, and I folded into him.

Taking his fire, meeting it with mine.

We were inseparable now.

Burning and light.

Untouchable.

We climbed into the night, rising high enough that I could see the entire bluff below. Our burning hut. The swarms of demons. The fires, hemming everything in.

The familiar sweep of the scythe drew my eye. Marcus was mounted on Ruin, Daryn in the saddle behind him. I saw Jode close by, on Lucent. A hail of arrows streaked from his bow, one after another, taking Ronwae and Bay's creatures down in a lethal barrage. Concussive sounds filled the air as demons erupted in bursts of claws and stingers, fur and thick, dark blood.

Jode.

He was a *machine.*

But there were too many for him. There was no end to the hordes.

At the center of everything, I saw Sebastian. He was still in the same place, the middle of the clearing, standing there like a statue. But he wasn't alone. Samrael stood next to him, holding one of his bone blades at his side.

Riot and I fell into a dive and soared down to the clearing. I spotted one of Ronwae's scorpions in the chaos and came in behind it, forming up with Riot at a gallop. I had my sword ready, and took its stinger clean off, then I reversed my grip, and drove the sword down, cracking through the armor on its back. Riot jumped aside, avoiding the whipping tail of the dying scorpion, and I almost flew out of the saddle.

Finding my balance, I put him into a hard charge toward

Marcus and Daryn. Jode was trying to keep them protected, loosing arrow after arrow, but he was losing ground against the tide of demons that were closing in around them.

I slashed at anything that got in my way. *Almost there.*

Ahead, I saw one of Bay's creatures make a wild sprint toward Marcus. Then another one. Marcus saw them and chose one, swinging the scythe. The blade hooked into the monster's thick back. As it fell aside, Marcus twisted hard, tugged like a fish on a line. Ruin saw the other monster and reeled. Caught between the two sharp movements, Daryn flew from behind Marcus and tumbled to the earth.

"Daryn!" I couldn't get to her fast enough. Bay's beasts came from all directions. Riot bucked beneath me, kicking at them with his hooves as I slashed at whichever one came closest.

Daryn shot to her feet and ran. Ran like a hurdler, strong and fast—but there was nowhere to go. We were on the side of the mountain with only two trails off the bluff. Pyro had set fire to both. I saw her reach the edge of the flames and pull up, then whirl and search around desperately for another way out.

There was no other way out.

I had to reach her. Marcus and Jode were in trouble. Sebastian was in trouble. But Daryn had the key. I went to shift to fire, but Riot resisted. He wanted to stand and fight.

"Riot!" I yelled, and he understood and finally relented. We folded in fast—finding the place where we were equal, perfect—and we soared to Daryn. Forming back up, I reached down for her hand. "Come on!"

She clasped it and vaulted into the saddle behind me.

The chaos across the clearing had intensified and the fires were climbing the woods behind the bluff. Pyro's burning missiles battled with Jode's bright white arrows. A frenzy had overtaken Ronwae's scorpions and Bay's beasts as they reacted in fear to the fires.

"Give her to me!" Samrael yelled from across the clearing. He laid the blade across Sebastian's throat.

But it wasn't Bas. It couldn't be him.

What if it was?

I was trusting my gut. But the price of being wrong was Bas's life.

I swung at a charging, stoop-backed beast with my sword, and it fell, howling.

"Gideon, go!" Daryn yelled, delivering a kick across the snout of another.

There was only one way I'd get her out. Hopefully she'd live through it. I ditched my sword, reached back, and pulled her in front of me. Then I put my heels to Riot's flanks.

He leapt forward in a thrust of sheer power, dead ahead.

Right into a wall of fire.

I did everything I could to wrap Daryn up with my body, my armor, all of me as Riot thundered through the heart of the fire. The world went bright orange, then white. A high, piercing sound filled my ears. Was that Daryn screaming? Even with my armor, my legs began to heat up, scalding, but worse by far was the feeling of Daryn's fingers digging into my ribs in pain. Hot went to searing. Then we went past searing and I wondered if I'd pushed too far.

Then we punched through, into open grass. Into cool dark night.

I reined Riot in and we came to a stop. Then I prayed the next few moments wouldn't destroy me.

"Tell me you're okay."

Daryn was trembling in my arms. "I'm okay."

She peeled away from me and slid out of the saddle. As she landed, she sucked in a breath and her right foot came off the ground.

I dismounted. "Where are you hurt?"

As I came to stand in front of her, a smell hit me. My stomach seized when I realized what it was. A wound spread over her calf. Red and raw at the center, charred around the edges. I couldn't look away from it.

Was it from Riot? Had Riot and I done that? Or had the fire?

It shouldn't matter—she was hurt. She was *hurt*.

But it mattered. I wanted to know—had *I* done that?

Focus. Next step.

"You need to get somewhere safe. You need a doctor."

She nodded tightly. "I'll go to Isabel."

My gaze went to the trail that led back to the tourist station. The Seeker. Daryn's friend would help.

Riot pounded the earth with his hoof. His eyes were bright, ferocious, and fire curled all over him. He looked how I felt.

"He wants to go back," Daryn said. "You want to go back."

I wanted to be everywhere. With her. Back in the fight.

"I can get down the mountain, Gideon. *You* have to go *back*."

"The key's around your neck, Daryn. They'll track you down."

"No. They won't." She lifted the chain over her head and dropped it around my neck. "It's no different. You've been protecting it all along."

I nodded, agreeing. I had Riot. I could fight to defend the key. And by taking possession of it, I'd take the heat away from her so she could get to Isabel. It was the least bad option.

I told her how to reach Cory at Fort Benning. "Tell him you're with me. Tell him we're in a live, hostile situation and that we need to get airlifted out of here. Have him pull our location up on a satellite." Cory was smart. He'd go to the right people.

I knew I was breaking this thing wide open but we were

losing. We needed all the help we could get. And I wanted Daryn out of there. As far and as fast as possible.

"I will," Daryn said, as she backed away. "I'll call him, Gideon. I know they'll come." She hesitated. "I'll see you," she said. Then she ran. . . . She ran into the darkness, her stride hampered by the burn on her leg.

I swung into the saddle. Riot and I folded right into fire and shot back to the battle zone. Back into madness. As we reached it, I searched for Marcus, but I didn't spot him. I didn't see Sebastian, either. Mounted on Lucent and firing bright arrows, Jode was easier to find.

He was in a standoff with the fire demon. Pyro had taken cover behind a cluster of rocks. Jode's arrows were keeping him pinned there, but Jode had the hordes to contend with, too.

Riot and I formed up behind Pyro at a full gallop. Jode spotted me and immediately withheld fire. Pyro popped up, thinking he had an opening.

Mistake.

I swung the sword with everything I had but Riot's power did most of the work, cleaving the demon in half.

That was one. Six more to go.

Riot and I kept on, picking the monsters off, but they never ended. There were always more and I saw why. The smaller scorpions rolled off Ronwae's body like marbles, and then grew steadily in size. And the gruesome humps on Bay's thick fur came off, like grizzly amoebas, forming into her mutated replicas.

Time took on a bizarre quality. I saw flashes of Marcus's scythe swinging in wide arcs. Jode and Lucent, at the center of a hail of bright arrows. Every second felt isolated, clear as a picture. Every instant was endless. I was in a fog. I was in the smoke and spatter of war, fighting to live. Nothing had ever felt more distant and real.

Nearby, Jode nocked an arrow, swung to the left, and fired. Behind me—almost *on* me—one of the smaller scorpions scuttled through shrubs, snapping branches.

I didn't have to tell Riot to go after it—he *went*.

The creature was fast on its six skittering legs, but Riot and I shifted and made up ground, re-forming as we came even. The scorpion let out a shriek as it saw us, and its stinger lashed down. Riot surged to the side, dodging, then let out a roar and responded with a burst of power, his legs and mane lighting up.

We came up on it, drawing closer. Close enough. I firmed my hands on my sword, reached up, and buried the blade in its armor.

The scorpion veered sharply. My elbows slammed straight, my shoulders almost tearing out of their sockets. I flew off the saddle, and my knees smashed into the ground, then I was dragging along beside it.

The creature jerked left and right, trying to toss me as I hung on to the sword buried in its side, trying to get my feet under me. Trying not to get trampled. The skin on my palms ripped as my grip slipped. I couldn't hold on much longer.

A flare of flames came up fast on my right—it was Riot, gone to fire. He flew a tight circle around the creature. It screamed and screeched to a halt. Then its body rocked up, rising like a boat on a swell. I knew what was coming before I saw the stinger whip down.

I released my sword, dropped, and rolled beneath the scorpion's body—the only safe place around. The stinger struck the spot where I'd just been, driving into the dirt. I saw it lash back up. Then I heard a sharp *crack* as the scorpion's underbelly shuddered above me.

Stupid thing had stung itself—and I was underneath it.

Tucking my arms, I rolled to my left as fast as I could. Not fast enough. A huge weight collapsed onto my leg. I felt a sharp jerk in my knee and pain shot up my thigh. I tried to free myself, but the scorpion weighed a thousand pounds, at least, and my foot was too far beneath it.

Riot thundered up, nostrils flared, his entire body blazing. One look at the frenzy in his eyes and I knew he didn't understand. He thought the scorpion was hurting me, which it was. But his answer was to slam his hooves into the creature's armor.

"Whoa, Riot!" I yelled. "Riot, no!"

He kept going, every stamp cracking the creature's thick shell into a mash as he worked closer to where my foot was trapped. He was going to crush my leg.

Marcus ran up. He took Riot's reins and pulled him back. I collapsed on the dirt, needing a second to absorb the relief. My own horse had almost maimed me. Marcus came back and stood over me.

"What did you go and do, Blake?" With a tug, he withdrew my sword and slid it beneath the creature's body, leveraging the weight off my leg.

As I rolled up, climbing to my feet, I felt a strain on the outside of my knee. My eyes burned. My throat was raw. A dull, muted ring sounded in my ears.

"Where's Sebastian?" I asked.

The fires around the bluff seemed to be losing some intensity.

"Not here," Marcus said. "It wasn't him before. It was Malaphar. Samrael was bluffing."

"Yeah, but where is he?" I focused in on the signals from the cuff. Bas didn't feel close.

Marcus's gaze fell to the key around my neck. "Where's *Daryn*?"

"Getting help."

Nearby, Jode fired at one of Bay's beasts as it tore out of the darkness, making a charge our way. Half the creature's thick gut disappeared, incinerated. It toppled to the earth and released a final yelp of agony.

Across the clearing Bay threw her head back and let out a roar. Her hordes immediately responded, flowing around her as they plunged through a gap in the fires, disappearing into the night. Ronwae and her multiples scurried after, and the battleground began to clear.

Were they going after Daryn? Why would they? She didn't have the key anymore. It was around my neck. The Kindred were drawn to its power—so they'd come after *me*.

At the center of the clearing where Bas had stood with Samrael, I saw a familiar whirl of darkness. Shadow formed up. She looked right at Marcus and me as she reared, letting out a desperate braying sound; then she took off, disappearing on the trail heading down the mountain.

Fear speared into my veins as Marcus and I mounted up and put our horses on a tear after her. Jode fell in with us, none of us saying a word.

We were doing exactly what the Kindred wanted. The key thudded against my chest as I rode, drumming right against my heart. But it was Sebastian. We had to find him.

We rode down the trail we'd walked a hundred times over the past few weeks. The fires receded as we left the bluff behind and descended to the river's edge. The darkness grew thicker and I knew exactly why.

As we reached the end of the trail, my grasp of time felt off. The ride had taken forever and it had been over in an instant. Our practice field along the river's edge—so familiar after all our time there—was a pool of darkness. I knew the river should be dead ahead, but I couldn't see it.

We slowed the horses to a walk. I moved to the outside, putting Marcus between Jode and me. Our horses put off more illumination than Ruin—but it didn't help much. I couldn't see more than five paces in any direction. Up on the bluff, the glow of the flames was visible. A long column of smoke lifted into the sky.

A distant sound caught my attention—one I hadn't heard in weeks. The drone of helicopter rotors carried through the fjord. Was that a Norwegian response to the fires, or had Daryn's message gone through? How much time had passed since I'd seen her? An hour? Two? Time felt elastic.

"I've had about enough of this," Jode said, drawing an arrow into his bow.

He fired, starting at twelve o'clock, and then moved on, working clockwise. Turning in a circle as Marcus and I stayed clear.

I spotted movement in the inky blackness. Alevar, flapping away in a clumsy, wounded flight. I signaled his position to Jode. He loosed another arrow.

Hit.

Alevar spiraled to the earth and sank out of sight.

Two down. Five to go.

I looked at Marcus. Bay leapt suddenly from the black void, teeth snarling, so much bigger than her monsters.

The horses startled. Riot bolted forward. Ruin and Lucent darted right. Marcus swung the scythe and missed—it was the last thing I saw. Riot galloped, surging into the darkness. I reined him in, leaning back, but he wouldn't slow.

I couldn't see anything anymore. I'd lost Marcus and Jode. I heard Riot's hooves hit gravel, then splash into water. We'd run right into the river.

I finally pulled him around and tried to orient myself. The sound of the helicopters was growing louder and the bluff was becoming more visible as Alevar's darkness dispersed. I put Riot in a walk, keeping my sword at the ready as I searched for Bas or Shadow.

I didn't expect to see him just seconds later.

Sebastian walked toward me through the darkness. He didn't look like he was under Samrael's control. He didn't look stiff or unlike himself, either. It was him. I *felt* that it was him through the cuff.

"Bas." I dismounted and approached him, sword still at the ready. It was him, but I wasn't taking any chances. "Tell me it's you, Bas."

"It's me. It's me, look." He stared into the darkness. Shadow came trotting over to him. Sebastian put his hand on her neck, and the mare settled at his touch. "See? It's me. Alevar came out of nowhere. He smashed into me when I stepped outside, and hit me right across the head. Next thing I knew, he'd brought me—" His eyes flew open. "What's around your neck? Oh, *no*. Gideon, is that—"

"Mount up, Bas." Now wasn't the time to explain. "Let's get out of here."

I heard a shrill whinny behind me.

Riot.

I spun as my horse twisted into flame and shot away.

"Riot!" I didn't understand—until I saw the massive form of a dragon emerging from the darkness.

Ra'om stepped forward, his claws pressing deep into the earth under his immense weight.

I had seen him in my mind once, thanks to Samrael's help. But I'd never seen a dragon in person before. It shook me.

Ra'om's red eyes were as I remembered them. As I'd seen them in my nightmares. In shadows. Penetrating. Evil. But his enormous body—scaled, serpentine, *powerful*—was more terrifying than I recalled. He was a thousand times my size.

"Gideon," Bas said behind me. "The *key*."

We definitely weren't escaping this without losing something. The key. Our lives. Possibly all.

Ra'om came to a stop, his long neck arcing high. Wings were folded at his back, liquid silver like the rest of him, and his thick, ridged tail settled on the grass behind him. He lowered his head, bringing it closer to my height, and opened his mouth slightly. Through his fangs, I saw the flick of a black tongue. And deeper, the orange glow of heat. A low growl rumbled from inside his throat and the glow of fire brightened.

As I stood, I felt him piercing my mind, pushing his way into it.

How are you, Gideon?

His cavernous voice echoed from deep within my head.

Samrael was right, it seems. You've caused us more trouble than we expected.

I felt the presence of other Kindred. Malaphar, Ronwae, Bay. I thought of Bas, behind me. I didn't know if he was in danger. But I couldn't help him even if he was. I couldn't even help myself.

Perhaps we should recruit you. I think you would make a good addition to my Kindred. It would be so rewarding to see you and your horsemen on my side. It's where you belong, I think. As one of us. Simply say the word, Gideon. And I can make you strong, like Samrael.

Then there he was—Samrael—striding toward me across our practice field.

He looked smug as he walked up to me. Ra'om's looming presence made me feel insignificant, but Samrael looked powerful. Victorious.

"I don't think so, Ra'om," he said, but he was looking me dead in the eyes. He brought his knife up and laid it under my chin, resting the cool blade on my neck. "He'll never be as strong as me."

The roar of the helicopters grew louder. They were close now. And I felt Jode and Marcus approaching, sensing them through the cuff. But I knew nothing would help now. It was too late.

Samrael drew the knife away. He hooked the point under

the silver chain around my neck, lifting it up over my head. Into his hands. He smiled. "Thank you for this."

The dragon let out a hiss of satisfaction—a horrendous, chilling sound.

What do you think, Gideon? I could give you power unlike anything you've ever known. Will you join us? Will you become our kin?

I pushed against his hold on me—and felt him ease back, relinquishing control. My body came back under my own power. My ability to speak restored. I swallowed, clearing my throat, and looked from Samrael to Ra'om.

"Interesting offer," I said. "How about I kill you both instead?"

Samrael lunged, slashing for my neck—but I'd expected it and twisted away. The blade sliced my shoulder, splitting skin and muscle. My hand opened and my sword dropped to the grass.

I braced myself for Samrael's next attack. Then Ra'om threw his head back and roared, spewing a cloud of fire into the air. Everything went white. I staggered, blinded by the sudden brightness, waiting for the knife to hit me again. To bite into my heart, my neck. But it didn't.

The brightness faded. Samrael wasn't even facing me. He was turned toward Ra'om—toward where Ra'om had been. The dragon was gone.

Not gone—*changed.*

Samrael was watching the shadowed figure of a man standing in the distance. He was nothing more than a dark shape but I knew it was Ra'om, and that he and Samrael were sharing a silent exchange. The man turned and walked into the night, and Samrael looked back at me.

"Ra'om has commanded me to spare you," Samrael said. "He thinks it would be a waste of potential. An error, in my opinion, but it is his decision. It seems your life continues. For now. I'll find you again, Gideon." He gathered the long silver chain into his hand, closing his fingers over it. "Right after I find her."

Then he followed Ra'om, taking the rest of the Kindred with him.

And the key.

CHAPTER 53

This pine room feels like a box after what I've said. After burning fjords and hordes of demons. After Ra'om.

I stare into Cordero's eyes, but it's not Cordero anymore. The face in front of me is a woman's, but all I see is Malaphar.

"And now we've come to the end, haven't we?" Malaphar says. "You were picked up on that practice field shortly afterward, correct? You and the other riders?"

I don't know why he's still pretending. I don't think I can do it much longer.

I'm going numb from the adrenaline running through me. I'm shaking from it.

"Where was Daryn, Gideon? Why wasn't she there? Did she stay with her Seeker friend, Isabel?"

Daryn actually *was* there. After she'd gone to find Isabel, she'd come back to our practice field. I picture it. The two Blackhawks that had touched down. The team of US Commandos that had arrived to get us out.

I remember the quick, furious exchange I had with one of them. With Texas—the guy in this very room. I'd asked him about Daryn. He'd had no idea who I meant and we needed to go. There was too much smoke. The Blackhawks's rotors hadn't even slowed. We needed to *go*.

I'd looked up to the trail and seen Daryn there. Standing on the exact same spot where we'd met that day Marcus had dropped me in the river. She was just standing there, watching.

Making no move to join us. To join *me*.

Seeing that, madness had come over me.

I'd lost the key. I'd lost her. I'd let myself down. I'd let the guys down. How many innocent people would the Kindred bleed of their goodness because of *me*? How much evil would spread because I'd given up that key?

The failure had crushed me. *Belligerent,* Cordero called me at the start of all this. It was true. I'd lost my head. I'd fought to get to Daryn, hitting anyone who came near me. Jode. Marcus. My rage was immense. I fought until there were too many descending on me. Then Texas threw his elbow across my temple. Next thing I knew I was waking up sedated and strapped to a chair, with a hood dropped over my head and a radiator clicking behind me.

Here.

Texas is watching me like he's remembering the exact same thing. He's perfectly still, except for the hand that moves slowly, millimeter by millimeter, toward his sidearm.

I swallow, and make myself answer the question. "Daryn would have gone wherever she could best protect the key."

"That's interesting, Gideon. Because, as you know, Daryn came *here*. Are you saying the key's here? Are you saying the Kindred took a false key in Jotunheimen? A decoy? Are you saying you know where the real key is? What are you saying, Gideon?"

There's no room for deception in this room anymore. There's no more time to wait for help. Not from Beretta, or from Daryn, or the guys.

"We both know where the real key is," I say. "Don't we, Malaphar?"

The door swings open. Samrael enters so fast, he's a blur.

Texas draws his pistol, but Samrael pushes his arm aside as he stabs—once, decisively. Texas drops. The floorboards bounce like a trampoline under my feet as he falls.

It's over in a second.

Samrael stands over him with a bone knife.

Cordero—who has transformed into Malaphar—is still sitting at the edge of the desk.

And me. I'm still sitting in this chair.

CHAPTER 54

I hear a terrible wheezing sound. Texas slumps against the wall. He's bleeding from his side, struggling to breathe. His baseball cap sits in the growing pool of blood beside him.

Sucking chest wound. Still alive.

Samrael picks up the gun on the floor and hands it to Malaphar as he steps around the desk. He looks at me, then at the cuff around my wrist with a fever in his hellacious eyes. Reaching into his pocket, he removes the silver chain with the false key. Daryn's necklace. "Don't need this anymore." He flips it toward me. It bounces off my chest and slides to the floor.

"When did you know?" Malaphar asks me.

My muscles shake with rage. "Does it matter?"

A smile spreads over Malaphar's crater-skinned face. "No. But I think it was the Lagos story. When Daryn said the key disappeared, she meant it. Do you know what day that was? Because she didn't mention that detail, did she? It was August second, Gideon. Do you know where the key reappeared? It was in four places, actually. I know even you can figure out at least one."

Breathe. Just breathe.

"Clever, don't you think?" Samrael says. "Very clever to separate it that way. Scatter the pieces across the globe and then hide them in plain sight." He gestures with the knife in his hand, like this room is the world. "Caused us a fair amount of confusion as we tried to follow its power. We didn't understand why it was weaker. Diffuse. Until that moment we took it—but then, you riders were all there together. A sound tactic. As was entrusting the pieces to people ignorant of what they even had. It made you immune to my capabilities. We had to do all of this. Mine you for knowledge you didn't even know you possessed. We've gone to a good deal of trouble."

He falls silent, and there's only the sound of Texas's labored breathing.

"Give it to me, Gideon," Samrael says.

I look at Malaphar. "It won't come off me. I've told you that."

"Daryn is the keeper," Samrael says. "Isn't she? The only one who can wield its power. It's another seal of protection. Isn't it?"

I shake my head. I don't know. I don't know and if I don't get out of this chair Texas is going to die and so will I.

"She is full of surprises." Samrael's gaze falls to the cuff again. He adjusts his grip on the knife. "Well, no matter. There are other ways of removing it."

He steps in, and hammers down with the blade.

The instant fragments.

I watch the pale blade come down. I watch it slice through my wrist and bite deep into the wood of the chair.

I hear the wood split and I see my hand fall.

I hear it thump as it drops to the floor.

Time moves again, and reality returns.

No. It doesn't.

What I see makes no sense. Where my hand should be there is nothing. I've been partially erased. And I'm bleeding. I'm bleeding like a leaky fuel pump.

Spots explode before my eyes.

Stay here, Blake. Stay, stay, stay.

Samrael grabs my forearm, keeping it in place with one hand.

With the other, he tugs on the cuff.

I feel warmth, wetness, slipping, and the cuff comes off.

The cuff, which is the key, which has been on me this whole time. On me and the guys—not around Daryn's neck.

Very clever.

Samrael straightens. "Thank you, Gideon," he says, giving the cuff a toss like it's a baseball. "I'm glad we could finally work this out."

He turns to Malaphar and they speak, but I can't hear what they say. The pain comes with a sound like metal bending in my ears. It expands, a universe inside me. I stare at the knots in the pine paneling and still see my handless arm. I blink and blink and I can't make it to go away. It's like a scratch on a lens.

The metallic groan recedes and I hear Samrael again.

"Fine," he says to Malaphar. "But you'll have to answer to Ra'om for it." He throws me a frustrated glance and leaves.

Malaphar smiles at me with his pinched features and beetle black eyes and I realize what just happened. An argument over who gets to kill me. Malaphar must've fought hard.

"It's just you and me again, Gideon. It's a shame you won't get to meet the real Cordero. She's here. Real nice lady. Smart. I think you'd have liked her. I think she would have liked you."

I don't want to die in this chair.

Malaphar disengages the safety and sets his aim on me.

I look right into the barrel.

This is the real deal, right here. Right now.

The gun goes off.

White noise—

Eclipses—

All.

CHAPTER 55

I'm here.
  I'm still here.
But I'm deaf and my heart isn't beating.
I count to five. Ten. Twenty.
The ringing in my ears starts at twenty-one, my heart at thirty.
Texas leans against the wall, holding his side. Blood pours through his fingers. He holds his knife in his other hand.
His knife. He used his bowie knife.
Malaphar is facedown on the floor. I can't see his neck, the front part, but deep black blood is forming a pool beneath him. It's touching the redder blood that belongs to me and Texas.
There's a bullet hole and splintered paneling to my right.
It looks bad in here. And I'm still making it worse.
Texas pushes himself off the wall and comes over. The ringing hasn't left my ears, but I can hear the big sucking sounds coming from him. He's dragging in air like he's going to dive deep underwater and the veins are bulging in his neck.
I'm not doing great, either. It's hard to think past the pain. It begins at my hand and has no end.
Oh, shit.
My hand.
"Hand? Where's my hand?"
Texas glances at the floor. He tries to tell me something but it comes out as a burbling noise, then wet coughing, then he bends over and spits.
We're making such a bloody mess. I hope I don't have to clean this up later.

He straightens and tries to talk again, but it's no better than last time and I can't stop asking him where my hand is.

Where is it, where is it, where is it.

Worthless question but I can't stop asking.

It still feels like it's part of me, only that I can't see it.

Between my question loop and Texas's wheezing, I hear something else. There's gunfire now. Outside this room. All over the cabin. Rounds are flying fast and furious.

Wood-paneled walls are shattering and windows are shattering. Tremors vibrate into the soles of my boots—the seismic ripple of the activity right outside this room. The jig is up. Everybody's in the fight now.

Texas runs a sleeve over his chin, like, *Okay. Enough of all this chatter. Time to get down to work.* He kneels by the chair and pulls a flex tie from his pocket. He wraps it above my missing hand and ties it off, making a tourniquet.

"Southpaw?" Texas rasps.

Am I a southpaw. He's been trying to talk for a full minute and this is what he wants to know. If I'm left-handed.

I want to answer him, but I also want to howl until my throat turns inside out. I want to know if Daryn knew. *I'm so sorry,* she'd said on our last night in the hut as she'd squeezed my hand. *Did she know?* What I want more than anything is to get out of this chair and pick my hand up off the floor. But I just nod and say, "Yes. Lefty."

"Righty now, kid," Texas says in his drowning voice.

Righty now. I nod. Okay. Okay. But it can't be that easy.

Then my eyes pull past him, to the door.

To Marcus, who explodes into the room.

CHAPTER 56

When Marcus sees what's happened to me, he loses his mind. He instantly starts yelling and swearing. Calling for help. Cursing the Kindred. More out of control than I've ever seen him.

It legitimately moves me. I have to put my head down because it's the nicest thing he's ever done for me, hands down.

Hand down.

My hand is still down on the floor somewhere.

Marcus's cuff is still on his wrist, which means we still have a chance. As long as we keep one, we still have a chance.

People stream into the room behind him. One is a stocky man wearing a black beanie. He picks up my hand, takes a quick look at it, then gives it to a red-haired guy about my age and barks some orders. The red-haired guy listens, nods, listens, nods; then he flees the room like a thief.

Black Beanie kneels beside me and opens a medical kit. He sprays something where my hand used to be, telling me that it's under control, don't rule anything out, reattachment is still a possibility.

I don't say anything but I'm not so sure, given the way I heal. The bleeding's already slowing. My nerve endings and muscular tissue may have already decided to move on, without my hand. Even the pain is lessening. Something's kicking in. Adrenaline or some internal defense mechanism has kicked in. I'm getting less shaky. Things are making more sense.

As my arm is being wrapped in gauze, Texas is helped out of the room. Malaphar's body is removed. The desk and chair where Cordero sat go next but I'm not clear on the urgency there. *Is there some kind of office emergency?*

Then Beretta comes back in. He tips his head, giving me a look like, *We pulled it off, kid, it could've been worse.*

Some part of me had begun to accept that he hadn't survived, and the relief of seeing him is intense. He doesn't look at the stump that's part of me now, which makes the vote unanimous: he's a human being of quality.

The bandage is tied off and it helps. It makes the end of my arm look better. Tidier.

I pull myself to my feet. I want to throw the chair against the wall, demolish it, but instead I wait for the room to finish taking a spin around me.

There are seven, eight people in here now. Wedged in this small room. Standing on human and demon blood. They're all Army. Strapped down with rifles. Pistols. Radios. Everyone is talking and listening at the same time.

"Where is he?" I ask Marcus. "Where's Samrael?"

"Outside, with the rest," he says. "Daryn, Jode, and Bastian are out there."

Information flows around me. The Kindred are digging in. Fighting for the other cuffs, of course. They won't leave until they have them all.

A man steps forward and regards me with a penetrating look. I remember myself and salute, fighting through another round of dizziness.

"At ease, soldier," he says.

At ease. It seems like an impossible thing to be.

Major Robertson's decorated, has the look of someone who's seen his share of combat. Nothing like this, I'm sure. But even this he seems to take in stride.

"Malaphar fooled us all," he says to me. His eyes move to Beretta. "We had no idea until Sergeant Suarez told us."

Suarez—that's Beretta's name.

"We'll have air support in twenty minutes, sir," Suarez says.

"Seventeen," amends a guy wearing an earpiece.

Marcus and I look at each other. What kind of damage can Ra'om, Samrael, Ronwae, and Bay do in that amount of time?

The answer is: Too much.

"Ready?" Marcus asks me.

"Yes." I'm ready to fight. But I didn't just lose my hand—I lost the cuff. I don't know if I still have my sword, my armor, or Riot.

I don't know if I'm still War.

CHAPTER 57

Outside, a battle is raging.

I pause on the front steps with Marcus and adjust to the scene. Our cabin is one of a dozen on the edge of a wide field where the fight is occurring. Dense woods surround the field, tall pine trees that rise like black spires. Gray clouds hover around the granite peaks of the jagged mountains in the distance. Snow patches spill like paint over the steep slopes. The terrain reminds me of Jotunheimen—if Jotunheimen were dropped and shattered.

"Wyoming," Marcus says, sensing my disorientation. A familiar flurry of ash circles ahead of us, and then Marcus is running. He meets Ruin as she forms and gallops into the fray.

Across the field, I see Jode and Lucent—a bright pair in the twilight. Jode is firing arrows at Bay's monsters and Ronwae's scorpions—a sight I saw constantly on our bluff—then my eyes pull to the black horse and rider. Sebastian is here. Bas, who was missing before. He's here. And *fighting*. But he has no choice. One of the cuffs is on his wrist.

I don't see Samrael, but Ra'om is flying over everything—a massive dark shadow wheeling against the steel clouds.

And there's another addition to this fight. The US military force on hand isn't significant in number, fifteen to twenty men, but they've dug into covered positions around the cabins and Humvees along the road, and they're laying down some serious brass. My ears fill with the steady chug of M249 SAWs and the staccato pop of M4s. Never have I heard a more welcome racket. I see that Bay's monsters are falling, but it takes a hail of firepower to break down the scorpions' shells. My sword pierces their armor with much less effort.

Then I see Daryn.

She stands with a cluster of soldiers behind a Humvee. Her calf is wrapped with gauze. Our gallop from the burning bluff feels like it happened a hundred years ago, but has it even been a day?

She sees me. She breaks away and comes running. Then she's flying into my arms. As I wrap them around her what I feel is a plummet from incredible to incomplete.

I don't know where I end anymore.

I don't know how I still feel my hand, but not *her*.

"Gideon." She steps back, and her gaze drops to the bandage on the end of my arm. Her eyes go wide and she freezes—but I don't.

I take off, summoning Riot on the run.

He comes up with a concentrated, furious burst of fire.

I still have him.

I fold in, and he sweeps me up. As we rise into the sky, it strikes me that Riot has become a bigger part of me than my hand, and I thank God he's still with me. I don't know what would've happened if I'd lost him.

Bonded as fire, we're something better than *alive*. In moments, I feel healed. Whole. There's no pain anymore, no shame. I shed all of it. Then I feel Riot's anger and his fear. He knows what's happened. I feel him clinging to me as we soar down to the field. I try to shift, but Riot wants to keep me as fire. We're untouchable like this. We can't be harmed. But to fight I have to become human. Vulnerable and dangerous. I push and Riot understands. He finally relents and we lock in. Horse and rider, formed again.

As we charge into the field, I loop the reins over my stump twice, ignoring the pain, fighting against it. Then I summon my sword.

It materializes in my right hand.

Righty now, kid.

Hopefully the reins will stay on my arm, and I can fight like this.

Marcus and Ruin fall in beside us, and together we make for Bay. With her monsters and Ronwae's scorpions flanking her, she's making a push toward Jode. He could shift and soar away with Lucent, but the demons have found a weakness. They're directing their attacks on the people by the cabins. Jode, who wields the bow's matchless range and power, is policing the entire battlefield. Marcus glances at me as we gallop closer. He knows it, too. If we lose Jode, we lose everything.

Reaching one of the beasts, I plunge my blade into the hump on its back. I swing again, inflicting a grazing blow on another, and Marcus is there to finish it with the scythe. We move through the clearing in tune, lethal as we fight. Marcus moves toward Jode, but I work toward Bay. By taking her down, I hope it'll call off the rest of her beasts, or at least stop the creation of more. It's our best shot. We can't beat an enemy that keeps regenerating in number.

The fog of battle settles over me, and I become instinct, reflex, reaction. The moments blur until one of Bay's beasts comes bounding at me from the left. Then it hits me—I can't parry or block to my left. I have a weak side now.

"Gideon!" Marcus yells.

Time slows as I recognize that it's *Bay*—and that she's coming with every bit of speed and power she possesses. She leaps, fangs bared, her claws slashing. I call to Riot urgently—*to fire*.

I'm too late and she slams into me. My left arm wrenches against the reins. I rock back, but I don't fall from the saddle. Bay tumbles off me as Riot kicks, but she isn't giving up. She slashes with long claws, tearing at Riot's hindquarters.

Riot roars. He goes ballistic beneath me, his body lighting up with flame. I try to send him all the way to fire, but he's seized by terror. He doesn't listen, and Bay won't let him go.

She rips my horse's thigh open again as he kicks and bites. I feel him buckle beneath me, his legs giving out. I swing at Bay, but I can't turn enough to reach her. I need the sword in my left hand, but that hand is gone.

I'm about to launch myself onto her when I hear my name shouted.

Across the clearing, Sebastian's seen Riot and me in trouble. Shadow is in a gallop as Bas spins the scales above his head. He launches them. They fly true, whirling, trailing smoke, and nail their target.

Bay topples to the dirt, kicking and thrashing, the scales looping around her neck. She reaches for them in panic, pawing with her claws, but the scales have twisted and locked.

Released from Bay's claws, Riot leaps away. He accelerates in powerful thrusts, mindless and wild from the attack. I slip my arm from the twisted reins and throw myself off the saddle. I land, stumbling, staggering, my balance off, my arm flaring with an ache that wants to consume me. I taste blood on my tongue as I push against it. Finding my forting, I walk to Bay.

She's still writhing on her back as I reach her, but she's hooked one of her claws under the chain. In seconds she'll untangle them.

She won't get the chance.

I toss my sword up to reverse my grip. Frenzied howls break out around me, and her beasts look to me with their soulless eyes. They already know it's over. I bring my sword down and plunge it into her heart.

Bay shudders and stills, her eyes going flat. Her monsters fall to the earth and scream like their hearts have been skewered, too. In seconds, they're all silent.

That's four. Four plus one horde.

We're at better than fifty percent, but it doesn't feel like it.

Samrael should count for extra. Ronwae, too.

Ra'om, too. Dragons should count for double.

I look up. Soaring above, Ra'om spews a furious burst of fire. I know he's seen Bay fall.

Kneeling, I unfasten Bastian's weapon from Bay's thick neck. Try to. Harder with one hand. I twist and untwist the links of the scales, trying to get five fingers to do the work of ten. How many things will be harder now? Not the time to think about this.

As I try to unlock the scales again, I sense a shift in the battle's quality. It's quieter without the snarl of the grizzly beasts. And there's no more gunfire. The Army force is out of ammunition. Not a surprise. They couldn't have anticipated a battle against demon hordes in Wyoming.

I'm not mounted, and it's made me vulnerable to the scorpions. Marcus and Jode converge on me. I reach down and tug on the chain again, to free the scales. Bastian needs his weapon. They untwist, and I pull hard. They finally slide from beneath Bay's head, but instead of relief, dread hits me.

If Sebastian needs his weapon, he can just call it back.

Why hasn't he?

As I lift my gaze and look for him, I see Shadow first, halfway across the field.

She's rearing and shrieking as several scorpions keep her from reaching Sebastian—Bas, who is on his back, pinned beneath one of Ronwae's massive claws. Bas is completely immobilized. Even if he called his scales, he couldn't use them.

Samrael stands over him, watching me like he's been waiting.

Stillness descends over everything. My vision tunnels. Everything fades except that point in the field: Ronwae pinning Bas. Samrael watching me.

They are a hundred paces away, but every detail is clear. Every sound. The strain on Sebastian's face at the pressure of the scorpion's claw. Samrael's satisfied smile. The quiet rattle of Ronwae's stinger.

I sense Jode and Marcus dismount and join me.

And Daryn. Daryn comes to my side, her gaze fixed on Sebastian.

Ronwae's multitudes draw around us, keeping us from moving.

None of us is moving.

Only Ra'om moves—a shadow drifting in the sky above.

Samrael lifts my cuff in the air. "I need the other three, Daryn," he says. His voice is ruthless. "Unlock them and bring them to me. Or I'll continue to remove them myself."

"No." Daryn shakes her head. "And they won't help you, Samrael. Even if I brought them to you."

"Will *you* help me?" he asks.

Daryn doesn't answer.

"I think you will," Samrael says. He turns to Ronwae, and motions with his hand. "Go ahead."

The scorpion's claw moves away from Sebastian, and then the stinger whips down. It strikes Sebastian on the chest. It stays there as the tail muscles flex, and I can almost see the venom moving into him. Then the stinger goes up and Bas sags against the ground.

Daryn is screaming. We're all yelling. Jode is the only one still in his right mind. He steps in front of us and holds us back. We can't stop this. It already happened. We can't stop it.

Then I hear Daryn speak words I never thought she'd say.

"I'll do it!" she yells. "I'll give them you!"

Samrael smiles. "I thought so." On the ground by his feet, Bas is gasping for breath. "Better hurry."

As Daryn comes to stand in front of Marcus, thoughts crash through my mind.

What are we doing?

How can we do this?

How can we not?

"Give me your arm," Daryn says. Her eyes are distant. She's

somewhere else. She's trying to get through a situation where every possible outcome is terrible.

Marcus's face is tight with anger as he extends his arm.

Daryn reaches out and frames the cuff with her hands. Her eyes drift almost closed. Soft, warm light builds within her palms. Gold, like her. And the cuff around Marcus's wrist loosens. It dissolves into pale ashes. Into a small tornado, circling Marcus's arm.

There is no wonder or awe on Daryn's face as she steps back, the ashes moving with her. Only focus. A focus that's *beyond*. She brings her hands together and the ashes consolidate, until Marcus's cuff is re-formed and pressed between her palms. She slips it over her wrist. Then she moves to Jode and begins again.

Under her guidance, her control, his cuff becomes a brilliant circle of light, and then transforms back into the cuff, resting in the palm of her hand.

I don't feel surprise as I watch her. The barriers of what's possible broke down when I first folded in with Riot. And I always knew there was something more to her. The feeling that's building inside me is dread.

I'm so sorry.

What did she mean? What does she *know*?

Daryn slips Jode's cuff over her wrist. It rests next to Marcus's.

Only Sebastian's cuff is left now.

She glances at me, and walks away. As she strides to Sebastian and Samrael, I tell myself it wasn't good-bye I just saw in her eyes.

She reaches them and kneels at Bas's side. Ronwae has backed off. There's no need to restrain Bas anymore. Even from where I stand, I can see that he's starting to convulse from the poison.

Daryn runs her hands over his forehead and it seems to steady him. Samrael stands close as she takes Bas's cuff, but his eyes are on me. He knows what it does to me, seeing him so close to her.

When Daryn has Sebastian's cuff, she stands and Samrael hands her mine.

She has them all now. All four.

"Do it," he says. He tips his head to Sebastian. "Quickly, if you hope to help him."

Daryn takes the four cuffs into her open palms. Each of them loosens and dissolves, transforming into dust. Into light and shadow and fire. They hover above her palms, turning in circles. But then they meld together and form a sphere. A small marbled globe, floating above her open hands.

Daryn steps back and the sphere expands, reaching her height and then larger. Twice her height. It turns in front of her, a world spinning above the trampled grass. A small universe of fire and water, ice and steel. Every element. Every star and every ocean. It's the most beautiful thing I've ever seen.

Miraculous.

It's the only word.

Samrael comes to Daryn's side and gazes at it with a look of triumph. "Now cede it to me," he says.

Daryn shakes her head, and tenses. Then I hear the distant howl of wind as a point of pure darkness appears on the sphere.

Samrael is focused on it, like he's the one feeding it, building it.

He is.

I know he's tainting it. I know how it feels to be tainted by the Kindred.

As the darkness expands, I see that it's a tunnel.

A *porthole.*

And through it, mountains appear. They're the same jagged Wyoming peaks, but they're cloaked in ice and it's night there. The ground is a smooth sheet of ice and the trees are coated with frost.

The wind howls louder and pushes at my back. It scatters leaves and rustles the trees around the clearing.

It's the pull of that place. An evil, leeching hunger. The kind I've seen in Ra'om's eyes.

Daryn staggers away from the porthole, but Samrael steps closer. He stands before it, gazing at the frozen world inside. His dark clothes whip with the force of the wind. He's mesmerized by what he sees. A refuge. A kingdom. An empire made of the same malevolent hunger that exists inside him. That feeds him.

I don't see Sebastian until he's running.

Running with effort. Like every step is a struggle.

But Samrael has his back turned and he's not expecting the collision.

Sebastian slams into him and they catapult forward.

They pitch into the porthole—and are instantly sucked inside.

Vanished.

Gone.

I loose sight of them and the passage pinholes shut. The sphere unravels in a violent tumble of elements, disappearing in a swirl at Daryn's hands.

Daryn clutches her hands close and bows her head. Her breath is ragged and her back shakes.

Spent.

She's spent by what she's just done.

What has she done?

"*Sebastian,*" Jode says with an exhale.

Then a deafening roar pulls my attention up.

Ra'om is ripping down the sky, coming right at us.

CHAPTER 58

I swing into Riot's saddle and tear toward Daryn. It's a short distance, but Riot struggles. His gait is lopsided and he's grunting with every stride. Dismounting, I reach Daryn in three strides.

"*Gideon,*" she says, tears brimming in her eyes. "It was supposed to be me! I didn't know Bas would do that! It was supposed to be *me!*"

"We'll get him back." Sebastian's scales are looped around my left arm. They give me hope that he's still alive. "We'll get him."

Ra'om sweeps down from the sky, strafing the cabins and trees with fire. Ronwae and her scorpions attack with no fear of death. They were moments away from attaining what they wanted. Failure has driven them mad, but I'm no different.

Vengeance beats through me like a pulse. I'm blinded by it. I *know* I am. All I want to see is the destruction of the Kindred who are left. All I want to do is join Jode and Marcus in demolishing Ronwae's scorpions.

Ra'om dives on us from above. Daryn and I lunge away, and Riot bolts. The dragon's huge talons gouge the dirt where we'd just stood. He climbs into the sky, pumping his massive wings, his long tail stretched out behind him.

"He won't stop," Daryn says. Her tears are gone. Now there's only fierce determination. In her hand is a small globe, alive with colors swirling inside it. I know it's our cuffs, formed together. Our way back to Sebastian. "I have to get this somewhere safe."

"And *you,* Daryn," I add, because now I know. It's not only the key. It's the keeper.

Riot comes back to us, bobbing his head. His breathing has become short and raspy. Shadow is with him and she's distraught, her movements jerky and her eyes wild. I know she's searching for Bas.

"I'll take her." Daryn grabs Shadow's reins. She steps into the stirrup and mounts the black mare. Shadow dances anxiously, but Daryn is firm and Shadow settles under her confidence.

"Daryn, wait," I say, before she leaves. I take Riot's reins. He jerks his head up, his amber eyes glowing with defiance. He wants to stay with me, but I can't let him. Not with blood hissing from the gashes on his thigh. *"Go, Riot."*

Daryn rides, and my horse goes with her, the fire rising over his legs.

Then I'm alone, surrounded by war.

Ready.

I see that Jode and Marcus have taken Ronwae down together. The red scorpion has no stinger. It's been severed, along with both claws. Jode is pumping arrow after arrow into her body as she shrieks. After what Ronwae did to Sebastian, it's not ruthless enough for me.

In the sky, Ra'om is easily contending with the two F-22s that have finally arrived. He twists and dives through the air, more agile than the planes. A perfect aerial predator.

I watch him as he sails down, blowing fire over the cabins, and I try to find his weakness. His eyes . . . his nostrils . . . the underside of his body . . . his joints . . .

You're mistaken, Gideon. I'm protected there, too.

"You're lying," I reply, watching him high above. "But that's okay. I'll find a better way to kill you."

He tucks his wings and plunges. In just seconds, he pulls up in the clearing in front of me with a thud that shakes the earth.

Ra'om unfolds himself, drawing up to his full size. There's a challenge in his red eyes. Pride, in his erect posture and the curve of his long neck.

You should have accepted my offer when you had the chance.

I walk toward him. "You're nothing without Samrael. He was stronger than you. What have you ever done but hide? You just show up for the glory. But there is no glory now, is there?"

Ra'om unfurls his neck and lifts his head high as he shuts his eyes. Fire tumbles from his mouth, rolling into the sky like a glowing orange wave. The sound of his anger penetrates through me, shredding across the woods and shaking the mountains.

I keep walking. "You know what I think, Ra'om? Samrael was never going to take you with him. He thought you were weak. He told me so."

No. He's my kin! Samrael is waiting for me. I'll join him and when I do, I'll take you with me. You'll bow to me, Gideon. I will break you. You will be mine.

Pride, I think, as I keep approaching him. That's his weakness.

Earned pride, Gideon. My pride is earned. You think you can defeat me with your sword and your one hand?

"Yes." I lift my sword. "I don't even think I need this," I say, calling it back. "You're just a giant lizard with wings. Except butt-ugly."

Ra'om lowers his head and extends his long neck. I know what's coming. It's what I wanted.

Grabbing Bastian's scales from my arm, I firm my grip on them—and *run*.

The fire comes like a wave and I keep running blindly through the flames. Run toward where I last saw him. Toward where I need him to still be.

Run.

Head down. Eyes closed. Feet digging.

When I'm through the fire, I'm almost at his lowered wing.

I step on it and jump, throwing myself onto his neck as I whip the scales out, holding on to one end. The chain loops around Ra'om's neck and locks. I jam my handless arm under it— then my face slams against dragon scales as Ra'om surges into the sky.

I grab the chain and hold on with everything I have as he shoots higher, higher, and my stomach isn't with me anymore. It's somewhere hundreds of feet below.

Ra'om makes a sharp turn and I twist, almost falling off. He makes another, trying to throw me. I hold on tight and catch a glimpse of the clearing far below. The cabins are just burning points. Ra'om thrashes and turns. Cold wind pushes against my face and my eyes water. His scales are smooth, impossible to hold on to, and I know I only have seconds.

I call my sword. I can't reach Ra'om's eyes and his scales are too thick where I am.

You should've thought of that beforehand.

He rolls into a shallow dive.

Do you remember, Gideon, sitting in the truck while your father fell? Do you remember how you felt as he looked at you in that last moment?

He levels his flight and banks to the left, and the mountain-side shoots past, a blur of trees and snow and rock.

Do you remember how you felt when he struck the ground? How you felt as you stood over him, watching the blood pool in his ear and then spill onto those red bricks?

"I remember," I say, adjusting my grip on the sword. "But you're going to have to do better."

I've forgiven myself. I know it wasn't my fault.

Ra'om turns his head in surprise.

His eyes are close, but he's given me a better option. A perfect angle into his ear canal. I reach out and drive my sword in, pushing until I can't anymore.

His body goes slack beneath me, his wings lose their tension, and I'm floating for an instant. Then I'm falling.

Out of the sky, but I have no fear.

Riot finds me. He wraps around me and I fold in.

Then we fly as fire.

As one.

CHAPTER 59

On the ground, I find Marcus and Jode waiting for me in front of the cabin where I spent the better part of the day tied to a chair. It's the only cabin untouched by Ra'om's fire.

Suarez is here too, and a handful of other people. They've been talking for half an hour. Or maybe an hour. It could be five minutes.

I tuned out after I asked about Texas, whose real name is Travis Low. He's been airlifted to a hospital, but I've been assured he's doing fine.

A Blackhawk helicopter sits in the distance and armored trucks make a line along the road. There are flares everywhere. People everywhere. Lights have been set up around the field. A light snow is falling.

It finally sinks in that it's over. I'll get to see my mom . . . Anna. I'll get to go *home*.

But Sebastian won't.

Then I see Cordero and my mind empties of everything else. She walks up with Major Robertson.

The expression on his face seems oddly informal and warm. I don't like it. Then I look into the dark eyes of the woman I've spent the past hours with. Anger shoots through me—hot and sharp—and Riot snorts behind me.

"Steady, Riot," Jode says, moving to my horse.

"This is Natalie Cordero," Robertson says. "She's with the Defense Intelligence Agency. The Kindred detained her at a nearby location."

Cordero doesn't offer her hand. "I've been investigating these kinds of matters for a long time, Private Blake," she says simply. "This time, I got closer than I would have liked."

I understand why they brought Cordero and me together now, rather than later. Clear the air. Right away before resentment can fester. But I'm not ready for this and I might never be. I don't know if I'll ever be able to look at her without thinking of Malaphar. She must sense it, because she excuses herself and leaves with Robertson.

"Where's Daryn?" I ask Marcus. I've been afraid to ask, I realize. Because if Daryn were here, then she'd be *here*. With us. With me.

Marcus runs a hand over his head and looks at me. "She's gone."

"We saw her last with Shadow." Jode says, watching me closely. "Shadow wouldn't settle. Daryn said she was going to walk her. Get her away from here to see if it would help . . . but she hasn't come back."

We look at each other, and the question is right there.

Will Daryn come back? Or did she just abandon Sebastian in that hellish world?

Is that it?

Is he gone?

Whatever Daryn's done, or has to do, or will do, I can't be angry with her. I've had the easy job. Slaying demons. She has the tough one. Following orders, even when it means hurting people you care about. She's much stronger than I am. But I know her. I know that wherever she is, she's suffering.

Someone comes up, wanting to look at my hand. At the place where my hand used to be attached to the rest of me. But Marcus snarls and the guy practically falls on his face as he rushes to leave.

He's such an asshole, Marcus. It makes Jode shake his head. It makes me wish Bastian were here to say something Bastianish to Marcus. *Don't throw stones at people who live in brick houses.*

The three of us stand and talk as floodlights go up. As

demon bodies are photographed, crated, and hauled away. We stand and watch the snow fall. Watch as it erases the evil that occurred here.

Suarez brings blankets. We throw them over our backs and search for things to say to each other, but no topic is safe. No topic helps us forget. But we try. We take turns making meaningless words, prolonging the moment. Stretching out *now*, because *later* is no good. *Later* will only be more of this—an accumulation of this feeling that none of us can escape.

We're lost.

We have nowhere to go. Nothing to do without Daryn's guidance.

Riot nudges me in the back. I turn and look at him. He's been making my neck sweat with his hot breath. Melting snow into puddles at my feet. I look into his big amber eyes and wish he could fix this for me, too.

We stand around in our blankets and watch the snow, but Sebastian and Shadow never join us, and neither does Daryn.

Still, we stand.

None of us calls what we did a victory.

CHAPTER 60

We'll be right back," Anna says to me. I look from her to Jode, whose arm is over her shoulder.

Jode. And my *sister.*

I still can't wrap my head around it.

"Where are you going?" I ask her.

Anna rolls her eyes. "To get something to drink, Gideon. Relax. We're not running away together."

Jode just laughs at me. They round Freedom Hall, heading to a tent set up with refreshments and food.

My mom slips her arm through mine. "How are you doing with this?"

"Well," I say. "On the one hand, I want to kick his ass. On the other hand—oh, wait. I only have one hand, so. I want to kick his ass."

My mom shakes her head at me. She hates it when I pull that one—about my hand. But I use it all the time. It's amazing how many expressions are based around hands. *I have to hand it to you. In good hands. Out of hand.* I notice them all now. I'm keeping a mental list so one day I can make Bas laugh. Someday it'll happen.

"I meant how are you doing with this," Mom says. Her eyes move to the group of soldiers standing a little way off.

The ceremony celebrating the newest graduates of RASP just concluded. Thirty-nine soldiers have donned the tan berets of the 75th Ranger Regiment for the first time. Private Marcus Walker finished at the top of the class.

Marcus looks about fifteen pounds lighter than he did a few

months ago when he enlisted. He was always shredded, but now he's ridiculous. I'm going to have to step up my workouts to keep us even.

"I'm good," I answer. "My baby's all grown up."

She smiles and squeezes my arm. "It's incredible that he did this, Gideon."

In the beat of silence that follows I hear the words she doesn't say: *for you.*

I didn't ask Marcus to enlist and become a Ranger. He and I never actually talked about *why* he did this, but it's obvious. To me. To Jode . . . to everyone.

With a prosthetic left hand, finishing the course wasn't an option for me. Supposedly I'll be getting a mechanical hand soon, one that's almost as agile and responsive as a real hand. When they find out you're War, the government goes out of their way to keep you happy. But RASP and I weren't meant to be. Plenty of guys who are Rangers become amputees. But amputees don't become Rangers.

I'd be lying if I didn't admit part of me wants to be standing where Marcus is. Surrounded by other guys who went through the program. Who persevered together, and formed a bond because of it. But I have done that. It's just that my own graduating class is much smaller.

Five of us were there at the beginning.

Now we're only three.

I can't dwell on that right now, though. Not today. Maybe I'm not directly honoring my dad's memory, but it's better this way. Marcus isn't just doing this for my dad and me. He's doing this for himself too. It's a pretty awesome trifecta.

"He's done good," I say.

Mom nods and squeezes my arm. "You all have."

As I watch, Marcus shakes Colonel Nellis's hand. Then they both look to me and snap a salute, which I return.

Mom wanders away to talk to some of the other parents. I watch her approach an older couple and introduce herself as Gideon Blake *and* Marcus Walker's mother. That's a first, but not surprising. Marcus and my mom had a bond from day one. She loved him about as quickly as I hated him—in the beginning.

Mom didn't ask a single question when I brought both him and Jode back to Half Moon Bay with me, straight from Wyoming. She'd just lined us up and asked us what we liked to eat. Then she'd broken up the chores between us. Laundry, trash, dishwasher. Like, *Fall in, children. You can either belong here or you can belong here. And by the way, I'm choosing for you.*

Greatest woman in the world. Well. Right at the top.

The three of us spent the first few weeks on self-imposed lockdown. We played a million hours of video games. We ate a hundred of Mrs. C's olallieberry pies. We started praying together, for Bas. I taught Jode and Marcus how to surf, while I figured out how to surf with one hand.

Jode hit on Anna. Anna hit on Jode. They both drove me crazy.

And Mom took care of us all.

After a couple of months, Jode shipped back to Oxford but Marcus stayed behind. One of the things I learned about him is that he grew up in foster homes. Lots of kids have great foster families, but he wasn't one of them. He struck out on his own as soon as he turned eighteen, which was right before everything started happening. He didn't say so, but my sense is that things went from bad to worse pretty quickly.

I still don't know how he died. Why he was beaten to death. Someday that story will come out. I hope it will. But I'm okay either way. Whatever he wants is good with me.

Jode, Marcus, and me—we haven't told anyone what happened. Before we left Wyoming, we signed contracts. We promised we'd never talk about the Kindred, or the key, or Jo-tunheimen, or any of it. We were given a cover story to explain how I lost my hand and how the three of us met.

The cover story goes like this: I can't tell you anything.

It's been effective.

I don't like keeping the truth from Anna and my mom, but it's not like I want to talk about what happened, either. That would only make it worse. Sharper. More real, the fact that two of us are gone.

Sebastian should be here. He'd be so proud, seeing Marcus do this.

So would Daryn. I think she'd also be proud of me.

I watch as Marcus hugs the guys in his class, as they take pictures and laugh, commiserating over their last weeks together. He's congratulating them, but he's also saying good-bye, even though no one else knows it. Tomorrow, the rest of the class will report to one of the Ranger Battalions, but he won't.

He'll be reassigned immediately to a newly formed regiment of the US military. A unit specializing in occult warfare, about as classified as you can get. Pretty small. Comprised of Suarez, Low, and myself. And a few other soldiers who were there in Wyoming. We report directly to Cordero, who's turned out to be pretty cool. She doesn't wear any perfume anymore. I think she does that for me.

We even have a British liaison if we need him. It takes some pull to get Jode out here—Oxford's pretty clingy about its students—but Cordero's up to the task. She got him here for this.

It's been half a year now, just about. And I feel different. I've gotten closure on my dad. I'm definitely carrying around less anger. But there's a new gap inside me. There are more people to miss. New images to try to unsee.

Bas, on the brink of death. Sacrificing himself to push Samrael into that spectral hell.

And Daryn. Wedged right next to me around our stone circle in Jotunheimen, her cheeks gold with firelight. Daryn a hundred other ways. Memories of her blurring with dreams of her, and yeah. She was right. We made some unwanted history. It's all I have left of her.

Jode comes back with a bottle of water. He twists the cap off and hands it to me.

"Don't tell me you already lost my sister?" I say, taking it.

He grins. "Queue for the women's loo."

Marcus comes over and joins us. A couple of the cadre instructors who knew me when I was in RASP come over, too. Suarez and Low wander over with a few guys I don't know. I wish Cory could be here but he's deployed, like most of the guys in my class who made it through.

The training stories start coming out. One after another. I laugh, listening to my brothers-in-arms. And I imagine what it would be like if I could add my story.

Man, you guys don't know anything. Talk to me when you've taken down a dragon.

Marcus looks at me like he's read my mind and smiles.

From the corner of my eye, I see my sister. She stands alone in the shadow of a building, watching me with a strange expression on her face.

I go to her right away.

"What's up, Banana? You look like you just saw a ghost."

"No . . . not a ghost," Anna says. "A girl just came up to me. She looked familiar, Gideon. She said she knew you."

Adrenaline moves through me in a hot wave. "What was her name?"

"She didn't say." Anna holds out her hand. "But she told me to give you this."

The silver key—the one that hung around Daryn's neck—rests in her palm.

"Where is she, Anna? Where was she?"

My sister turns. I follow her eyes.

And I'm running.

ACKNOWLEDGMENTS

It takes a team to make a book; I've been very fortunate with my team on this one.

Thank you to everyone at Tor Teen for your efforts and your enthusiasm, especially Kathleen Doherty, Amy Stapp, and Melissa Frain. (Mel, I couldn't have picked a better champion and editor for this story. A banana-free world for you!) Thanks also to Adams Literary for everything you do.

Research was one of the most rewarding parts of writing this novel. It gave me a small window into the lives of real heroes, who were gracious enough to share their experiences and knowledge with me. (Any errors within are, of course, unintentional and mine.) Colonel Andy Juknelis, US Army; Colonel Kyle Lear, US Army; and First Lieutenant Wesley Milligan, US Army: I appreciate every single phone call and e-mail, but more important, I'm so grateful for your service. This world is a better place because of you.

Cheers to Lia Keyes, Katherine Longshore, Lorin Oberweger, Terri Rossi, Pedro Carvalho, Jarrett Jern, and Trish Doller, who all read versions of this story along the way and provided excellent feedback. Taylor McGarry and First Lieutenant John Decker, US Air Force, were also kind enough to give me their input. Sebastian Luna, thank you for letting me borrow your name. It's such a good one!

Last, but not least, a universe of love and thanks to my family for their patience, understanding, and unconditional support. I'm blessed beyond measure to have each and every one of you in my life. Now . . . ready for another story?

TOR TEEN
READING AND ACTIVITY GUIDE
Ages 13–17; Grades 8–12

ABOUT THIS GUIDE

The questions and activities that follow are intended to enhance your reading of *Riders*. The material is aligned with Common Core State Standards for Literacy in English and Language Arts (www.corestandards.org); however, please feel free to adapt this content to suit the needs and interests of your students or reading group participants.

Prereading Activities

1. *Riders* is a work of apocalyptic fiction set in a realistic contemporary setting. "Apocalyptic fiction," which can be looked at as a sub-category of science fiction, explores events surrounding the end of human existence, or a marked shift or change to human existence as it is known. Examples can be found in the *Terminator*, *Mad Max*, and *Matrix* film series, and in young adult book series including *The Maze Runner* by James Dashner, *The Hunger Games* by Suzanne Collins, *Divergent* by Veronica Roth and *The City of Ember* by Jeanne DuPrau. Invite students to share the titles of favorite works of apocalyptic literature or cinema, particularly noting which elements of these apocalyptic (or post-apocalyptic) worlds they found most memorable.

2. Discuss with students why they, and others, may find themselves drawn to works of apocalyptic fiction, par-

ticularly in terms of events happening in their present-day real world. Have each student select a recent newspaper article and consider how its subject might be a source—or outcome—of an apocalyptic incident. Have students write fictionalized versions of their selected articles including an apocalyptic element.

Supports Common Core State Standards: W.8.3, W.9–10.3, W.11–12.3; and SL.8.1, SL.9–10.1, SL.11–12.1

Developing Reading and Discussion Skills

1. The novel is narrated in first person—present tense and flashback—by Gideon Blake. How do you think this point of view affects what readers learn about Daryn, the other horsemen, Cordero, and the Kindred? Is Gideon a reliable or an unreliable narrator? Explain your answer.

2. Do you think Gideon is right to abandon his family as his adventures begin? Do you think he had any other choice? Why or why not?

3. On page 28, Gideon says that, "Setting goals is how I do things." Do you identify with Gideon's strategy? How do you get things done in your life?

4. In Chapter 44, Gideon realizes he is talking not to Cordero but to Malaphar. Does this change your experience of reading the novel? In what ways?

5. What are the names and powers of each of the four horsemen? Describe moments in the novel when each of them endangers himself (and others) by his inability to understand or master his power? What unique interpretation of the meaning and use of powers does Sebastian offer? Might this be related to the sacrifice he makes at the end of the novel? Why or why not?

6. Why doesn't Daryn want to pursue a romantic relationship with Gideon? If you were her friend, what advice might you offer her about her reasoning? Have you ever

worried about the risks of getting to close to a person? Why and what conclusions did you reach?

7. Who are the seven Kindred? Most simply defined, the word "kindred" means relative or related. Why do you think Veronica Rossi chose this name for the evil group in her novel? What relationships do you think she is positing by using this term?

8. On page 190, Gideon explains why he became a soldier. Do you think this is a complete explanation? Do you believe Gideon has "zero problem doing whatever it took to keep harm from coming to innocent people"? Explain your answer.

9. What happens to Gideon when Ra'om invades his mind? Why can't the Kindred invade Daryn's mind?

10. At the end of the great battle in chapter 59, Gideon says, "None of us calls what we did a victory." Do you think Daryn and the Riders were successful in their defeat of the Kindred? What risks does the world still face at the novel's conclusion?

11. At the end of the novel, Gideon's connections to the other riders, to Riot, and to Daryn are what have enabled him to both forgive himself for not saving his father, and to begin moving forward in his own life—things he was struggling to accomplish at the story's start. How might this novel be read as an exploration of the challenges of defining and understanding the notion of the self?

Supports Common Core State Standards: RL.8.1–4, 9–10.1–5, 11–12.1–6; and SL.8.1, 3, 4; SL.9–10.1, 3, 4; SL.11–12.1, 3, 4.

Developing Research & Writing Skills
Setting & Background

1. Analysis of *Riders* must begin with a look at one key inspiration, the notion of the Four Horsemen of the Apoca-

lypse described in Revelations, the last book of the New Testament of the Bible. If possible, read Revelations Chapter 6 (one long paragraph) to see the original literary source for the four horses imagery. At the library or online learn more about scholarly interpretations of this final biblical book, including its use as inspiration for works of literature, art, and music. Use this information to create a PowerPoint or other multimedia-style presentation about your discoveries to share with friends or classmates.

2. In an interview on National Public Radio, Professor Elaine Pagels notes that the author of the Book of Revelations was likely a refugee from Jerusalem writing in a time of rebellion against the Roman Empire. "I don't think we understand this book until we understand that it's wartime literature . . . it comes out of people who have been destroyed by war." (Book Of Revelation: "Visions, Prophecy And Politics." *Fresh Air,* (radio program) http://www.npr.org/2012/03/07/148125942/the-book-of-revelation-visions-prophecy-politics.) Consider reading Veronica Rossi's *Riders* as another work of wartime literature. Write a short essay arguing that a contemporary, real-world war situation of your choice should be interpreted as the backdrop for the novel.

Character

1. On page 86, Daryn tells Gideon that her journal is about "everything I care about." In the character of Daryn, write at least three entries into her journal, possibly including a reflection on leaving home, your first meeting with Gideon, your frustrations over getting the Riders to cooperate, or your thoughts about your future.

2. *Riders* invites readers into the worlds of four very different young men who share the experience of "death" and

being brought together by Daryn. With friends or classmates, discuss the term "death" as it is used in the novel. What do you think has truly happened to Gideon, Sebastian, Marcus, and Jode? Role-play a conversation between the four Riders in which each character discusses how the death experience influenced his decision to join Daryn. (Note: Riders in this exercise can be played by male or female students.)

Plot

1. *Riders* posits a catastrophic, alternate-world-of-evil scenario against which Gideon, the other riders, Daryn and, ultimately, a small division of the American military commit to fight. In the character of (the real) Cordero, create a military-style presentation describing what you know of the Kindred and the risks posed by the evil alternate universe they seek to reopen, to give to friends or classmates. Then, for each of the four horsemen, create a recruitment-style poster entitled "Why I Fight." Include graphic images, names of people or places, a short essay, and quotations from the novel, such as Gideon on page 133 ("After a while, I couldn't look at those stars without thinking *God*. And then thinking, *Oh my God. You're really real.*")

Supports Common Core State Standards: RL.8.4, RL.8.9; RL.9–10.4; RL.11–12.4; W.8.2–3, W.8.7–8; W.9–10.2–3; W.9–10.6–8; W.11–12.2–3, W.11–12.6–8; and SL.8.1, SL.8.4–5; SL.9–10.1–5 ; 11–12.1–5.

3-16